THE LAST ACT OF
HATTIE HOFFMAN

THE
LAST ACT
OF
HATTIE
HOFFMAN

MINDY MEJIA

Quercus

First published in Great Britain in 2017 by

Quercus Editions Ltd
Carmelite House
50 Victoria Embankment
London EC4Y 0DZ

An Hachette UK company

A CIP catalogue record for this book is available
from the British Library

HB ISBN 978 1 78429 576 9
TPB ISBN 978 1 78429 593 6
EBOOK ISBN 978 1 78429 594 3

10 9 8 7 6 5 4 3 2 1

Printed and bound in Great Britain by Clays Ltd, St Ives plc

For Myron, Blanche, Vic, and Hilma,
who farmed the hills of southern Minnesota and
cultivated a legacy of hard work, forbearance,
laughter, and love. All my stories start with you.

HATTIE / *Saturday, March 22, 2008*

RUNNING AWAY sucked.

Here I was, standing in the exact place I'd daydreamed about in math class so many times, right in front of the departures board at the Minneapolis airport, and every detail was just like I'd pictured. I was wearing my travel outfit – black leggings, ballet flats, and an oversize cream sweater that swallowed my hands and made my neck look even longer and skinnier than usual. I had my beautiful leather suitcase and enough money in my purse to fly anyplace I'd ever imagined. I could go anywhere. Do anything. So why did I feel so trapped?

I'd snuck out of the house at three o'clock this morning and left a note on the kitchen table that said only, 'Back later. Love, Hattie.' Later, of course, meant anytime after now. Ten years later, maybe. I didn't know. Maybe it would never stop hurting. Maybe I could never get far enough away. The 'Love, Hattie' part was pushing it a little. My family wasn't the kind to leave love notes lying around the house, but even if they suspected something fishy, they were never in a million years going to think I was flying across the country.

I could practically hear Mom's voice. *That's not like Hattie. For Pete's sake, she's got less than two months of school before graduation and she's playing Lady Macbeth in the school play. I know how excited she's been about that.*

I shoved the imaginary voice aside and read the destinations again, hoping to feel any of the exhilaration I'd thought I would feel when I finally escaped Pine Valley. I'd only been on a plane once before, when we'd visited some relatives in Phoenix. I remembered there were a lot of buttons and lights on my seat and that the bathroom looked like a spaceship. I wanted to order something off the snack cart, but Mom had fruit roll-ups in her purse and that's all we got to eat except peanuts and I didn't even get those. Greg knew I didn't like nuts and took mine. I was mad for the rest of the trip, though, because I was pretty sure I would have liked airplane peanuts. That was eight years ago.

Today was going to be my second flight, to my second life.

And I wouldn't be standing here, feeling paralyzed and miserable, if there had been a seat open on any of the flights to La Guardia or JFK. That was the problem with impulsively deciding to run away from home the day before Easter. The airport looked like Black Friday and the security lines stretched out to the drop-off curb. The earliest available flight to New York was at 6:00 a.m. on Monday and that was too long to wait. I had to get out of this state today.

I could fly to Chicago, but that seemed too close. Too Midwestern. God, why couldn't there be a seat to New York? I knew exactly what shuttle to take from either airport, exactly what hostel I would stay at and how much it cost and how to get to the closest subway station. I'd spent hours on the internet memorizing New York City, so long that it felt like I'd already moved there and I'd assumed that's where I was going when I left the house this morning. Now I was stuck looking at this stupid departure board for some second-choice destination. If I couldn't go directly to New York, I needed to at least get closer to it. There was a 2:20 to Boston. How far was Boston from New York?

Even though I knew it was dumb, I kept glancing at the doors, watching people pour into the airport with their mountains of luggage and their keys and wallets and tickets all jumbled up in their hands. No one was coming to stop me. No one even knew I was here. And even if they did know, would anyone really care? Except for my parents, nobody in the world loved me enough to bother bursting through those doors, yelling my name, desperate to find me before I was gone.

I tried not to cry as I went to the counter for the Boston flight. A tanned, overly perky lady told me there was one seat in coach left.

'I'll take it.'

It was $760.00, which was more than I'd spent on anything besides my computer. I handed her my driver's license and eight crisp one-hundred-dollar bills from the horrible envelope that started all this in the first place. There were two bills left. I stared at them, looking so small and alone in that big white space. I couldn't put them in my wallet. I'd earned every penny in my wallet and I didn't want my money to even touch the contents of this envelope. Lost in another wave of depression, I must not have heard what the woman said next.

'Miss?' She was leaning toward me, obviously trying to get my attention.

There was a man with her now and both of them stared at me like that dream where the teacher's asking you questions and you didn't even know there was a homework assignment.

'Why are you going to Boston today?' the man asked. He looked at my small suitcase.

'To have a tea party.' I thought that was pretty witty, but neither of them laughed.

'Do you have a secondary form of ID?'

I dug around in my purse and pulled out my school ID. He looked at it and then the computer.

'Do your parents know where you are?'

That made me a little panicky, even though I knew I was a legal adult. A few stories popped into my head. I could say my parents were already in Boston waiting for me, or maybe just my dad. He'd separated from my mom and sent me the money at the last minute to spend Easter with him. Or I could go the straight-up orphan route. The tears stopped me, though. Emotion clogged my throat and I knew I couldn't pull it off. Not when they were already suspicious. So I let the emotion take over instead.

'Why don't you mind your own business?' Outraged customer. The airport seemed like a good stage for that.

The people behind me stopped grumbling and started to watch the show.

'Look, Miss Hoffman, there are certain protocols we have to follow for a cash purchase of a same-day ticket, especially a one-way ticket. I'm going to have to ask you to come with me while we check this out.'

There was no way I was going to get locked in some Homeland Security office while he called my parents and made this day ten thousand times worse. What if he could figure out who withdrew the envelope money? Did they have ways to do that? I reached over the counter and grabbed the bills and my IDs.

'Then I'm going to have to ask you to shove your ticket up your ass.'

'Should I call security?' The woman – who had totally dropped her perky act – picked up the phone and started dialing without waiting for an answer.

'Don't bother; I'm leaving. See me leaving?' I grabbed my bag and wiped my eyes with the back of the fist that had crumpled all the money into a sweaty ball.

'Why don't you calm down, Miss Hoffman, and we'll–'

'Why don't you calm down?' I cut the guy off with a glare. 'I'm not a terrorist. I'm sorry you don't want my eight hundred dollars for your crappy seat to Boston.'

Someone in line shouted out a cheer, but most of the crowd just stared as I wheeled my bag away, probably trying to decide what kind of bomb I was going to smuggle on the plane. *Takes all kinds, Velma.* Nudge, nudge. *You wouldn't suspect her of anything, would you?*

I ran to the parking garage and had no idea how I got to my truck or paid the attendant, it was such a blur. My heart was pounding. I checked behind me every second, paranoid that some security guard was going to chase me down. And then once I got on the freeway, the sobbing started. I almost hit a minivan, my hands were shaking so bad. It wasn't until a half an hour later that I realized I was headed back to Pine Valley. The Twin Cities had already disappeared and unplanted fields stretched as far as I could see.

This was what happened when you let yourself need someone.

This crap heap was what you turned into when you fell in love.

I was so happy – so free and above it all – when I started senior year last fall. That Hattie was ready to take on the world and she would have, damn it, she could have done anything. And now I was a pathetic, sobbing mess. I had become the girl I'd always hated.

Suddenly the radio cut out and the lights on the dash started flickering. Shit. I panicked as other cars flew past me. Spotting a turnoff up ahead, I swerved onto a gravel road that bisected two fields, eased off the gas, and let the truck coast to a stop. When I put it into park the engine coughed and then died completely. I tried the key. Nothing. I was stranded in the middle of nowhere.

Falling across the seat, I sobbed into the scratchy fabric until I had to puke and then stumbled out of the truck into the ditch, heaving up only coffee and stomach acid.

A cool wind whipped across the fields. It dried the sweat that had broken out on my forehead and helped the sickness to pass. I crawled away from the vomit and sat on the side of the ditch, letting the soggy ground turn my pants and underwear cold.

I stayed there for a long time, long enough that I didn't feel the chill anymore. Long enough that the tears stopped and something else started.

I was totally alone except for the cars passing on the freeway and I realized that – for the first time I could remember – I didn't want to be anywhere else on earth. I didn't want to be trapped in a cramped airplane seat, flying to a strange city with nowhere to go after the plane landed. I didn't want to be onstage with the lights up and a full audience watching my every move. I didn't want to be lying in my bed alone while Mom cooked some dinner I didn't have the stomach to eat. There was something so comforting about the blankness of the land around me, the empty fields edged with naked trees and patches of stubborn snow.

No one knew I was here. Suddenly that fact was wonderful. I could have said it my whole life to everyone I'd ever met – *No one knows I'm here* – and they would have laughed and rolled their eyes and patted me on the back. *Oh brother,* they'd say, but it was true. I'd spent my entire life playing parts, being whatever they wanted me to be, focused on everyone around me while inside I'd always felt like I was sitting in this exact spot: curled up in the middle of a dead, endless prairie, without a soul in the world for company. Now that I was here it all made sense. Everything clicked, just like it does in the movies when the heroine realizes she's in love with the stupid guy, or she can achieve her All-American, underdog dreams, and the music amps up and she walks, like, determinedly out of some random room. It was just like that, except without the sound track. I was still sitting in a ditch in the middle of nowhere, but everything on the inside suddenly changed.

I heard my mother's voice again. I remembered what she said last night when I was too busy sobbing on her shoulder to listen or understand.

Get off the stage, sweetheart, she said. *You can't live your life acting for other people. Other people will just use you up. You have to know yourself and figure out what you want. I can't do that for you. Nobody can.*

I knew exactly who I was – for maybe the first time ever – and exactly what I wanted and what I had to do to get it. It was clarity. Like waking up from a dream where you thought things were real and then feeling the actual world come into focus all around you. I stood up – ready to ditch this pathetic, crying girl forever. Good effing riddance.

Gerald's old camcorder was tucked in the top of my suitcase. I pulled it out and set it up on the back of the pickup, hitting the record button on a brand-new tape and centering myself in front of the lens.

'Okay, hi.' I wiped my eyes, breathing deep into my diaphragm the way Gerald taught me. 'This is me now. My name is Henrietta Sue Hoffman.'

And by the time I was done with Pine Valley, no one would ever forget who I was.

DEL / *Saturday, April 12, 2008*

THE DEAD girl lay faceup in a corner of the abandoned Erickson barn, half floating in the lake water that flooded the lowest part of the sinking floor. Her hands rested on her torso over some frilly, bloodstained cloth that must have been a dress, and below the hem her legs stretched bare and shocking into the water, each swollen to the size of her waist and floating like manatees in the dirty lagoon. The upper half of her body had no relation to those legs. I'd seen slashed-up bodies before and a share of floaters, too, but never both nightmares lying side by side in the same corpse. Even though her face was too mutilated to ID, there was only one report of a missing girl in the entire county.

'Must be Hattie.' That from Jake, my chief deputy.

Dispatch had gotten the call from the youngest Sanders boy, who'd found her when he and some girl snuck out here. There was a fresh spot of puke, just inside the crooked door, where one of them had lost it before they'd made their escape. I didn't know if it was that or the dead stink that made Jake gag a little when we first came in. Normally I would've made a point to rib him about it, but not now. Not staring down at this.

I unhooked the camera from my belt and started snapping pictures, angling out and then in, trying to get her from every side without slipping into the water next to her.

'We don't know it's Hattie yet.' The sudden stone in my gut aside, we had to do this by the book.

As soon as we'd walked in the door I'd called the crime lab up in the cities and requested a forensics team to tag and bag every last scrap of evidence. We had maybe an hour alone with her before they got here.

'Who else could it be?' Jake moved around her head, watching his step as the boards groaned underneath his ex-defensive tackle weight. He leaned in closer and I could see the lawman had clicked on in his brain.

'Can't make a positive ID with her face like that, especially since she's already bloating. No rings or jewelry. No visible tattoos.'

'Where's her purse? I've never met a girl that didn't keep one glued to her hip.'

'Taken, maybe.'

'Hell of a place for a robbery/murder.'

'Don't get ahead of yourself. ID first.' I crouched down next to her. With a gloved finger, I nudged her lip open and saw her teeth were intact. 'Looks like we can go dental.'

Jake checked the dress for pockets, didn't find any.

'Cause of death, stabbing, most likely.' I pulled up one of her hands and saw the knife wound either right at or just above her heart.

'Most likely?' Jake snorted.

I ignored him and lifted her arm up a little farther to reveal where the white skin on top met the red skin underneath.

'See that?' I pointed to the line separating the colors. 'That's liver mortis. When the blood stops pumping it gets sucked down by gravity and pools at the lowest spots. That's how you can tell if a body's been moved, if the red isn't on the bottom like it should be.'

We checked a few other places on her. 'Looks right. This is probably our murder scene.'

I kept at the teaching line and focused on the body as just another set of remains. I'd seen hundreds, mostly in Vietnam, of course, and right now I would've even gone back there rather than think about who belonged to this wrecked corpse.

I showed Jake the poke test.

'If you poke the pale part of the skin and it flushes red, it's been less than half a day.'

'So the blood settles within twelve hours.'

'Mm-hmm.' The skin under my gloved finger stayed white. There wasn't any blood to show beneath it. So she'd been here since at least the early morning.

The barn floor croaked a warning and we both eased back.

'This place is going to fall in on our heads.'

'I doubt it. It's been like this for the last ten years at least.'

I'd seen this barn almost every weekend during the summertime, from fishing opener to frost, leaning into the east bank of Lake Crosby like it was watching the sunnies dart under the surface. Seen was probably saying too much, though. Sure, I knew it was there, as good a landmark for fishing as the public beach on the exact opposite bank, but I'd never stopped to look at the old Erickson barn for who knew how long. That's how it always was with things right next to you. Lars Erickson abandoned the building twenty years ago when he sold most of the lakeshore to the city and put up new barns next to his prefab house on the other side of the property, a good mile away. The only visitors this old girl had, besides the lake itself that lapped up during flood years, were teenage kids like the Sanders boy who wanted somewhere private to have sex and smoke joints.

Just about all the place boasted was privacy. It was one big room, a twenty- by thirty-footer, with empty rafters except for the remains of a hay loft on the end that dipped into the lake. The double-wide doors opened on the opposite side and there was a hole in the wall where a window used to be.

With the heavy rains and unseasonably early snowmelt this spring, the water had come up to cover a fourth of the floor and it was full of cigarette butts and empty rolling paper packets, along with something that might have been a ziplock bag or a condom.

Jake followed my gaze.

'Think our murder weapon is in there?'

'The team will find it if it is. They're thorough.' Some counties had their own crime labs, whole departments of analysts and investigators, but not us. This was misdemeanor country and most of our felonies were the usual drugs and domestic violence, nothing that justified the extra payroll. It had been over a year since I'd called the boys from Minneapolis out for anything.

'If this isn't Hattie, it's a transient for sure. There's no one else reported missing in five counties.'

'You include Rochester in that deduction?'

'Hmm.' He thought about that.

'See if you can find anything outside the entrance.' I handed him the camera and crept back out toward the edge of the water. It hardly creaked without Jake there – compared to him I suppose I was tiny, whittled down to bone and gristle after thirty years on the job. I squatted next to the girl and cupped my jaw in one hand, looking for what I wasn't seeing. She was drained pale and her face was turned slightly to one side. Her eye sockets, pooled with dried blood, had caught some of her hair. The cuts were mainly to her eyes and cheeks, short jabs except for one long diagonal slash from her temple to her jaw. An exclamation point. Except for the stab wound to the chest the rest of the body was fairly clean. Someone wanted this face to go away pretty bad.

I glanced over at Jake to make sure he was out of earshot, before leaning close.

'Henrietta?' It always riled her when I used her given name, which was why I'd done it for practically eighteen years. Everyone'd called her Hattie since the day she came home from the hospital with a lacy bow tied around her sweet, bald head. That memory just about undid me, so I cleared my throat and made sure Jake was still busy before conceding the name I'd jokingly refused to use in life. 'Hattie?'

I wasn't expecting a reaction or a dove from God or anything, but sometimes you have to say something out loud and see how the words land, how they end up sitting in your gut. These words felt like knives inside me. I stared at her build, the long brown hair, the skimpy dress too early for the season. No matter what I'd said to Jake, these details told me who I was looking at when I first walked in the barn.

When Bud came into my office this morning and told me he had to file a missing persons on Hattie, both of us figured she'd taken off. Nothing that girl ever wanted more than to get out of town, but Bud's wife wasn't so sure. Hattie was starring in her high school play this weekend and Mona didn't think for one second that Hattie would leave town before finishing the show. Some Shakespeare play. Mona also said Hattie wouldn't've left two months before graduation. What she said made sense, but hell would freeze over before I bet on the common sense of a teenager. I put out the standard missing persons alert, all the while thinking Bud and Mona would get an email from her next week saying she was in Minneapolis or Chicago.

Now, as I stared down at what was probably the remains of my fishing buddy's only daughter, a worse question started tearing at me, the question that would gut Bud's life as easily as we'd gutted sunnies and carp not five hundred yards from this very spot.

Who could have murdered Hattie Hoffman?

By the time the crime lab team arrived and the ambulance negotiated the overgrown trail to the barn to load up the body, I'd already gotten two dozen phone calls. The only one I answered was from Brian Haeffner, Pine Valley's mayor.

'Is it true, Del?'

I stood off to the side while the forensics boys combed over the entire barn like ants at a picnic.

'Yeah, it's true.'

'Accident?' Brian sounded hopeful.

'Nope.'

'You're telling me we've got a murderer on the loose?'

I walked outside and spat near the side of the barn, trying to loosen the dead taste from my mouth. The grass was untrampled, waving toward the lake in a light wind.

'I'm saying we've got an open homicide case on an as-yet-unidentified victim and that's all I'll be saying.'

'You'll have to make a statement. We'll have every news station in the state calling.'

Brian always exaggerated the hell out of everything. He'd likely get a few calls from the *County Gazette*. The truth was, his wife probably wanted to know all the details so she could spread it around at Sally's Café, where she baked muffins every morning. Brian and I went back pretty far, since we were both long-standing public officials. We endorsed each other every time an election rolled around and he was a good mayor, but I couldn't take more than one drink with him at a time. He yammered on about every little thing and was always wanting to know about cases and 'crime trends.' Sometimes he reminded me of one of those excitable dogs that can't stop licking your hand.

'You just got my statement, Brian. We'll release the victim's ID when it's confirmed.'

'I need to know if the town's at risk, Del.'

'So do I.'

I hung up on him and pocketed the phone as one of the medics walked over.

'Sheriff, we're ready to take her in.'

'Okay, I'll follow later. I've got some things to check first.'

'Some leads?' The girl looked hopeful. I'd never seen her before – she wasn't from the county.

'No such thing as leads.' I walked back into the barn. 'You either got the guy or you don't.'

<hr />

The forensic boys bottled and bagged everything that wasn't nailed down and dragged every inch of the water in the barn. They turned up an empty wine bottle, a kerosene lantern, five empty cigarette packs, some generic matchbooks, and three used condoms.

I watched as they taped up the door and window.

Jake came up next to me. 'No murder weapon.'

'Nope.' We waited for the team to finish up and clear out. They'd found a few hairs and were going to test the condoms, too, to see if there was any DNA left. Beyond that, they'd hold the rest until we either told them what we needed or closed the case.

After their vans disappeared over the horizon, there was only the sound of the wind drying out the fields and an occasional sparrow call from the lake. It was easier to think that way.

'She was in the far corner from the door.'

'So she either got backed up into the corner or someone found her there.' Jake was right with my line of thought. This was why I'd picked him as my chief deputy.

'No visible wounds or marks on her hands, so there wasn't much of a struggle.' I walked toward the barn door and faced out, like I'd just left. Farmland stretched to the horizon in gentle hills in every direction, empty fields shedding the last of their snow. There wasn't a single house or building in sight of the barn. 'He kills her and heads out. Doesn't leave the knife. He needs to get away and deal with the weapon and his clothes.'

Jake pointed at the trail that circled around the lake toward the beach and the boat launch. 'That's our best bet. He parked in one of the lots and went back the same way.'

'It's either that or cross-country to the highway or past the Erickson house to Route 7. Both are about a mile.'

'Why would he park so far away? Doesn't make sense.'

'No, it doesn't. But most killers are stupid. And they usually don't plan on killing anybody, so they don't think about details like the best getaway route.'

Jake grunted to let me know he wasn't on board with a cross-country escape.

'We're going to need dogs to go over the fields. A mile in every direction. Call Mick in Rochester. And get the boat out on the lake with a metal detector. The killer might have tossed the knife in on his way back to the car.'

'I agree with that. I'll have them go over every inch of the lake and shore.'

We left the scene and bumped the cruisers back over the fields to Winifred Erickson's house. Jake kept on going toward town, but I tried her door first. No answer. Didn't mean she wasn't home. Most folks around here threw open the screen door at the first dust trail over the horizon, but Winifred took her notions. Sometimes she'd go weeks without showing her face in town, and I'd been sent more than once to see if she'd fallen over dead in her kitchen. She never answered the door until I was ready to bust it down and then it was with curlers tying up the leftover strands of gray on her scalp and Lars's old pipe jutting out of her mouth, asking me if I knew how much doors cost and was I damn ready to buy her a new one. A few days later she'd appear on Main Street again, as friendly as you please. She'd been odd like that ever since she killed her husband.

I left her a note about the dog search and headed back to town.

The phones were ringing like fire alarms when I got into the office, but Nancy wasn't at the desk. I found her in the break room getting a cup of coffee. Jake was scarfing down a sandwich while holding his phone.

'I'm on hold with Rochester,' he got out between bites. Glad to see the kid's appetite wasn't affected by a mutilated corpse.

'Grab me some coffee, too, Nance, will you?'

'They won't stop, Del. They've been pouring in like water since about twenty minutes after you got called out there.'

'Who?' Jake asked.

'Everybody I've ever met, for starters, and I'm telling them to keep their noses in their own business. But the papers, too, and Shel called to see if you wanted him to come in.'

Shel was one of our four full-time deputies. With only twelve people in the whole office, we were gonna be pretty thin on the ground during a murder investigation.

'How the hell did he hear about it so quick?'

'He's cousin to the Sanders. They called him as soon as the boy came home.'

'No, tell him we're fine. Jake can take any emergencies from here.'

'But I've got to open the case,' Jake protested.

'I'm opening this case.'

'I lead the investigations unit, Del.'

'And I'm the sheriff of this county.'

I didn't pull rank on him that often and he didn't look any too pleased that I had now. Didn't matter. This was my case. Nancy followed me into my office with the coffee.

'No calls for the next twenty minutes. And this case needs to be locked down. Not a word or a nod to anyone before I tell you. We can confirm one dead female by stabbing. That's all.'

'You know me, Del. I'm a black hole.' She made to leave and then turned around. 'Was it bad?'

I looked up the number on my phone and sighed. 'It's going to get worse.'

'I'm sorry, Del. I'll get a press release ready for when the ID is confirmed.'

Nancy shut the door behind her. I sighed and looked at the picture on the wall of me holding up a thirty-pound muskie on Lake Michigan, the biggest fish I'd ever caught in fresh waters. Bud had called him my monster and then practically outdid me the very next day with a twenty-six-pounder of his own. Jesus Christ. I hit the call button before I could think any more about it.

He answered on the first ring. 'Is it her?'

I gritted my teeth, took a breath. 'You've heard.'

'Mona's out of her mind for worrying. What do you know?'

'Can't say who it is yet.'

'Can't or won't?' Bud's voice didn't rise or change at all, but I'd never heard him ask that kind of question of me in the twenty-five years we'd been friends.

'Can't, Bud. There was some . . . trauma . . . to the face and we can't make a positive ID.' He didn't say anything to that, although I knew he was taking it in somehow, and his picture of the dead girl who could be his daughter just got a whole lot uglier.

The last time anybody'd seen Hattie, according to Bud, was on Friday night after her play up at the school. Bud and Mona'd gone to see it and they hugged her afterwards and said not to be too late, but Hattie never came home.

'You remember what Hattie was wearing last night, Bud?'

'Her costume. It was a dress.'

'A sundress?'

'No, a white dress with blood all over it. Fake blood. And she had a crown on.'

'Would she have changed out of that before leaving?'

'I guess.'

'Does she own a yellow sundress with some ruffly stuff on it?'

'Hell if I know.' Bud checked with Mona. I could hear their voices low and tense.

'No, Mona says she doesn't.' He came back on the line, sounding almost relieved. I didn't share the feeling.

'Hmm. Still no idea who she got a ride with from the school?'

'Mona and I keep thinking it should have been Portia. She was in the play, too, but she says she didn't see much of Hattie afterwards.'

'Okay, Bud. Listen, I need you to release Hattie's dental records to my office. I'll have Nancy stop by with the form and you'll be the first to know about this girl one way or the other. I promise you that.'

He made a sound like a shaky acknowledgment and hung up the phone.

Before I could think too much about what I'd just asked of my best friend, I called Rochester and confirmed the autopsy was scheduled first thing tomorrow. It didn't matter that tomorrow was Sunday; morgues didn't keep business hours.

While Nancy took care of the paperwork and pictures, I opened the case file with Jake's fancy new software that made it impossible to get any work done. Couldn't grumble about it now. After getting the damn thing open, I filled in the few details we had. It was bleached bones, almost nothing.

Female.

Caucasian.

Stab wounds and possible head trauma.

Body found by two local juveniles at the old Erickson barn on Saturday, April 12, 2008, 4:32 p.m.

I swallowed and rubbed my jaw, looking at all those blank fields. I was worried for the first time I could remember, thinking about what I might have to type in there. Girls didn't get murdered for nothing, not in Wabash County. There were no drive-by shootings here, no angry boys unloading an arsenal inside the high school. All that crazy city shit was a world away from us, and that's why a lot of the folks who lived here stayed. Sure, the Pine Valley storefronts were always half empty. When crop prices were down, people might not scrape out their mortgage payments, but this was a community. A place stuck on the idea that people still mattered. Something certainly had mattered enough to draw this girl out to the Erickson barn in the middle of nowhere. And whatever it was had also mattered enough to someone else to kill her over it.

It was getting late so I walked home, but who knew why. I ate most of my meals at the station and hardly slept anymore. It used to be just during big cases, but lately I was only down about four hours a night. I owned the top half of a duplex a block off Main Street. The Nguyens, the folks who ran the liquor store now, lived downstairs. They were practically the only Asians in the county and although their cooking smells were downright pungent – nothing like Chinese restaurants – they were quiet and never banged on the plumbing to tell me to shut up like the last old woman did before she had a stroke and died. I kept it down anyway, especially in the middle of the night when I wasn't sleeping. I played records sometimes, but I never watched the TV anymore; it just made me feel dead already. I got my news in the paper and listened to ball games on the radio, so there was no point even having the thing except the Nguyens' cat liked to jump in through the window and lie on top of it. Even though I'd never liked cats, this one was all right. He didn't strut around demanding food or rub his fur all over the place. He just sat on the TV on one side of the living room and I sat on the couch on the other side, and we were okay.

I sat up all night long thinking about that body. If I dozed off a little, I didn't remember it. I made notes and lists of people to talk to and watched the clock turn slowly toward 7:00 a.m., while the cat's tail twitched.

———◆———

'Well, Sheriff Goodman, whose remains should I thank for the honor of this visit?'

Dr. Frances Okada hadn't changed. Sure, her hair was a silvery bun now and there was a stoop in her back, but she still sauntered around the morgue like the unholy queen of the dead and she still separated my name – 'Good man' – like it was some great joke nobody got except her.

'That's the same question I've been waiting to ask you for an hour while I sat in that damn lobby, Fran.'

'Yes, such a shame for you that this young man' – she tossed her head in the direction of a body in the corner that a technician was working over – 'had the nerve to have an aneurysm during his baseball practice last night. He should've had the courtesy to check your schedule first.'

I walked over to the table wordlessly. My mother always told my sisters and me that silence ends an argument quicker than words. It worked pretty well with snooty medical examiners, too, and pain in the ass or not, Fran was going to give me an ID. Bud and Mona were waiting.

The body had changed again. She was gray under the lab lights and the bloating had gotten worse. She didn't look like anyone anymore, let alone Hattie.

'I sent your girl down to Radiology as soon as she arrived. These are her teeth.' She slid the pictures into the viewer. 'And here's the film that arrived on your suspected victim, Henrietta.'

'Hattie,' I corrected, stepping forward to inspect the pictures.

'See the cavity here and here.' She pointed to both sets. 'The fillings are a spot-on match and there's an identical profile from either side.'

Fran's finger lingered on a slightly crooked tooth in the bottom jaw. 'There's no need to go to DNA for this one. She's Henrietta.'

'She's Hattie.' It came out a little angrier than I meant.

'I'd estimate she was dead for twelve to eighteen hours before she was discovered, judging by the rate of decomp.' Fran snapped on a new set of gloves and her voice softened a bit. 'You knew her?'

'Doesn't matter now, does it? I need a full workup with a mind toward murder. Foreign blood, hair, anything she's got on her that can point somewhere. And I need it quick, you understand? Call me when it's ready.' I was already on my way out the door.

'Why don't you just stay and witness the autopsy for yourself?'

I glanced back to see she was finally looking me straight in the eye, standing like a guardian over the disfigured remains that, two days ago, had been Hattie.

'I've got something to do.'

Bud's truck was there when I pulled into the driveway, even though it was still early on Sunday morning and church couldn't

22

have let out yet. Bear, their black Lab, came panting at my leg for his usual scratch behind the ears as I headed up to the house. I didn't look at him. Before I'd gotten halfway up the sidewalk, Mona jerked the door open.

She wore a big flowery apron and her hair was tied back with a handkerchief. She was the only woman her age I knew who kept her hair long, and it made her seem timeless somehow. She had a strong, calm face and a manner to match, but today there were tremors behind her eyes.

'Well?' She bit it out.

'Mona.' I removed my hat. 'Is Bud around, too?'

'Just say it, Del.' Her fingers rapped a rhythmless beat on the side of her thigh while she stood as rigid as a board. It was like her fingers didn't belong to the rest of her, and I had a bad flash of Hattie half in, half out of the water, her strange dead body disconnected from itself.

'Can I come in?'

'Course, Del.' Bud appeared behind Mona and opened the door wider. He took his wife by the shoulders and backed her up so I could get by. She shook him off and went into the living room ahead of us.

Once I stepped inside, the smell of butter and chocolate overwhelmed me. The kitchen was full of cookies – pinwheels and chocolate chip and sugar cutouts stacked on plates all over the room.

Bud followed my glance. 'She was making some for the church bake sale yesterday when we got the call about that body, and then' – he shrugged helplessly – 'she just didn't stop. She wouldn't go to church and I don't know if she slept at all last night.'

His voice sounded far away, like I wasn't standing right next to him, and I didn't know if that distance was coming from him or me.

I went into the living room and stood by the fireplace, where Hattie's and Greg's senior class pictures both hung above the mantel in gold frames. Hattie was leaning on a tree with her arms crossed, wearing a white shirt with a flower pinned on it and a smile that barely lifted the corners of her mouth. She looked happy. No, not happy, really. Satisfied. She looked like a girl who knew what she wanted and just how to get it. She was the child who was going to succeed and make a new life away from Pine Valley and marry some hotshot lawyer and come home only for holidays with a shiny career and a kid or two to show off around town; she wasn't the child who was going to die. I glanced at Greg's picture, posing with Bear and a shotgun. He'd had that razor-cut hair long before he signed up for the army and was eager as hell to ship off for Afghanistan the minute he graduated. He was the one who was supposed to die. He was the child Bud and Mona had hardened their skin for, so they could take the news if it ever came.

Bud sat on the couch next to Mona, holding her hand and waiting. How many times had I been in this living room? Hundreds, and every time Bud had made me feel like it was my living room, that those were my family pictures hanging on the walls. I took a deep breath and looked at him now. His hair was going silver and his shirt stretched tighter around his middle than it used to. He looked me dead in the eye, and I told him.

'The dentist sent Hattie's dental records over to Rochester where the girl's body is and they compared Hattie's teeth to the victim. It was a match. It's Hattie.'

Mona swayed forward like someone had hit her from behind and Bud let her hand go, but neither of them made a sound.

'God, I'm sorry, Bud.' My throat tried to close up, but I forced the words out. 'Mona, I can't tell you how awful I feel. I promise you I'll find this son of a bitch.'

Mona stared at the faded green carpet. 'Teeth?'

Bud looked right through me to the pictures on the wall. 'What happened? How did she . . . ?'

'She was found at the old Erickson barn down on the lake and it looks like that's where it happened. She was attacked by someone with a knife and she died from a chest wound.'

Bud sat perfectly still through the whole description while Mona kept shaking silently.

'You said you couldn't identify her by her face.'

God damn my mouth. I'd been trying to keep it as simple as possible, to spare them from something.

'The attacker got to her face with the knife, too, but that may have been after she died. We won't know until the autopsy's finished.'

Mona let out a low kind of howl. Bud woke up from his trance and reached for her, but she threw him off.

'Get away from me!'

She stumbled up and back into the kitchen, hitting walls and choking on her own sobbing. The farther away she got, the louder her grief poured out. Mona wasn't a hard woman, but she was as no-nonsense as they came. I don't think I'd ever seen her spill so much as a tear in all the years I'd known her. Listening to those wrenching cries come from a woman like Mona was just about the worst thing I'd ever heard.

I leaned in toward Bud, who was still frozen on the couch.

'Bud, what was Hattie going to do after the play on Friday? I need to know as much about that night as you can tell me.'

He didn't act like he'd even heard me, but after a minute he passed a rough hand over his face and cleared his throat, staring at the floor.

'Going out, she said. She was going out with some of the kids to celebrate opening night.'

'She didn't say who specifically?'

'No. We figured it was the whole crew of them. They'd all gone out the weekend before, too, after they finished building the set.'

'She wasn't standing with anybody in particular?'

'She was standing with us.' His voice broke and he swallowed. 'She was right there with us.'

The crash made us both jump. I ran through the kitchen toward the back bedroom that Bud and Mona shared. Mona lay on her side on top of the remains of a small spindle table. It looked like her legs had buckled underneath her. Her back shuddered uncontrollably among the mess of tablecloth and books and wood. When I tried to see if she was hurt, she started wildly hitting at me and her cries changed into a high, keening sound. I walked back to the living room to see Bud hadn't moved. His hands were turned palm up on the couch, fingers curled in like a baby's.

'Bud.'

He didn't answer. His eyes were unfocused. There was a smear of flour in his hair where Mona'd shoved him.

'Bud.'

Woodenly, he stood up and walked into the bedroom. He bent over Mona, covering her sobbing body with his own. I wiped my eyes and let them alone.

❖

Pine Valley High School was a one-story brick building on the south side of downtown, marking the point where the storefronts on Main Street turned into houses and gas stations. It hadn't changed since the sixties, when they put on the addition of the new gymnasium.

Pulling into the half-full parking lot, I met Jake outside the front doors and we followed the signs to the 'new gym,' where the play was already under way. Three weeks and a lifetime ago I'd promised Hattie I would come to the Sunday matinee performance. Now here I was.

Jake skimmed a program. 'Says Hattie was playing Lady Macbeth.'

We sidled inside and took some empty chairs in the back. Two kids were on stage, both wearing white costumes and standing in front of some castle scenery. I recognized the Asian girl, Portia Nguyen, but didn't know the boy. They were talking in that flowery Shakespeare language I never cared for, but eventually I tuned in to what they were saying. She was trying to get him to kill somebody and he seemed on board with it. At the end of the scene, she crossed over to him, plotting their reaction after the murder.

'We shall make our griefs and clamor roar upon his death.'

He took her hand. 'I am settled and bend up each corporal agent to this terrible feat. Away, and mock the time with fairest show.'

He led her offstage, speaking to the darkness.

'False face must hide what the false heart doth know.'

Afterwards I pulled the teacher in charge aside and told him I needed to talk to the whole cast and crew. He went pale, but didn't ask me a thing. Peter Lund was his name, a young guy with glasses and no dirt under his nails.

Lund told everyone he wanted to do a 'quick wrap,' and called them into the music room. After the doors closed, it was dead silent as the kids waited.

'Great show, uh – everybody. Portia, you . . . you did well. We'll break the set down in a minute, but Sheriff Goodman needs to talk to all of us right now.'

He walked to the back of the room, leaving me and Jake alone in front. Some of the girls were already crying. Pine Valley was as small-town as they came, and I knew all of them had heard about the body within hours of the discovery.

I didn't beat around the bush. I gave it to them straight and they acted about the way you'd expect a group of teenagers to act when one of their own got stabbed to death and showed them all for the first time they were mortal. There was shock and a lot of tears and wailing. Most of the boys turned into cardboard, frozen and ready to be knocked over with a feather. Most of the girls held on to each other. Lund hunched in the back of the room with his head in his hands.

I gave them a little bit for the news to settle in but got to the reason I was there before the trauma took over completely.

'She was killed on Friday night after the play. Now I need each and every one of you to think. Do this for Hattie now. Who did she leave with that night? Did any of you meet up with her afterwards for a party, anything like that?'

'Some of us went down to Dairy Queen, but she didn't show up there,' said the boy who played Macbeth. He looked more like he was losing his mind now than he had up on stage a few minutes ago.

'Tommy was at the performance, wasn't he? Didn't she leave with him, Portia?' one of them asked.

Portia Nguyen unwrapped herself from another crying girl and looked up with a flat, wet face. Her crown was tilted in her hair. 'Maybe. I don't know. I didn't talk to her much. I didn't even say congratulations.'

'Tommy would have given her a ride if she asked. He would have done anything she wanted him to.'

'Tommy who?' Jake asked.

'Tommy Kinakis,' I answered. Hattie'd been dating him for most of the year, if I remembered right. I'd watched him as an offensive lineman on the varsity team last fall. He was solid, hard to get around, had never let his quarterback get sacked in any of the games I'd been to. If a kid like that wanted to put a knife through somebody, there wasn't much that would stop him.

'I know what killed her.' Portia stood up and faced me like she was ready to start rattling off one of those long speeches from the play. 'It was the curse.'

'Come again?'

Some of the kids gasped and covered their mouths.

'The curse killed Hattie. The curse of *Macbeth*.'

PETER / *Friday, August 17, 2007*

CONGESTIVE HEART failure was going to kill me.

I was twenty-six years old and in the best shape of my life. Granted, I had nowhere to go but up. I'd evolved from the skinny high school nerd to a guy who ran at least fifteen miles a week. I could've probably even benched weight if I ever dared go into those weight rooms full of sweaty, meathead guys. I ate an organic, vegetarian diet and I didn't smoke – but congestive heart failure was ruining my life.

'What do you want for dessert?'

I watched Mary across the table. She'd scarcely spoken since they brought our entrees and kept glancing at her watch like we were out past curfew.

'Chocolate mousse?' I asked with a grin. After seven years together, I knew she couldn't resist anything with chocolate in it. I'm sure a lot of people say that about their wives, but I'd once watched Mary eat chocolate-covered bacon at the state fair. Fried pig fat dipped in chocolate. And she'd laughed at my green face and said it wasn't all that bad.

'I guess so.' She shrugged.

I waved the waiter over and ordered a coffee along with the dessert. This was the kind of place where you could wave a discreet waiter over, order a *caffè americano,* and they nodded in approval. Drop lights hung over the tables, wrapping each party in their own cocoon of light. It was modern yet romantic, a place that probably catered to the medical crowd from Mayo. Mary hadn't wanted to drive all the way into Rochester, but the restaurant choices in Pine Valley were a Dairy Queen or a café that closed at 7:00 p.m. Besides, there was no movie theater in Pine Valley and this was our traditional dinner-and-movie date, except that unlike most couples we always switched the order. Movie first, then dinner, so we could discuss what we saw. That's what we'd done on our first date when we watched *American Beauty* and argued over each character's moral superiority until the waitress actually asked us to leave so they could turn over the table. Lengthy, flirtatious debates weren't going to cause any seating issues tonight.

The coffee came and I sipped it right away, burning my tongue. I didn't care. I kept drinking and watching Mary, trying to figure out where I'd gone wrong.

Her hair was down tonight, reflecting a luminous gold halo from the light, and it fell in her face as she stared at the table, the other diners, the bay windows, anything that wasn't me. Mary had an apple face, the kind of wide cheeks that could scoop up happiness and share it with buoyant democracy, but I couldn't find any joy in her tonight.

She wore her 1950s blue shirtwaist dress, and I'd hugged her when she came downstairs at the house, kissed her cheek, and whispered, 'Hello, beautiful.' She smiled and ducked away. I assumed it was because Elsa was sitting on the couch watching us, but Mary acted the same way the rest of the night. Polite. Distant. Like the entire evening was more of a chore than mucking out Elsa's chicken barn. The movie didn't help and that was completely my fault. I picked *Knocked Up* because Mary liked romantic comedies and it had gotten good reviews, but neither of us laughed much. We hadn't used birth control since our wedding night and after three years of trying for a baby, she had to sit there and watch two idiots pretend to get pregnant in a sloppy one-night stand.

'I'm sorry about the movie.'

She finally looked up at me. 'It's okay.'

'I should have thought of it.'

'No, really, Peter.' Mary sat up straighter as someone came and quietly put the dessert on the table between us. 'Babies haven't been on my mind lately.'

'That's too bad. After this I wanted to go park the car somewhere and neck. Or more.' I winked at her. She said nothing so I continued, hopeful.

'It feels like we're back in the dorms again. Waiting for our roommates to leave, or finding a quiet park. Remember the second floor of the Fourth Street ramp? The side where the lights didn't work?'

She took a spoonful of chocolate and shook her head. 'We have to get back. We've already been gone too long.'

'Elsa's done fine on her own for seventy-three years. She'll make it through another hour.'

Mary took another bite, ignoring me. Then she abruptly set the spoon down and crossed her arms.

'What is it?'

'Ten dollars for chocolate mousse. That's crazy.'

'Well, it's even crazier to order it and not eat it then.' I dug in. It was damn good. Light and rich and not too sweet.

'Try another bite. This one's the ten-dollar bite.' I hovered a spoonful in front of her face and she sighed before taking it.

She started eating again, but quietly, unwilling to engage. I drank the rest of my coffee and tried to draw her out. Nothing worked.

When the bill came, Mary immediately grabbed it. She paid the waiter and picked up her purse. 'Are you ready?'

'Elsa's fine,' I said, rubbing her arm as we walked to the car.

'I know,' she replied, even though we both knew her mother wasn't fine.

'Then what's the problem?'

'Sixty-eight dollars for dinner, Peter. On top of twenty for the movie. Who do you think is going to pay for all that?'

'I've got a job. We'll have money.' Her irritation was slowly seeping into me now, too.

'You haven't even started working yet and you're already spending it.'

'I just wanted us to go out and have a nice time,' I said over the car roof before we both got in and slammed the doors.

The road to Pine Valley was a dark, flat, two-lane highway lined with crop fields. Neither of us bothered with the radio. The evening seemed, unfortunately, past the point of salvation.

If I was going to be honest – which, with every passing mile of towering cornstalks, sounded like an increasingly reasonable idea – I still couldn't quite figure out how I'd gotten here.

I was a Minneapolis kid. I grew up hanging out at uptown coffee shops, debating the cover art of my high school literary magazine over pasta at Figlio's, and spending every weekend flipping through CDs at the Electric Fetus. I met Mary at the U and we got married the summer after graduation. We were probably too young, but Mary's parents were old. She'd been a late-life baby, their ultimate surprise after years of infertility and relinquished dreams. They gave Mary every opportunity, lavished her with love and support, and in return she wanted to give them the gift of seeing her married and settled. I maxed out my credit card and put that diamond on Mary's finger and we stood at the altar of her hometown church while Mary's parents beamed from the front row. The wedding comforted both of us when, the very next spring, her father had a massive heart attack and died planting his soybean fields.

After the wedding, we found a Victorian one-bedroom rental on the bus line, and I started grad school while Mary got a job at one of the banks downtown.

And then congestive heart failure came along.

Elsa, Mary's mother, started getting weaker and weaker. Mary began driving down once a month to check on her and help out around the farm. There was always some canning to do or an out-building to repair or doctor appointments to keep. I tried making jokes about my farmer wife, but Mary laughed less and less. Then she was making trips every weekend and since some of my classes were at night, I wouldn't see her for days at a time. By the time I graduated and got my teaching license, Mary was spending three days a week in Pine Valley and working ten-hour days in the city to make up for it.

She was exhausted all the time. I tried to convince her that Elsa needed to sell the property, but she would grind her teeth every time I mentioned it, roll her eyes, and say, 'Don't you think I've tried that?'

We couldn't find anyone to come help Elsa; the only qualified nurse who was willing to drive out to the farm wanted a thousand a week to check in on her and administer her meds.

I looked for a teaching job so Mary could quit the bank or at least scale back to part-time. I was trying to be a good husband. Isn't that what good husbands do? Except I couldn't find anything. The only openings were in elementary special ed and I had no experience with behavioral disorders. They wanted me to promise to go back to school for the specialty, but I wanted to teach literature, not social skills.

Then last March, Mary came home with a newspaper clipping. She showed me the ad – Pine Valley High School English teacher, the exact job I was qualified for – and told me that Elsa knew the principal personally and had put in a recommendation for me. The principal was waiting for my call.

God, I did not want to move to Pine Valley. But she looked so hopeful and tired, and I don't know how it happened but two months later we moved in with her mother and I lost my entire life. Although she said it was only temporary, we both knew that meant we were staying until Elsa died, whether that took months or years. Lately, I hated to admit it, I'd been hoping for months.

The entire summer everything was Elsa, Elsa, Elsa. How was Elsa feeling today? Did she need a new oxygen tank? Could she take a shower by herself? It felt like we did have a baby, except our baby was an old, set-in-her-ways woman with a failing body.

Elsa was grateful, but all her gratitude seemed reserved for Mary. Me, she treated like a mildly irritating foreign exchange student.

It started with the vegetarian thing. She questioned everything I ate, from kale to black bean burgers to tempeh. When I went running, Elsa shook her head like she'd never seen a human move faster than a brisk walk behind a plow. And if I cracked a beer at night, she sniffed and pointedly looked away.

I honestly didn't care what my mother-in-law thought of me, but she was coming between me and Mary. Every time Elsa cold-shouldered me, she stretched Mary's peacemaker position a fraction thinner, pulled her daughter a little further away. One day I fixed the fence around her chicken barn while she toddled out after me to supervise, and we even had some good conversation about Mary's childhood, except by the next week she'd forgotten all about it. The deprivation of oxygen to her brain was robbing her memories, especially the most recent ones, so all my attempts to improve our relationship were pointless.

And then there was the squawking. Even though the chickens were housed on the far side of the main barn, the clucking and rustling and scraping of those birds were omnipresent, no matter what time of day. It was enough to drive anyone insane. There were only about fifty of them, the last of Mary's father's flock, but they seemed to provide eggs for half the county. People stopped by all the time to pick up a carton, and Mary personally delivered them to our neighbor, Winifred Erickson, who usually followed Mary right back to our house and chatted with Elsa for hours. Mary collected eggs twice a day, starting at 6:00 a.m., cleaned the nests out, cleaned the floor, and hauled the feed – without making more than a few bucks a day as far as I could tell – and she wanted to talk about not having money?

'Why don't you get rid of the chickens?' I kept asking her.

'I don't mind it. I grew up doing this. I just don't know how Mom managed it by herself.'

'Why do you have to manage it? We can buy eggs at the store.'

'Mom won't hear of selling them,' she said, which had become her standard line of the summer. Our seventy-three-year-old baby wants this. Our seventy-three-year-old baby won't tolerate that.

It was creeping into everything. Mary wouldn't discuss books with me anymore. She said she had no time to read, yet she watched those awful shows with Elsa every night. She didn't want to drive into the city to see any plays or even spend a night with our friends.

She'd shake her head. 'It's too far, I'm tired just thinking about it.'

Thank God the house got internet service. I set up my computer in a little bedroom upstairs that warehoused Christmas ornaments and dusty cardboard boxes marked with phrases like *Uncle Joe's funeral* or *Dewitt 1938*. That's where I read, made my lesson plans for the fall, and checked Facebook every night, watching my friends go to bars, literary readings, parties, and conferences.

I wasn't going to lie; I had a lot riding on tonight's date. I was desperate to remove our relationship – even for a few hours – from the farm and Elsa, to resurrect the kind of fun, spontaneous times we'd had in college, before grad school and illness had claimed all our Friday nights. Mary liked the idea. She'd been excited when I mentioned it earlier in the week.

'A night out,' I'd said, 'before the school year starts. We won't do a single productive thing.'

She laughed. 'Promise?'

Now, driving back to Pine Valley with a silence that was building even higher walls between us, I wondered again where I'd screwed up. Or did she screw up? Any stranger watching us tonight would have been embarrassed at how hard I was trying, but I was obviously trying the wrong things. The wrong movie. The wrong restaurant. Would it have been better if we'd gone to the local Dairy Queen and traded bites of Blizzard while teenagers flirted their way around our booth?

The lights of Pine Valley warmed the horizon, and as much as I hated personification, it was like the town itself was visually shoving the answer down my throat. Yes. Yes, you tried too hard. You wanted a Minneapolis date, but you don't have a Minneapolis wife anymore.

With that uncomfortable thought in my head, we drove into town, a small grid of streets surrounding one main drag of businesses underneath the soybean plant's smokestacks on the horizon. A few gas stations, the Dairy Queen, and a CVS pharmacy were the only places still open at 9:00 p.m. on Friday night.

'Can you stop at the pharmacy? I need to pick up Mom's medicine and some pictures.'

Obediently, I pulled into the parking lot and killed the engine, following her inside. She went to see the pharmacist and sent me to the photo counter in the opposite corner of the store. The salesgirl didn't notice me approach and I didn't care enough to try to grab her attention.

I didn't have a Minneapolis wife anymore.

To say that I wasn't prepared for this change in Mary was a laughable understatement. It had never occurred to me that I'd need to prepare for it. The trouble with vows was that they were too damn generic. I'd stood in that church a block away from here and repeated, 'For better or for worse,' imagining the worst to be Mary laid low with a cute, flu-like sickness requiring chicken soup and boxes of Kleenex. Maybe we'd lose our jobs. Maybe we'd have to deal with infertility. I'd projected every normal scenario into those vows, everything people told me to expect, but the minister never said, 'You might move away from everyone and everything you love into a rundown farmhouse in the middle of a desolate prairie, where you won't have sex or even any conversation that doesn't revolve around the state of a dying woman who hates you.' No, he'd stood smiling in front of us and said, 'For better or for worse.' Better or worse what? I'd agreed to adjectives. I'd happily squeezed Mary's hands and made vows with unknown placeholders for nouns. For someone who aspired to be an English professor, binding my life to someone else's with a game of Mad Libs suddenly seemed like a terrible joke.

'Can I help you?'

I blinked. The salesgirl stood on the other side of the counter now, obviously waiting for me to say something.

'Oh. Yeah. Pictures for Mary Lund?'

She promptly went hunting through the bin.

'Nope, nothing for Mary Lund.'

Usually I asked clerks to take a second look whenever the first answer was no. Most of them were young and bumbling and found the item on the second or even third try. This girl was young but looked like she'd never bumbled over anything in her life. She'd already straightened back up to face me, supremely confident, equally ready to hand me my hat or let me try again. I was the one fumbling now under her attention.

'Um, how about Elsa Reever?'

'You have some interesting aliases.' She grinned this time before diving into the *R*s.

'A rose by any other name . . .'

'Would still have pictures at CVS,' she finished, pulling an envelope out of the bin and waving it with a flourish.

'Apparently.'

She rang up the pictures on the cash register. 'So, Elsa, did you need anything else today?'

'Um –' I glanced back in the direction of the pharmacy, looking for any sign of Mary. Did she mention anything else? I couldn't remember, and given the course of the evening, it was probably safer not to spend extra money.

'No, that's all.'

I handed her my card and watched her complete the transaction. There was something about her: a brightness, a presence. Usually teenagers gave distracted or grudging service in these types of jobs, but this girl was wholly and happily in the moment. A distinct flash of hatred ran through me as I assessed her. Tall and lean, she had a conscious grace about her limbs. Her skin was honey-tanned, her too-wide mouth gleamed with some kind of gloss, and her eyes sparkled with the kind of sly intelligence that said her *Romeo and Juliet* retort barely qualified as an easy volley on her part. This was a girl who hadn't made any mistakes yet, one who recognized the world as only a giant cupcake for her careless sampling.

She turned to hand me the pictures and her slyness evaporated. 'What's wrong?'

'Excuse me?' Her sudden concern startled me out of my fixation.

'You. You looked angry.'

What kind of town was this where total strangers called you out on your moods?

'No, I mean, well . . .' I stumbled around my words like an idiot. 'I'm not . . .'

'You're totally angry.' She enjoyed my stuttering, stretching her too-wide mouth wider. 'I can see it here and here.' She pointed to her eyebrows and her jaw, imitating me with crossed arms until I dropped mine to my sides.

I shrugged. 'Not about the pictures.' Why not admit it?

'Is it one of the aliases?'

'How do you know it's not you?'

'Duh. We don't even know each other. Oh, I'm Hattie, by the way.' She reached out a hand and I stared at it a second before shaking it.

'Peter.'

'Hi, Peter. You know what I do with an alias that starts sucking?'

'What?'

'I trade it in for a better one.'

'Yeah, you can do that when you're sixteen.'

She giggled. 'What are you, eighty?'

'Eighty-two.'

'Well, maybe you just need some stool softeners, then. They're in aisle six.'

I burst out laughing and she nodded like she'd finished what she set out to do, and then Mary appeared with her bagful of prescriptions.

'Ready?' Mary asked.

'Yeah.'

I nodded to Hattie the cashier, who waved at both of us. 'Good night. Thanks for stopping in.'

On the way back to the farm, I reached across the seat and laid my hand lightly on top of Mary's, ready to try again. When we turned onto the gravel road that led to the farm, a light flashed across the sky.

'Look!' I switched off the headlights and hit the brakes.

We watched the shooting star race through constellations until it burned up and was gone. For a moment neither of us spoke. Then Mary turned her palm over so we were holding hands.

'Did you make a wish?' she asked.

'I thought that was for first stars.'

She shrugged. 'Maybe it could be for first shooting stars, too.'

'Okay.' I linked our fingers together, happy to play along. 'Star light, star bright . . .'

'No, you have to keep it a secret or it won't come true.'

'Everyone knows that. I was just doing the prologue.'

She smiled and let me finish. Even though we didn't talk for the rest of the drive, the tension had eased and it started to feel like the night I wanted us to have. I made a wish – silently – as we headed back toward the farm.

After five minutes of winding, gravel hills I pulled into the box of trees sheltering Elsa's house and barns from the prairie winds. I turned the car off and let my gaze wander, in no hurry to go inside. Mary's father had done a great job maintaining the place, but three years after his death signs of neglect were starting to show. Paint peeled off the corners of the main barn. Weeds overran the vegetable garden where green beans and peas used to grow in military formation. In the daylight you could see a few gnarled shingles scattered over the building roofs, caused by storm damage that no one who lived here anymore was capable of repairing. Elsa leased the fields to a neighbor, but the land, buildings, and chickens inside this windbreak of trees were still her domain. It made no sense why she wanted to stay here. My mother had moved to a condo in Arizona within a few months of my graduation. Why did Elsa want to grow old in a place that reminded her, with each broken fence and chipped windowsill, of her every disability? It was the worst retirement home I'd ever seen.

One of the barn cats ran through the yard as Mary sighed. I could feel the effect of the farm trickling into her, too, and tried to salvage the good mood.

'Hey.' I jiggled her hand playfully. 'Come here.'

I was the one who closed the distance, though, kissing her lightly. She accepted the kiss at first, but her face tilted away when I would have prolonged it. For a moment neither of us moved or spoke.

'I wished that things were different,' she finally said. 'On the star. I wished that Mom was healthy.'

'You're not supposed to tell, remember?'

'It doesn't matter. It's not going to come true.' Her voice broke and automatically I reached up, rubbing her shoulder.

'You're doing too much.'

She shook her head, looking out toward the fields. 'They gave me everything. They loved me better than any child could hope for . . . and this is what I can do now, the only way I can show them that love back.'

'We need some help. There are other ways.'

'It's fine. I'm fine.'

'You can't even enjoy a dinner away from her. Look what this is doing to us.'

She looked at me then with an expression I'd never seen on her face before. It was cold. My Mary, my sweet and generous, vintage-loving, apple-cheeked Mary looked at me like I was some annoying stray begging for scraps.

'I'm sorry I can't take care of you right now, Peter.'

'I don't want you to take care of me. Jesus, I just wanted us to have fun tonight.'

'Don't say *Jesus* like that.'

'Are you fucking kidding me?' It wasn't, maybe, the most eloquent response I could've made to an attempt to censor my language.

'My mom' – she shook her head, glancing at the house – 'has gone to church every Sunday her entire life. Her faith is important to her. Can you please respect that while we're here?'

'I don't see Elsa here now.' But even as I said it, I knew she was. She was everywhere, sitting in the movie theater between us, sniffing at the prices on the restaurant menu, and pinching Mary's profile tight and unrecognizable here where the ammonia stink of chicken shit seeped in from the yard.

'I'm just saying.'

'Fine.' I got out of the car and slammed the door, which brought squawks from the chicken barn.

The house was dark, with only the stove light on to welcome us back. Elsa must have gone to bed early, maybe trying to be considerate of our date night. Usually Mary tucked her into bed and brushed the wispy strands away from her face while Elsa looked at photo albums and told stories about people I didn't know and the two of them laughed and reminisced. There was never a place for me during these nightly rituals.

'I'm going to check on her quick,' Mary said.

'Okay.'

Mary disappeared and I went upstairs to our bedroom. Soft voices drifted up through the heating vents and I could picture Mary perched on Elsa's wedding quilt as they filled each other in on the last three hours, both of them refusing to look at the empty place on the other side of the bed.

My shooting star wish had been for Mary and me to be happy again. Maybe it would never be like before, but there had to be a new happiness somehow, a way for us to thrive that I couldn't see yet. I got undressed and lay down, staring at the water-stained ceiling while waiting for Mary to come up, and that's how I fell asleep. Waiting.

HATTIE / *Monday, August 27, 2007*

MOST PEOPLE think acting is make-believe. Like it's a big game where people put on costumes and feign kisses or stab wounds and then pretend to gasp and die. They think it's a show. They don't understand that acting is becoming someone else, changing your thoughts and needs until you don't remember your own anymore. You let the other person invade everything you are and then you turn yourself inside out, spilling their identity onto the stage like a kind of bloodletting. Sometimes I think acting is a disease, but I can't say for sure because I don't know what it's like to be healthy.

The first character I remember playing was Fearless Little Sister.

Even when we were little, my brother, Greg, had all the gleeful meanness of a teenager with a sack of cherry bombs and one of his favorite games was trying to terrorize me. He'd hide things in my room – frogs, chameleons, spiders, snakes, everything in a farm kid's arsenal – trying to get me to scream and that's exactly what

I wanted to do. Instead, I made myself scoop up each wriggling, disgusting little critter and I carried them back to his room, asking him questions, calm as peaches. *Where'd you get this snake? Look at the stripe on its belly. What should I name him?*

He tried to spook me by telling me it was going to turn my hands green or make my hair fall out, but I just laughed and called him a liar. Oh, I was still scared. I hated the sight of a shoe box, because I knew he'd trapped something slimy or scaly inside it, but I learned how to turn a cry into a grin and how to talk loud when I wanted to curl up and whimper.

I didn't mind when Greg signed up for the army right after graduation and shipped off to Afghanistan. I knew he'd come home changed; I just didn't know if it would be changed better or changed worse.

The first and most important lesson in acting is to read your audience. Know what they want you to be and give it to them. My Sunday-school teacher always wanted sweet smiles and soft voices. My middle-school gym teacher wanted aggressive baseball players, swinging like Sosa even if you couldn't hit a parked car. My dad wanted hard workers – finish the chores well and without complaint. And even though I didn't like my chores, I became Cinderella and slogged through them as patient and graceful as you please. Fit the character to the play.

You knew you were playing it right when your audience was happy. They smiled and praised you and told each other how wonderful you were. Maybe part of you wished they'd see past the act, even once, and tell you Bridget Jones-style that they liked you just for who you were, but that never happened. No one wanted to go see independent movies with you. They laughed at the books you were reading and thought you were snobby because of the way you talked. So you put on the show, waiting for your real life to begin someday. And the applause made things inside of you warm that you hadn't even known needed to be warmed up. The real you might be so much colder. So you kept doing it.

I'd acted my entire life and so far it'd only gotten me here, to the first day of senior year at Pine Valley High School. My last year in this building EVER. The last year of mandatory pep fests, the last year of rubbery macaroni and cheese smells in the hallways, the last year of showing my work on math formulas with sine, cosine, and the other one.

I'd always been good at school, not because I was so interested in most of it, but because I could remember anything I read or heard. And that was pretty much what school was, just reading things and then saying them back. Teachers loved that. What I really hated, though, was doing group projects. The teachers always paired up the smart kids with the stupid or lazy kids, which was completely unfair. Sometimes we got to pick our own groups, but even then I always ended up with someone who didn't understand what we were doing. In American history last spring, Portia and Heather and I did a project on the civil rights movement and Heather kept confusing MLK with Malcolm X. Seriously. And at the end of class one day, Portia said, 'I totally understand why you mix them up. I mean, they're both black.'

And Heather just said, 'Yeah,' like Portia was serious.

Portia looked at me like she couldn't believe it – she's very sensitive to race issues because she's Hmong. But she's sensitive to everything else, too, and that's because she's Portia.

Later Portia passed me a note that said, 'Don't u hate it when ur dumb friends r dumber than u think they r?' I almost died laughing and had to hide the note before Mr. Jacobs saw it.

Portia's family moved here from Chicago when we were in ninth grade. Before then I'd been sure there was something wrong with me. Everyone else seemed to belong here without even trying; they didn't have to pretend to like things like 4-H or

American Idol. Then Portia came, bursting with stories about the Magnificent Mile and the lights on the marquee of the Goodman Theatre, and I realized there were places where it didn't matter if your cow won a blue ribbon at the state fair. We'd been best friends ever since.

I pulled up to school in Greg's old truck and waved at Portia, who was just walking in. She waited for me.

'OMG, I love it,' Portia said, eyeing my outfit as I walked up. 'Turn around.'

'You like?' I did a catwalk turn. My first-day-of-school outfit was the best New York impression I could find in the Apache mall in Rochester – a black pencil skirt and a gray twinset with my black church heels that had the pointy toes. My hair was long and straight, light brown because mom wouldn't let me dye it, and I usually wore it like today, swooped over my forehead and tied into a low, sleek ponytail.

'You're so East Coast, darling.'

'And you are totally California chic.' I grinned at her sundress and chunky sunglasses. 'I guess it makes sense that we're meeting in the middle.'

Portia laughed, slung her arm through mine, and pulled me inside.

'You just missed Becca Larson. She's got tan lines all over her boobs and half the football team was checking her out. I tried calling Maggie like three times to compare schedules, but she didn't answer or text back, so I don't know what her deal is.'

Portia kept chatting as we roamed the hallways and I put in a word here or there, but really, Portia didn't need a lot of replies. So I pretended I was at the ten-year class reunion. *Look at how small everything is! There's my old locker. Oh yes, I've been living in New York for the last decade. Manhattan, darling. I couldn't possibly live north of 96th Street.* Not that I knew where 96th Street was, but I would. In less than a year I would be there and my new outfit officially kicked off the countdown.

We got to our lockers and found Maggie flirting with Corey Hansbrook, who still had acne all over his neck. Gross.

'So.' Maggie turned to us after Corey left for class. 'Have you seen the new English teacher?'

'No! Dish.' With the promise of new gossip, Portia completely forgot about being snubbed. At least for now.

'I saw him when Dad and I were pulling into the parking lot and asked who it was.' Maggie's dad was the vice principal, but that never seemed to interfere with her sexcapades. My dad would've freaked out if he saw me hitting on everything with a penis.

'He's got gorgeous dark hair and cute squareish glasses and he looks like he's in college.'

'Ass?' Portia demanded.

'Couldn't tell. He was walking toward us. Kind of skinny, but hot, like library hot. Sweaty in the stacks, you know what I mean?'

I laughed along with Portia as the two-minute bell rang and didn't give the new teacher another thought until we walked into our fourth period AP English class. Then something changed.

I'd felt out of place in my New York outfit all morning, which was the whole point, really – I was taking my first, deliberate steps away from trying to fit in – but when I walked into English and saw the new teacher, somehow I felt exactly right. He was lounging in his desk chair wearing chinos, facing the window, and completely oblivious to the stream of students talking and laughing as they picked out where to sit. I didn't pay much attention to them either, only enough to slide into the front row and crack a notebook. Portia and a few other people settled in the desks around me and Maggie leaned over to whisper, 'See, he's totally hot.' I flashed her my Mona Lisa smile and started doodling random patterns on the notebook cover.

When the bell rang, the class quieted down and the new teacher moved to half-sit against the front of his desk. 'Right, I'm Mr. Lund and you're in Advanced Placement English Literature and Composition. If that's not the class it says on your schedule, you're in the wrong place.'

It was then, seeing him face-to-face, that I realized we'd already met. He glanced at me, but his attention kept moving around the class. He didn't make a big deal about his name or introductions like some teachers did and he didn't seem to care about the whispers that still lingered at the edges of the room.

'I'm sending some papers around. Mark your name on the attendance sheet and take a copy of the syllabus and read through it. This is what we'll cover for the first semester, but you'll need to sign up for the spring semester as well in order to take the test for college credit. Everyone clear? Questions?'

When no one spoke up he kept going, and a hint of a grin tugged the corner of his mouth up. 'This is by far the best class they gave me this year. You're all seniors on a college track so you're smarter than the average bear. We don't have to beat our heads against the five-paragraph essay or any of the standardized testing crap in here. We've got some room to play and do some actual learning. I'm going to expect you to do your own thinking, speak up about your opinions, and be prepared to debate and either defend or relinquish those opinions as our discussions demand. If you're quiet, I'm going to have trouble passing you. Speak up. I'm not Robin Williams in *Dead Poets Society*, all right? I'm not going to draw you out of your little self-conscious shells and show you that you're a closet poet.'

Most of the room started snickering.

'And on that subject, we won't be writing poetry in here. No poems allowed. I can't stomach them. Don't write a poem in response to one of our texts and expect me to pass you. This is about reading and critically thinking about what you've read and how the text has changed you. Every book changes you in some way, whether it's your perspective on the world or how you define yourself in relation to the world. Literature gives us identity, even terrible literature. *Moby-Dick,* for example, defined how I feel about rope. I don't know how anyone can write pages and pages of thinly veiled rope metaphors. If there are any Melville fans in the room, I might have trouble passing you.'

More laughter and this time I couldn't help joining in. He pushed away from the desk and collected the attendance sheet.

'I expect this class is going to be the highlight of my day. Don't let me down.'

As he started going through the syllabus I felt something good happening deep in my stomach, the same kind of feeling I got when the casting call for *Jane Eyre* was posted for the Rochester Civic Theater a few weeks ago and I knew I was going to get the lead role. Mr. Lund was smart, funny, and urban. He looked as wrong in the cement brick building of Pine Valley High School as I had felt for the last three years. And even though it seemed like he must be a mirage or some product of my bored-to-death-by-Pine Valley imagination, I could feel the heat coming off him from my seat in the front row. I could smell the soapy spice of his deodorant. He was real and he was talking to us like we were actual people, which was a teaching strategy no one had ever tried in this building before. The feeling in my stomach grew throughout the whole period and when the bell rang, I gathered my books with a huge smile on my face.

I was walking out with Maggie and Portia when Mr. Lund stopped me.

'Hattie the cashier.' He smiled as he erased his notes on the board.

'Peter the customer.'

'Let's go with Mr. Lund, all right?'

'All right.' I gave him a little wave and left for lunch.

Maybe it was Mr. Lund's attitude or just the promise of some actual literary discussions, but whatever the reason, I forgot about being excited for the end of the year. Now I was excited for what the year might bring.

◆

I worked the photo counter at CVS. It was way easier than working on the farm and they actually paid me here. All I had to do was develop pictures and run the cash register and sometimes I helped the old ladies pick out greeting cards for their grandkids. They always wanted to get the 99-cent ones with generic teddy bears on them. I thought they were being cheap until one of the pharmacy techs told me how much they spent on their meds every month. Jesus, remind me not to get old. *I must keep in good health, and not die.*

The store was pretty quiet when I punched in after school. Usually the rush came when the first shift at the plant finished and then again after five when the Rochester commuters got back into town. I pulled a blue smock over my New York outfit and started downloading picture files from the website and sending them to the printer. They were mostly kids' birthdays and holidays, sometimes a wedding or a vacation to Branson. Once there were two hundred pictures from Hawaii and another time someone had gone to Paris. I must have stared at the Paris pictures for hours, seeing myself sitting in those little cafés and strolling over the bridges, meeting a fashion photographer and going backstage at a runway show. I had the whole trip completely imagined, but when the lady came in to pick them up, she said it was just a layover on a business trip. My version was so much better.

It was always women who got pictures. Ninety-nine percent of the time when a guy came to the counter, they were picking up for someone else, like Mr. Lund did last week. The scrapbook ladies developed the most and they always told me what kind of album they were working on and showed me a picture or two, like I hadn't already peeked at all of them.

As I finished today's downloads, Tommy Kinakis walked over.

'Hey, Tommy.'

He nodded and opened his mouth, but nothing came out.

'You picking up some pictures?' I prompted, trying to help him out. He looked flustered and kind of wet.

'Yeah, for my mom. Told her I'd get 'em after football practice.'

'Is that why you're all sweaty?'

He huffed out a laugh and ran a hand through his hair, leaving it standing up in spikes. 'Coach rode us pretty hard today. First game's Friday night. You coming?'

Tommy and I had gone to school together since kindergarten, just like most Pine Valley kids. I'd known him when he was throwing rocks on the playground. I'd watched him give his country report on Germany in sixth grade, when he didn't know anything about WWII and flushed like a Red Delicious in front of the whole class. By high school he'd grown bigger and taller than my dad and he didn't talk much since his voice changed. He had dirty-blond hair and baby-blue eyes that darted around skittishly.

I pulled his mom's pictures and rang him up. 'I don't think I can. They've got me scheduled to work on Friday.'

'Here?' He looked around like he wasn't sure the place was real.

'Yeah, somebody's got to keep an eye on the store.'

'Don't know why. Everyone's going to be at the game.' He pulled out a faded leather wallet and handed me a twenty.

'Right? That's what I keep saying.' To no one. Ever.

Tommy nodded, all serious as he took his change. The subject of football seemed to loosen his tongue.

'You should come. We're going to destroy Greenville. Wipe the field with those bastards.'

'I know we will.'

'They're not going to lay one finger on Derek.' He pounded the counter with a fist. 'We got the best QB in the region this year.'

I had zero responses for that, so I just tossed him a flirty smile. He softened immediately and ducked his head as he stuffed his wallet away.

'I'm sure your boss can find someone else to work.'

'That would be awesome.' I was never in a million years going to ask my manager about it.

He finally raised his eyes and took the pictures from me, blurting, 'I'll watch for you in the stands.'

Half a grin, a spin, and he hurried out of the store.

I was confused for the next half an hour. Tommy Kinakis? What had I ever done to interest Tommy Kinakis? He sure wouldn't like me if I told him I had specifically asked to work Friday nights.

Football was just one more thing that separated me from everyone else in this town. I'd never gotten what was so great about smashing into a bunch of beefy guys and throwing a pointy ball around, but no one else in Pine Valley agreed with me. Every resident from age ten to a hundred and ten could tell you the names of the varsity roster, and they all showed up for each home game, screaming and cheering so loud I could hear the roar from in here. I liked working during games because the store was always completely dead; I could read books from the bestseller rack or paint my nails until the game was over and then everyone remembered some pictures or a card they had to pick up and mobbed the place. Before I knew it the shift was over, and all my coworkers loved that I let them have the night off.

After today's shift, I punched out and drove home on the winding dirt road that I knew as well as my own face. Our farm was about six miles from town, surrounded by nothing except fields and wind turbines. We got some of the money for the electricity created by the ones on our land. Wedding money, my dad always chuckled when I asked him about it. Even though I didn't think I was ever going to get married, I didn't tell him that. I always said, 'Holiday Inn wedding or Hyatt Regency wedding?' and he pretended to cuff me on the head and we laughed. With Greg gone in the war, he liked to think about me living one of those safe, normal lives – going to college, having a career, getting married, and giving him grandkids who would play tag around the hay bales and call him Pop-Pop.

When I pulled into the driveway I was surprised to see the kitchen light still on. Usually Mom and Dad had already settled into bed on the nights I worked. Dad sat up watching the bedroom TV and Mom would be reading whatever the library just got in, since she'd gone through everything else on their shelves. She never wanted to talk about her books though. She just swallowed those pages up and kept them tucked inside. Maybe that's what made her so hard to read sometimes, all those books floating around in her.

The table was set when I walked in and Mom pulled a chicken hot dish out of the oven, serving up two plates while I took off my coat and shoes.

'Late supper?'

'I wanted to eat with you, hear about your first day of school. Dad couldn't wait.'

'You don't eat supper at nine forty-five at night!' he bellowed from the bedroom. 'It'll give you heartburn.'

'That's what Tums are for!' I yelled back. He liked a good yell. Made him feel like the house was alive.

'Sit down, eat up. Did everybody like your new outfit?' Mom glanced at my clothes like I was still ten years old and playing dress-up with my cousins.

I shrugged. 'I don't know. It doesn't matter. I like the outfit.'

'You look . . . different. I suppose that's what you wanted.'

'Yeah, that's what all us rebellious teenagers want. Bucking the system with our pencil skirts and twinsets.'

'Eat your peas.'

I did and we fell quiet for a bit, while I tried to think of something worth telling her. It was a normal day for the most part.

'There's a new English teacher.'

'I heard.'

'He seems nice. Different, you know, from the other teachers.'

'Elsa Reever's son-in-law. He and Mary came to live with Elsa this summer.'

A few more bites. Dad's clock on the wall that was radio-synced with the international standard clock in Denver said it was 9:52. Mom's clock on the microwave read 10:03. She said it felt like it gave her a cushion.

But Dad's clock is right there, I always pointed out.

I don't look at it, she always replied.

'Tommy Kinakis came in for some pictures.' I said, just to make some conversation. Dad walked in to refill his water in his undershirt and boxers. He used to drink root beer while he watched the news every night, until the doctor told him he was pre-diabetic. He wasn't fat, not like some people with all their jiggles and bulges. He was just – solid. But I guess he was getting more solid than the doctor wanted, so now he drank water at night.

'Tommy Kinakis? He's looking to be one hell of a linebacker this season. They're expecting he'll get a pretty good ride at the U.'

'I think he was trying to ask me out.'

Dad grunted like Tommy had to be reevaluated now. Mom scraped off the last bits of hot dish from the pan and tossed them out the side door for the barn cats. She looked like she was talking to the cats when she replied.

'Tommy's a good kid. You could do a lot worse than a Kinakis.'

'I don't know. I guess.'

'You don't have to date anyone, Kinakis or no Kinakis.' Dad gave my shoulder a squeeze on his way back to the bedroom.

'Did you get those convent brochures you've been waiting for?' I yelled at his back and heard him chuckle.

I helped Mom clean up the table and load the dishwasher. She never said thank you or anything, but she appreciated it when I helped out. That was at least one thing I knew about her.

'Thanks for having supper with me.' I picked up my book bag and was on my way to my room when she stopped me.

'Hattie.' She wrung the dishrag out in the sink and draped it over the faucet to dry.

'Yeah?'

'Maybe you should go out with Tommy. It would be good for you to socialize, make friends in the real world, instead of surfing away on your phone like you do all the time lately.'

I should have just agreed, but ever since I bought my Motorola this summer she acted like I was carrying Satan in my purse. Like I wasn't going to school, and work, and rehearsals. Why couldn't I text my friends and check my forums? 'The internet's not full of made-up people, Mom. They're real, too.'

'Yes, but it's important to talk to people face-to-face. You don't know who some of these people are.'

'Of course I do. They're people just like me.'

'Oh, honey . . .' She shook her head and looked at me, looked right through me until I really did feel like I was nothing more than a ten-year-old girl playing New York dress-up by way of Rochester, Minnesota.

'There's still a lot for you to learn about the world.'

'Like what?' I bristled, ready to argue with her, but she just smiled like I'd proven her point.

'Don't stay up too late.' She came and kissed me on the cheek, her library book in one hand, cholesterol pills in the other. I watched her walk down the hallway into their bedroom and turn on her nightstand lamp. Her hair was almost half gray now. And for about the millionth time in my life, I wondered who my mother wanted me to be.

DEL / *Sunday, April 13, 2008*

JAKE AND I headed over to the Kinakis place right after the play.

'You think Tommy had something to do with it?' he asked.

Jake was still acting a little sore because I'd made him leave his cruiser at the station and ride with me. He didn't think two seconds ahead sometimes. I wasn't going to spook Tommy with two cop cars pulling up in front of his house. Out here, intimidation is never the right way to go, no matter what the city boys say. Country people know themselves. They don't do anything they think they shouldn't just because you wave a badge at them. And the more badges you wave, the more stubborn some of them get. It was all the Norwegian and Irish blood.

'I don't think anything about Tommy, except from what we know so far, Hattie might have left the school with him.'

'And she was definitely dating him,' he added.

'Yep.'

'Big kid.'

'Hmm.'

I could tell Jake was thinking along the same lines as me. Last year, sixty-five percent of all the women killed in Minnesota were done in by domestic violence. The number rang true around the station when the stats came out. We were a quiet county and we didn't have the murders, but we still saw a fair amount of domestics. Too many.

'So he takes Hattie out to get a little action at the Erickson barn after the play. Friday night, springtime, kids are going to be kids. They get into a fight about something and things get out of hand.'

I snorted. 'You're no more than a damn kid yourself. Sound like some TV cop.'

'I'm just putting together the story.'

'That's Tommy's job.'

We pulled into the Kinakis place and right away the wife came to the screen door. Martha, I think her name was. Jake and I took our time getting out of the car. If you weren't there to arrest somebody, it was always a good idea to give them a minute or so to puzzle out why you were there. They drew their own conclusions, and sometimes when you got to talking, they'd fill in blanks you didn't even know were there.

'Mrs. Kinakis.' I pulled my hat off as we approached. 'Is Tommy home?'

'He is.' She looked between each of us, not willing to step aside and let us in quite yet. 'He's in pretty bad shape, though. We just got the news.'

'That's why we're here.'

'Can't it wait till tomorrow? I was going to let him stay home from school.'

'Afraid not. This is a murder investigation and we need to talk to everyone who saw Hattie on Friday night. Now, we can do it here or down at the station. You decide.'

She looked torn for a minute, kind of scared and mad wrapped up together, before opening the screen door and waving us in.

We waited in the living room while she got him. Jake paced around, tapping his hat on his leg, while I looked over the pictures sitting on top of an upright piano. Lots of football shots, lots of Tommy riding tractors and posing with dead deer and pheasants.

Tommy came into the room with a parent on either side. He looked about five years old – round face blotchy with emotion, flannel shirt untucked, arms hanging like he didn't know he had them. At first he seemed like he wanted to say something, then just dropped his head and waited.

'Tommy, we've got some questions.'

Mrs. Kinakis jumped in again. 'He's really in no state to answer questions right now. I thought he was coming down with something even before we got the call. I'll bring him to the station first thing in the morning if you want.'

'This is a murder investigation, ma'am.' Jake was eager to do some talking. 'We don't have time to waste if we want to find Hattie's killer.'

Tommy flinched a little at the word. His mother steadied him with a hand.

'Best to talk while the memories are fresh,' I said.

'Well, sit down. Let's get this over with.' Mr. Kinakis waved a beefy hand at the couch and shot his wife a look that told her to hold her peace.

None of the Kinakises were what you'd call delicate flowers, so after they sat down on the wraparound sofa, there wasn't much room for Jake or me. I went to the window instead and gave everyone a minute to situate themselves. The sun was still well above the horizon, melting the last bits of snow that hugged the north side of their outbuildings.

'Hattie left the play on Friday night with you, Tommy?' A flock of Canadian geese honked overhead and landed in a field across the road. There was no answer behind me.

'How long were you dating her?'

There was a pause and a murmur before he managed to speak up. 'Since Sadie Hawkins, I guess.'

'Five, six months. You must have been pretty close.'

'I don't know.'

'Did you like the play on Friday? Did Hattie do all right?'

'I guess.'

Kid wasn't much for talking. I finally turned around and put myself dead in front of him and waited until he looked up. He was big; he could probably bench my whole weight, but he didn't look it right now. He looked small and scared, hunched between his mom and dad.

'Where'd you and Hattie go after the play, Tommy?'

'Out for a drive,' he admitted.

'For a drive where?'

'I dunno.'

Jake jumped in, hell-bent on playing bad cop. 'We can take you down to the station, if you'd prefer, or to the murder scene. Maybe that would jog your memory a bit.'

'What are you accusing my son of, Jake Adkins?' Mrs. Kinakis asked, standing up.

'No one's doing any accusing, Mrs. Kinakis. All we know is Hattie left the school with Tommy on Friday night and the next time anyone saw her she was dead. Now we need to know what Tommy knows. I understand it's hard to talk about, but it's going to be a lot harder if he chooses not to talk to us. For us and for him.'

Mr. Kinakis cleared his throat and motioned to his wife to sit down. She walked to the other side of the room instead, and we all waited for Tommy. After a minute, he took a breath and started in.

'I thought we were going to Dairy Queen, but she wanted to go out to Crosby instead.'

Mrs. Kinakis gasped and covered her mouth. 'You didn't tell us you took her to the lake.'

Tommy looked away.

'Where on Crosby?' I asked.

'The parking lot by the beach. We went there sometimes to . . .' He glanced at his dad. 'Just to make out. Nothing else. She hadn't wanted to go out there for a while.'

'What then?'

'Well, I thought she wanted to – you know, but she didn't. She said she couldn't see me anymore.'

'She broke up with you?' Jake asked.

Tommy nodded. 'She acted so strange. I told her there was still another couple months before graduation, and prom, too. Didn't she want to go to prom?'

He was looking at his hands now, almost seeming to forget we were all there.

'She got real quiet then. Looked sad for a minute. And she said some girls weren't meant to go to prom. It was like she already knew. Like she knew she was gonna die.'

He broke off and put his head in his hands.

'What happened then, Tommy?'

'She left.' His voice was muffled and I wished I could see his eyes.

'She got out of the truck and told me to go find some other farm girl who'd let me fuck her. Sorry, Mom. She said, "'Bye, Tommy," and then she walked off into the night. She never swore. I didn't know why she was acting like that. I didn't know what I did wrong.'

'Did you follow her?'

'No.'

'Must have made you mad, what she said.'

He lifted his head again and his eyes were dripping. 'It was cold out. I thought, let her walk home then. Fuck *her*, you know? Sorry, Mom.'

'Anybody else in the parking lot?'

'No.'

'You pass anybody on the way in?'

'I don't think so.'

'And you just let her walk off and went home?'

'I – yeah, I left, but I drove around for a while before going home. I was pretty mad.'

'You pick anybody up? Call any of your buddies to talk about it?'

He shook his head. 'I didn't want to tell anybody. I even . . . doubled back and drove around the back roads for a while, think- ing I might see her and maybe she'd apologize. She just wasn't like that, you know? We were going to do things. We were getting a limo for prom and all of us were going up to Derek's cabin in July. It's been all planned for months. Everyone's bringing their girlfriends.'

'Did you go back to the parking lot? Try to find her there?'

'I just drove by without stopping.' He swallowed and took a shaky breath. 'It was cold.'

'Then what?'

He looked at the door. 'I came home.'

'When did he get home that night?' Jake asked his parents.

'Didn't hear him,' Mr. Kinakis said. 'We were already in bed.'

'I'm sure I heard him come in.' Mrs. Kinakis jumped in. 'It couldn't have been later than ten thirty.'

'Tommy?' I turned back to him.

'Yeah, it was probably around then,' he mumbled.

We kept after him for more details and his story didn't waver.

He kept his head down and wiped tears from his eyes with meaty forearms. As we wrapped up the interview, Mrs. Kinakis wasted no time shooing us out the door. Before she got us all the way out, I shot Tommy one last question.

'Hattie ever talk about a curse?'

'Curse? Like a voodoo curse?' He looked up blankly and shook his head as Mrs. Kinakis hustled us out of her house.

After that Jake and I headed over to the east side of Crosby to check on Shel, the deputy who'd won the coin toss to search the lake. The rest of the boys had made a full search of the shoreline first thing this morning and turned up nothing. Most of them were combing Winifred's fields with the dogs now while Shel had the boat out on the lake, scanning the bottom. It was a shallow lake. Twenty feet at the deepest point. If there was anything to be found, Shel would see it soon enough.

While Jake radioed him, I poked around the parking spot by the beach. The gravel was dry and snow-free, so no chance of pulling tire tracks to see who else might have driven in here. I walked over to where the trail started and squatted down. It was a dirt path that you could hardly see in the summer, winding through the surrounding weeds and grasses, but now, just after the thaw, it was exposed plain as day. The ground was smooth, tramped down by years' worth of feet hiking around the lake. There were a couple half-prints here and there – not much to go on. A dozen people could have walked this path Friday night and you wouldn't know.

I followed the trail around to the barn – it wasn't far, maybe half a mile – and checked the shoreline to see if anything had washed up in the last few hours. Nothing.

When I got back, Jake was fiddling on his phone next to the beach. 'So far Shel's got a case of empty beer bottles with the labels all washed off. Looks like leftovers from last summer.'

'How much area has he got left?' I asked.

'He's covered over half the lake. Or so he says.'

I glanced at Jake, who sneered. 'He drives a boat like a twelve-year-old girl.'

'Better than whining about opening a case file like a twelve-year-old boy.'

Jake grunted.

'So Hattie gets out of the truck and Tommy thinks she's walking home, but she walks to the barn.'

'The barn window's on the other side of the building. You wouldn't be able to see any lights inside from here.'

'Exactly.' I faced it again.

Physically, it was the same decrepit pile on the horizon I'd seen every fishing season, but its substance had changed. Now it held a horror inside, the memory of a dead girl who'd been so bursting with life and plans, who'd swatted me on the shoulder every time I called her Henrietta and told me once with a cheeky grin, 'I'm going to arrest you for defamation of character.'

I'd laughed and explained you couldn't defame someone's character by calling them their legal name. And then we'd had a long talk about free speech and what was and wasn't legal, with Bud looking on, shaking his head like he was proud and kind of confused all at the same time about where this girl came from.

'So, if Hattie went there by herself, either the killer was waiting for her, or knew she was there and came later.'

I turned away from the barn and the memories I didn't need right now. 'Agreed. Odds are strong against a chance meeting out here. Someone knew she was going to the barn on Friday night.'

'You don't like Tommy as a suspect.' Jake said, watching the water.

'He's all we got at this point and he admitted a fight besides.'

'You don't like him for the killer,' he said again.

'Mmm.'

A yell came off the lake and Shel waved wildly at the monitors. I waited motionless, hoping for the knife, while he hauled up his find and motored back to the launch. It was a purse instead, found about twenty yards from shore and one-third of the way down the trail from the barn. A quick check revealed Hattie's license and school ID inside, which told us the killer probably tossed it as he left through one of the parking lots.

'You want to call off the field search?' Jake asked as we cataloged the contents on the cruiser's hood.

'After today. Keep them tracking along the main field paths until sundown, just to see if anything else turns up.' There was no sense wasting the borrowed manpower I had from Olmsted County.

We bagged and tagged everything in Hattie's purse, from her waterlogged phone down to the empty Lifesaver wrappers that littered every pocket, and after ten minutes of methodical examination there was only one thing that interested me.

'This guy.'

I held up the bag with a business card we'd found in Hattie's wallet. It was black on one side, white on the other, and some fancy writing said *Gerald Jones* with a website underneath. On the white side someone had written a phone number.

'I want to know who this is and why Hattie had his card. Check the number. Find out where he is.'

Jake nodded while he fiddled with another evidence bag. 'I think the phone's completely toast. Too bad.'

'Suppose we'll have to do our police work the old-fashioned way.'

Jake slid right into our standing argument as he gathered up the purse evidence and we got back into the cruiser.

'Del, the old-fashioned way is antiquated. You want to know about this Gerald Jones? If the phone had worked I could've just looked him up in her address book and seen when she last talked to him.'

'So you have to get a warrant for some phone records. You're breaking my heart.'

We argued until we got back to Pine Valley and then Jake went to pick up some Dairy Queen while I had Nancy finalize the press release. Neither one of them seemed to think about going home on a Sunday night. Usually if Jake had to work overtime, he would've started complaining by now, but I didn't hear a word out of him. Nothing about some date with legs up to there or the beers he was missing with his buddies. There was a silent understanding that we were all in this case together, to whatever end.

I talked to the field teams while we ate. Shel hadn't turned anything else up in the lake and the dogs were coming up empty. If we couldn't find the murder weapon, our hard evidence depended completely on the autopsy results and the forensics report on the items they'd found in the lagoon. We needed some prints or some DNA, badly.

'Man, you won't believe this stuff, Del. Listen to what I found.'

Jake brought his laptop into my office and started reading aloud. Nancy hovered at the door.

'The curse is one of the most widely held superstitions in theater, dating back centuries. It's rumored that Shakespeare wrote actual witches' spells into his play, which angered the real witches living during that time. Every performance of *Macbeth*, or "The Scottish Play" as generations of frightened actors refer to it, is considered dangerous and ripe for accidents and foul play.'

'What curse?' Nancy asked.

'What are you looking up that shit for?' I balled up my sandwich wrapper and threw it away.

'You're the one who asked Tommy about it.'

'Then you weren't listening too well.' I left the two of them and found some leftover coffee in the pot, smelled it, and put the whole thing in the microwave. By the time I'd gotten back it seemed like Jake had filled Nancy in. I glared at her big, frightened eyes.

'I didn't ask Tommy about the curse. I asked a murder suspect if he wanted to deflect some suspicion somewhere else. And he didn't.'

'So what does that tell us?'

'Either he killed her and he didn't know about the curse, or he didn't kill her and someone else did. Someone who isn't some goddamn ghost story.'

'Witch's spell,' Nancy corrected.

'Witches' spells, my ass.' The microwave beeped and I went out and poured the sludge into a cup.

'Listen to this,' Jake said when I came back again. 'Laurence Olivier nearly died several times while he was performing *Macbeth*. Three people died in a London performance in 1942. In Manchester in 1947, the actor playing Macbeth said he didn't believe in the curse. He was stabbed during a swordfight in rehearsal and died.'

'So some guy didn't like him and thought it was a good opportunity to off him.'

Jake wasn't paying attention to me. 'When Charlton Heston played Macbeth, he was severely burned.'

'That's what happens when you stand too close to a fire.'

They were both sucked into it now. Nancy read over his shoulder as Jake clicked through web page after web page.

'The legend is that Lady Macbeth died in the very first production back in 1606 for King James. The actor collapsed and died backstage. No one knew why.'

I shook my head over the coffee, draining the cup. 'You two are acting like that girl, Portia.'

'It's a lot of stuff to happen around one play, and now Hattie, too. Makes you wonder.'

'Makes *you* wonder, maybe. Makes me think I need another deputy on this case.'

'Come on, Del.'

Grabbing my coat, I left them both with their heads full of nonsense and headed back over to Bud's place. I needed to dig into Hattie's life more, see where she was spending her time, and I also wanted to see Bud and Mona. Make sure they had pulled themselves off the floor.

Curses. Jesus. It took all kinds. There wasn't anything to a curse but words. Just like blessings and prayers and all the rest of it. People used words to try to change what they should be changing with their own two hands. And if the problem was too big to fix, no words called up into the air would make a lick of difference. I drove past the turnoff to Bud's and kept going for a ways, just to let the land settle into me and put everything back in perspective.

They called Montana big sky country and that's what it was here, too. This land was all soft hills of corn and soybeans rolling out into the clouds in every direction. Farmhouses hid in clumps of trees here or there, but there wasn't anything to break up the horizon. The sky ruled, whether it was the sun baking the crops or the wind whipping dust devils across the roads. Some mornings the sky wouldn't even let you see the land; it'd lay a fog so thick you couldn't make out the car ahead of you. Everything came from the sky and it put you in your place, made you feel how small you were. For years after Nam, I parked out next to the highway and watched those big old thunderheads roll in. It was like a balm, seeing how they made everything under them dark and cowering, like seeing a piece of my soul laid out. That's why we had such good church people here. In the city the sky was all covered up by buildings and bridges and everything else. People forgot how little they were. They forgot they weren't in charge. Out here it was plain as day. You just looked out in front of you and saw God. Now, I didn't take to those ministers who said God listened to each and every one of us and intervened in our daily lives like some meddling boss. I used to believe it as a kid, I guess, but I'd seen too much to put any stock in it now. Look at Hattie. Who could see that mutilated, bloated body and tell me it was God's will? No, God had nothing to do with that. He had bigger things to worry about than how we managed to muck up our lives and deaths.

Just as I was turning back toward Bud's I got a call from the morgue.

'Sheriff Goodman,' a voice said. Fran didn't say hi like everybody else. Made you feel like you were being allowed to talk to her, even when she was the one calling you.

'What do you have?'

'No foreign fibers or hairs anywhere on her. No sign of a struggle either.'

'So she didn't see it coming?'

'I would say the blow to the chest came first and she either didn't have the time or the inclination to fight before it was delivered. The slashes to the face were postmortem.'

'How can you tell?'

'No struggle. The trauma to the face wasn't deep enough to cause her to lose consciousness, so it would have elicited a defensive response.'

'So it was quick.'

'As quick as any of us can die.'

Well, that was something. At least I could tell Bud that. 'Anything else?'

'Yes. There were traces of semen on her underwear.'

'Jesus Christ.' I swung over to the side of the highway and hit the brakes. A few cars swerved around me, slowing down like I might ticket them for speeding. I rubbed my forehead, thinking it through.

'Someone raped her before killing her?'

'It doesn't appear to be rape. I noted some mild abrasion. Nothing more serious.'

'What the hell does that mean?'

'It was aggressive, but probably consensual sex.'

'And the semen survived the water?' I asked.

'Only her legs appeared to be submerged. Her torso was dry, otherwise we wouldn't have been able to observe any sexual activity.'

'Can you tell when it happened?'

'It could have been anytime within a few hours of death, based on the abrasion.'

Had to have been after the play, then. Either Tommy wasn't telling all about parking with her at the beach or she'd gone off to meet a lover, an aggressive lover, who might have done her in.

'Well, we've got some DNA now.'

'That you do.'

'Good. I've got at least one suspect to test against.'

'The Hennepin County crime lab can do the comparison. It could take weeks, depending on their wait list. Have him come in to Mayo to submit the specimen.'

'He'll be there in the morning.' I'd make sure of that.

After I hung up with Fran, I stared at the sky for a minute, took a deep breath, and then continued out to Bud's.

There were trucks and cars littered all over the driveway, family pouring in to help out any little way they could. The minister was there and all the church ladies. I found Bud out in the barn with some of the men. They were talking about helping him get his corn in this year, and weren't taking no for an answer. I nodded at each one as they filed out, leaving Bud sitting on the arm of a combine, staring at the floor. I didn't ask him how he was doing. I didn't push my sympathies on him like another load I expected him to carry. There wasn't anything I could do except take him inside and sit him and Mona down in their bedroom away from all the hens and tell them matter-of-factly everything Fran had said. That Hattie didn't feel a thing. It was as quick as falling down. That she wouldn't have had two seconds to be scared.

Then I told them about the sex.

'What?' Bud shot up, looking like he wanted to take a swing at me. I hadn't even mentioned the aggressive part.

'God damn that Kinakis kid. God damn him.' Bud wasn't in any mood to think beyond that, so I turned to Mona.

'Was she seeing anybody besides Tommy Kinakis?'

She shook her head once, a tight denial. 'She'd been seeing him since before the holidays.'

While Bud stormed around the room, probably planning Tommy's death, I sat on the bed next to Mona. She was working her hands one over the other, staring hollowly at the remains of the table she'd fallen into that morning.

'Did you know she was having sex, Mona?'

Bud swung around, all ears now.

'No.' Steady tears leaked into the crows' feet around her eyes. She didn't bother to wipe them away. 'No, I didn't know that. I thought there was something she wasn't telling me, but I didn't think it was to do with sex. Hattie was never starry-eyed about a boy in her whole life. Honestly, I never thought she liked Tommy that much. I couldn't pin down exactly why she was dating him.'

'That kid's got some answering to do.'

'Hold on there, Bud. We're going to talk to Tommy again in the morning, and have him submit a DNA sample to test against what we found on Hattie.'

'You're sure it wasn't rape?' Mona whispered.

'It wasn't rape. The medical examiner was positive. Don't be thinking that, either one of you.'

Neither of them seemed able to speak anymore.

'I'm going to need to look through Hattie's room. If you remember anyone else she was close to or in contact with, call me
right away. Doesn't matter what time.'

Mona resumed crying in earnest now and Bud went over to her.
I left them alone and went to Hattie's bedroom upstairs, without a
word to the hens hovering by the kitchen doorway.

I was surprised there wasn't much to see. A twin bed, dresser,
and desk. She didn't have posters splashed all over like most teenagers, just one picture – framed – of the New York City skyline
above her bed. Her closet was about as messy as you'd expect but
it was all clothes and purses holding lip gloss, bobby pins, movie
ticket stubs, and loose change. Nothing that helped. Her desk
seemed about the most personal thing in the room. The drawers
were full of magazine pictures of subway stations, neon signs, and
women walking down city sidewalks with little rat dogs tucked in
their purses. I couldn't find a diary or a journal, which struck me as
odd. Hattie'd seemed like the type to keep one. Her laptop had a
lot of stuff on it though and maybe we'd find something there. Jake
could dig into those files with his computer tricks.

In the bottom drawer I found a program for a Rochester play
where Hattie had gotten the lead. I remembered Bud saying something about that last fall. Scratching his neck, shrugging his shoulders as we winterized his boat. *Kid's a natural. Damned if I know
where she got it.*

Flipping through the program, my eye caught on a particular
name.

Gerald Jones, director.

Now, why would Hattie be carrying, on the night of her death,
the card and phone number of a man she hadn't seen in over six
months? A man she was connected to through the theater?

I smiled grimly, ready to put Jake in his place when I got back to
the station. Look what old-fashioned police work turned up.

PETER / *Saturday, September 8, 2007*

SHAKESPEARE WAS one cunning SOB. I didn't care much for his comedies, the farces full of village idiots and misplaced identities. I'd always gravitated to the tragedies, where even witches and ghosts couldn't distract the audience from this central psychological truth: by our own natures, we are all inherently doomed. Shakespeare didn't write anything new. He didn't invent jealousy, infidelity, or the greed of kings. He recognized evil as timeless and shone a spotlight directly, unflinchingly on it and said, *This is what we are and always will be.*

Of course, right at this minute, I had no idea what my wife was.

'So Peter just found out he'll be directing the spring play at school,' Mary said conversationally as she sliced through the tender breast meat of a chicken. She smiled at me, encouraging me to jump into the conversation, but I couldn't concentrate on anything besides the chicken. It had been alive a few hours ago and now wafts of rosemary and cooked skin rolled off it, turning my stomach as Elsa and our neighbor Winifred lifted their plates for the entrée.

'Do *The Music Man*. I like the songs in that one,' Winifred ordered. She often joined us for Saturday-night dinners and usually I looked forward to the bang of the screen door that announced her arrival. She was wiry and opinionated and had all the strength of heart that Elsa lacked.

I shook my head weakly. 'The principal said it had to be Shakespeare.'

He'd told me he didn't care which play, except it couldn't be *Romeo and Juliet*. Nothing suicide-related, he said.

Elsa smiled fondly as she scooped up some peas. 'Lyle always likes his Shakespeare.'

'Remember when he had them do *A Midsummer Night's Dream* in Will Davis's bean fields?' Winifred scoffed. She glanced over and filled me in on the joke.

'All the chairs were set up on what they found out was a giant anthill, and before the first act was over, the whole audience was covered in biting ants.'

Elsa put a quavering hand on Winifred's, changing the topic back to how she didn't like Winifred living alone anymore. Having Mary and me around helped her see how much better it was to have support, she said. Winifred dismissed her friend's concerns with a practiced flair and steered the conversation to the new furnace that was being installed in the town café.

Everyone enjoyed Saturday-night dinners with Winifred. The conversation was more animated. Elsa perked up and her complexion looked healthier, which made Mary relax. Once, we played cards afterwards and Winifred even had a beer with me, but it became obvious that Elsa didn't have the capacity to play hearts anymore, so the game ended and the TV was switched on before she could become too flustered.

I was always the third wheel at these dinner parties, trying to find my way into conversations that debated the merits of different furnace brands or analyzed the year's weather predictions from the *Farmers' Almanac*. All my references to literature or pop culture fell flat, despite Mary's or my attempts to explain the context. They didn't intentionally ostracize me, but I was outside all the same. To-night, though, I couldn't even try to engage. My attention was torn between the chicken in the center of the table and Mary's profile as she refereed the conversation.

'That doesn't look very good.' Winifred leaned over my plate and poked at my veggie burger.

'Try it if you want.' I got up and grabbed a Coke from the fridge.

'They're actually pretty tasty,' Mary put in. 'Especially grilled and with some cheese and tomato on top. They make great lunches.'

'No, thanks,' Winifred replied. 'I only eat food I recognize.'

Then she and Elsa launched a discussion of the quality of vari-ous TV dinners. I took a long drink.

After dinner Mary and I tackled the cleanup. She washed the dishes and tossed comments into the older ladies' discussion via the pass-through window between the kitchen and living room, just like everything was normal. Her hands were scalded red from the hot water. I couldn't stop staring at them. She laughed at some-thing, then caught my expression and sobered as she handed me a plate to dry.

As soon as the kitchen was in order I excused myself and went upstairs. I'd been spending more and more time in the spare room, which was obvious from the piles of books and stacks of student papers covering the tops of the dusty storage boxes. The heat from the oven had drifted up, stifling the air in the tiny space. Opening a window that screamed against its sash, I began picking up books at random. Lifting one, I traced the gilt in the cover, then grabbed another and checked a copyright date I already knew. I flipped to arbitrary pages and read a few lines, then turned to the next book and the next. I couldn't settle into any of them, couldn't make myself forget what happened today.

The worst part was that it had been my idea in the first place.

Show me what to do with the chickens and I'll take some shifts with them. Give you a breather, I'd offered the other day. It was a desperate move on my part. I could think of a thousand things I'd rather do to reclaim my marriage besides clean up chicken shit, but all my efforts with Elsa were failing. Whether it came from pride or shame, she allowed only Mary to help her with most tasks, and whenever I asked her how she felt the answer was the same. 'Fine, fine.' So chicken shit it was. Although she raised her eyebrows when I made the suggestion, Mary agreed.

Since school started I'd been sleeping in on Saturday mornings, but even after grading papers late into the night I staggered out of bed at 5:30 today and trudged along behind her through the yard, which wasn't even touched by the gray before dawn.

She showed me how to collect, wash, and store the eggs, how to clean up the excrement, and how to replace the straw as needed. We fed them while they lurched around and pecked at our boots, following us with their blank, beady stares. She lectured about how to look for disease and sickness and then she picked up one of the hens and carried it to the back of the main barn and killed it.

I didn't even realize what was happening until Mary had the knife in her hands.

'What are you doing?'

'What does it look like I'm doing?' Her voice was matter-of-fact. The blade flashed pink from the sunrise and the bird struggled to free itself from her grip.

'Is it sick? What's wrong with it?'

The bird's eyes were rolling frantically now and I couldn't seem to focus on anything else.

'Nothing's wrong with it. Winifred's coming over for dinner tonight.'

And with that she severed the bird's head from its body and blood spewed onto the ground. The body flopped and rolled, as if unaware of its own death and frantically trying to recover the piece it had lost. I stumbled backward until I ran into the barn wall. If there'd been anything in my stomach, I would have heaved it right over that fountain of blood. Mary went to a nearby hose and washed off the knife like she'd been slicing a birthday cake, angling it to one side and then the other until I could see her face in the blade.

The bird bounced over to me and I ran away from it, which made Mary roll her eyes.

'It's just a chicken, Peter. You don't run away from them in the grocery store.'

'They don't run at me in the grocery store!' I yelled.

'I'll probably roast it with some potatoes, but I'll throw on something separate for you.'

I didn't answer. She stood on one side of the headless chicken and I stood on the other without any idea how to respond to her polite offer to make me a vegetarian meal.

The thing was, most of my friends would have been impressed. *Chick's got brass balls,* I could hear them saying. Even when she'd outmaneuvered them with her easy logic on whatever issue being debated at the bar – raising minimum wage or the literary effect of Harry Potter on the millennials – she always bought them a beer and made them laugh in the end. If I told them about what happened today, they would've raised her status to legendary.

I didn't know why it bothered me so much. I'd probably seen Mary eat a hundred chicken wings during those times at the bar.

Would I be okay with my wife eating dead animals if she couldn't bring herself to kill them? It was ludicrously hypocritical. I knew that. But that damn chicken's eye wouldn't go away. It stared up at me from the lifeless head, surrounded by a pool of its own blood.

Someone laughed in the living room and then I heard footsteps on the stairs. Mary appeared in the doorway and leaned against the jamb, mirth infusing her features.

'I found an Old Maid card set and thought it might be fun. Then Winifred said there were too many old maids in the room already.'

'They're old widows, not old maids.'

'True.' She shrugged and grinned. 'Do you want to play?'

'I don't know that game.'

'It's easy. Even Mom can handle it, I think.'

'No, I don't feel like playing.'

'What's the matter?' Mary came into the room and sat on the edge of the desk next to me. She brushed some hair out of my eyes.

'Nothing.' I pulled back.

'Are you still upset about the chicken?'

'You could have at least warned me beforehand.'

'Oh, come on, Peter.'

I pushed away from her dismissive tone and paced the edge of the room. 'It didn't bother you even a little, did it?'

'What do you want me to say? This is how I was raised.'

Everything about her demeanor told me I was the one with the problem. I was the aberration in the room. After seven years she either didn't understand my moral choices or she didn't give a shit. I shook my head and picked up a book on top of a stack by the window, turning pages like there was something important inside, if only I could find it.

'You're not coming down?' I could hear the hurt in her question and I didn't care.

'No. I think I'll pass on the exciting card game with the seventy-year-olds.'

'Would it kill you to be part of this family?'

I advanced on her, jabbing the book in the direction of the barns outside the window. 'What do you think I was doing this morning? You think I was collecting eggs and hauling straw bales for fun?'

'No, I know you hated every second of it. You couldn't have made it more obvious if you tried.'

I barked out a laugh. 'Oh, trust me, I could have made it a lot more obvious.'

'I didn't think it was going to be like this.' She blinked back tears. 'I knew it would take some adjustment to move here, but it's like you're not even trying.'

Shaking my head, I turned back to the window. If she thought 'some adjustment' would turn me into a butcher, there was nothing else I could say to her.

She lingered and drew a breath, as though on the verge of saying something else, then I heard the creak of the floorboards in the hallway and her slow descent down the stairs.

I sunk into a chair and dropped my head to the book in my hand, drilling the imprint of the spine into my forehead. The truth was, I *did* want to be part of this family. What wouldn't I give to relax and joke away the evening with Mary, or the Mary of before? To unlearn what I knew about her?

Aggravated, I sat up and tossed the book on the desk and that's when I noticed the title for the first time. *Shakespeare's Complete Tragedies.*

Nothing suicidal, the principal had said, sitting jovially in front of his glass cabinet full of model tractors, each green body carefully polished to catch the light. *I don't like putting suicide out in front of teenagers. Don't want to give the misguided ones any ideas.* He didn't want to disturb teenagers who were learning to behead chickens on their fathers' farms, who were guiding cows and pigs into trailers and driving them to their deaths.

I paged through until I landed on *Macbeth*.

Macbeth – arguably the most violent play Shakespeare ever wrote. I could pour buckets of red corn syrup all over the stage, let them kill and feast on each other's blood. No romantic suicides here; *Macbeth* was pure carnage fueled by greed and madness and revenge. The Bard always reveals our natures and in this play he'd said that in the right situation, with the right motive, all of us are murdering monsters.

I marked the page and pushed the book to the far side of my desk, away from everything else, as if afraid of what was inside.

BY SEVEN o'clock Monday morning I had Jake digging into Hattie's laptop and was knocking on the Kinakises' door. Mrs. Kinakis was none too pleased to see me again, especially when I explained that I needed Tommy to give DNA samples that morning. Both parents were royally ticked off that Tommy'd landed on the suspect list, but Tommy himself didn't have anything to say about it. He was as quiet as yesterday, sitting at his mom's kitchen table and poking at a bowl of oatmeal turning to concrete in front of him.

'I'll do it.' He finally spoke up, killing his parents' arguments mid-word. He put his varsity letterman's jacket on without a backward glance at either of them and we were on our way to Rochester.

Tommy stared out the passenger side window the whole ride, wiping his eyes every once in a while. He'd asked if he had to sit in the back before we got in and that was the last he'd spoken.

When we were almost into the city, I told him he was doing

a good thing. 'I could've easily gotten a warrant, you know. You saved me the trouble.'

He nodded and a minute later asked, 'Will the blood clear me?'

'Semen.'

'Semen?'

'Found some on her body. You sure it wasn't yours?' I wanted to ask him without his parents staring him down.

'No.' He was mighty quick to answer. 'I already told you, she wouldn't let me.'

Another pause, while the fact of it must have sunk in. 'Some-one . . . raped her?'

He seemed to have trouble with the word.

'Can't say.'

'So my . . . stuff . . . won't match and then you'll clear me, right? That'll take me off your list?'

'We'll see.' I didn't tell him that, apart from Gerald Jones, he *was* the list.

He was quiet for the rest of the morning, letting nurses lead him around like some overgrown pup. After dropping the kid off back home, I swung by the Erickson place again. Winifred's Buick was in the garage and a Chevy pickup was parked out front. I banged on the screen door for what felt like ten minutes with no answer and then headed around to the outbuildings. Winifred leased most of her land to one of the big farming cooperatives and I'd never seen her set foot in the fields since the day she shot Lars, but she had to be here somewhere.

I poked around until I heard voices coming from the machinery shed.

'– don't know what I'm going to do.'

'You're not going to say a word, that's what.' Came the reply. The first person was kind of muffled, but Winifred's old, crackly voice carried clear as day.

'Can't keep it a secret forever.'

'Can't say nothing till you decide what you're going to do.'

'We're not talking about this.'

'You have to talk to someone and I know exactly what you're feeling.'

'It's murder.'

'Murder has its place, just like everything else. When I was–' Winifred's voice cut off and there was a pause. Then a gunshot deafened me.

I threw myself against the side of the shed, my gun already drawn.

'God damn it, Winifred!'

'Who's there? You better get the hell off my property before I let another one fly.'

'It's Sheriff Goodman. I'm coming in there and if I don't hear a gun hit the floor in five seconds, I'm going to come in shooting. Do you hear me?'

Silence.

'Winifred? I'm counting.'

There was a thud and a grunt. 'Fine, then.'

I crept into the half-lit building, my aim trained on the two women by the right wall. Winifred was dressed in a checkered housedress. She had stringy, tight curls all over her head, a pipe in her mouth, and a put-out expression on her face. An old rifle lay by her feet. The woman next to her was at least forty years younger and drawn up into herself like a fetus perched on a stool. She had a blond ponytail and round, tear-streaked cheeks. Neither of them posed any threat, but I kept a bead on them just to make a point.

'You shooting at all your visitors now, Winifred?'

She crossed her arms and sniffed at me. 'Sure, when they're sneaking up on me and there's a murderer on the loose.'

Sighing, I holstered my weapon and fixed a stare on the younger woman. Even though I didn't recognize her right off, she seemed familiar.

'I got a few questions for you, Mrs. Erickson.' One of the most pressing ones was why these two had just been talking about murder, but I had a feeling I'd get more out of the younger one on her own.

'I'm in the middle of something.'

'No, no. I'll go.' The woman uncurled herself and was trying to leave when I stepped in her path.

'I didn't catch your name.'

'It's Mary Beth Lund, Sheriff.' She reached out a hand. 'Or Mary Beth Reever, you probably remember me as.'

'Sure, sure.' I shook her hand, which seemed strong enough despite her red eyes. 'You and your husband moved in with your mom last year, right?'

'Yeah, Mom's not doing too well and she won't move off the farm.'

'Lot of stubborn old people out here.' That got a snort out of the one standing next to me.

Mary Beth smiled. 'Anyway, we're just up the road and Winifred's been so great, always letting me borrow something or stop by to chat.'

'I'll walk you out, sweetling.' Winifred put her arm around the woman and used her free hand to puff on her pipe. 'Del, you can head on up to the house.'

I watched them go, walking slow and talking quiet. There was no reason the two of them couldn't be friends, but their conversation didn't sit right at all. You didn't come talk murder with Winifred Erickson for the hell of it.

I glanced out at the strip of woods on the north side of the property where Winifred shot Lars twelve years ago. I remembered it like it happened that morning, which is always the way it is with killings. They stick to you after everything else falls away.

I found him laid out on his back, shot clean through the side with a .308 Winchester. It was a bad year for coyotes and the Erickson chickens were suffering. Lars had been coming home from the Reevers' at the same time Winifred was chasing a coyote away from their coop. She told the jury she shot at it and hit Lars by mistake. Even though she inherited a $500,000 life insurance policy and the entire farm, which Lars owned free and clear, unlike most in these parts, the jury still let her off on account of the number of chickens she could prove they lost plus the fact that she shot Lars in the side from a distance. Apparently the jury thought that to want to kill someone, you had to be facing them and up close.

Lars was a regular son of a bitch, always going on about who was cheating him today and raising stinks about every little thing. Most people figured it was on account of losing both his boys so young – one to pneumonia and the other to Vietnam – but for my money Lars was just born like that. Nothing good enough for him. Didn't think anyone was on his side. Winifred told the jury, as plain and sober from that witness stand as when I found her standing by him, that there'd been nothing she could do to help him. And I think she meant it, except I doubt she was talking about that morning.

'I don't know a thing about it, so you can save your breath.' Winifred stumped up the porch steps as Mary Beth's truck kicked up a dust cloud over the driveway.

'What was she crying about?' I nodded in the direction of the road.

'That's her business.'

'Everything's my business in a murder investigation.'

'Marital troubles didn't get the Hoffman girl killed.' Winifred opened the front door and waved me in behind her.

'You must know a lot about it then, if you can say what did or didn't cause it.'

She poured out a cup of tea that must have gone cold and set the kettle on for another.

'I know as much as the next person about Hattie Hoffman.'

'The barn's on your property.'

'When's the last time you think I made it out there? My arthritis wouldn't let me get halfway.'

'Oh, I think you could do anything you put your mind to, Winifred.'

She cackled at that and slapped a second cup down on the table. 'It's Earl Grey or go thirsty.'

'Earl Grey's fine.' I sat down and watched her fix the tea. After she got everything situated, she puffed at the steam over her cup and her tongue loosened up some.

'Course I knew the kids were using it, that's why I put the No Trespassing sign up on the east side over there, so no one could sue me if the roof fell in on one of their heads. But I haven't been out that way in years.'

'You didn't see or hear anything strange on Friday night?'

'Not a thing. Came home from the play and went to bed.'

Something sank inside me when she said it and it wasn't only because I knew she was telling the truth. I should've been up at the school, too, cheering Hattie on, watching her shine for the last time. Drinking in silence, I watched a cardinal land on one of Winifred's bird feeders out the window. The tea was bitter.

'Mona must be beside herself,' she said after a while.

'She is.'

'I been there. Something shifts inside you after your child dies, like things that were liquid before turn hard and brittle.' She nodded out the window absently, lost in an old, familiar sorrow that was as part of her now as the curls on her head.

I finished the tea and made my way to the door. 'Nothing else you know offhand about Hattie, is there?'

'Seemed a little uppity this last year, talking about going to New York and being on Broadway, but I didn't think so on the way home on Friday. That girl could act. It was something to see.'

'Well, I'm not going to rule out making more sweeps of the property, and the barn's off-limits until I tell you personally otherwise.'

'Sure, sure.'

'And stop shooting at people or I'll confiscate your rifle.'

'Mm-hmm.' She walked me out to the cruiser, not worried at all about losing her gun. She probably had five more where that one came from.

'Is Mona still out at the house or did she go to her mom's?' she asked.

'I don't know. She was there yesterday.'

'I'd better go see her.' Winifred pulled her worn sweater around her middle, even though the sun was warm today. She looked up at the sky and then around the horizon, sighing. 'Kids leaving all the time and the ones that haven't are getting killed. Men dropping off with heart attacks every other day. Pretty soon this is going to be a country of nothing but old women.'

I flashed her a cheeky grin. 'That suits me fine.'

She gave me a nice slap on the shoulder for that as I got in the car. 'Oh, go on.'

◆

As I followed my nose over to the Reever farm, I saw I'd missed two calls from Jake and phoned in at the station on the way.

'Del, where are you at?'

'Checking a few things out. Did you find Gerald Jones?'

'He's in Denver until tomorrow. Says he's been there since last Wednesday. We're confirming, but it sounds like a pretty tight alibi.'

Damn. Now my suspect list was down to Tommy.

'I want to talk to him when he gets back.'

'Should we bring him in?' Jake asked.

'No, I'll go to him. Anything from the forensics team?'

'No, not yet, but—'

'What about Hattie's computer?'

'You're not going to believe what I found.'

'Well, you've been calling me like a spurned woman all morning. Must be something worth telling.'

'Jesus, Del, I've got a lead on the killer. Did you want me to wait around until you've had your Dairy Queen?'

I pulled into the Reevers' driveway and bumped over the mud ruts to park in front of the house.

'What do you have?'

'It looks like Hattie was talking a lot to some guy named L.G.'

'The hell kind of name is that?'

'It's a handle.'

'A what?'

'I'll explain it to you when you come in. Pick up some Dairy Queen, will you?' And he hung up, the little shit.

I'd known the Reevers since they'd found out they were pregnant with Mary Beth. The whole town could spot them coming a mile away – John hustling to open doors and lift grocery bags, Elsa rolling her eyes at him with one hand hugged to her belly, both of them well into their forties and grinning like fools on their first date. Happiness like that was polarizing – it either drew you in or pushed you out, and in those years after the war, I didn't know how to be drawn in. I was a patrol cop, which was the only thing I was good for then – handing out tickets and laying down the law, everything in black-and-white – and it got to be whenever I saw the Reevers coming down Main Street, I found something that had to be done on the other side. It wasn't until I pulled John over for speeding a few years later, Mary Beth bouncing and babbling in her car seat, and John looking bashful, saying, 'It makes her giggle' that I found myself laughing, standing outside their Pontiac on the shoulder of Highway 12. I finally got drawn in.

'Why, Del, what brings you out here?' Elsa answered the door, wearing an oxygen line in her nose and looking like a mild breeze could knock her down. She'd been fading more and more ever since John died.

'I'm looking for Mary Beth.'

'Oh, she's over at Winifred's.' She braced a hand on the door-jamb and squinted toward the woods that separated the two farms.

'I don't think so. I stopped by there and saw her leave.'

'Oh?'

'Looks like her truck's in the driveway.'

The evidence of it seemed to confuse her, so I switched gears.

'I met your son-in-law up at the play yesterday.'

'The play.' She said it like she was trying to bring a memory into focus. 'I think we were supposed to go see a play this weekend.'

'Must be nice to have some extra hands with the farm.'

'Mary Beth does it all. He doesn't do enough around here to fill a thimble.'

'The fields and the animals, huh? That's a lot for one person.'

'No, she doesn't work the fields. We rented them out when John passed on. Just the chickens and the gardens.'

'Nice to have fresh chicken on the table.'

'Exactly.' Elsa pointed at me, inexplicably vehement. 'That's what any regular man should say.'

'Mind if I check around for her?'

'Go on ahead. I better not. She gets after me when I try to pull this oxygen tank through the mud.'

I touched my hat and headed across the way, poking my head in a few buildings until I found Mary Beth in the chicken barn collecting eggs. A group of hens pecked around her feet, some white, some brown and orange, all of them scratching and clucking away. They weren't packed in like I'd seen in some farms, where you could barely see the floor through the sea of animals. This flock looked more like a mismatched extended family gathered around their matriarch.

'Mrs. Lund?'

She yelped and jumped about a foot out of her skin, scattering the chickens in all directions, but managed to hold on to her basket. She had the look of her dad, now that I knew who she was – fair and sturdy, the kind of bones built for weathering storms, and it seemed like she was in the middle of one right now. The basket trembled on her arm and her breathing didn't quite settle down, even after she saw me.

'Sheriff. My God.' She put one hand over her heart and checked her harvest for breaks.

'Didn't mean to scare you.'

'That's okay,' she said without looking up.

'How are things going out here?'

'Fine.' She wasn't the chatty type, apparently. Mary Beth had never been a troublemaker growing up, so I didn't know her too well. I think she played volleyball in high school and had been in the paper for National Merit Scholar things now and again.

'I was just up at the house talking to Elsa. She said you do most everything around here these days.'

'I do what I can. I'm not my dad, that's for sure.'

'He'd be the first one to say thank God for that.'

She parted with a small smile, but it disappeared as quick as it came and she busied herself checking the remaining nests.

'What brings you out here?'

'Eggs, to tell the truth,' I lied, watching the chickens dart in and out of a low door that must have led to an outdoor space. 'When I saw you at Winifred's I happened to remember you'd started selling them again. I used to buy some from John from time to time.'

'Sure.' She went through the last of the nests and then motioned me to follow her to the main barn, where a series of old refrigerators lined one wall.

'How many do you need?'

'A dozen'll do me fine. How much?'

'No charge.' She handed me a carton and waved off the five-dollar bill I'd pulled out of my wallet.

'Sorry, I can't take them for free. Got into a bit of a sore spot with that once. Had a bartender who let me drink free for about a year during one of those years you don't want to remember too well anyway. It seemed like a great deal until I found out he was selling the marijuana his cousin grew in the middle of his cornfields. He thought I owed him. Never forgave me for throwing them both in the clink.'

'I'm not growing marijuana,' Mary Beth said with a nervous laugh.

'All the same.' I held the money out until she took it.

'I don't have change on me, so you'll have to take another dozen.'

'Sure, I'll come back when these run out.' I shifted the carton under my arm and switched topics. 'You didn't know Hattie Hoffman, did you?'

'No,' she answered quickly, starting to unload the eggs she'd just collected.

'She was practically family to me.'

'I'm sorry.' Whatever else she might have been feeling, she sounded like she meant it.

'You okay, Mary Beth?'

'Yeah. There's just a lot going on right now.'

'Mmm. Your mom and the farm and everything.'

She nodded and kept working.

'Why were you talking about murder with Winifred?'

'What?' Her head shot up and she finally looked me in the eyes. Hers were surprised and tense, the kind of tense that builds up over months and years, where the muscles don't even remember how to relax. Winifred had said something about marital troubles.

'I heard the two of you before she open fire on me. She said murder has its place.'

'It was nothing. Not what you think.'

'How about you tell me what it was and then I'll tell you if it's what I think.'

'It was just . . . Peter, my husband.' She swallowed and stopped, then her eyes darted around the floor. 'He's a vegetarian. Thinks it's wrong to kill animals. Winifred was trying to reassure me.'

Even though it explained Elsa's comment, the rest of the conversation still didn't jibe.

'Anything else?' I asked.

'It's between me and her. I don't . . .' Her mouth became one firm line and I knew I wasn't getting any more out of her.

'I need to see your knives.'

'Why?' Her eyes flashed, but there was no fear in them.

'Hattie was stabbed to death.'

She nodded and silently obliged. The autopsy report had come in last night and it said the wounds were caused by a straight, single-edge blade about six to eight inches in length. I measured each of Mary Beth's knives and none of them fit the specs. The only one with the correct length was curved and none of them had the right blade width. I didn't think I was going to find the murder weapon on Mary Beth Lund's tool bench, but there was something she wasn't telling me.

She walked me back to the cruiser and lifted a hand to Elsa, who watched us through her lace curtains.

'Hey, does a handle mean anything to you?' I asked. Mary Beth was only a few years older than Jake.

'Like a bucket handle?'

'No, like a name.'

'Sure, that's what people call their screen names for websites and blogs and stuff.'

I thanked her and started whistling as I backed out of the driveway, ready to put my chief deputy back in his place.

———◆———

I pulled into Pine Valley proper and cruised down Main Street, nodding to the men outside the feed store who usually stood around jawing about the price of hogs and corn seed. They watched me for the whole stretch of road with cap-shaded eyes and grim mouths, leaving no doubt about today's topic of discussion.

When I got into the station, Jake was hunched over Hattie's computer like it was showing the ninth inning of game seven of the World Series. I dropped a sack of burgers on the desk.

'You're not going to believe what I found.' He fished out a burger and bit in without a glance at what he was eating.

'So' – I sat on the desk – 'Hattie met someone online with a handle named L.G.'

'How'd you know?' Jake managed to look genuinely disappointed with a mouthful of bun. Clearly he'd been looking forward to explaining handles to the old man who knew squat about the internet. I swallowed a smile.

'Stands to reason.'

'Well, I don't think she saved everything. See? She was copying and pasting messages into a text document. Some of the messages don't seem to pick up where they left off and there's no names on any of it, except this one.'

He swung the screen toward me.

HollyG,

I should probably use your real name now, but I can't bring myself to do it. This last fragment of duality will allow me to say what I must. Our friendship is over. It was a dangerous idea in the first place, no matter who you were, but now that Jane Eyre has unmasked us it's obvious how painfully wrong this is. Please know that I wish you well and blame myself entirely.

We can never speak of this. Tell no one.

Goodbye,
L.G.

'When's this from?' I asked.

'She saved it last October. There's dozens of these files, filled with hundreds of messages. Del, Hattie was having a secret relationship.'

'L.G.,' I muttered.

Jake pulled up the next one and we read, finished our burgers, and read some more.

HATTIE / *Tuesday, September 11, 2007*

'WHEN YOU think about it, there's really only three people worth bothering asking to Sadie Hawkins.'

'That's three more than I would look at twice.' I processed Mrs. Gustafson's photo order – thirty pictures of ugly kids – while Portia leaned on the counter and examined her fingernails. She'd collected four new shades of polish from the beauty aisle and was consumed with figuring out which one went best with the traditional Sadie Hawkins flannel. Like there was a winning possibility there. Ignoring me, she lifted one of the bottles up to the light. It looked like blue Gatorade, the kind of color that looked awful on me and gorgeous on her with her light-brown skin.

Portia visited me a lot at work since her parents' liquor store was only a block away. She didn't like trying to do her homework while people bought beer and asked her mother to repeat herself just because she had trouble with *R*s. Even though it took me a while to understand her, too, I'd always loved going to their house.

Mrs. Nguyen would scold us in her low staccato while she ladled spoonfuls of spicy pho into our bowls. Portia was embarrassed by all of it, of course. She didn't understand how amazing it was to be from somewhere other than here.

'There's Trenton.' She started ticking off date possibilities, lining them up like the nail polish bottles.

'He's dating Molly.'

'For now,' she conceded. 'Sadie's is still a month away. And then there's Matt.'

'He's like three feet tall.'

'Yeah, well, so am I. Not everybody's a giraffe like you.'

'I prefer the term gazelle.' I slipped the photos into an envelope and stuck on the label. 'Or undiscovered supermodel.'

Portia snorted. 'Keep dreaming.'

'Who's your third?'

'Hmm? Oh, Tommy.'

'Which Tommy?'

'Kinakis.' She kind of looked away when she said it.

'Tommy Kinakis? What the hell, Porsche?'

'What? Don't you think he's cute?'

He was, sort of. He had nice hair and pretty eyes, but he was dumb as a rock. A giant rock.

'What would you even talk about?'

'Who says we'd be talking?'

I debated before telling her. 'He asked me to come see one of his games.'

'Really?' She stopped playing with the nail polish. 'Are you going to?'

'Yeah. Rah, rah. You know me. Hi, Mrs. Gustafson.'

Portia disappeared with the nail polish as I gave Mrs. Gustafson her pictures. She told me about every ugly grandkid while I nodded and laughed at her stories about them.

After we'd gone through all of the photos, she laid a hand on my arm. 'Now, you're just about graduated, aren't you, Hattie?'

'Yep. Next spring.'

'And what are you going to do?'

I knew what the right answer to that question was. My line was supposed to be that I was going to the U, majoring in nursing or something else productive, and delivered with an upbeat smile that ended the conversation. Instead I gave her the real answer.

'I'm moving to New York City.'

She raised her eyebrows. 'What are you going to do out there, honey?'

'I'm going to be an actress on Broadway,' I said.

'Well, I guess you will then. Goodness' sakes.'

I patted her blue-veined hand, rang her up, and told her to watch for me in the newspapers someday. As she left, smiling and shaking her head like I was delusional, a happy shot of adrenaline coursed through me the way it always did whenever I said it out loud. I was going to New York, and for the first time I didn't care what anyone thought about me. I wanted a life that was bigger than Pine Valley, a life that made everything different.

I wasn't stupid. I'd probably have to transfer to a CVS in the city and work there for a while. That would be the easiest thing, and then I'd have rent money coming in while I looked for something better. And yeah, maybe I wouldn't make it as an actress, but I had the rest of my life to figure it out and it wasn't like anyone had a career anymore the way they used to with one company and a sad little briefcase and a pension. The 2000s were all about recycling, reinventing, and fusion. I could be an actress-photographer-dog walker or a gallery aide-waitress-model. Geez, look at me now. I was a million different things depending on who I talked to or how I felt. All the Mrs. Gustafsons in the world needed to realize their 'What are you going to do?' pop quiz was completely defunct.

Portia bought a pink polish and a *People* magazine and went back to her parents' store. She texted me just as I was closing up the counter, telling me to ask Tommy to Sadie Hawkins and I replied, 'Y don't U?' She didn't answer.

I went home and ate a sandwich before going to my room.

'Homework first!' Mom yelled after me as I went upstairs.

'I know!' I yelled back.

I shut my door and took out my history text book and a notebook and pulled up a website about the Middle Ages in case Mom checked on me, and then clicked on the site I was really going to: Pulse.

Pulse was a forum for New Yorkers I started visiting this summer because it posted tons of casting calls. I checked out every call and googled the play, the theater, and the director now, too, because since rehearsals began a few weeks ago for the Rochester Civic Theater I'd learned that our director, Gerald, loved to gossip about other directors. So I found directors to ask him about. He really just liked being asked questions so he could give a lot of bitchy opinions, but it was fun to listen to him talk about the New York theater scene.

I logged in with my handle, HollyG, and my avatar popped up on the screen, a picture of two of Heather's dad's pigs real close up on their snouts. If you weren't a farmer's daughter, you had no idea what you were seeing. It just looked like a smashed, tired pink canvas with sharp black cuts through the frame. People on the forum always commented on it. They thought it was great art. One of them even asked for the link to my portfolio when I told him I took the picture. So I guess it was pretty easy to fool New Yorkers, too.

Although I didn't comment on all the threads, I read absolutely everything. People talked about plays opening, plays closing, a new building that looked dreadful, the latest restaurant that lived up to its hype, the horrible, ongoing road construction, and the closest subway station to a trendy gallery. They never brought up the weather or television, which were the two main topics of conversation at CVS. I wanted to roll my eyes at all the customers and say, 'Who cares if there's a frost advisory?' except I knew my dad cared and it was important for his crops, so I talked about it like it was the most interesting thing in the world. I even kept a *Farmers' Almanac* behind the counter. Still, I think that's why I liked Pulse so much, because I could act like myself. I could say what I really felt and ask what I wanted to know. Mom said that the internet was dangerous because everyone was anonymous and you never really knew who you were talking to, but I think that's what gave me the courage to open up. I found myself in the forums. Every day in school I became what my teachers and friends wanted, then I went straight to work or play practice and became what they wanted, then I came home and had to cram in homework and try to figure out what my parents wanted – when, honestly, all they *really* wanted was for Greg to be home and for me to be about ten years old again (Sorry, Mom and Dad. Not gonna happen.) – and by then it was 10:00 p.m. When I logged on to Pulse, it felt like I was breathing for the first time all day. I let myself relax and look around, and that's when I saw a post from a newbie that needed to be intercepted.

> **LitGeek:** Hi everyone. I'm new to the forum. I saw the discussion on Thomas Pynchon's book signing next week and CAN'T BELIEVE IT. I won't be in New York then, but if anyone is planning to go, can I send you a book for him to sign and $50.00 for your trouble?
>
> **HollyG:** $50 for your trouble? You must be from the Midwest.
>
> **LitGeek:** Guilty. How did you know?
>
> **HollyG:** Because nobody would do it for less than $200 and it's not going to happen anyway. Thomas Pynchon's an urban myth.

LitGeek: Hmm. I've read his books and bio and he seems pretty corporeal to me.

HollyG: Not the guy. The book signing is an urban myth. You're a newbie so you don't know the Thomas Pynchon book signing is like Giuliani running for president, like the construction finishing on the crosstown, like Amelia Earhart's plane landing at JFK.

LitGeek: Oh. Right. That sucks. I was excited. So why are people posting about this event like it's going to happen?

I sent the next message in a PM.

HollyG: Some people think it's funny, but most of them just want your $200. I flagged the thread for the moderators to take down. They can be pretty slow, though.

LitGeek (replying to the PM): I guess I should thank you for saving me the cash and the disappointment.

HollyG: Can't let a fellow Midwesterner get suckered by the scammers.

LitGeek: You're from or live there now?

HollyG: Live there now, temporarily. I'll be in NY by this time next year.

LitGeek: Where are you now?

HollyG: Southern MN.

LitGeek: Me too(!), unfortunately. What town are you in?

HollyG: Too embarrassing to say. Besides, you're probably a child molester and I'm not going to meet up with you at the local Perkins.

LitGeek: We're definitely not from the same town then, if you can boast of a Perkins. So, to clarify, if I'm a child molester, are you the six-year-old on your dad's computer?

HollyG: Of course.

LitGeek: Then let me give you a tip. Don't go through Daddy's temporary internet files.

HollyG: lol

LitGeek: Oh – I get it now.

HollyG: ??

LitGeek: HollyG. Except you're still Lula Mae at the moment, aren't you?

HollyG: Took you long enough if you're really a LitGeek.

LitGeek: What can I say? I'm as slow as this internet connection. It's a good thing I don't actually have anyone to talk to.

HollyG: Poor, friendless LitGeek. [Violin playing]

LitGeek: I know, I know. It's just that I moved out to the sticks pretty recently and feel out of touch with all my friends.

HollyG: You came here voluntarily??? As a consenting adult?

LitGeek: That's a matter of debate. I came because of my wife.

HollyG: So why don't you talk to your wife?

LitGeek: Uh . . . I do.

HollyG: No, you said you didn't have anyone to talk to, remember? What about your wife?

LitGeek: Oh, right. You're obviously not married.

HollyG: I'm six. I can't even legally work in a sweatshop yet.

LitGeek: lol

HollyG: So, LitGeek, who are your favorite authors besides the elusive Mr. Pynchon? Obviously not Capote . . .

◆

It went on like that for weeks. September turned into October and everything else seemed normal. The entire school went crazy when the football team made regional playoffs. I got fitted for costumes at the theater and rehearsals were off-script now. Midterms started and Portia's dad freaked out when she got a D on her trigonometry test.

I was practically oblivious to all of it. Instead, I constantly checked the forum on my phone. Every time I looked at the PM he'd left a new message. Sometimes we started new PMs for new topics, and a lot of nights we were online at the same time, talking in real time for hours. He told me about Don DeLillo and David Foster Wallace and we debated the best works of Tom Stoppard and Edward Albee. We agreed on how fabulous the new Guthrie Theater building was and disagreed on how awful the Rochester theater scene was. I didn't tell him about my role in *Jane Eyre*. We were both careful to not say too much about our lives. He called his house a death camp once, but he never talked about his job or his wife. He asked me things like if I could inhabit the life of any character in a book, who would I be? I had no idea. I became the main character in every book I read. I felt myself inside their skin, but it didn't have anything to do with liking them or wanting to be them. He said when he was young he wanted to be Charlie Bucket and when he was twenty he read *Love in the Time of Cholera* and felt strangely jealous of Florentino Ariza, who I guess loved a woman he couldn't have for fifty years. I said if he wanted to be frustrated and sad his whole life, why didn't he just become a guidance counselor? He laughed and then he said, 'Florentino knew what he wanted. Even Charlie knew what he wanted. I guess I'd just like to know what my chocolate factory is.'

He was married and probably bald and fat and gassy, too – and none of that mattered because we weren't in the real world. I told him how I really felt about everything, how I wanted to move to New York more than anything but that sometimes I was scared, because I didn't have a plan or know anybody and I couldn't tell anyone that. He said anything worth doing should scare you a little, and that some of the greatest stories began with a journey. Then I started posting Journey lyrics and pretty soon we were both rocking out to 'Don't Stop Believing.' I started imagining LitGeek when

I was in bed at night, feeling my skin and my heartbeat under the sheets, my head bursting with everything I was going to see and do, and I pretended my hands were his as they skimmed up my thighs, that he was exploring me, that he wanted me, too.

> **LitGeek:** You know today is our month anniversary of PMing?
>
> **HollyG:** Aren't you the chick this evening?
>
> **LitGeek:** I guess that makes you the man in our relationship.
>
> **HollyG:** I don't know if you can call a couple of messages a relationship. And a month? God, I don't think anniversaries start until a year.
>
> **LitGeek:** Of course it's a relationship. Everything is. You can have a relationship with a chicken, for God's sake.
>
> **HollyG:** Only a country girl could read that and not take it the wrong way.
>
> **LitGeek:** So you admit it at last, Lula Mae.
>
> **HollyG:** I admit nothing. That was only a general statement. For all you know, I took it completely the wrong way.
>
> **LitGeek:** Oh really? :P
>
> **HollyG:** <Imagining> Come here, pretty hens. LitGeek won't hurt you . . . much.
>
> **LitGeek:** rotfl
>
> **HollyG:** ☺
>
> **LitGeek:** How little you know me. I wouldn't lure them like that. I'm much more subtle.
>
> **HollyG:** So what would your approach be?
>
> **LitGeek:** Hmmm . . . I never thought about seducing a chicken.

I held my breath as his last reply lingered on the monitor. I typed slowly, deliberately, feeling the anticipation bubble in my chest.

> **HollyG:** Pretend I'm a chicken. Give it your best shot.

He didn't answer for a full minute.

LitGeek: Are you sure?

And that's when I fell, when I knew I was in love with this ghost of a man. He didn't try to make it funny or play it off. His reply told me that he was tempted, but he wouldn't do it unless I was absolutely certain. My heart started racing as I typed.

HollyG: Yes.
LitGeek: Well . . .

My eyes were glued to the screen.

LitGeek: First . . .

He was never this slow a typer. I could practically hear him thinking, see his eyes scan my body as he decided on the first caress.

LitGeek: I would brush my fingertips up your back, starting at
your hips and tracing all the way up to your neck, to the
hollows beneath your ears where you said you were ticklish.
But this won't tickle . . .

That was the first night we had sex.

I sat in English class one day in the middle of October, trying to concentrate on the lecture because Mr. Lund would call on anyone without warning, yet also daydreaming about last night's chat with LitGeek. I'd cracked him up after he randomly mentioned *Jane Eyre* and I replied that it would have been a much better book if the wife had burned Mr. Rochester in his bed, pinned it on Jane, and then taken London by storm. He said that would blow the morality tale completely, then I pointed out the only one who wouldn't get exactly what they deserved was Jane, and she should have caught on to the whole setup by then anyway. Stupidity probably sent a lot of people to the gallows. Why should Jane be an exception? That's when he told me I would make a good dictator and we both laughed.

I startled out of my daydream though, when the stacks of our next book were passed around the class.

It was *Jane Eyre*.

'I know it's not the most thrilling read for the guys, but trust me when I say any Brontë is better than Jane Austen.'

'Why can't we read something from this century?' someone asked.

'This century's only a few years old. It would be a lot slimmer pickings and all the books are still in first-run prints, so they're pricier. The school district's not going to pay for that, although you did not hear it from me.'

'Isn't this the one where the wife's bonkers and locked in the attic?' Jenny Adkins asked while reading the back cover. She was a total anglophile, watched any British movie ever made, and was completely in love with Hugh Grant. I tried to tell her once what a horrible actor he was, but she just sighed and said, 'He's not an actor. He's a star.'

'No spoilers, Jenny. Come on.' The class laughed as Mr. Lund leaned on the edge of his desk the way he always did when he settled into a lecture. 'Actually, someone just told me the other day that this book would be a lot better if the wife burned the hero in his bed, pinned it on the heroine, and then blew all his money in London.'

I barely heard the class's laughter. Oh my God. OH MY GOD. His face blurred in and out of focus. His face, LitGeek's face, the face I'd been dreaming about for weeks. The face I'd been dreading to see and dying to touch was right here in the same room with me. I froze, and my heart started pounding so loud I thought for sure Portia would hear it. Oh my God.

'Hattie?'

I jumped, snapping out of the shock. 'What?'

'Welcome back.' He grinned, and I swallowed hard. 'I said I assumed you've read this already.'

'Yes, I have.' It had become kind of a joke between teacher and teacher's pet. I'd read everything in the syllabus except for some book about Vietnam that wasn't assigned until Thanksgiving.

'Any thoughts to share with the class before we all dive in?'

I could do it right now. I could make some flip comment about the book being a morality tale, quoting him exactly from last night, and he would know. His eyes would widen, his skin would pale. I could see the scene play out, how the knowledge would flood him and make him weak and shocked and ashamed. He would break off all contact with me and I would never get to talk to him outside of English class.

And that's why I didn't.

'I liked how Jane took control of her life. She made her own fate.'

I stared out the window as I said it, unable to make eye contact with him. I was afraid he'd somehow see it in my eyes, that he'd guess the truth and our cyber affair would be over.

◆

It was surprisingly easy to be in love with Peter – I thought of him as Peter in my head now even though I still called him LitGeek online and Mr. Lund in school. It felt like he was playing parts, just like me. I watched him at pep rallies and memorized his wardrobe and his class schedule. I even knew what car he drove – a beat-up blue Mitsubishi that some of the jocks made fun of because it was foreign and anyone who drove anything besides a GM or Ford around here was suspect. The only teacher I saw him talking to was Mr. Jacobs, who was totally lame. All he ever wanted to teach in his history classes were wars; he always went on about what country attacked who and drew endless diagrams of battlefields on the board. As far as friends went, pickings were pretty slim and it didn't take long to realize Peter didn't have anyone besides me.

But oh, how he had me.

I was restocking product one day at CVS when Mary Lund came in for her mother's prescriptions. I didn't recognize her. She'd grown up in Pine Valley, but was eight years older than me, so I'd never known her. It wasn't until I heard her and the pharmacist talking about Elsa Reever, Peter's mother-in-law, that I realized who she was. I froze for a minute, feeling flushed and guilty, even though I knew she had no idea her husband spent almost every night talking to me. I grabbed a carton of antihistamines and took them to the cough and cold section to get a better look at her.

She wasn't too tall or too short, or too fat or too thin. She wasn't too anything. Her hair was dishwater blond and pulled back into a ponytail. She was sunburned, dressed in old jeans and the kind of plain pullover hoodie that you bought at Fleet Farm for ten bucks. I couldn't see anything special about her, any reason why Peter would have chosen her. The only distinctive thing about her was a couple of large moles in front of her right ear. From a distance it looked like a vampire had missed his mark and bitten her face.

I stood close enough to hear the whole conversation while stocking the shelves, and made my expression look bored so no one would think I was eavesdropping.

'How is she doing on the oxygen?' the pharmacist asked.

She shrugged. 'I don't know. Her energy level isn't any different, but she says it makes her feel better.'

'Sometimes that's the most important thing.'

'I guess so. She still can't move farther than one room at a time before she has to sit down and rest.'

'Elsa's lucky to have you out there. Most folks in the same condition would be in a home by now.'

I could hear her sigh ten feet away. 'Maybe she should be in a facility. I worry about leaving her, even for little trips like this.'

'But your husband's with her.'

'Right.' There was a pause. 'You're right.'

They talked about the drugs for a few minutes, dosage and side effects stuff, and then she left.

Mom had already told me that Peter lived with his wife at the old Reever farm and now the story started to come together. I tried to remember the last time I saw Mrs. Reever. She went to the same church we did, but I hadn't noticed her in the congregation lately. Maybe she was too weak to go, which meant she might be close to dead or maybe they'd put her in a nursing home like Peter's wife just mentioned. Either way it meant Peter would leave town. That horrible thought created a bubble of panic in me that I couldn't shake for the rest of the week.

The next Sunday, Mrs. Reever came to church. Peter and his wife helped her up the steps, one on each of her arms, and it looked like they were moving in slow motion. They finally got her settled in the last pew and she clutched the oxygen tube, breathing shallow little gasps that made the polyester flowers on her dress stir pathetically. Peter set the oxygen tank down and his wife looked briefly grateful, but he didn't see it. After that, she spent the rest of the service helping her mother. He tried to talk to her once, but either she didn't hear him or she was ignoring him. When it was time to sing the hymns, she was the only one of them who stood up. Mrs. Reever mouthed the words, apparently by heart since she had no hymnal, and Peter didn't even bother to pick one up. He just stared at the pew in front of them, sometimes glancing up at the pulpit or around the church, and then he caught me watching him.

My heart jumped and even though I felt my cheeks start to color, I didn't whip around to the front. That would have been a dead giveaway. While I tried to figure out what to do, he smiled. Not just the smile a teacher gives his student when they cross paths outside of school, but a genuine, I'm-happy-to-see-this-person smile. His eyes crinkled up and his teeth flashed and for the briefest second he looked exactly like I'd dreamed when I fantasized about telling him the truth. I couldn't breathe, let alone keep singing the stupid hymn. I returned his smile and lifted my fingers in greeting, then swiveled back to the front slowly, hoping he was still watching me, that his eyes lingered on my silhouette and liked what they saw.

And that's when I decided. With my heart thumping, feeling the secret words I prayed every week burning in my throat, I was flooded with a need more powerful than I'd ever felt before. The realization almost dropped me to my knees in the middle of the service. I wanted Peter to smile at me like that every day, to grab my hands and tell me everything he was thinking. I wanted to wrap my legs around him and feel him sink into me. I wanted to smell the sweat of his sleeping body in the summertime while the cicadas screamed in the night.

It was time for HollyG to meet LitGeek.

PETER / *October 2007*

RUNNING WAS the best part of my day because it let me forget. There was something about the balance of the quiet land against a cadence of steady footfalls that wiped every higher thought from my head. I regularly jogged the lake trails in Minneapolis, and after we moved here I started running the back roads by the farm until I found a better route. I joined the Pine Valley High School cross-country team.

Not officially, of course. One of the math teachers coached the team and he tried to rope me into the assistant coach job, but there was no way in hell I was giving up every Saturday morning from now until Thanksgiving for their meets. I just ran with the boys. They knew every shortcut and trail in a thirty-mile radius and on Tuesdays and Thursdays after school we tackled the country, a small herd of humans trekking by pastures where cows chewed and stared. Most of the kids looked like I had in high school – awkward and sunburnt and hollow between their bones – but they understood endurance through uneven terrain. We practiced hills between rows of corn and did laps on freshly harvested fields full of soft dirt. We sprinted the easy straights on the football field to practice getting the lead position early and ran the trail around Lake Crosby dozens of times to work on maneuvering on a confined path. Most of them tried to pass each other where the trail opened up by the abandoned barn and it became a joke, all of them tensing as we approached it, grinning and preparing for the mad dash to the front. I stayed at the back to encourage the stragglers, saying things like, 'Pacing, pacing,' 'It's not about tempo, it's about effort,' and 'Keep it up. Don't lose sight of it.'

I would forget.

I'd run for miles, measuring my breaths, feeling my calves burn and then go numb, and watch the wide, empty horizon with a feeling of utter happiness. Her words would filter through like raindrops, unconnected to anything, and quench something inside me, a bone-deep aridity I'd barely let myself acknowledge.

And I would forget what a complete sack of shit I was.

I was cheating on my wife.

I tried to rationalize it most of the time, telling myself I hadn't even met HollyG. She was just a screen name, an internet Siren. Was my increasing fixation with her functionally any different from buying a *Penthouse*?

I knew her completely and yet not at all. I could say exactly how she'd feel about any given book or play, what her favorite drink was, why she hated reality TV, the kind of people that made her nervous. Yet I didn't know her face, her age, her weight, or her life. She could be divorced with six kids. She could be waiting on a job transfer so she could leave her husband. How could I be cheating with someone I couldn't pick out in a lineup?

Yes, we'd had sex. Three times. It was cyber sex, though. What was the difference between that and one of Elsa's romance novels?

There was no one I could ask, no one I trusted besides HollyG, and when I did break down and ask her one day, she told me that everyone cheats in their heart and she was happy to tell me that I wasn't any better than anyone else. I laughed, of course, but answered that I was more worried about being worse than everyone else. Then she said something I'll never forget. She waited a long time to respond before she wrote, 'You're no worse than me. That's all that matters.'

God, I was euphoric when I saw those words. Absolutely euphoric in a way only a complete sack of shit can be. I read her reply a dozen times, loving how she paired us together in a few simple phrases, how we had become the only ruler against which the other could be measured. You're no worse than me, she said. So she was married, too. It made it somehow better, to know that she was as culpable as I was, that even our sins were compatible.

I locked myself in the spare room upstairs, telling Mary and Elsa that I was grading papers and developing lesson plans.

'How many lessons do you need for those kids?' Elsa asked me one night as I was clearing the table and preparing my exit.

'It's a lot of work the first year. I'm starting from scratch and I've got six classes with different ages and abilities, not to mention teaching for the standardized tests. I have to go in with a game plan every day.'

'But it's Friday, isn't it?' Elsa looked to Mary for confirmation, who nodded silently while scooping the leftover potatoes onto a scarred metal tray that she always set outside after dinner for the barn cats. Since the chicken butchering day, she'd said less and less to me, and nothing that mattered.

'All the more reason to get a jump on it.' I grabbed a Coke from the fridge and ducked out of the kitchen before she could inquire further. I should've asked Mary if I could help wash the dishes or what she wanted us to do over the weekend, anything that would tamp down the raging guilt that raced through me every time I looked at her during the last month, but she seemed to want nothing from me, as if my total incompetence as a farmer had excluded me from every other area of her life. I didn't pursue it. I didn't try to reach her anymore, and as I shut the door to the spare room and logged onto my computer, I actually felt somewhat justified – complete bastard that I was – because she had turned away from me first. Mary was the one who'd left our marriage for someone else, and when HollyG found me in that forum I was desperate. Every night I'd been searching for first editions, signed copies, and rare or out-of-print books. It was my knee-jerk reaction to loss, ever since my parents' divorce when I was ten. It wasn't only the escape that attracted me; it was the predictability. Books were finite, a world contained between two covers that could be repeated as many times as I turned the first page. No matter how much misery Tolstoy unleashed or how often Chuck Palahniuk's characters fucked their lives up, their stories became charted, inevitable. I could count on them. Lonely and hungering for connection, I went searching for books. What I found was something else entirely.

HollyG: There you are.

Her words, always so vital and direct, able to cut through all my bullshit, appeared on the screen and erased every thought of Mary or infidelity. Everything in me came to attention, but I was surprised. She usually wasn't online this early.

HollyG: Things are slow tonight. I'm bored and want to see your face.
LitGeek: I'll take that as a metaphor.

I'd been a teacher for less than two months and I was already doing that speech correction crap.

HollyG: No, actually I meant it literally.

LitGeek: ??

HollyG: Do you want to meet me?

I sat bolt upright in the creaky dining room chair, scanning the words again to make sure I hadn't misread. I typed, deleted, started again.

LitGeek: I do, but it's not a good idea. You know my situation.

HollyG: Yes, I know. So how about we meet without meeting?

LitGeek: Again with the '??' What are you up to?

HollyG: There's a community theater production of *Jane Eyre* in Rochester next week.

LitGeek: Does the wife take all in this version? ☺

HollyG: You'll have to come see to find out.

LitGeek: I don't understand. You'll be there?

HollyG: I'll be at the Thursday matinee. I'll wear a gray dress with white cuffs. We won't talk or even sit near each other. Just a glance across a crowded room. We'll meet without meeting.

LitGeek: I can't. We're walking a fine line already.

HollyG: Don't worry, I won't let you fall. Think about it. I'll be there, whether you go or not.

God, I couldn't get the idea out of my head. For two straight days it tortured me. The temptation to see, to give face and form to the only person in a hundred miles who gave a shit about me was overwhelming. By Sunday night I'd all but given in. What could be less illicit than two strangers watching a play on opposite sides of a theater? And I had this hope that seeing her in the flesh would kill my demented infatuation. Maybe she'd be sixty or covered in eczema. I could dream.

Calling in sick wasn't an option. Mary would hear about my sick day before the play even hit intermission, thanks to Elsa's cozy chats with the principal. I wasn't eligible for vacation time yet either, but when I walked into school Monday morning I had a plan. We were reading *Jane Eyre* in my senior Advanced English class, so why not take a field trip? I'd have eighteen kids with me, all eager for a day out of school with their cool, new teacher. It was the perfect cover. I got the principal's approval, reserved a bus, and printed out permission slips, all before the first student walked into my classroom that morning.

As Mary and I got into bed the night before the play, though, my duplicity was making me nauseated.

'What's wrong?' Mary asked.

I told her about the field trip. 'I guess I'm just nervous about what could happen.'

'It'll be fine,' she said, yawning.

I flipped around to face her, seized with an idea. 'Why don't you come? You could meet us at the high school and ride along on the bus. It'd be just like Minneapolis, except I get educator rates now.'

Hope leapt in my chest, but she shook her head and fluffed her pillow before settling on her side, facing the wall.

'I'm taking Mom to the cardiologist tomorrow. Remember?'

'Reschedule it.'

'No, Peter. We've waited three months to see this guy. You'll be fine.'

'Why can't you ever make time for me anymore?'

Swiveling back toward me, she pulled the covers toward her side of the bed. 'Are you kidding? You ask me the night before and expect me to drop everything?'

'I thought it would be fun. Excuse me for wanting to have fun with my wife.'

She shook her head and jabbed a finger at my chest. 'No, you just said you were nervous to go by yourself. Don't try to pretend like you were thinking about us. If you want to take me out, ask me when you don't have twenty teenagers tagging along.'

She tossed herself as far away from me as possible on the bed and fell asleep a few minutes later while I lay awake, staring at her back in the darkness.

The next day I couldn't concentrate on anything. I made all my morning classes work in small groups. I had no appetite at lunch, and when Carl asked me what was wrong I mumbled something about a cold or my sinuses. On the bus, one of the kids had to remind me to take attendance and only then did I remember that Hattie Hoffman, my favorite student in that class, was out with an excused absence. The drive to Rochester was short and before I was ready we filed into a small two hundred-seat theater with faded red velvet chairs. The room was over half-full and I scanned the crowd as subtly as I could, but no one was wearing a gray dress. Even after the lights dimmed and the play started I kept watching that damn door. HollyG would show up, I knew it. She might show up late, though, just to be perverse. I had no idea what was happening on-stage until the student sitting on my left gasped and elbowed me in the ribs. 'It's Hattie!'

'What?' I whispered and she pointed at the stage.

I focused on the play and saw Hattie Hoffman in center stage, exchanging lines with an older woman sporting a severe bun. Flipping through the program I saw her name listed at the top of the page in the title role. The little shit. She didn't mention a word about it when I passed the permission slips around. I had assumed she'd say something about the field trip, because Hattie always had an opinion on everything, but she'd kept silent with her head buried in a notebook. Had she been embarrassed about being in the play?

I paid attention for a few lines, enough to realize Hattie was ac-tually good. She didn't try for the English accent, which was smart, and she delivered her lines cautiously, with the exact trepidation Jane would have shown when she announced her decision to leave Lowood School for Girls and seek out her destiny at Thornfield Hall. The longer I watched her the more eerie it got. Hattie usually moved with a deliberate grace; I'd always noticed it because it set her apart from the rest of the kids. On stage that assurance disappeared; she'd become Jane completely. As the scene drew out, the back of my neck tingled. I held my breath when Hattie held hers, looked to the places where her eyes strayed. I was captivated to a point I didn't totally understand. Maybe it was because she was my student and I felt a sense of pride. Except it didn't feel like pride, not completely. It was more intense and nagging, like I should know something I didn't. The other kids and I exchanged smiles, bound in the hushed excitement of discovering a secret about one of our own.

Now Mrs. Fairfax was telling her to put on her best dress to meet Mr. Rochester, and Hattie stood solemnly, smoothing the pleats of her gray dress and nervously straightening the bright cuffs. 'This is my best dress, Mrs. Fairfax.'

Her dress. Oh. Holy. Fuck.

The nagging sensation in the back of my head exploded and everything blurred. I swayed forward and when I could see again, the two women were crossing the stage into the adjoining set. The back of Hattie's hips receded calmly, covered in gray, gray, gray. Oh, God.

No. I wrenched around and searched every single body in the crowd, desperate to find someone else. Anyone else. I was not having an affair with one of my students, for the love of Christ. But there was no one. No one else in the entire theater that could be HollyG. And I knew there wouldn't be. Subconsciously, I'd known it since I first laid eyes on Hattie on that stage.

The rest of the play passed in a fog. I slid down in my seat until one of the kids asked if I was all right and then I used the excuse to go to the bathroom. All I wanted to do was get the hell out of there; run through the front doors and never fucking stop.

I splashed a gallon of water on my face and sat on the toilet for ten minutes, trying to figure out what I was going to do. It wasn't until the second act that I realized I still had an out. HollyG didn't know who LitGeek was – I hadn't given her any clues to pick me out of the crowd. And why would she suspect me? I was providing a field trip, for God's sake. She was expecting our whole class to be there.

I held on to that and went back to my seat, but nothing suppressed the insanity raging in my head for very long. It wasn't until Mr. Rochester proposed to Jane that I snapped back to reality.

'Do you doubt me, Jane?' The actor grabbed Hattie by the arms and drew her close.

'Utterly and completely.'

When he caught her in an embrace my pulse started jumping. He was older than me, maybe in his early thirties, so not as old as Mr. Rochester was supposed to be, but close enough. And Hattie was almost exactly Jane's age, the young innocent who captured the world-weary Rochester's heart. As Jane realized Mr. Rochester was serious and accepted his offer of marriage, several things happened at once in my head. The detached academic in me thought they'd done a good job casting, except for the fact that Hattie was too pretty to play Jane. The teacher in me observed the two of them embrace, her delicate pink cheek brushed up against his grizzly five-o'clock shadow, and felt uncomfortable and protective. And the rest of me just watched her lithe frame wrap around a man twice her age and took a long, hard swallow.

And that reaction was going to stop right now. Jesus, how many headlines had I read about some teacher having an affair with a student? It was usually female teachers, all desperate, insecure,

123

unevolved women who deluded themselves into thinking they loved these idiots. I never blamed the kids. Teenage boys would have sex with a banana peel, but the teachers had no justification worth the breath it took to say. They should have done what I was going to do right now. End it. Stop it before it even began, or at least before it knowingly began. There was no way I could've known HollyG was Hattie. HollyG was Hattie was Jane. Her identities shifted in front of me, none of them quite capturing the girl on stage who was now running away from Mr. Rochester in her wedding dress. Their definitions couldn't hold her any more than the actor could make her marry him. At least she was running away from an already married man. It was the only flash of comfort as I waited for the torture to end, that at least some version of her was doing the right thing.

When it was finally over, the cast filed out in front of the curtain and we all stood and clapped. The actor who played Mr. Rochester pushed Hattie out in front of the line and the applause multiplied as she took a bow. Then, in the middle of the ovation, she looked directly at me and slowly, deliberately, ran her hand down the arm of her dress to her cuff. The corners of her mouth crept up and her eyes lit with a hundred meanings. I felt the obligatory return smile fall off my face and my hands froze in mid-clap.

She knew.

She cornered me after the play when the cast was mingling with the audience in the theater lobby, knowing I couldn't run away while we were surrounded, our roles as clearly cast as the actors' had been only minutes ago.

'Hello, Mr. Lund.'

'Hattie.' I clung to the name, a little girl's name, and tried to force myself to speak to that person alone. 'That was a wonderful performance. I didn't know you were in theater.'

'This was my first production.' If she could tell how uncomfortable I was, she didn't show it. If anything, her smile only grew wider.

'You're a natural. It's like you've been acting your whole life.'

She laughed at that and was twirled away by another student before she could torment me further.

Before I deleted my account at Pulse that night, I reread every message we'd sent each other. I'd saved them all and it was mortifying to realize what should have been obvious from the beginning. She was leaving for New York in less than a year. Of course, because she had to graduate high school first. I'd been so impressed about the books she'd read, but that was because I was assigning them to her. It would have been funny if it weren't happening to me. After debating half the night over it, I decided to send her one last message. It was better to be absolutely clear about what had to happen. I agonized over the diction, wanting to tell her how much she'd meant to me, but I knew I couldn't give her a single encouraging word.

Over the next week I could tell Hattie was trying to find a way to talk to me and I did everything possible to prevent it. As soon as the bell rang to dismiss Advanced English, I would shoot out the door and play hall monitor or find a reason to run to the main office. I became paranoid about being alone in the school and invented excuses to see Carl during my off-periods. I asked Mary out for a proper date that Friday, but the cardiologist had confirmed Elsa's heart only had a year left at best and Mary was too depressed to want to do anything. When I asked her if she wanted to talk about it, she just shrugged and turned away.

A week later, Hattie cornered me in the middle of class. I had the students working in pairs and she left her partner talking in mid-sentence, strolled casually up to the front of the room, and leaned against the stack of essays I'd just collected.

'Do you want something, Hattie?' I didn't look up from my

computer, but somehow I could still sense the curve of her hip and the tilt of her head. I knew she was wearing the wide-necked blue top that was too loose and sometimes fell off her shoulder. Her fingers tapped a beat into the desk; she always had nervous fingers. She didn't say anything for a minute and I felt her gaze, waiting for me to look at her. I refused.

'I had some questions about the essay.'

'Yes?' I kept typing.

'I wasn't quite sure how you wanted it structured.'

She was lying and not even bothering to lie well. The essay was a simple comparison paper between the *Jane Eyre* book and the play. Hattie never had a question about homework and the tone of her voice was all wrong. It was too quiet, subdued. Finally I looked at her and tried to keep my face and voice impassive. She was close enough to smell, her eyes wide and serious. Her fingers fell still as our eyes met.

'I'm sure your essay's fine.' The words were hard to get out.

'I was worried about the third paragraph in particular. I hope you'll think it's okay.'

God, why was she so young? Why was she my student? Why was I still compelled by this attraction when any worthwhile human being would have stopped thinking about her as anything but a felony?

'I'll look at it. Go finish up with your partner.' I glanced at the clock, then turned back to the computer. 'There's only a few minutes left.'

That night after dinner I put the stack of essays in the middle of the kitchen table and dug in with a red pen. I muttered comments to myself about some of them and wrote with loud, scratchy hand-writing, making sure Elsa and Mary could hear me, not that either of them cared. Since the cardiologist's diagnosis, Mary had spent every possible minute with her mother and it seemed pointless to bring up the idea of going on a date again. It felt like I was the one fading out of this house.

When I got to Hattie's paper I was tempted to stuff it in the bottom of the pile or, better yet, just mark it with an A and move on to the next, but the perverse Humbert Humbert in me couldn't resist reading. It was a fairly standard analysis, nothing too in-depth. She thought the book did better with character backgrounds, although the play gave them living, breathing vitality. Her words, not mine. I flipped the first page over and skimmed ahead to the third paragraph.

> . . . *in the case of Mr. Rochester's wife. Due to time constraints, the play couldn't address her moral ambiguity or even her history. Peter, if you're reading this, meet me at the old Erickson barn on the lake at 8:30. I have to talk to you. However, the play allows Mrs. Rochester to be a three-dimensional character . . .*

I did a double take, read it twice more to be sure, and then looked at the clock. 8:39 p.m. My heart began pounding. I glanced through the door to the living room where Elsa and Mary were watching *American Idol* from their matching rockers, cheerfully critiquing the contestants like every other Thursday night. The paper suddenly felt like a billboard in my hand, even though neither of them even glanced in my direction. I folded it twice over and stared at the white square. Perspiration broke out on my armpits and back.

I didn't think. I walked upstairs and changed into sweats, then came back down and pulled on my running shoes, all with that white square of paper burning through my palm.

'Where are you going?' Mary asked.

'I've got some heartburn from dinner. Going to try and jog it out.'

'This late? It's already dark.'

'I'll take a flashlight.' I grabbed one from the front porch and ran down the driveway and over the hill toward Winifred Erickson's farm. I clicked the flashlight off after the house disappeared from sight and picked up my pace, running blindly over the gravel, sprinting into the faint edge of the horizon, hoping I'd hit a pothole or land wrong and twist my ankle. I pushed harder, crushing the paper into garbage, sharpening my breath, cold muscles stiffening, then I veered off the road into the woods, praying now for a root to trip me and knock my teeth out or at least give me a nasty concussion on a tree stump. But nothing touched me. I was a ghost runner, inviolate, racing into the clearing with insane luck burning through my legs and then the barn was in sight. I stopped dead and stood there, chest heaving. A giant oak tree stood next to the barn, shadowing it from the moon. There was nothing to do except face her now.

The door gave way with a deep croak. It was dark inside, except for the glow of a small camp lantern on a stool in the corner. I didn't see her at first, but as my eyes adjusted I found her silhouette leaning against the window underneath the oak tree. She must have watched me approach. Her hair was pulled up and she wore a red plaid jacket. I crammed my hands in my pockets. I probably should have thought about what to say before I got here.

'Hello, LitGeek,' she said softly into the darkness.

I swallowed. 'Hello, Hattie.'

'Why don't you call me HollyG?'

'Because that's not your name.'

'Neither is Hattie. Hattie's a nickname.'

'But that's who you are. You're Hattie Hoffman. You're a teenage high school student and I'm your married English teacher.'

She didn't say anything or move from the window.

'You have to understand that it's over. Whatever it was is over and I should have never – I shouldn't have . . . Christ.'

I turned back toward the door, frustrated beyond words. The floorboards creaked.

'No, you shouldn't have. But you did.' Her voice trembled slightly underneath the vowels.

'I'm married, Hattie.' Maybe repetition would help the idea sink in. 'I have a wife.'

The barn creaked again and her voice was closer this time, stronger. 'You were married a week ago, too, but that didn't stop you from wanting to see me. It didn't stop you from becoming the chicken whisperer.'

I laughed before I could help it. That's what she'd nicknamed me after that first night of cyber sex, when it was all under the ridiculous pretense of seducing a chicken. The laugh died, though, as the words came back, with full-color images now of things we'd done, places I'd told her to caress, imagining my lips there instead of her fingers. The boards groaned underneath us and I spun around before she could come any closer. She'd crept most of the way across the barn and was near enough that I could read the longing and hesitation in her eyes. They were open wide and her mouth was parted and she looked so damn young. A child with a woman's body. She didn't even know how young she was. She probably thought she was grown up and ready for the world, with her acting career and her endless quips and comebacks and that brain that soaked up everything around her. She probably thought there were only a few years between us, but it was a lifetime – dark, undiscovered caverns of disappointment and compromises. She was the adult idealized. I was the adult that really happened.

'I'm your teacher, Hattie. Can't you understand how wrong this was?'

The corner of her mouth tipped up. 'What have you ever taught me?'

She took another step forward and my hands went up automatically, holding her back by the shoulders, keeping those last two feet of sanity between us. 'I can teach you a few things about statutory rape laws.'

She looked down at my hands on her. 'So you've thought about it.'

Christ, she wasn't even listening to me. She was on a completely different planet having a completely different conversation.

'No. Well, yes, but only in terms of how long my prison sentence would be. You're a child, Hattie.'

That got her. She stepped back, crossing her arms. 'I'm seventeen.'

'Exactly.'

We squared off for a minute in silence. Agitation made her chest rise and fall and the movement squeezed her breasts against her arms. The fact that I even noticed only made me angrier.

'Look, Hattie, I only came here to tell you in person that I made a horrible mistake, but it's done now. Over. You're a good student and—'

'Good?' She raised an eyebrow.

'Great student, all right? You were my favorite student in class before this.'

'And what am I now? Your favorite what?'

I gritted my teeth. 'You're still my favorite student, or at least you will be if you drop this right now.'

Her face changed, became vulnerable. The arms crossing her chest looked more like they were hugging her body now for support. She dropped her face to the floor and her words were just above a whisper. 'I don't think I can, Peter.'

'Don't call me that.'

'It's your name.'

'Not to you it isn't. Open your damn ears. You're the child. I'm the' – I barked out a laugh – 'responsible adult and this?' – I waved a finger between the two of us – 'will never fucking happen. I should be home right now grading papers while my wife and her mother watch bad TV, not running off to meet children in vacant barns in the middle of the night.'

'You keep calling me a child.'

'That's because you are.'

She looked up and her face had changed again. She was like quicksilver, how fast she processed information and emotions and moved on. Now she had a speculative, smug look, like she'd figured something out. My body tensed up, wary at the lightning change.

'I think you're calling me a child so much because you're trying to convince yourself of it.'

'No, that's just the fact of the matter.'

'I'll give you some facts, Peter. Fact one: You're unhappy in your marriage. You don't love your wife anymore and you've realized that you chose the wrong woman.'

'You don't know what–'

'Fact two: We met online and you found someone who shares your interests, who excites you and makes you think and laugh. And now that you know who I am you're scared, because I could make you lose everything.'

She stared with an intensity that bore right through me and her voice fell to little more than a whisper. 'But I would never do that, Peter. Because I'm the right woman.'

She was so close. I could reach out and touch her again, but this time to pull her in and kiss her. I could tip her head to the side and run my mouth down her neck, taking bites out of her, tasting the skin that smelled so fresh and sweet against the rotting wood of the barn. She would let me. She would let me do more.

I backed up two quick steps until my heels hit the door, opened it, and walked outside, breathing deep. The wind had picked up, and the swift muddy scent of the fields and lake cleared my head.

Hattie walked out and stood next to me, facing the same horizon.

'I could transfer out of your class, if that's the problem. You wouldn't be my teacher.'

'I teach basic English for seniors, too. You'd still be my student, just surrounded by idiots.'

She laughed. 'No, thank you.'

'How can I make you understand?'

She waited, and I sensed a satisfied silence, as though she'd rather stand next to me arguing than be anywhere else.

'You're too young. You're too innocent.'

She laughed again, but it was a different laugh, edgier. 'I'm not a virgin.'

'That's not what I meant.' It *was* what I meant, but I couldn't concede any ground. My resolve weakened the longer we stood here, where even the shadow of the oak seemed complicit. I silently counted all the reasons I couldn't kiss her, shouldn't even think about kissing her.

'I'm good at being what people want me to be. Watch me, Peter. You'll see. I'll become the last girl in the world who would be having an affair with her English teacher.'

I swallowed and when I finally spoke, my voice was hoarse. 'That's because you're not having an affair with your English teacher.'

She walked out of the shadows into the moonlight at the edge of the clearing, her slim hips jutting from side to side, and paused at the walking path that led around the lake. It was the same spot where the boys broke out of rank for their mad dash to the front, where their order and steady pace turned into the chaos of shifting and merging bodies. She glanced back at me, her eyes shining with blatant confidence.

'Fact three, Peter: I'll be eighteen on January fourth. See you then.'

And she disappeared into the night. I stood there for what felt like an hour, knowing I'd lost a key battle. I'd sprinted for the lead with no strategy and stumbled, giving up any chance of victory. My gut churned with dread and disgust at myself. This had to stop. If I had any decency at all, this affair had to be over.

From this point on, as far as I was concerned, Hattie Hoffman was as good as dead. She had to be.

**TEENAGER STABBED IN PINE VALLEY.
FRIENDS BELIEVE CURSE RESPONSIBLE**

Just weeks before her high school graduation, an eighteen-year-old girl was murdered outside Pine Valley. The Wabash County Sheriff's Office confirmed the identity of the victim as Henrietta Sue Hoffman, known as Hattie to her friends and family. The body suffered multiple stab wounds and was discovered in an unused barn near Lake Crosby on Saturday night. The Sheriff's Department has no suspects in custody at this time, but confirmed they are following 'all possible leads.' One such lead may be from an unusual source: a four-hundred-year-old curse. According to Portia Nguyen, a close friend of the victim . . .

'Hell.'

I threw the paper back on the table without glancing at the rest of the story. It was front-page news in the Minneapolis newspaper, and the *County Gazette* had run Hattie's senior picture under the headline along with a two-page spread of other pictures from her high school yearbooks. Hattie's murder was already big stuff in the local news – everyone demanded details when a young, pretty girl got killed – but now that this *Macbeth* nonsense had hit the wire, every nutcase and reporter in the state would be all over us. Pressure like that might make the killer nervous, and who knew what a jumpy murderer would do next.

It was 5:30 a.m., too early to go downstairs and pound on the Nguyens' door, so I went over my suspect and evidence lists, ate my oranges, and tried to forget about the media.

The oranges were a birthday gift from my sister in Florida. She sent a huge crate every year and spoiled me for those pale, watery ones at the grocery store. I ate one from the crate every morning, peeling it right over the garbage, and watched the droplets spray with each rip of skin. The scent of it got on my hands and lingered all day, no matter how many times I washed. It was a good scent, bright and tangy, and I needed that this week. The further I dug into Hattie's life, with the picture of her bloody, bloated-legged corpse waiting each time I closed my eyes, every bite of orange tasted sweeter, sharper.

I ate and read over my lists. We had two possible suspects now: Tommy and the person who'd signed that letter L.G., so Jake was working on ID'ing him through Hattie's internet records. The guy was connected to her by two things, we figured from the messages Hattie saved. They both liked art – acting and reading and stuff – and neither of them cared for country life. They never mentioned names, their own or anybody else's, or any places or events, so it was hard to pin him down. Boy was educated. Liked throwing the five-dollar words around and sounded pretentious as hell most of the time, but Hattie seemed to take to it. Girl like her probably would have. Probably thought he was refined. We knew they traded messages for about a month – talking books and then talking dirty – until they figured out who the other person was, somehow through *Jane Eyre*. That's when he seemed to end it. In any case, that's when Hattie stopped saving the messages. I couldn't prove a relationship beyond October of last year, but the whole thing smelled wrong. So far he was the only person who'd clearly wanted Hattie to disappear, and that was enough to land him on the suspect list.

The evidence list was a little more promising. I had the semen on Hattie's underwear, and the forensic boys had emailed their report over last night, saying there was more semen in one of the used condoms they'd found at the bottom of the lagoon in the barn. I had them send it over for analysis along with the underwear and Tommy's sample. No latent prints turned up on any of the other recovered items, which meant they'd been down there at least a few days and weren't part of our crime scene. I included Hattie's purse on the evidence list, and the business card from Gerald Jones that was inside it. His Denver alibi had checked out clean, but as a play director he was plenty arty. Not a bad candidate for L.G. He'd caught the red-eye into Rochester this morning and I planned to drive over there first thing.

What I really wanted was the damn murder weapon. We were four days away from the murder now, a hundred hours that the killer could have used to stash, bury, or clean it. Shel had finished dragging the lake yesterday and hadn't turned it up. The farther away we got from Friday night, the less likely it was that we'd find it.

I heard the Nguyens stirring around six o'clock and gave them until 6:30 before I went downstairs. Mrs. Nguyen answered the door and waved me inside, calling something to her husband. Mr.

Nguyen came out, all smiles and hospitality until I asked to see Portia, then his forehead creased and he paused before nodding and calling her out. While I waited I noticed the cat lounging on the sofa, facing away from me like we'd never met before in our lives. I turned my back on him, too.

Portia had her father's height and her mother's round cheeks, but the manners of neither. She barreled into the room in a pink robe with bare feet and hair flying out behind her, demanding, 'Did you find out?'

Her father chastised her in their own language and she backed off a little.

'We've found out a lot of things, Portia. Which one are you thinking of?'

'Who killed her? Who killed Hattie?'

'If I knew that, I'd have better things to do this morning. As it is . . .' I unrolled the newspaper and dropped it on the coffee table with a loud thwack. 'You've been feeling chatty, haven't you?'

She shrugged. 'They were outside school at lunch yesterday. I wasn't going to lie to them. The curse is real.'

'You didn't mind the attention, did you? And you sure didn't seem to mind getting to play Lady Macbeth in Hattie's place.'

'What are you saying?'

'All these nuts are going to come rolling into town looking for interviews now, and if you jump in front of the microphone like you did here, maybe your face'll be splashed on newspapers and TV programs all over the country. Mighty nice for you.'

'Stop it!' she yelled and then started crying. Mr. and Mrs. Nguyen stood behind her, motionless. 'I was her best friend. I can't believe she's dead.'

'If you're her best friend, you must know things about her. Private things. Things she wouldn't have told anybody else.' I waited until her crying quieted down. 'I need to know those things, Portia.'

'Like what?'

'Who was she seeing before Tommy?'

'Nobody.'

'She didn't have a crush on anybody?'

'No, she used to make fun of Maggie and all the girls that dated a lot in school. She called them "he-tarded." '

She laughed a little and I couldn't help joining in. It sounded like one of Hattie's quips.

'Okay, no boy at school. How about someone she met somewhere else, like at the play over in Rochester last fall?'

Portia shook her head.

'Is there anything else that you know about Hattie? Something she confided? Anything that didn't seem quite right?'

She shrugged and looked up, wiping her eyes with a sleeve of her robe. 'I don't know. I mean, I thought we told each other everything, but . . .'

But obviously Hattie hadn't trusted her best friend enough to tell her about L.G.

'A couple weeks ago,' she huffed, hiccuping, 'Hattie's truck broke down on some nowhere road south of Zumbrota. I dropped everything to go pick her up – and I'd just flown home from the choir trip the day before – but she wouldn't even tell me where she'd been or why she had a suitcase with her. She made me drive her to the Apache Mall in Rochester and said she had something to take care of. She wouldn't tell me what and she wouldn't let me come with her. I was pissed. I spent an hour at the Gap waiting for her to text me. When she finally came back, the suitcase was gone and she looked, I don't know, like sweaty but happy.'

'What did she do with the suitcase?'

'I don't know. When I asked, all she would say was *It's waiting*.'

'What did it look like?'

'Small, carry-on size. Black with wheels.'

'And you don't know where she was earlier that day or where she went while you waited at the mall?'

'No, her cheeks were all red and she was out of breath when she came back, but she totally changed the topic whenever I asked. She bought a sundress for herself and randomly bought me a shirt, like a total afterthought, then spoke like two words to me on the ride home. She didn't even ask about my trip.'

The anger and grief were all churned up together in her voice and she kept wiping at her eyes.

'After that day, she seemed all right except like, not there anymore. Even though we still talked and hung out, she acted weird.'

'How's that?'

'I don't know. Like on Friday after the play I told her she'd been great, and she just laughed and said she was done acting. And I was like, Oh, you're retiring at eighteen? Can you be more dramatic? But then she was. She was done, she was done.'

Portia broke into full sobs. Both her parents stood at the door, her mother clutching a dish towel, her father's head bent.

'All right.' I pointed to the ceiling and waited until she registered the gesture. 'You think of anything else and you know where to go, right?'

She nodded and walked out of the room, melting behind the wall of her parents' bodies. I nodded at both of them and let myself out. Maybe it was unrelated, but I wanted to know what Hattie did with that suitcase and why she was carrying it around in the first place. I called Jake on my way into Rochester and filled him in. He was busy requesting a warrant on a few websites that he thought Hattie'd visited a lot, but said he'd check with the Rochester police for reports of abandoned luggage.

I chewed on the interview for the rest of the drive. Hattie hadn't told her best friend about L.G. or where she'd been that day her truck broke down, and wouldn't let Portia see what she did with that suitcase. Usually when someone stashed a suitcase they were getting ready to run away, but what did she need to run away from? The list of Hattie's secrets was growing. What would Bud do if I had to tell him any of this? If I had to take his girl away all over again?

Part of me couldn't help hoping the DNA would come back as Tommy's. It was a simple story, one I'd heard dozens of times over the years with different variations, yet always the same key parts. A couple has a fight, things get out of hand, and he kills her. It wasn't a crime I understood, but it'd become awfully familiar. The rest of this – a curse, a secret lover, a possible runaway attempt – came from someplace else entirely. Her body flashed into my head again, stabbed and bloody on top, legs bloated and floating in the water below, with me kneeling next to her, trying to fit her disjointed pieces together.

I turned off the highway into downtown Rochester, looking for another piece.

◆

'Of course, she was an amateur. That was abundantly clear from the first day of rehearsals.'

Gerald Jones was built like a beanpole and dressed all in black. Not like Johnny Cash black, more like Fred Astaire pretending to be a cat burglar. We were in the front office of the Rochester Civic Theater, and he'd spent the last ten minutes wiping his dry eyes and showing me 'stills' from the *Jane Eyre* play he'd directed Hattie in last fall. They looked like run-of-the-mill pictures to me.

'She didn't even know stage directions at first. I had to ride her a bit, but by the second week she'd gotten up to speed and apart from the technical side of the business, she was a director's dream.'

'Why's that?'

'She was the perfect actor. Unformed clay. All I had to say was "more vulnerable" or "urgency" and she'd make the adjustment. It flowed through everything she did – her gestures, face, posture, tone, volume. I'd cast her because she had a good read and her appearance was exactly what I was after. See?'

He held up a picture of Hattie clutching a shawl and staring at a man in an overcoat and hat.

'She was thin, so she could pull off that gaunt look, but there was a fire in her – something always unspoken – which gave her a beautiful stage presence. The audience fell in love with her as much as Mr. Rochester did every night.'

'Mr. Rochester, he this guy?'

'Yes.'

'Anything going on between them backstage?'

He was genuinely surprised by the question. 'No. God, no. Mack's happily married with two kids.'

'But you just said he was in love with her.'

'His *character* was in love with her *character*.' Now he sounded as if he was talking to a small child.

I worked out the last bit of orange pulp caught in my teeth and flicked the pictures around on his desk. 'And how about your character? Did you have any feelings for Holly?'

'Jane.' He sounded out each letter in the word, slowly, like he'd downgraded me from a child to an idiot dog. 'The character's name was Jane. And no, I didn't have any feelings for her. What are you trying to get at?'

'Maybe you were feeling cozy with your new star. Looking to squeeze some of that unformed clay.'

He gave a quick bark of laughter. 'I don't think my partner, Michael, would appreciate the insinuation.'

The way he said 'partner' cleared things up quick.

'Hmm.' I looked away, clearing my throat. 'Right.'

Jones clearly wasn't L.G. Even if he didn't bat for the other team, he had zero reaction to Hattie's screen name. I sighed.

'Why did you think I had a relationship with Hattie?'

'We found her purse in the bottom of the lake. The murderer had thrown it in the water after he hacked her up. You want to tell me why your business card was one of the only things she was carrying?'

'Oh.' His smug superiority dried up and it finally seemed to register that Hattie was dead. He sat down in front of his pictures and stared blankly at them.

'I hadn't talked to her in months. I gave her my card after the play ended, to help her out. She was set on New York, you know, and I still have some contacts there. I told her to call me when she was moving.'

'Did she say when that would be?'

'After she graduated, I thought.'

'When's the last time you talked to her?'

'Christmas. I sent her one of my old camcorders and she called to thank me.'

'Video camera?' There hadn't been anything like that in Hattie's room. 'What for?'

'It helps some actors rehearse. To record and review their takes. Hattie had talent and I wanted to help her refine it.' Then he smiled ruefully. 'Also, I'd just bought myself a new one and Michael had forbidden me to bring any more equipment into the house without getting rid of some of the old.'

'Right. Can you think of anyone else she might have been close to during the play? Anyone she maybe met while doing it?'

'Not that I ever saw. She was always so busy, between her classes and work schedule. She was in and out of rehearsals without talking to much of anyone, and she even did her homework during the few scenes she wasn't in.'

'Do you have records of who bought tickets to come see the play?'

It turned out he did and after a little finagling he let me go through the sales slips on site without having to get a warrant. It was grunt work, something I should have sent Shel to do, but I needed to be on the front lines of this. Sitting back in the office signing payroll or doing a press conference while someone else looked for Hattie's killer would have driven me mad. I sat on the visitor side of Jones's desk, pulling all the receipts for male customers to scan back to Jake. There were a lot. Who knew this many people went to plays?

Jones grabbed some coffee for both of us and watched me work. After a while, he quietly commented, 'This wasn't the play that killed Hattie.'

'Save it.' I kept flipping through receipts.

'You don't believe in the curse.'

'No. I don't believe a spook story can murder someone.'

'Then you've never heard of the Astor Place riots.'

He went to a file cabinet and rustled around, pulling out two pieces of paper.

'William Macready was one of the finest British actors in the early eighteen hundreds. Here he is.' I glanced up at a drawing of a little guy with a wig, tossing his head back and smiling at something outside the frame. Looked like the tax-evasion type.

'Great.' I went back to work.

'At the same time in the US, Edwin Forrest was making a name for himself in the New York theaters.'

He showed me the other picture. This one was a stocky, ruddy-looking guy with black hair sticking straight up. A brawler.

'The two were friends early in their careers, until Forrest performed *Macbeth* in London. The audience booed him and Forrest got it into his head that Macready had orchestrated the reaction out of jealousy. A few weeks later, while Macready was playing Hamlet, Forrest stood up in the middle of the audience and heckled him. He was immediately cast out of London society and had to return to New York.'

'Is this going anywhere, Jones?' I checked my phone and saw two missed calls, both from Jake.

'In May 1849, Forrest and Macready performed competing versions of *Macbeth* in New York on the same night. An army of Forrest's fans stormed the Astor Opera House, determined to put a stop to Macready's production. The rioters pummeled the theater with rocks and tried to set the building on fire, which prompted the militia to start firing into the crowd.'

'All this over a couple of theater actors?'

'These men were the movie stars of their time. Over twenty people died that night and a hundred more were injured. It was the worst tragedy in the history of theater. And it happened because of *Macbeth*.'

'It happened because of a bunch of idiot rioters and some policemen who couldn't do their jobs.'

'But what set it off? *Macbeth*. Forrest's terrible performance in London, which started the whole rivalry in the first place. What were they both playing that night? *Macbeth*. It's the story of a man who murders his way into a crown. Not an insane man. Not a manipulated man. Just an ordinary man, drawn to extraordinary evil. That's what *Macbeth* is, and for four hundred years, violence has been drawn to that play like a moth to the flame.'

He put the pictures away and looked at the one of Hattie lying on top of the desk. His voice dropped, as if the story had exhausted him.

'You'll find your murderer, Sheriff. You'll have a weapon and a motive and everything you need for your day in court. The curse is what you won't be looking for, what you'll never be able to prove with forensics. It's the catalyst. It's what makes things boil over.'

I'd fallen still, my hands lost in the papers. Something about his words brought the memories back. They could be gone for years, healed over and laid to rest, and then out of nowhere the gun smoke stung my eyes, the wet jungle invaded my nose, and I had to bury them all over again. You could leave a war, but it never left you.

'Ordinary men commit extraordinary evil all the time. Trust me.'

He smiled a bit and nodded in deference. 'You would know.'

I started working again and shook my head. 'You know what that play really is? An insanity defense from heaven.'

Jones laughed just as Jake phoned again and I answered this time.

'What have you got?'

'Why didn't you answer any of my calls?'

'Good God, Jake. When you get married you better find some girl who likes wearing the pants.'

'We could've found the murder weapon. Or there could've been an explosion at the plant.'

'Dispatch would've called for something like that.'

'You don't know, that's all I'm saying. It could be important.'

'Well, is it?'

'Damn right it is. I found out who L.G. is.'

Finally some good news today. And I was in just a mood to haul this pervert through the ringer. 'The warrant came through?'

'Yes, so I accessed her account information and found hundreds of messages to a guy named LitGeek.'

'L.G.,' I muttered.

'Exactly. So I accessed his account information and there was an email address. I traced . . .'

I didn't hear much of the techno talk, because at that moment

I flipped a piece of paper and saw a name that clicked everything into place. I dropped the other papers and stared at the black type, thinking back over the last few days.

'. . . so when I got the gmail registration it said the guy's name is–'

'Peter Lund,' I interrupted.

'How did you know that?' He was pissed as all get-out.

Gerald Jones wasn't so good an actor that he could pretend he wasn't eavesdropping, and the last thing I needed was another juicy bit leaked to the press. If Hattie had had an affair with her high school teacher, they'd be on Pine Valley like white on rice.

'Never mind. I'm headed there now. I'll have him at the station in thirty minutes.'

'I'm coming with you.'

'You're staying right there and printing out every email you've got off of Hattie's computer. And take that busted fax machine out of the interrogation room. And make sure there's a fresh pot of coffee.'

'You're going to try the friendly angle?'

'No, I'm thirsty.' I hung up and tossed the half-full coffee cup Jones had given me into the trash. He grinned.

'Somehow it's heartwarming to know the crusty-sheriff cliché is alive and well.'

'Happy to oblige.' I got up and shook his hand. 'Jones.'

I took the highway back to Pine Valley at a hundred miles an hour, lights flashing. The speed felt good. It got the blood up, helped clear the morning away. I walked into Pine Valley High School less than fifteen minutes later and the principal met me before I'd even crossed the front door.

'Sheriff. This about Hattie?'

'I wouldn't be pulling one of your teachers out of the classroom otherwise.'

'Which one you need?'

'Lund.'

He made a sort of sucked-in face before hollering to his secretary to call for a sub.

'This way.'

We walked back to the classrooms and he led the way to the end of a hall.

'Anything I should know about Peter?' he asked, just as we got to the right classroom.

I knocked on the window. Lund looked up from his computer and froze a bit. I pointed at him and then at my feet. *Get your ass out here.*

'A lot of things you should probably know about him.' We both watched him fumble around and say something to the students. 'I'm only interested in one.'

Peter came out and glanced between the two of us. 'Sheriff. Do you have more information about Hattie?'

'Matter of fact. Need you to come down to the station.'

'Can't it wait until the end of the day? I've got classes.' He waved behind him, looking at the principal, who was eyeing him like he was trying to picture the knife in Lund's hand.

'We'll take care of the kids,' the principal said. 'Go get your stuff.'

Lund did as he was told and we headed out to the cruiser. I let him ride in front.

'What's your take on this curse nonsense?' I asked as we pulled out of the parking lot. I could sense his whole body relaxing as he heard the question.

'Bullshit.'

I laughed once and he eased up a bit more.

'The legend part of it, anyway, is a load of superstitious paranoia. The real curse is dealing with actors – or in my case, kids –

who believe in the bullshit and make the director's life a living hell. You saw how Portia Nguyen got everybody scared on Sunday?'

I nodded.

'She's been like that the whole play, feeding this curse crap to anyone who'll listen.'

'Did Hattie listen? She and Portia were mighty close.'

'No.' His voice quieted down. 'No, Hattie was one of the only ones who didn't buy it. She . . . she was different from most teenagers. She understood the space between reality and illusion.'

He started to say something else and then seemed to think better of it.

When we pulled up to the station I had Jake take him into the back while I got a cup of coffee and waited for it to cool. Two news vans drove by the front window and I could hear Brian bugging Nancy out on the sidewalk to set up another press conference. I took a drink and headed to the interrogation room.

Jake, who was playing bodyguard by the door, handed me a folder when I walked in. Lund looked a lot more uncomfortable than he had a few minutes ago. I sat down and flipped the folder open, reading the emails and sipping my coffee. After a moment, Lund leaned in and saw enough to drop his head into his hands.

'So, LitGeek, huh?' I tapped the name on one of the pages.

'God. I . . . I didn't know who she was. It was all anonymous.'

'Anonymous, like strangers?'

'Yes.' He lifted his head while I kept drinking and flipping pages. 'Yes, exactly.'

I picked up a paper and leaned back until I could read it clearly. ' "I'm running my hand up the inside of your thigh and into the crease of your leg. My fingers are a whisper on your skin, a suggestion you can't ignore." '

Jake snickered. I read the crap same as I'd read my breakfast order at Sally's. I glanced up at Lund. He'd gone beet-red.

'You make . . . suggestions like that . . . to complete strangers?'

'No, I knew her. I mean, I didn't know her identity but I knew who she was, I thought. We'd been chatting for weeks. We'd become close.'

'Mmm-hmm. Appears that way.'

'What did she print? God, did she just print the sex stuff? As soon as I found out who she was, I ended it. I mean immediately. Doesn't she have that in there, too?'

He'd worked himself into a pretty good sweat and tried to see what I was reading. Jake was trying for all the world to look tough and disinterested again after the snicker.

'Matter of fact, she does.'

He heaved a sigh out, deflating like a balloon. 'So you can see. It was over. It was nothing.'

'Don't suspect your wife would think this was nothing. Don't suspect Hattie did. She seemed pretty bent on you here.' I shook my head. 'For some reason.'

'Hattie did try to talk to me after we realized . . . the situation. I even met with her once, to end it face-to-face, because she wanted to . . . to continue the relationship.'

'And you weren't the least bit tempted? Pretty, young girl like that. Smart, just like you. Liked all those books and big cities.'

'No. No.' He shook his head, looking between me and Jake. 'She was a student, a . . . a child. I could have gone to jail, for Christ's sake. Not to mention losing my job and my marriage.'

'You still can, Lund. We can arrange all those things for you.'

'But nothing happened. I told her she had to drop it, that I would never return her feelings, and she moved on. She started dating Tommy Kinakis. That's when I finally felt like the whole nightmare was behind me, when I began seeing them in the halls. It seemed like they were together for the rest of the year, but I have no idea why. He's a big, hulking idiot. Have you even talked to

Tommy yet? He acted like she was his property, always draping an arm over her and steering her through crowds in the halls like she couldn't walk by herself.'

'You must have been watching her pretty close to know all that.'

'With the rest of the students, I couldn't care less. But yes – I watched Hattie.' He slumped a bit as he said it, maybe ashamed, maybe relieved to get it off his chest. 'How could I not? I was paranoid that she'd decide to turn me in.'

'Well, then, this all worked out pretty nice for you. Can't hurt you now, can she?'

'No! How can you even say that?' He snapped back up, indignant as hell. 'I fucked up, okay? I know it. I'm an asshole and a lousy husband.'

'No arguments here.'

'But that doesn't have anything to do with the fact that Hattie was the brightest and most promising student in that entire school. She . . . understood people, she could peg you with a glance. It was unsettling sometimes, like she could see right through you. She was going to New York in the fall and I knew that she would fit right in with that fast-paced East Coast mentality. I knew she would do something amazing with her life. And I was relieved, too, okay? That she would be gone and I could move on with *my* life.'

'Maybe next fall wasn't fast enough for you. Or maybe Hattie decided she needed some cash for her trip to New York or a little bump in her GPA.' It grated, having to talk about Hattie like that, heaping ugliness on her, but I couldn't spare her from it. I had to bare all her secrets, and just hope I could keep some of it from Bud and Mona.

'The only time I spoke to Hattie in the last few months was in class or at the play. She wasn't blackmailing me. She wouldn't do that. You need to talk to Tommy. Hattie was going places and

Tommy wasn't. If she tried to break up with him . . . these last few days . . . it's the only thing I can think of.'

I nodded and shuffled the emails back together in the folder, flipping it shut. He was working up a good sweat trying to put the knife in Tommy's hands.

'Where were you on Friday night after the play, Lund?'

'I had to wait until everyone left and then lock up the school. Carl helped me. Then we went over to his place for a drink.'

'Carl Jacobs?'

He nodded.

'Okay, let's go.' I stood up and handed the folder to Jake.

'To Carl's? He's still at school.'

I led him out the door, practically cuffing him on his sweaty collar. 'We're going to Mayo. I'm gonna give you a chance to clear your name, Lund. Or clean it up some, anyway.'

I put him in the front seat again, in case any of those news vans happened to be watching, and walked Jake back to the station door, talking low.

'You think he was the one that had sex with her?' Jake asked.

'Lab'll tell us one way or the other. He wanted to, that's for damn sure. Comes down to whether he was more horny or scared, I guess.'

'I'd go with scared. That guy reeks of chicken shit. You want me to pull Carl Jacobs in?'

'Just do a phone interview. The less people we parade into the station, the better. Corroborate the alibi. I want to know when they left the school, what they drank, what they talked about, and when Lund left Carl's house. I'll get the same from Lund on the way to Rochester. Call me as soon as you know.'

'You'll pick up this time?' He was too excited to put much sarcasm behind it.

'I might at that. And Jake?'

'Yeah?'

'Not one word of this to anyone outside this conversation, you understand? Not dispatch, not Nancy or any of the boys, not even your mother. The press would have a field day.' I passed a hand over my face. 'And I'd have to arrest Bud for murdering this sorry excuse here.'

'What do I say if someone asks about Lund?'

'You tell them to keep their big noses out of an ongoing investigation.'

Jake seemed to like that idea and I left him to it, walking over to the cruiser. Lund was sunk into the seat, his head turned away from the window like the whole damn town didn't already know where he was. LitGeek liked to hide. Now the question was, how much was he hiding?

HATTIE / *Wednesday, November 7, 2007*

'COME ON, Hattie. You know you're going to.'

Portia took a bite of her hamburger, made a face, and set it back down. 'Didn't I say no pickles?'

Maggie leaned across the Dairy Queen booth and picked off Portia's pickles, popping them in her mouth. 'I don't know. She's a big, fat community theater star now. Probably too good for our spring play.'

'Shut up, both of you. I said I hadn't decided.' I squirted some ketchup in my basket.

'It still tastes like pickle,' Portia complained.

'Then give it to me.' Maggie grabbed the burger.

'It's only November,' I pointed out and offered Portia some of my onion rings. 'I'll decide when they post what play it's going to be. I'm not auditioning for a musical. I can't sing.'

'I heard Mr. Lund's directing it this year. There's no way he would pick a musical.'

My stomach lurched at his name and the onion rings turned to concrete in my mouth. Luckily a group of football players barged into the restaurant and started horsing around by the registers.

'Maggie, did you ask Derek to Sadie's yet?' I changed the subject.

She shot a coy look over her shoulder at the testosterone display. 'Yep. We're going to double with Molly and Trenton.'

Derek had someone in a headlock by the Dilly Bar case, but he paused to shoot Maggie a grin with a licking motion. Charming.

'What about you, Porsche? Did you ask Matt or Tommy?'

'Matt's going with Stephanie.'

'Well, Tommy's right there. Go ask him.' I waved an onion ring at him, but Tommy startled like he'd been watching me and walked over to our booth, hands shoved in his letterman jacket.

'Hey, Hattie.'

'Hey, Portia had something she wanted–' I got violently kicked under the table.

'– to go do,' she finished, smiling at Tommy. 'You can have my seat.'

'Mine, too. I'm going to grab a Blizzard.' They exchanged a look and suddenly they were both gone. I got the uncomfortable feeling that I'd missed a conversation.

'Er – d'you mind?' Tommy flapped his jacket at the empty booth and I shrugged. He sat down, cleared his throat, and started playing with the napkin dispenser. Gerald always said hands were a shortcut to the character. Ignore the words, he said. Pay attention to what the hands were doing. Tommy had thick hands and dirty fingernails and he clubbed the dispenser around like a hyped-up hockey player. He was nervous as hell.

'So, what's up?' I finally asked.

'Nothing. Just got home from hunting with my dad. Bagged a twelve-pointer at two hundred feet.'

'Killer,' I deadpanned, nodding.

It seemed like most of the restaurant was watching us, with Tommy's football buddies in the front row, elbowing each other and shoving fries in their mouths.

'What's up with you?' he asked.

'Just grabbing a bite before work.'

'Oh. Cool.' He scratched his hair, which wasn't exactly curly. It looked more like he'd just gotten out of bed.

I took a drink and my straw made that slurping noise when you get to the bottom. Tommy eyed the cup hopefully.

'Do . . . do you want me to grab you a refill?'

'Sure.' I handed it to him. 'Half orange, half Sprite, three ice cubes.'

I watched him go to the soda fountain and fill my ridiculous order exactly. He even dumped out a little orange to make sure it only filled half the cup. When Derek walked over and punched him in the arm, Tommy shoved him mercilessly into the condiments counter and came back to the booth without spilling a drop. Amazing. It was like a social experiment. I took a sip and tried experimenting some more.

'So what do you think of Portia?'

'Portia Nguyen?' he asked, and I tried not to roll my eyes. There were no other Portias in the entire town.

'Yeah.'

'I don't know. She's nice, I guess.'

'What would you say if she asked you to Sadie's?'

'Oh.' He flushed bright red and started playing with the napkins again. 'I, um, I didn't think . . . she was gonna ask me.'

Then he swallowed and met my eyes. Funny, I'd never noticed his were a perfect blue, like the kind of sky that made you forget there was anything behind it.

'I thought maybe you might ask me,' he blurted out.

I offered him an onion ring while I considered. There was a lot to consider all of a sudden.

'Why do you want me to ask you instead of Portia?'

'I don't know. She's just kind of loud. She's always talking about people. I know she's your friend and all, but . . .' He let the sentence hang, looking completely uncomfortable, and shoved the onion ring in his mouth.

'She is pretty loud,' I agreed with a smile. He smiled back, a half grin that made his baby face cute and crooked. So he wanted a quiet girl.

'Are you going to ask me then?'

'I don't know.' I leaned forward and let my hair fall in my face. 'I think I need to see you dance first.'

'What? Right here?' He seemed confused.

Okay – a quiet, simple girl. I offered him another onion ring and watched his face light up. He liked being fed. The list of characteristics grew. And just like that, Tommy Kinakis's girlfriend started to form.

◆

For our first date, we went to see *No Country for Old Men*. He picked me up in a gigantic truck that he clearly worshipped. He pointed out the new seat covers, the sound system, and even showed me how he'd built a secret cubbyhole in the driver's side door that held a flask of whiskey, which he tipped my way in the theater's parking lot. I declined. We shared a monster-size popcorn during the movie although it was gone before I'd had more than a few bites; I was too engrossed in the performances.

'I love the Coen brothers,' I sighed on the way home.

'Was one of them the hit man?' Tommy asked. 'He was awesome.'

We didn't talk again until he pulled into my driveway and then he fiddled with the radio and mumbled for me to hang on.

'For what?' I asked, but he was already out of the truck and walking around to my side.

As he opened my door he held out his hand awkwardly. I took it to jump down and would have let go if he hadn't closed his fingers around mine and put his other hand gently on my shoulder.

'You . . . said you wanted to see me dance.'

And then it registered – the country music he'd turned up and the bashful expression on his face.

'Oh.' I flushed and dropped my gaze, thrown off balance by the gesture.

He drew my hand in to his chest and turned me in a few circles until the song ended and I backed up.

'So will I do?'

I smiled. 'I think so.'

The next weekend we went to Sadie Hawkins and a postseason football party afterwards, where Tommy kissed me next to Derek's dad's beer fridge. Yells went up all around and after that everyone started talking about us like a couple. It even sounded right. Tommy and Hattie, high school sweethearts.

By Thanksgiving we'd established a routine. We went out on Saturday nights, and since we didn't have any classes together – I took all advanced subjects and he was mostly on the remedial track – we only saw each other during lunches at school. I sat with him at the football table and let him eat most of my lunch while I played on my phone. On the days with chocolate chip cookies, though, he always gave me his.

Tommy obviously liked me – all I had to do was smile at him and he lit up – although it wasn't me he liked so much as just having a girlfriend. He gave me bone-crunching squeezes whenever the other jocks corralled their girlfriends and we usually spent Saturday nights double- or triple-dating with some of them. I think he felt like he truly belonged, now that he had his own plus-one, and even though he was dumb as a box of rocks, he was still a sweetheart. I was glad I could give him that kind of acceptance from his friends.

Mom and Dad were happy, too. I think they thought having a boyfriend grounded me here, like maybe I would change my mind about New York. They invited Tommy over for Sunday dinner and he and Dad watched the football game afterwards, just like Greg and Dad used to do.

For me it was all learning. I'd never dated anyone before and had no idea how to be a girlfriend. It turned out to be easy – mostly physical, no-brainer stuff. It was more about leaning in to listen than actually listening, or putting a hand on his arm instead of telling him to stop. I watched the other girls on our double dates and saw how they teased and giggled. They looked so happy and I wondered whether, if I looked happy enough, I would belong, too.

One day after lunch I walked him to English class. We meandered down the hall with Tommy draping an arm over my shoulders and my book bag slapping lightly against his thigh, seemingly in no hurry, but inside my body started to hum. The football players called their usual shout-outs to each other as the warning bell rang and then we got to Peter's door. I looked up and smiled that hinting smile at Tommy, leaning toward his huge dinner-plate face. He took the bait, smashing his mouth down on mine and tightening his squeeze where he had tucked me under his shoulder.

'Have fun in English,' I teased after he let me go, running a fingernail up his biceps.

'Yeah, right.' He rolled his eyes and walked into the classroom.

At the teacher's desk, Peter stared at me, completely frozen. His eyes darted back and forth between me and Tommy and I could tell he was in total shock. He did cafeteria duty with Mr. Jacobs and could have watched me with Tommy for weeks now, but he'd refused to even glance in my direction since that night in the barn. I ignored him and blew Tommy a kiss before waltzing down the hallway. It was beautiful.

After that I could tell Peter was watching me. In Advanced English I made sure my hand was up as much as ever. If anything, I worked extra hard on the assignments so I could always make some point about the book's theme or subtext that would impress him. For a while he tried to gloss over me, but after he saw me kissing Tommy, he loosened up a little. He began admitting I was bringing up interesting viewpoints, then he started debating my ideas for the benefit of the class to try to get someone else to jump in on the argument. A few weeks after Thanksgiving, he opened the discussion by saying, 'Does anyone besides Hattie have anything they want to say about the ending?'

The whole class laughed, including me, but I stuck my hand up anyway.

'Anyone?' Peter looked around hopefully.

After another minute, he sighed theatrically and called on me.

'I thought it was a terrible ending. Nothing was resolved.'

'Anyone else feel that way? Show of hands, please.' He perched on the edge of his desk, which was my favorite position to watch him in. It meant he was going to launch into a lecture and try to make us think about some of the issues in the book. His sleeves were rolled up to his elbows and my gaze drifted to the hair sprinkled along his forearms before I blinked and made myself listen to what he was saying.

'It's a book about war. War always leaves society with difficult questions that may or may not be able to be answered. Is it O'Brien's place to answer those questions for us or is it only his responsibility to point them out so that the reader has to confront them?'

Becca Price answered that one. 'I think everyone would have a different answer about whether the war was right or not. I mean, look at how it is now in Iraq and Afghanistan. No one can agree on the right thing to do or whether or not we should even be there. But everybody says it's the Vietnam of our generation.'

'Yes, lucky you,' Peter said. Some people laughed. Others just stared at their notebooks. I wasn't the only one with family over there.

'So back to Hattie's complaint that nothing was resolved–'

'Wait, I didn't mean that I wanted him to answer big, philosophical questions about war. But none of the characters' story lines were wrapped up.'

'Maybe O'Brien wanted his characters to symbolize those bigger questions. If the plot wrapped up too neatly, would you still be thinking about the implications of war on ordinary men and women?'

I sighed and pursed my lips, knowing I'd lost my point. But then I had an idea.

Peter kept the discussion bouncing around for a few more minutes and then handed out our essay assignment just as the bell rang. I jumped up and followed him back to his desk while everyone packed up their book bags.

'Mr. Lund, I still have some issues with the book. Could I stop by after school to talk about them?'

I kept my face completely innocent, biting my lip and tilting my head for effect. Peter swallowed and glanced around the classroom. Everyone was talking and laughing, pushing their way toward the door.

'Why don't you just use those issues as subject matter for your essay?'

'But I can't write the synopsis if I'm not sure I understand the book correctly. It'll only take a few minutes.'

I left before he could tell me no again and was on pins and

needles for the rest of the day. Would he be there? I knew he had a free period during the last hour of the day – yes, I had his schedule memorized – so he could bolt out of school before I even got out of chemistry. I practically ran out of class when the last bell rang and beat the crowd down to the first floor. A few people tried to call me over as I passed the locker bays, but I just waved and kept walking with my science book clutched to my chest.

When I got to his room, I stopped to catch my breath and peeked in the window. Peter sat at his desk reading. My heart flip-flopped and I pushed through the door, eager to watch his face look up and see what expression it would have. When I opened the door, though, I saw two other students working at desks in the back. One of them was Tommy.

Tommy grinned when he saw me, but I looked away and let my hair fall in a curtain over my cheek, stalking over to Peter's desk.

'Oh, Hattie.' He glanced up from his computer. 'I forgot you were stopping by. I've got a couple students doing last-chance re-visions.'

Behind me, Tommy snorted softly. Peter ignored it, giving me a bland smile.

'Did you still want to talk about O'Brien?'

'Yes,' I managed after a minute.

'Well?'

I wanted to slap the pretend nonchalance off his face. Instead I rummaged around in my bag to find the book, buying myself some time, and decided two could play this game.

'Here.' I set my book on his desk and grabbed an empty chair by the whiteboard, pulling it over next to his.

'I can't remember the exact passages right now, but I've got them marked.'

He sat up straighter in his chair while I made a show of flip-ping through the book and making thinking noises. Tommy kept shooting me looks, confused, until I sent him a small grin and a wink to give him the idea I was here for him. It worked. He put a hand over his mouth to hide his smile and went back to work, probably turning all his commas into periods or capitalizing random words.

'Here it is.' I found a page where I'd written all over the margins, venting about how depressing the whole thing was. I do that a lot. I like to add my words to a book, as if I'm talking to the author and we're having a conversation that makes the story come alive in a way that it wasn't before I started reading it.

'You know this is school property, Hattie. You can't deface it.'

'So bill me.' Tommy and the other student laughed, then both tried to pass it off as coughing.

'Like here. I don't get this guy's through line at all. He hangs himself after he gets home? He survived a war and then decides to kill himself? He should've just walked toward the Vietcong with a big white flag over his head.'

'Think about all the flashbacks he keeps having, the guilt he feels over his friend's death. Maybe if he truly had survived the war, he would have been able to move on. The truth O'Brien wants us to feel in this story is that some part of the character did die in Vietnam and he just didn't realize it yet.'

'But look at how long this story is.' I moved to flip the pages and accidentally brushed my fingers over his hand.

The touch was electric. It shot through my entire arm and I froze for a second, unprepared. I glanced at Tommy, but Peter's computer hid our hands and the book. We were in plain sight in the middle of the school, twenty feet from my boyfriend, yet no one could see us.

My heart started racing and my breath sped up. Peter hadn't moved a muscle. It seemed like he was stunned, too.

Carefully, so carefully, I paged back to the beginning of the story, staring at his hand. It was a beautiful hand, with long fingers and blunt nails and a dusting of hair on his knuckles and wrists.

'It's at least twenty pages long,' I said, low and kind of breathlessly. I didn't think Tommy could hear me. 'And nothing happens in it.'

'The character can't move forward. That's why he keeps circling the lake. If he only did it once, you wouldn't fully appreciate his impotence.'

His voice fell, too, although neither of us looked at each other. We both stared at the desk and the book in front of us.

'If he can't move forward' – I swallowed and reached out, deliberately this time, and set my hand next to his, barely touching him – 'then what's the point?'

His skin was tough, not like Tommy's babyish skin, and I felt the warmth radiate from his pinky finger into mine and through my whole body. I wanted to slip my palm over his and thread our fingers together, but I didn't dare. Tommy could stand up and see us at any moment. Someone could walk by in the hallway and glance through the window in the door. A second ticked by, then two, while Peter left his hand next to mine and I thrilled at this tiny, forbidden contact.

Peter took a deep breath and spoke, carefully and deliberately. 'The character made his choices already. That's the point of the story. He has to face the consequences of his decisions.

'Read this section again.' He picked up the book, breaking contact, and my heart sank. He found the paragraph he wanted and gave it to me, then scooted a safe distance away.

The words swam around on the page. I had no idea what any of it said. I remembered my first date with Tommy, how he'd held my hand and twirled me around so sweetly and I didn't feel anything, not even a single drop of the reaction I'd just had to the barest touch of Peter's skin. If I was a normal girl with normal dreams, I would have been giddy about Tommy Kinakis's hesitant touch. I would have giggled over him with all my girlfriends and pulled him closer instead of ducking my head and turning away. It would have been so much simpler and I took a moment to mourn for what I could never be. No matter how well I played the part, I would never become the role.

So it was time to pull back the curtain and take a bow.

'Okay, I think I see your point.' I closed the book and put it away.

'I hope you'll at least think about what I've said before you write the essay.'

'Of course.' I added, in a softer voice, 'I always do.' Before he could say anything, I pulled out a sheet of paper and wrote something, then stood up and pulled on my coat and book bag. I positioned myself between the guys and Peter, so they couldn't see him, and handed him the piece of paper with the note in the middle of the page.

What do you think of Hattie's new boyfriend? – HollyG

Peter's head snapped up and he stared at me, confusion all over his face. I let my heartbeat settle down and gave him a slow smile, the kind of smile that conspirators exchange, that revealed everything without saying a word, the kind of smile that lit up an entire stage and said to every person in the audience, *I'm yours and only yours.* I smiled at him with everything buried inside me that longed to break free.

Just as the understanding started to filter through his eyes, I turned and strolled out of the classroom, winking at Tommy as I passed.

PETER / *Thursday, December 6, 2007*

WHAT DID I think of Hattie's boyfriend? What did I think of Tommy Kinakis?? I thought he was dating a sociopath, that's what I thought of him.

My footfalls were hard and driving, chewing up the cartilage in my knees with grim satisfaction. I needed to destroy something and my body was the only available option.

Since cross-country had finished I'd started running at night again, and these holiday nights were endless. The snow we'd gotten for Thanksgiving had melted and given way to a dry, dark December. The sun gave up the horizon as soon as I pulled into Elsa's driveway after work, casting a final weak flare against the metal silo before the darkness swallowed everything and the silence began. All the summer chirping of insects had vanished. Even the chickens were quiet. There was nothing to interrupt my constant guilt except exertion.

I'd bought a headlight to see the road and its beams bounced

167

jarringly over the rocks. I ran in the middle of the gravel, passing farmhouses that glowed like tiny ships on a rolling, frozen sea. Trees loomed at the edges of the road, their naked branches ghostly in the moonlight, but I barely noticed them.

She was dating Tommy as a cover.

In the three hours since she'd sauntered out of my classroom, I'd been incapable of thinking about anything else. She'd told me at the barn that she would become the last girl in the world who would be having an affair with her English teacher and apparently this massive deceit was her plan. Tommy was a convenience, nothing more to her than a prop. I'd stumbled through the rest of the afternoon and dinner, trying to digest the magnitude of what she had done. She had multiple personalities; it was the only explanation. She was dangerous, calculating, diabolical, and . . . brilliant. She was fucking brilliant.

After that night at the barn, I severed any connection with her, refusing to engage or ignore her in class, because ignoring her would single her out and I couldn't afford to differentiate her in any way. I slipped up once during lunch, though. Carl had caught me looking at her in the cafeteria.

'Trouble?' he asked. Nothing else. Carl was nothing if not succinct.

He glanced in Hattie's direction. Even though we were supposed to be monitoring the students for fights and other inappropriate conduct, Carl and I usually just ate and kept to ourselves.

'No.' I looked away quickly, stuffing a bite into my mouth.

'Should be illegal for them to wear sweaters like that until they're eighteen.'

It was suddenly hard to swallow.

'Some of them don't even seem like kids. The boys do, of course. Boys don't become men real fast anymore. These girls, though . . .'

'I know.' I kept myself from looking at Hattie again, but I felt like it was written all over my face. I stared down at my sandwich, as engrossed as it was possible to be with egg salad.

'Out here they sometimes still get married right out of high school,' Carl kept on, feeling conversational that day for some reason. He added that – 'out here' – occasionally when he talked to me, like he was my reluctant tour guide to rural southern Minnesota.

'You've got to be careful,' he said.

I didn't respond or even look up and we spent the rest of the lunch period lost in our own heads. If he suspected anything about me and Hattie, he didn't say so and I never made the mistake of glancing in her direction after that day.

The only interaction we'd had in the last month was through her homework assignments. I read them upstairs in the computer room, ashamed of how much I reacted to her words on the page. Regardless of anything else that had happened, she was still one of the brightest, most agile-minded students I had known. She introduced argument after argument, defeating her own points and turning on a dime to embrace some entirely new theory that she later questioned and half-hung at the end of her paper like both a prize and a warning. She clearly didn't draft her essays, but I loved that she didn't. It was like watching her think out loud, as if the page itself was breathing. I didn't give her anything less than an A, even when her narrative structure obviously needed some improvement, because I knew she would challenge me on the grade and I couldn't risk any chance of having to talk to her one-on-one.

And after all of that careful distance she ambushed me anyway, just when I'd started to relax and think she'd moved on. She handed me that piece of paper and tossed me right back into the fucking fire.

Turning into the parking lot for Lake Crosby, I passed an empty pickup. There was no one around; the truck looked like it could have been left for dead weeks ago. I slowed my pace as I reached the uneven terrain on the trail that circled the lake. Soften your stride, I'd told the boys. Tense your core.

Then I didn't need any reminders. My gut clenched as I jogged around the far side of the empty barn and spotted a small glow coming from the window under the oak tree.

No. It couldn't be.

I stopped, not nearly as winded as I'd tried to make myself. The nightly runs – supposed to be both punishment and escape – had only made me stronger, but apparently not strong enough to keep running.

It was just kids, I tried to reason even as I clicked off my head lamp. Just a couple of kids having beers or smoking pot. I crept closer, tempering my breathing, all the while calling myself a damn idiot for not turning away and sprinting for the woods.

I got close enough to see inside and there she was.

She had a blanket spread out on the floor and a camp lantern next to her. She sat cross-legged with a book in her lap and a bottle of water nearby. Her long hair was tucked away in her hood and her cheeks gleamed orange in the lantern light. Despite the recent warmth, I could see small puffs of her breath against her jacket. Something about her straight posture or the tilt of her head re-minded me of Alice in Wonderland and a vertigo came over me, like I was the one tumbling down the rabbit hole.

I turned and walked silently to where the trail picked up again. I could just make out the line of trees that marked the border of Elsa's land. All I had to do was click the light on again and run. My calves were cooling off and stiffening up. It was time to move, but I couldn't.

I looked back at the barn and the empty horizon behind it. She was alone, exposed, and suddenly all my anger vaulted toward her with a stunning satisfaction. I crossed the clearing in five paces and shoved open the creaking door. She looked up, startled at the intrusion.

'What the hell are you doing here?'

A smile broke over her face as she registered it was me.

'Studying.'

'Bullshit.'

'No, I'm studying history. The Renaissance was definitely not bullshit.' Her smile only grew wider, until she saw the strap on my head.

'What's that?'

'It's a headlamp.' I ripped it off and shoved it in my pocket.

'Okay.' She seemed amused by my sweaty clothes and my rage.

'Answer the question, Hattie. What are you doing here?'

'I told you already. I'm doing some homework.'

'No, you should be doing homework in your house or at school or the library.'

'The library's closed.'

'In a warm, well-lit room.' I bit out each word, ignoring her attempts at cute quips. 'Not in a condemned, unheated building in the middle of the winter.'

Setting the book aside, she stood up and faced me earnestly, pushing the hood back on the quilted blue jacket that made her look about five years old. 'Come on, it's like forty degrees. We could have a pool party.' She laughed, and then added, 'I was waiting for you.'

'How did you know I'd be running out here?'

'I didn't, but I thought you might come. After what I told you.'

'And if I didn't? Would you just sit out here freezing every night waiting for someone to stumble on you?' I stalked toward her.

'Who would be out here?'

'Anyone! God, Hattie. Don't you think?'

'I think you're overreacting.' She was starting to get irritated. Good.

'You could be raped or mugged.'

'Morbid much?'

'No one would hear you scream.' I stood on the edge of her ridiculous picnic setup, looming over her.

'This isn't Minneapolis, Peter. In case you hadn't noticed. This is Pine Valley, where nothing bad ever happens except maybe drought. And see? I've got some water right here.'

She was trying to lighten the mood again. Screw that.

'Why are you dating him?'

'Tommy?' She instantly brightened, like I'd asked the question she'd been hoping for. 'What do you think? Is he a good choice?'

'Tell me you like that moron. Tell me you're not using him to get closer to me.'

'I look at it as more of a public service. Everyone's happy. You have no idea.' She looked infinitely pleased with herself and it sent me over the edge.

'Why?' I grabbed her arms and shook her over the top of the lantern, throwing her shadow violently across the walls and ceiling. The force of it wiped the pleasure off her face. She understood I wasn't playing her little game.

I shook her again, pulling her up and bruising her arms. 'Why are you doing this?'

'Because I love you.' Her eyes were wide and dark in the lantern shadows. Her voice broke a little and I realized how close we were: one furious, aching breath apart.

Instantly I dropped her and turned away, fighting for control.

'It's a crush. An infatuation.' I wiped the cooled sweat from my forehead and tried to put some distance between us.

'No one will suspect, Peter.' She was right behind me.

'Stop this.'

'No one will know I'm yours.'

'You're not mine.' I turned around and she paused, too. She wasn't confident enough to bridge that last gap. Still a child. I took advantage of her hesitation, of that last flicker of innocence.

'Can't you see how wrong this is?'

'I didn't know it was you. I didn't know until it was too late. I'd already fallen.' Her voice was low, pleading now, and it started to break things inside me, things I'd spent weeks fortifying. 'I just want you to look at me like you feel it, too. I know you do. I didn't imagine it.'

'What were you planning on doing, Hattie? Sleeping with us both?'

'No.' She swallowed. 'Just you.'

My mouth went dry and my blood shifted from a pound to a dangerous pulse.

'But you let him kiss you.'

'Are you jealous?' A smiled flashed across her face and was gone. 'It's just acting, Peter. There's not much to being Tommy's girlfriend. I could have nailed it when I was twelve.'

I took a step closer, compelled beyond reason toward this girl who kept shedding masks like a matryoshka doll, each one more audacious than the last, a psychological striptease that racked me with the need to tear her apart until I found out who or what was inside.

'Is your entire life an act?'

She dropped her head and something like shame finally crossed her face.

'Yes,' she whispered.

'And what role am I supposed to be playing?'

'None!' Her head snapped back up.

'You've planned this whole scene.'

'No! It's not like that.'

'Who am I, Hattie? The big-city teacher who throws his whole life away for you? Who sweeps you off your lying feet? Like this?'

In a heartbeat I closed the distance between us and hauled her up again. 'Is this the part where I declare my love? Where I tell you I can't get you out of my goddamn head?'

'Yes,' she choked out.

'How does the fantasy go, Hattie? What comes next?'

Her eyes swarmed with fear, anger, and arousal, everything that had been torturing me since the *Jane Eyre* play, and then I knew what came next, what I couldn't stop myself from doing any longer.

We moved at the same time. I took her mouth in a race of lip, tongue, and teeth, and pulled her down to the floor with me, straight into the welcome blood rush of hell.

HATTIE / *January 2008*

I LOST my virginity when I was fifteen, although *lost* is a funny word for it. I didn't misplace it like a homework assignment or a cell phone. It wasn't like I could find it again and tuck it back in there. I gave it away in Mike Crestview's basement on an old sofa with a cabbage-leaf print while we watched *Lord of the Rings*. I suppose it was a pretty typical first time, except I wasn't all starry-eyed about Mike. I was curious more than anything. You can't watch that many seasons of *Sex and the City* without getting a little curious. And Mike was a nice enough guy, a senior all excited to leave for college. I probably liked that excitement as much as anything else about him.

We were watching the part where Gandalf fights the fire monster and falls into hell or wherever when I asked Mike if he wanted to have sex.

He seemed pretty surprised. He was actually better friends with Greg than with me, but Greg was gone for the weekend, so I'd come over alone.

'Do you have a condom?' I asked him. 'If not, we can forget it.'

It was kind of hilarious how fast he found a condom and made sure his parents were still at the grocery store.

The sex itself was bumpy and weird and I didn't help very much. Mike said he'd done it before, so I just lay back and let it happen, observing more than participating, I guess. The thing I remembered most, besides the scratchy fabric rubbing my butt, was the vein that popped out in Mike's forehead, like a curvy blood river. After that I figured I understood what sex was all about, and didn't have any urge to try it again.

Last fall, as my junior year started and Mike was off enjoying life in Minneapolis, my grandpa passed away right in the middle of harvest and my parents had to go to Iowa to take care of the details.

He'd been in a nursing home for years, ever since my grandma died and he had a stroke. Before the stroke he was just like my dad – a tough, matter-of-fact guy. Dad had a sense of humor, though, while Grandpa always seemed tense, like he was waiting for the other shoe to drop, but if it ever did he wouldn't say a word about it. After the stroke, it was like he'd been turned inside out. He cried all the time. He cried when we came to visit him, when the nurse put him to bed at night, even about stuff that should have made him happy like when the Twins were winning. It was as if eighty years of buried emotion started leaking out his eyeballs.

The nursing home was a sad-looking concrete building outside Des Moines where all the old ladies sat on the cracked patio and tried to wave us over to their wheelchairs. We ignored them and kept our eyes on the backs of Mom's shoes as she walked inside. Grandpa always had stale Bit-O-Honeys that just about broke your jaw and we had to sit there chewing them while Mom chatted to the walls as she fussed around his room and he stared at us, silent tears running down his grizzled, old face.

When he died I wondered if my dad was more upset about missing the harvest. Nobody talked about their feelings around here. They just absorbed the hurts and the losses and barely nodded if anyone said anything about it. It was okay to be funny or crack a joke like Dad, but any other emotion just got the *American Gothic* treatment. It was all hidden and sometimes I wondered if it was even there. I guess Dad really did love his father, though, because he left in the middle of the harvest and hired a migrant contractor to take over his fields while he was gone.

I stayed behind to finish school that week and was supposed to come down for the funeral on Saturday. One afternoon I was reading on the log swing by the house, tracing the outside of one breast absently while I flipped pages, when I glanced over and saw Marco standing twenty feet away, staring at me. He was tall and thick, the kind of fat someone got when they did manual labor and probably ate a bunch of fast food, layers of muscle over fat over muscle. Dad had said he was Guatemalan, with dark skin and hair, but his eyes were bright and fixed on the hand on my breast.

I jumped up and muttered an apology, then ran back to the house. I even locked the front door, which I don't think had ever been locked before, and watched his comings and goings through the curtains of my bedroom for the rest of the afternoon. Maybe it was the book, or the way his eyes seemed to be on fire, but that night was the first time I had an orgasm. I'd tried masturbating before, but apparently it was all about motivation.

Since I'd fallen in love with Peter, motivation was never a problem.

Still, nothing I'd imagined in my bed at night had prepared me for what happened in the Erickson barn. His anger scared me and I'd almost lost hope, until suddenly he grabbed me and dragged us to our knees. I remembered everything, how he ran his hands over every part of me he could reach, how I burned every place he kissed me. He was sweaty and hard and demanding and then it was over as quickly as it started.

'We can't do this,' he'd said, pushing me away.

I dove back into him, kissing his neck, running my hands through his hair. He smelled so good. I wondered when boys stopped smelling like boys and started smelling like his tangle of musk and soap and heat. Or maybe Peter had always smelled that way. What would I have done if he'd walked by me in a mall when he was sixteen? Would my eight-year-old nose have smelled its match and followed him through the food court? I smiled into his collarbone and murmured, 'I have condoms.'

He groaned and nuzzled my temple, then framed my face in his hands. 'You're trying to kill me, aren't you?'

'No, Peter.' I shook my head as much as his hold would allow. 'I'm trying to help you live.'

'Drop the act, Hattie. Tell me what you really want.'

'I want you. I just want you.' I said it over and over again, closing my eyes and rubbing my cheek against his hand. His thumb ran over my mouth and I let it fall open, hoping he'd keep kissing me, but he didn't.

He stood up and dragged himself away.

'You're not eighteen.'

My heart flip-flopped. 'What's a few weeks?'

'Legally, it's the difference between getting fired and getting fired, arrested, and thrown in jail.'

I noticed he didn't say anything about getting divorced, but I didn't want to bring it up and spoil my chances. 'So what are you going to give me for my birthday? A party? A present?'

'A spanking,' he said, almost to himself, and then shook his head and started laughing. It wasn't a happy-sounding laugh.

'Hey, I'm going to be eighteen.' I stood up and crossed my arms. 'You can't talk to me like I'm a kid after that.'

He just covered his face with his hand. I walked over and pulled it down so he had to look at me.

'If anyone's getting spanked, it's you. You're the naughty one here, having lusty feelings for your underage student.'

I tsk-tsked him in my best sexy-teacher voice, but he wasn't in the mood to play. His eyes raked over my face like he was desperate for something and not finding it. I didn't know how to assure him when he didn't believe anything I said. Finally he groaned again, a self-defeating groan, and wound me into a hug, resting his forehead on mine. It was the sweetest gesture he'd made toward me yet, and my heart slammed in my chest. The hope almost choked me.

'There's not enough punishment in the world for either one of us, but that's not why we're here, is it?'

I didn't want to say the wrong thing, so I said nothing. I just closed my eyes and leaned into him.

'When will you be eighteen?'

'January fourth,' I whispered.

He was quiet for a minute. And then he said the thing that threw my heart into a cardiac trauma level of happiness.

'I'm taking you to Minneapolis.'

◆

We set the date for the weekend after my birthday. He told his wife he was visiting some old friends and I told my parents I was going to look at the U of M. Dad had insisted I apply there in case I decided to go to school closer to home next year and they were both thrilled – or as thrilled as they could get – when I told them I was going to take a campus tour. When Mom offered to drive up and back with me, I told her I'd arranged to stay with a girl I'd known freshman year whose family had moved up to the suburbs.

'She wants to take me to the casino for my birthday,' I told them one night over beef stroganoff. Dad chuckled and Mom frowned and both of them told me I wasn't allowed to lose more than twenty dollars, but that's all it took for my story to become rock-solid. That was usually key with my parents. By admitting a slightly bad thing, I could blind them to any other possibilities of misbehavior. And even if they suspected anything else, it was probably along the same line of things I could do now that I was turning eighteen – getting a tattoo or buying cigarettes. Sleeping with my married English teacher was so far off the radar it was laughable.

The rest of December moved like a freaking iceberg. Every day dragged out. My shifts at CVS were an endless line of customers. Tommy took me to the drive-in and tried to feel me up under my sweater. Portia got a cold and then gave it to me, with a sore throat and cough and everything. The only good part was Peter's class, where I sat in front as always and pretended not to ogle his every movement. I chatted with Portia and Maggie and argued most of Peter's lecture points, just like I always did. The only physical contact we had was when he collected homework assignments; he had everyone pass their papers to the front and then he walked along the front row picking up the stacks. I handed him my row's papers and our fingers brushed. That was all.

One day, though, the week before Christmas, I was just finishing a text on my phone when the bell rang, and Peter immediately said, 'Hattie!'

It was loud and everyone stopped talking to see what was going on.

'Yeah?' I hit send before looking up.

'Phone on my desk. Now. You can pick it up after school.'

I trotted my phone up to his desk, ecstatic about violating the no-cell-phone-in-class policy. I thought it was genius, finding the excuse to see me alone, but after school that day a whole group of sophomores had invaded his room to study for the MCAs.

He glanced up from the middle of the horde when I came in and said, 'Oh, Hattie. Your phone's over there. Leave it at home next time, okay?'

I nodded and grabbed it, completely deflated after spending half the day dreaming about a brush of skin, a murmured promise, or even a stolen kiss behind the door.

It wasn't until I'd finished collecting books from my locker that I noticed the message. I had a new text, sent from myself, to myself, a half an hour ago.

'From her hair the heads of five crucified also looked on, no more expressive than she.'

Is this you? I keep looking, can't help myself. Looking for you is my only sustenance.

Check your right front tire.

I practically ran out of the building, through the parking lot, and found a rectangular package on top of the tire, hidden from view in the wheel well and wrapped in gold.

I got inside the truck and opened it, making sure no one was watching me. It was a book, a hardcover edition of *V,* by Thomas Pynchon – the book he'd wanted to get autographed the first time I stumbled on him in the chatroom. It felt like a lifetime ago. There was nothing written inside. He'd been careful not to create any link between us, but I couldn't care less about that right now. He'd given me a Christmas present.

I smelled the wrapping paper and whispered it – 'sustenance' – feeling as giddy as I ever had in my life.

I got another unexpected present, too. Gerald sent me a camcorder with a note in his swirly handwriting about hard work and dedication to perfection. Portia and I spent the last few nights before break performing our favorite movie scenes for the camera and it helped the time to pass.

Christmas was so strange this year. Although I didn't miss Greg, exactly, it was weird not having him there, ripping open his presents and shouting his surprise or excitement. There was no one to dilute Mom and Dad's attention. They sat on the couch blowing the steam off their coffee cups and watching me with that fake kind of happiness, the kind where you try to pretend things are normal, as I opened a big box that sat by itself under the tree.

My present turned out to be a suitcase, a gorgeous suitcase. It was compact and simple, with smart pockets and dividers inside and wheels that looked like they were made of titanium. They made a sleek whirring sound on the laminate floor as I walked it around and around the kitchen table.

'I love it,' I told them honestly and gave them each a big hug.

'If you're going to be seeing the world next year, you'll need to look the part,' Dad said and ruffled my messy bed-head hair.

Mom showed me how to wipe stains and dirt off it to keep the black material looking nice, and then she made me an enormous Denver omelet that I couldn't half finish.

I packed the suitcase up immediately and set it in the corner of my room. December turned into January, and then on the morning of Saturday, January 5th, I put it in the passenger seat of my truck – where it looked absurdly out of place – and drove to the Crowne Plaza in downtown Minneapolis.

I was breathless as I knocked on the door to his room and when he opened it we both stared at each other.

'Hi.'

I just smiled instead of answering, not trusting my voice.

'Come in.' He stepped aside and gestured awkwardly.

There were lilies in a vase on the desk. I crossed over to them and touched one of the ragged-edged, white petals. 'Nice hotel.'

'No – I mean it is, it's not bad, but I brought those. You said once they were your favorite.'

Even though he seemed a little jumpy, he walked over to me. I let go of the suitcase handle and lifted one of the flowers out of the bouquet and smelled, closing my eyes.

'Thank you.'

'Happy birthday.'

It made me warm to hear his voice, so low and close to my ear. I didn't think I could be any happier than I was at that moment, standing quietly next to him, with the whole evening ahead of us and no one else in the world to intrude. I turned toward him and gave him a flirty grin.

'Is this my only present?'

He lifted a finger and brushed it along my jaw. 'I don't know yet.'

I stepped closer, angling my head up. 'How can I help you decide?'

He didn't disappoint. Slowly, so slowly, he leaned in and kissed me. It was unlike any kiss I'd had, made up more of air and promises than actual flesh. I felt myself getting weak, getting wet. I reached for his shirt buttons, but he stopped me.

'No.'

'No?' I said it like I'd never heard of the word before.

He laughed and wound my scarf around my neck. 'We're going out.'

It was effing cold, so we took the skyway, walking from sky scraper to skyscraper in the second-story labyrinth of shops and corporate offices. Most of the stores were closed for the weekend so we just window-shopped and wandered into the few that were open. Peter led us on a meandering route over Nicollet Mall and then we hit the streets to walk through the more crowded theater district. I recognized one of the old lightbulb marquees where I'd gone to see *The Nutcracker* when I was ten.

'You mean last year?' he teased.

'I don't know, old man. Why don't you carve it into a stone tablet so I can understand how young I am?'

'I left my chisel at home.' He casually slid my glove into his and we kept walking like we did this every day, and no one we passed even glanced in our direction.

We went on – playing, baiting each other, both of us acting drunk even though we were completely sober – until we came to a restaurant with blue lights that rose three stories high.

'Hungry?' he asked, opening a door made out of bright mosaic tiles.

Since it was early afternoon, there weren't a lot of people eating and we got seated right away. It turned out to be a tapas restaurant, one of Peter's favorites, and he told me to order anything I wanted. Soon our table was filled with tiny plates of exotic food and I tried everything. Although a few things tasted weird, most of it was delicious. My favorite was a beef tongue wrapped in cabbage with this amazing dipping sauce. When I offered some to Peter, he declined.

'I'm a vegetarian.'

'What?' I was thrown. I scanned the table, like I could find some evidence of him eating meat, and realized all the dishes on his side were cheeses, vegetables, and breads. It was such a mundane thing, but somehow it shook my confidence, took us another step apart.

'What else don't I know about you?'

He smiled and thought for a second before answering.

'I hate tofu.' His lip even curled as he said it. 'It's probably a vegan sin, but the stuff always reminds me of *Soylent Green*.'

'I've never eaten tofu.'

'Lucky.'

I laughed. 'Why'd you become a vegetarian?'

'My mom was. She basically raised me as one.'

'I love my mom's chicken and biscuits.'

'I love my mom's roasted portobellos.'

'Mushrooms are gross,' I declared. 'Who decided it was okay to eat fungus?'

'Fungi.'

'Thanks, fun guy. I also kind of hate speech correction.'

Peter closed his eyes and shook his head in apology. 'Believe me, I do, too. It's out of my mouth before I even know it.'

'I do that so much. I'll be halfway through a conversation before I realize I don't actually believe anything I'm saying.'

I was glowing, caught up in our game of reveal, but Peter fell silent just as the waiter came to check on us. When we were alone again he leaned in and took my hand, eyes intent on me, and in that moment there wasn't anywhere else in the world besides this table with the two of us wrapped taut in its circle of light.

'Tell me something true,' he said.

'I just did. Chicken and biscuits. Mushrooms.' My teasing smile faltered.

'That's different. Those are tidbits. They're facts – meaningless, weightless. Facts are everywhere. Tell me something visceral, something that's as part of you as your breath or teeth, that you don't even know how to lie about. Tell me something that can hold you here with me.'

For a moment I stared at the plates on the table and then the memory was there, like it had been hovering right at the edges of my mind, waiting to be told. I smoothed my fingers over his and wondered where to start, then I wondered what he would think of me when I was done. Taking a deep breath, I chose my words carefully.

'When I was a kid, I used to tag along after my brother, Greg, and the Beason twins from the next farm over. They were older jockish boys I could hardly keep up with on my bike and they weren't very nice. If I had anyone else to play with, I probably wouldn't have followed them around. When you live in the country, though, you play with whoever lives nearby.

'Sometimes we chased barn cats or went swimming in the lake. Sometimes they had me steal stuff from the drugstore, because no one ever stopped me except to say *How's your mom doing?* Other times they just made me go home.

'One day they biked down to the quarry and I followed as usual. An old wire fence circled the place, but it was broken in a few spots and no one had worked there for years. It was easy to get in. We left our bikes on top and climbed down the rock face. It looked like a giant staircase cut into the ground, like we were going to another world. I was excited and started exploring as soon as we reached the bottom. The boys set up tin cans and tried to knock them down with stones. I wasn't paying attention and walked in front of them as they were throwing. The rock hit me here.'

I brushed a finger over the scar line just beneath my right eyebrow. The skin always felt too smooth there, glossy and slightly indented.

'I fell down and the blood gushed everywhere. It got into my eye and I couldn't see. The boys were all yelling at each other and at me. I don't think we were supposed to be playing in the quarry. When I accused them of hurting me on purpose, one of them – I don't know which one – got really close to my ear and told me that if I ratted them out, I would pay for it. They'd never let me play with them again and if I tried to tag along, they'd throw more rocks at me.

' "It"ll be on purpose then,' he said.

'They tried to push me back up the rock wall, but I still couldn't see anything and my head was pounding so bad. I fell a couple times and finally Greg told me to stay there while they went to get help.

'I was lying on the bottom of the quarry for what felt like forever. There was no shade and the sun made me nauseated. I knew my dad was coming and that I had to lie to him, and I was convinced that God would strike me dead. Honor thy father and mother, they said in Sunday school. I pictured God himself walking down those giant stairsteps, pointing a finger at me and never letting me come back up to the regular world.

'When Dad got there I told him I'd climbed down into the quarry on my own, even though the boys told me not to, and I'd fallen. I was crying and shaking, waiting for the judgment I was sure was coming, but Dad just scooped me up in his big arms and carried me the whole way back to his truck and drove me home.

'No one got punished that day. Not even me.'

I rubbed the scar absently as the waiter cleared our plates.

'Greg and the Beason boys were grateful. They even stole me some SweeTARTS – my favorite candy – but I was petrified all week. I was still waiting and I couldn't bear it. I knew something awful should happen to me for what I'd done.

'At church that Sunday I said the first and only prayer I've ever prayed for myself. *Dear God,* I said. *If you're mad at me, strike me down right now.*

'But nothing happened. The organist kept playing. My parents kept singing the hymn. A rush of relief washed over me as I realized I was safe. God didn't mind at all. I started pretending more, being accepted more, and I prayed the same thing the next week and the week after that. I've said it every Sunday since I was eight years old. *Dear God, if you're angry, strike me down. Strike me down here and now.*

'And every week when He doesn't I leave the church feeling . . .

absolved. Like I'm still covered in dirt but the dirt's clean. I know I'm not good, Peter. I don't think I can be. And that's something I don't know how to lie about. I can't walk into church and say *Bless me, for I have sinned.* I know I shouldn't be blessed. I walk in and say *Strike me down.* And even though I know God will take me up on it someday, I still can't change, because as much as I should want to be good and one of the blessed ones' – I lifted his hand and kissed the palm and laid my cheek in it – 'I want you more.'

I rubbed my face into his hand to absorb the texture of his skin completely, to memorize it for all the days ahead. His thumb brushed my cheek and he studied my face, like he was memorizing, too.

'What do you think?' I asked, shakily. 'Was that true enough for you?'

'I think . . .' – he drew a deep breath and let it out slowly, then brought our hands down to the table and kissed the back of mine – 'he'll have to strike us both down now.'

We went back to the hotel and undressed slowly, savoring the revelation of each other. When our clothes were in piles on the floor he laid me down on the bed and traced me lightly all over. He murmured while he roamed, telling me how beautiful my breasts were and how sweet they tasted. He explored my stomach, my hipbones, the inside of my thighs, and his words created something inside me, a wild animal that bucked and clenched, forging a thousand invisible emotions trapped underneath my skin. When he lined our bodies up and pushed inside me, it became too much to contain and the happiness welled up in my eyes, trickling down my temples.

Out of nowhere I remembered my grandpa's silent, tear-streaked face in that depressing nursing home room. It was probably the last time anyone should be thinking about their dead grandfather, like some final proof of how unnatural I was, but in that moment

I understood, finally, how love could be too much for our bodies to hold.

When Peter saw my tears he stopped moving and got the strangest expression.

'What is it?' I whispered.

'I was going to say your name, but I don't even know what to call you.'

I pulled his head down to the crook of my neck, hugging my entire being around him. 'Call me yours.'

DEL / *Wednesday, April 16, 2008*

THE PROBLEM with DNA was it took too damn long. It wasn't like in the movies where they poured something in a test tube, swirled it around, and got the name of the killer. You had to send the samples up to the crime lab in Minneapolis and they put your stuff in line behind everyone else's stuff and they got to it when they got to it, which could take up to a year depending on the type of evidence. Lab people, working nine-to-five and looking at dead-girl cells all day long. They didn't care about your dead girl. It didn't make any difference to them. At least that's what it seemed like from here in Pine Valley, where we only had one dead girl and she'd torn a wide, ugly hole through this town.

Hattie was all anyone was talking about, the only thing filling their eyes when they passed me on the street. Word got around about Tommy Kinakis's DNA test, probably from Tommy himself, the big goon, and about Lund being pulled out of school for questioning. Phone calls poured in to dispatch and Nancy told most of them to stuff it, but she felt it was her duty to keep me up-to-date on the gossip as she tucked sandwiches and fresh coffee into the few bare spaces on my desk. Brian Haeffner kept playing politician, trying to set up daily press conferences. Every parent in town wanted to know about security for the high school. Thanks to Portia, the curse story had spread like wildfire and two vans from the cities' news stations had camped out on Main Street last night. I'd stopped answering my phone unless it was Jake . . . or Bud. He had called around six this morning.

'Del.'

'Bud.' I was sitting at the kitchen table staring at today's front-page picture, which was a 'still' from the play on Friday night of Hattie wearing her bloodstained dress and her crown, looking haunted and holding one arm out against the darkness. It gave me goosebumps. I imagined Bud was looking at the same thing. Neither of us spoke again for a minute.

'Do you have the DNA results?' His voice sounded rough.

'No. No, it takes a little while. I'm checking other things in the meantime, getting the timeline down.'

'You brought Peter Lund down to the station yesterday.'

It wasn't a question, but I heard the demand behind the words well enough. Twenty-five years of friendship will do that.

'We're talking to a lot of people.'

'You think Lund had something to do with it?'

'He was the director of the play, knew all the kids. You've heard all this curse bullshit. If any of them had a mind to act it out, I thought Lund might have a bead on which one.' It grated to be lying outright, to be using that stupid curse as a reason for anything.

'So you don't think it was Tommy?'

'I don't think anything, Bud. When I start to think things are one way, then it closes off a lot of other ways that might be just as probable. I'm just getting as much information as I can while we wait on this DNA, trying to piece the whole night together and everyone who was in it.'

There was another long silence, a sigh on the other end of the line, and a hitch in Bud's voice when he spoke again. It sounded like this call was costing him almost more effort than he could bear.

'Del, Jesus. All I can think about is her poor body lying there on that slab yesterday. Me and Mona went to claim her and she looked like a piece of meat, all bloated and – and wrong. My little girl, my little girl was a piece of meat on a slab.'

His next words were racked by sobs. I could hardly make them out.

'And I'm going to gut the son of a bitch that did it. I'm going to make him wish he'd never so much as looked at her.'

'Bud, you listen to me. Bud?'

There was only scraping and heavy breathing in response.

'I'm going to find this guy, Bud. Hattie's got me for that. She doesn't need her dad going to prison. Mona needs you, too, you know, and Greg needs you here for him when he gets home. You gotta remember them.'

I didn't know if he heard me until the breathing evened out. The sun was starting to rise, turning the kitchen a deep, burning orange.

'Are you saying you're going to arrest me?'

'Bud—'

'My girl is dead. I held her in my hands yesterday, held her sweet, bald head and watched her cry for the first time. I taught her how to drive a tractor on my lap with her little pigtails bouncing in my face. I watched her play a queen – a queen with all the power and wickedness you could imagine. She owned that stage. She lit it up. And I hugged her and told her what a good job she did and let her go. I just let her walk out of that school and die. And I'll be damned if I'm going to sit around and pick out her funeral dress while her killer walks around free.'

'That's exactly what you're going to do.'

'Damn it, Del. What aren't you telling me?'

'I'm telling you we're in the middle of an ongoing investigation and you'll know who killed Hattie the minute the cuffs are on him.'

There was a pause and then the line went dead. I dropped my forehead on to my hand.

After a minute, I got up and walked to the window, where the sky was lightening up behind the houses. Normally it was the kind of sunrise I liked to watch, all hellfire burning against the clouds, the kind where Bud and I would ignore a pull on the line to just sit in the boat and stare at the horizon. Over two decades we'd been fishing together. Every year he invited me to his house for Easter dinner and this year we'd all sat around their dining room table eating honey-glazed ham. Hattie'd been trying to get me to tell her how fast over the speed limit she could drive without getting pulled over, while Bud and Mona and I all laughed, and now she was never going to speed anywhere again. Bud, who'd told me to slap a ticket on her right then for 'conspiracy to speed,' was threatening vigilantism. And I – if I couldn't find Hattie's killer fast and quiet enough – I might end up losing Bud, too.

The badge weighed heavy this morning. I downed the rest of my coffee and left the house with a blazing need to do something, anything, that would push this case forward.

I went to Carl Jacobs's house. When Jake talked to Carl yesterday, he'd corroborated Lund's story and most of their answers had matched dead-on. Both said they'd gone to Carl's house after locking up the school, driving separately, Lund following Carl. They sat in Carl's basement having a beer – Budweiser, by both accounts – and shot the shit for a while before Lund left. Carl estimated the time at 10:25, because he'd turned on the last of the news afterwards.

What wasn't so clear was their topic of discussion. Lund said they talked about the play and about work. Carl didn't remember straight off, according to Jake. Then he claimed they talked sports – how the Twins were looking this season. He didn't think they'd talked about much else.

It was a quarter to seven when I got to his house, early enough that Carl wouldn't have left for work yet. He answered the knock like he'd been waiting right on the other side, dressed and shaved for the day.

'Sheriff. Little early, isn't it?' He glanced past me toward the cruiser.

'Early enough that you can spare a few minutes.' I nodded behind him and he let me in. His boy stood in the hallway, still in his pajamas but wide awake and half afraid, by the looks of him.

'Morning.' I tipped my hat to him, which put most kids at ease, but not this one. He just dropped his eyes to the floor, not moving.

'Maybe Lanie can watch him for a minute while we talk.'

'Lanie!' Carl shouted and his wife appeared, also in pajamas. She didn't look very awake or pleased.

'What?' She didn't greet me.

'I've got to talk to the sheriff.'

'Again?'

'Just get Josh ready, okay?'

She shook her head and collared the boy, taking him back down the hall and slamming a door.

Carl gestured me into the kitchen.

'Not a morning person, is she?' I asked pleasantly.

'What is it, Sheriff? I answered everything your deputy asked me and lost an entire period of class doing it. You know how people are looking at me?'

'How's that?'

'Like I was –' He shook his head. 'Like I had something to do with this mess.'

'Did you?'

'What are you asking me?'

'What do you know, Carl?' I put my hat on the table and stared him down.

'I know Hattie Hoffman's dead, that's all. I had her for history two years now. American history last year and European this year. She liked Europe better.'

'That's not what I'm getting at. Why'd you lie to Jake?'

'Lie!'

'I want to know what you talked about in your basement on Friday, and you'd better not say the Twins.'

He stared at me, frozen for a minute, before going to the doorway and glancing down the hall. Then he dropped into one of the chairs at his kitchen table and spoke quietly.

'Lanie.'

'What about her?'

He sighed. 'We talked about her a bit. When Peter came back with me on Friday she was upset. We started fighting. We're always fighting these days. And after she stomped upstairs, Peter and I talked about it.'

'About what?'

'About getting married young. Not knowing what the hell you're getting into. He got married right out of college, too.'

'Was he having marital troubles? Did you talk about that?'

He was quiet for a second. 'No. Not exactly. He asked me something, though, and I'm not proud of what I told him. That's why I didn't tell your deputy.'

I waited and eventually he came out with it.

'He asked if I would've stayed with Lanie before Josh was born.

If I could've done it over again when there weren't any kids to think about, would I have stayed?'

His voice dropped even lower. 'I said no. I said I thought even Josh wished we were divorced sometimes. The stupid things we fight about . . .'

'What kinds of things?' I smelled a domestic brewing.

'Everything. You ever been married, Sheriff?'

'Yep.'

'Huh. I didn't know that. What happened?'

'Vietnam.'

'She left you while you were gone?'

'Nope. About two minutes after I got back. Turned out she liked me better on the other side of the world.'

I never talked about Angie. Not that I was torn up about it anymore. There was a time, a long time, when I was bitter about how she left, but that all faded. She hadn't known what to do with an angry war vet anymore than I knew myself. She just wanted a happy, regular life. Before I shipped out, she'd begged me to go to Canada with her. I took the honorable path, though; I put my country before my girl. Her letters were one of the things that got me through my tour and that's what I remembered about her now. When I heard she'd died in a car crash outside Dubuque a few years ago, I pulled out all those letters again. It was a strange thing, reading all the warnings to be careful and not let myself get hurt, all that concern pouring out of Angie's dead hand. I put them away in the box with the medals and the note from the president and hadn't looked at any of it since. No need to dig up the past, except I felt for Carl. Angie and I had been kids ourselves, no property or children to muck up the divorce. There was just a *See you later* and a few papers to sign. But Carl and Lanie had a life together – a home, a son.

'That's horrible, Sheriff.' He looked mad. 'Leaving a war hero as soon as he gets home.'

'What's done is done.'

I picked up my hat and made my way back toward the front door. 'Lund never complained about his wife?'

'Not really. Mostly his mother-in-law. Seems she doesn't care too much for him.'

'You talk about Hattie that night?'

'No.' He opened the door and walked me out to the cruiser. 'No, I would've remembered that.'

'Okay. Thanks for taking the time this morning.'

He nodded and Lanie appeared in the screen door behind him, her face pinched and closed. Whether or not she heard what Carl had said in the kitchen, it looked like they had some more fights ahead.

———

I found myself driving toward Bud's house, but what could I say? I couldn't tell him what he wanted to know, which was who to point his gun at. This was an active investigation, not to mention a media nightmare, and the less Bud knew the better.

Passing the turnoff to Bud's, I headed out to the lake. On the way I called the crime lab to check on the samples. They told me the file was still pending and they couldn't give me a date on when it would be processed. They were working through an 'unusually large number of files,' according to the pissant who finally answered my call.

I pulled into the lot where Hattie and Tommy went parking on Friday night, looking across the lake to the Erickson barn with its old roof bowing down toward the water. There were a few trees along the shore next to the barn, enough cover to hide in even without the long grasses that would wave up in a few more months. According to Tommy's story, she'd gotten out of his truck and walked to the barn on her own. Meeting someone. Why would she go there if she wasn't meeting someone? It probably would have been around 10:00 p.m. Lund could easily have met her out there after he left Carl's place. Someone could have followed her, too – Tommy, or even someone else, but whoever it was had to have a reason to be out here in the middle of the night. I rubbed my face and thought through my short list of suspects. Lund and Tommy both had motive, both might have had reason to want her dead.

I got out of the cruiser and retraced Hattie's last steps – across the parking lot and then along the lake that lapped up the shore with a warm, lazy wind. It was cooler and partly cloudy last Friday, in the low fifties and dropping after sundown. She would have been cold, probably walking fast, both from the chill and to put distance between her and Tommy. There weren't any houses or barns on the horizon in any direction. The security light in the parking lot would have been on, but it didn't have enough wattage for more than a hundred-foot radius, so she only had a partial moon to light the way. Was she afraid? I didn't know. If she was alone, no. Walking alone in the cold and dark wasn't anything to a country girl. Maybe Hattie was aiming toward the city, but she was as much a part of this land as any other Pine Valley kid, and the land comforted folks here. Its openness and vastness were a balm. No, if she walked to her death alone, she walked unafraid. I crunched along the trail and scanned along the edges of the grass again. Nothing was trampled, no mud kicked up. There were no signs of any struggle. We'd already been over this ground; me, the forensics team, and Jake to boot, but it never hurt to retrace your steps, especially when you were thinking things over or waiting for a lab tech a hundred miles away to squirt something into a vial.

Halfway to the barn I stopped and looked back. The parking lot had disappeared under a slight rise in the land. I couldn't see the cruiser anymore. Had Hattie looked back? Was Tommy – alibi-less

Tommy, who didn't know why she'd broke up with him; horny, angry, hormone-riddled Tommy – following her?

I hadn't followed Angie. When she left, over thirty years ago, I'd let her go. I was angry, maybe even angry and drunk enough a few of those dark nights to kill somebody, but I never pursued her. She made her choice just like I'd made mine. I'd chosen war. She chose Iowa. She sent the divorce papers in the mail and got herself married to a pharmaceutical salesman the next spring. I went to school on the GI Bill, got a patrol job in Wabash County, and didn't have anything good to say to anybody until Bud started waving at me from across Lake Crosby.

He was only a few years younger than me, but it was the difference between being drafted or not. He and Mona were newlyweds starting out on the farm and that first summer all we talked about was fish. Just a quick wave and confirmation on what was biting. I could handle that. By the next summer, he got me to come over a few times and Mona would fry up our catch. The year after that we took our first trip to Lake Michigan. He was the first person to put up a *Goodman for Sheriff* sign in his yard, until he realized no one would see it and then he stuck it on the back of his pickup truck instead.

By the time I heard from Angie again, when she sent a letter congratulating me on getting appointed sheriff, all the hard feelings were gone and that was probably all due to Bud. I wrote her back and she sent me a Christmas card every year after that until the year she died. There was usually a picture included of her and her husband and some kids who were on the chubby side. She was a handsome woman, stayed that way, too.

I turned back toward the barn and kept walking. It had been awhile since I'd had Angie on the brain, but I supposed it made sense. Carl and Lanie. Hattie and Tommy. Relationships hitting their breaking point. Tearing apart.

The yellow tape was still all over the barn, courtesy of the crime scene boys. I ducked under it and went inside. Stagnant water, mildew, and rotting wood were the smells that greeted me, just like they would have greeted Hattie. She'd left Tommy and walked to the barn. Then she'd had sex with someone in the barn. Then she was killed by someone in the barn. That was up to three different people who could've interacted with her. Or just one.

I paced, not caring one bit about the wood hollering under my boots. It could fall if it wanted to fall. I was narrowing in on the timeline, the story, but it didn't mean anything if I couldn't put it with a suspect. I needed that DNA back, needed to know who was lying to me so I could lean on them until they told me exactly what happened, not to mention get a warrant to search every inch of their life for that murder weapon.

I pulled out my phone and dialed the number before I could think about it too much.

'Sheriff Goodman,' she greeted me on the third ring.

'Fran, I need that DNA. Who do you know in the Minneapolis crime lab?'

'I'm well, thank you. And you?'

'I'm serious.'

She dropped the sarcastic tone. 'And why is your murder any more important than any of the other thousand bodies that come through my morgue every year? Because it's yours? Because Cowboy Goodman needs to save the day?'

'There's no day to save, Fran. She's dead.' I kept pacing, trying not to curse because I knew it riled her. 'This isn't about me. You can take shots at me until the cows come home, okay? You're probably right – you always are – but this is my friend's child. His baby girl. I've got two prime suspects for the semen and I need to know which one it is and I need to know today, while there's any shred of evidence left.'

She was quiet after my rant. I kept walking, ready to argue with whatever she said next, until she sighed.

'All right, Del. I have a few contacts. I'll make a call.'

'Good. Good.' I ducked out of the barn and started making a sweep along the perimeter of the building. It was old ground, already covered, but the momentum soothed me. 'You tell them I need it today.'

'What you need and what they can do are two unrelated things. I'll ask them to expedite the samples. That's all.'

I squatted down by a tuft of dead grass outside the window, pushed it aside, and saw a mouse skeleton. It was picked clean and almost completely intact. 'Thanks, Fran. I owe you one.'

'One what, exactly?'

'I'll take you out in the cruiser someday. We'll give tickets to out-of-staters.'

She laughed – actually laughed out loud, which was a small miracle – but then became suddenly serious again and sent me in an entirely new direction.

'If you really want to track down this murderer, Del,' she said, 'there's someone else you need to talk to.'

PETER / *Friday, February 15, 2008*

IT WAS amazing how life simply kept moving forward. You could do the most despicable, amoral thing you'd ever imagined and just drive home afterwards. Go to work. Get your dry cleaning. Pick up some wine at the liquor store and chat with the parents of the best friend of the girl you'd slept with behind your wife's back. Pay for your wine. Go home.

Mary scarcely acknowledged my trip to Minneapolis in January. I'd taken the money for the hotel out of my personal savings account, which she would never see. When I got back, she'd asked about the friend I told her I was visiting. I said he was fine and it was good to catch up with him. She went back to mopping the floor and I went upstairs, laid on our bed, and relived every detail of what happened that weekend: Hattie's confession at the restaurant, what followed on the hotel bed. And on the desk. And in the shower. *Dear God, strike me down.*

No one looked at me differently. No one even suspected. It

made me wonder what else I could get away with, how far I could push this double life, and that question depended solely on Hattie.

In the month since our trip we'd barely spoken. There was no safe channel of communication. We couldn't use email, phones, or the internet, nothing that could be traced, and so our relationship became a game of silent voyeurs. I watched her eat lunch with Tommy every day across the cafeteria. She watched me make notes on the board during lectures. When we passed each other in the hallways she looked right through me and kept chatting with her friends. I stood at the door to the classroom when the bell rang just to inhale her scent as she walked by. She always smelled light, airy, with a hint of fruit; either strawberry or raspberry, I could never tell. It was maddening, being so close to her. She must have felt the same, because she stopped by the classroom after school one after-noon under the pretext of having a question about the spring play, but I didn't trust myself not to touch her. I moved the conversation quickly into the hallway, looking beyond her as I monitored the flux of bodies, sensing her mounting frustration. Finally she wrote a note in light pencil on one of her assignments – just a location and a date – that I frantically erased in the upstairs storage room as my blood started racing.

It was a rest stop along the Mississippi, a scenic overlook into Wisconsin, but no one toured the bluffs this time of year. I only saw one other car in the half hour before she arrived. I pulled her into the backseat without a word and we wrestled clothes off, panting, tugging, and twisting until she was straddling me, and then her long, tight body drove me insane.

I wanted her like I'd never wanted anyone. At the same time I was terrified of what she'd do with the immense power she had over me. She thought she looked up to me, that I was the one in control, but little by little she was going to realize that my life was like a house of cards at her feet and all it would take to destroy me was one stray kick from any of her myriad selves. I craved her, I was obsessed with her, and I feared her more every day.

The Friday after the rest stop I got home from work to see Mary walking around the outside of the house with a guy I didn't recognize. He looked about our age, wearing a baseball cap, snow-covered work boots, and a tool belt, and he nodded in my direction as I headed up the walk to the house. These days I looked at every-body one second longer, just to see if this was the person who was going to raise their finger and expose me for what I was. Not this guy, not today. He resumed his conversation with Mary and I went inside. Elsa was asleep in her rocker in the living room. I grabbed a Coke and drank half of it while staring at the contents of the fridge, wondering how to see Hattie again. She could 'visit' another col-lege on spring break. We could go to Duluth, or Chicago. Hattie would love Chicago.

Mary opened the front door and I quickly shut the fridge. She went to the sink without a word to me and started washing dishes with the air of someone finishing an interrupted activity.

I moved toward the door, my body automatically retreating. Apart from eating and sleeping, I lived in the storage room now. Even if Mary hadn't acted like an island for the better part of the winter, it was ludicrous at this point for me to make the effort to reach her. Before I disappeared tonight though, curiosity got the best of me.

'Who was that?'

'Harry Tomlin.'

'What did he want?'

'I asked him to come out.' She almost didn't elaborate, but then she shrugged as she tipped a pitcher upside down into the rinse rack. 'He's an old friend from high school. I'm having him put in some new windows.'

'Windows?'

'It's too drafty in here. There's no point in replacing the boiler until the windows are done.'

'Boiler? What the hell, Mary?' I didn't know what stunned me more – her plans or that she was actually sharing them with me. I paced to the living room door to make sure Elsa was still asleep. 'You're the one who freaks out whenever I spend a dime. Why are you pouring money – my money, I might add – into this crap heap of a house?'

'I won't touch your precious paycheck, all right? Keep it. Mom's got her social security and I'll make my own money.'

'Doing what? Selling eggs at fifteen cents a pop?'

A hint of a smile played with her mouth. 'Thirty-five cents, actually.'

'What?'

'Organic, free-range, family-farm eggs.'

'What the hell are you talking about?'

She didn't answer at first. It was frustrating, talking to her pro-file. She wouldn't even turn around to have a conversation with me. Never mind that she had every right to shove me down, stomp on my balls, and kick me out of her mother's crap heap of a house. She didn't know that.

'Remember going to the farmers' markets in Minneapolis? How you always spouted off about organic this and cruelty-free that?'

I did remember, but the memories weren't splashed in her sar-casm. I'd honestly – and obviously stupidly – thought those were our good times. We were living in our Victorian walk-up and every Sunday morning in the summer we read the paper over coffee, commenting on and tossing sections until the dining room table was covered with tented and folded stories, cartoons, and the re-mains of the coupon pages after they'd met Mary's scissors.

Later we'd walk down to the market and stroll through the stalls. Sometimes we only bought a baguette for brunch and ate it on the way home, tearing off chunks and washing them down with a smoothie. A few times we decided to make things on the spur of the moment and came home with forty tomatoes and peppers, splattering the kitchen with a blind attempt at salsa. Those were usually my ideas. Mary always had a shopping list and a plan; she coolly checked off items as we made our way down the rows.

When we first started going, she raised her eyebrows at the number of Hmong vendors, but she never said anything beyond, 'They don't farm out by my family,' and she bought anyone's produce as long as it was good quality and not overpriced. She talked shop with the farmers, discussing rainfall and temperatures. She didn't care about herbicides or how the cows were treated. I was the one who insisted on the organic stalls while Mary would roll her eyes and laugh. When I tried to show her articles about the effects of chemical fertilizers and insecticides, she scoffed and said, 'There's a study for everything. You know you're going to die anyway, don't you?'

She was never interested in organic farming. So where the hell had this come from?

'I've been talking to a guy near Rochester who has the whole operation down. Mobile coops and vegetarian feed. He sells to restaurants in the cities at a premium price, and we're going to start doing the farmers' market circuit in the spring.'

'We?'

'Me and him and a few other farmers in the area. There's a demand. All those people in the cities like you, wanting their eggs from happy chickens, wanting their meat grass-fed and humanely slaughtered.'

She shook her head on the last two words. It was a point we agreed on, but for cosmically different reasons.

'Where is this coming from, Mary? You know Elsa's not going to last the year.'

She flinched at the words and I backpedaled, lowering my voice.

'I'm sorry. I didn't mean to say it like that, but it's obvious the doctor was right. She's weaker every day. She remembers less and less of what anyone tells her. The other day she didn't even know who I was.'

I didn't mention that – because she didn't know me – she was nicer than she had been since my wedding day. She patted my hand and called me Hank and asked me to read her a few obituaries. Hank was happy to oblige. It was the first time in months I'd felt welcome in this house.

The retention-rate issue was becoming hard to ignore. She'd weakly asked Mary every day for two weeks why we'd bought 'that five-dollar pepper' until it was finally drilled into her head that it was 'Peter's fancy pepper.' She watched the weather forecast on the news at least two times a night and still acted surprised when it snowed the next day. If the oxygen wasn't sufficiently reaching her brain anymore, how much longer could the rest of her body survive?

I phrased the next question carefully. 'Why would you invest in a whole new business when we're only here on a temporary basis?'

She didn't say anything and, to be honest, I already knew. The answer was right in front of me.

'You're not just here for Elsa.' I dropped into one of the kitchen chairs and stared at her profile. She didn't confirm or deny. 'You like it here. You're not going to move back to Minneapolis when she dies, are you?'

Still she didn't speak. She just kept washing dishes, her hands idly squeezing the rag over a saucer as she gazed out the kitchen window into the abyss of white.

'Dammit, Mary, answer me. I think I deserve an answer. Have you been planning this since before we moved?'

She rinsed a dish and set it in the rack, then slowly pulled a coffee cup out of the suds. 'You wouldn't understand.'

'Clearly I don't. How can I understand what you won't say?' I crossed my arms, determined not to leave this room until she came clean.

'It's . . .' She stopped, shook her head, and started again, moving the soapy cup from one hand to the other, still staring absently through the glass framed by faded gingham curtains. 'I don't know how to say it. It's like the trees.'

'What?'

'In the city you can't see them.' She paused, thinking. 'They're all squished together, tangled into each other until you can't tell where one tree stops and another starts. Their branches are sawed off so they don't hit power lines or roofs. Some of them have those red spray-painted death rings around their trunks and they're chopped down when their roots grow too big under sidewalks. They're sad to look at, all contorted and disfigured or pruned down into nothing.

'But here, here you can see the trees for what they really are. My whole life I watched them growing at the edges of the fields like cross-stitches holding a quilt together.' Her gaze focused on the pines behind the garage and her voice lost that hardened edge she'd acquired around me.

'They stand tall in windbreaks around the farms and you can really see them. You can trace their silhouettes, follow how their branches bend and curl. Some are craggy. Some are thick and strong. Some are stooped like old men against the wind. You can understand their nature here. I didn't realize it until we moved back and I felt myself breathing again. I was walking home from Winifred's one day and I just stopped and stood there studying the shapes of the trees on the horizon. They were like portraits, each one of them, and it was the most beautiful thing I'd seen. I knew then that I couldn't go back. I couldn't breathe in the city; I was suffocating more every day.'

'But we live in the city.' I felt compelled to make some stab at an argument. 'Our lives are there. Our friends, your job. Your boss said you could come back anytime.'

Logic was all on my side. I knew it, could taste it on the words, but they felt hollow against Mary's eloquence.

'And work in a beige, five-foot cubicle for ten hours a day? With no sunlight? Surrounded by stale air and browbeaten, angry people? No, Peter. I can't spend my life like that. I'm going to terminate the lease on the front forty this year and buy more chickens next spring. I'm going to be a farmer, like my father, and his father. I'm going to sow my fate with the land.'

Neither of us spoke for a while. The weight of her decision blanketed the room, silencing both of us, forcing us to confront what we'd both known. Eventually she finished the dishes, hung the rag over the faucet to dry, and sat down across from me.

I looked at her, really looked for the first time in months. The transformation I'd sensed, and resented, in her was complete. The girl I'd married had long, glossy locks of blond hair streaming from beneath her veil. Her cheeks had been flushed as she walked up the aisle and her eyes glowed with tears and simple, untainted emotion. The woman in front of me sat practically emotionless, radiating only a calm confidence. All the romance had been carved from her like baby fat, making her strong, making her whole. Her description of the trees echoed through the air between us, plain poetry that could have graced the pages of any number of pastoral novels, and I realized how beautiful she was, and how insignificant I'd become to her.

'So this is it? It doesn't matter what I want?'

'You'll have to make your own choice. Whether you want to stay with me or not.'

'How am I *with you* now? We don't talk to each other. We haven't had sex since last fall. Christ, what happened to us, Mary?'

She was quiet for a minute, to the point where I thought she'd retreated into her silence again, but then she drew a breath and made a quiet admission.

'I think it was easier to be angry with you because you hated it here than be angry with myself because I hated the reason we were here.'

Before I could reply, Elsa shuffled into the kitchen, coughing weakly and asking about dinner. We went through the motions. I helped Elsa to her chair and Mary served something from the crockpot that I ate without tasting. By the time I went upstairs to stare out our bedroom window at the chicken barn, any ire I'd harbored toward Mary had turned inside out. Her honesty was contagious. I'd always assumed I was a good person – eating right, running, living consciously, whatever the fuck that meant – when the exact opposite was true. I was the guy who cheated on his wife while she took care of her dying mother. I was absolute slime.

I stripped off my clothes and was searching for pajamas when Mary came upstairs.

'Under the sheets in the basket,' she murmured and brushed by me, changing into her own.

We both climbed into bed and lay there for a minute. Mary turned on her side and I felt her looking at me. Jesus, she would have been better off with anyone else. Maybe that guy, that window guy, had a crush on Mary in high school. They could have had three kids and a chicken farm dynasty by now. Instead she had a dead father, a dying mother, no children, and a selfish, asshole husband. She deserved so much more.

'You're right about the windows,' I said.

'I know.'

Another minute passed while I stared at the ceiling and neither of us pretended to fall asleep. Then she propped herself up on one elbow.

'Will you stay?' she asked. 'I know things haven't been good, but that can change, can't it?'

What changed was that her hand moved under the covers, snaking over my chest.

'Mary.' Everything I couldn't say was wrapped up in the two syllables of her name. No, Mary. It's too late, Mary. When you shut me out I didn't wait for you, Mary.

Her lips touched my neck and I closed my eyes. Inhaled. Her hand slipped down my stomach and I caught it, holding her off.

'This isn't a good idea.'

'Peter,' she murmured. 'Let me try.'

I had no right. Self-loathing coursed through my veins as her hand wriggled free and found a rhythm. And then I was trying, too, rolling her to her back and trying to return her unexpected gesture, trying to act like a husband should, trying to make up for the fact that, even now, Hattie beckoned from the shadows of my mind.

HATTIE / *March 2008*

SPRING BREAK in Minnesota sucked. There was always still snow on the ground and only the choir people got to go anywhere, because they competed in a tournament in Nashville. I hated country music and Nashville was probably the last place I'd visit, but it was better than Pine Valley. Portia was an alto and she'd brought up the trip constantly ever since Peter posted the cast list for the spring play.

I'd gotten the female lead of Lady Macbeth. Portia was cast as my understudy.

And go figure, that's also when she started getting really weird about this curse stuff. At first when Peter posted the casting call, Portia had mentioned the curse of *Macbeth*, but it was all in her gossipy, I-know-more-than-you voice. After she found out she wasn't in the play, all of a sudden the curse was real. She spent every rehearsal telling us about famous *Macbeth* accidents, and by the time we held our last session before spring break, everyone was doing her insane cleansing ritual.

The deal was this: if anyone said 'Macbeth' inside the gymnasium when we weren't directly rehearsing the lines, they 'invoked the curse.' To pacify the curse gods, they had to immediately run out the door, race around the outside of the gym, spit over their left shoulder, and recite, 'Angels and ministers of grace defend us.' Then someone else had to officially admit the person back into the gym before we could continue rehearsing.

The first time Peter said 'Macbeth,' Portia tried to get him to perform her routine and he totally snapped at her. He threatened to ban her from the production if she even so much as mentioned it again. After that she operated in whispers until everyone said 'the Scottish play' or 'Mr. and Mrs. McBee.' Portia even started running out on Peter's behalf when he said the word, and all the underclassmen followed her, so every time Peter called Macbeth up to the stage, half the cast dropped their scripts and ran like lemmings into the hallway. It was hilarious. Sometimes while we waited for them to do their penance I crossed myself 'in the name of the father Macbeth, the son Macbeth, and the holy Macbeth spirit. Amen.' Peter couldn't help laughing whenever I did it.

After the last rehearsal before break I went over to Portia's house to hang out for a while. Instead of watching movies like we normally did, she just tried on a bunch of outfits for her Nashville trip and pretended to want my opinion.

'How about this one?' She spun around in a short-sleeve twinset and knee-length skirt that looked exactly like my back-to-school outfit.

'That seems a little too prep school. Shouldn't you go for more of a southern belle?'

'It's not a costume, Hatts. I just want to look like me on vacation. Like a me without parents.'

She slid on a pair of sunglasses. Show-off. I lay down on her bed and hung my head over the edge, looking at her upside down. '*Très* parentless.'

'What are you going to do all week?'

'Work. Run lines.' I threw a jab of my own. At first I thought it was a little mean of Peter not to give Portia any part, but the more she rubbed in her 'fabulous' trip, the less mean it seemed. And I really was planning on working on it. Opening night was only three weeks away and I didn't have all my longer speeches down yet.

'You can call me on Thursday if you need help. We have a free day and I'll probably be all over the Opry Mills, but I can spare an hour or so to rehearse.'

'We'll see. I might get Tommy to help me.'

Portia snorted and I couldn't help smiling, too. Tommy Kinakis reading Shakespeare sounded as wrong as Carrie Bradshaw plowing fields. He'd been bugging me about seeing each other during break, though, and Portia knew why.

'Are you finally going to do it with Tommy?'

I stared at a corner of the ceiling where a small spider was busy making a web. It had been over two months since Peter and I stayed in Minneapolis, and to say we *did it* was just so middle school. It felt like an ocean had opened up between me and Portia and I would never be on her side of it again. It made me embarrassed for her, and lonely for me.

I hadn't seen Peter alone since the night we parked at the scenic overlook in February. It was like I was fasting for weeks and weeks before getting these sudden feasts, where I had to eat as much as possible to survive the next fast. Before we drove away that night, he told me the same thing he had before we'd left Minneapolis, that we didn't have a relationship. *I can't be with you,* he said, *not the way you want.* And I ignored him again. Graduation was only a few months away and then our biggest obstacle was gone. Peter didn't know that I had plans; I could see how the whole play would unfold.

In the meantime I still had to wear this other life. Part of me had wanted to break up with Tommy since the first night Peter kissed me, but the show had to go on. Everyone thought of us as a couple, a single unit. Every day someone asked if Tommy and I wanted to do this or that and I always answered, 'I don't know what Tommy wants to do. I'll ask him.' Then during lunch I *asked* Tommy about our plans until he said what I wanted him to say. I always tried to spend our dates with other couples, especially since he'd started trying things.

'I told him waist up only.'

Portia tucked her jewelry bag into the suitcase next to me on the bed. 'You said he wanted to do more.'

'It's not my problem if he doesn't listen.'

'It might be your problem.' She put on a jacket and quickly shrugged it off again. 'What am I doing? I won't need that in Tennessee. It's going to be eighty degrees.'

Then she sat down next to me and got really serious. 'Look, Hattie, I know you think you've got Tommy wrapped around your little finger, but look at him. He's a giant.'

She stopped, tongue-tied, which was so not like her.

'What are you saying, Portia?'

'I'm just saying be careful.'

I left her on the bed and stood in front of her full-length mirror. It felt better to have this conversation through a reflection. 'You're saying be careful in case my boyfriend is a rapist?'

'Pretty much.'

'And this has nothing to do with the fact that you wanted to ask him to Sadie's?'

'Are you kidding me? He was just one option. It's not like I liked him.'

'Obviously not, if you think he's going to force himself on me.'
I started giggling. 'Come on, Porsche. Tommy? Really?'

She looked put out by my laughter; she just sniffed and went
back to picking out clothes and talking about all the fabulous
things she was going to do in Nashville. We didn't talk again before
her trip, but as soon as their plane landed she started compulsively
texting me, which was typical Portia. I just replied with stuff like,
'Great!' and 'That sounds awesome!,' which was typical Hattie.

Tommy ended up coming over on Tuesday during spring break.
Mom was home, putting together a care package for Greg in the
kitchen. We hadn't heard from him in a few weeks because he was
on an active assignment. No one really knew what it meant except
that Mom had to start working on a package for him. She bought
magazines she thought he'd like, made cookies and wrapped them
in bubble wrap, and tucked in all sorts of odds and ends with sticky
notes to tell him why she'd included them. She sent cartons of cigarettes, too – even though she hated smoking – because Greg said
they were better than money over there. It sounded a lot like prison
to me. He was scheduled to come home in July, and sometimes I
caught Mom flipping the calendar pages back and forth like she
was counting down the number of flips until she could breathe
easy again. You didn't notice when she was moving around, which
was like always, but when she sat at the dinner table or read books
at night her hands trembled. I didn't remember them doing that
before Greg left.

When Tommy came over, he asked about Greg. I always forgot
they'd been on the football team together when Greg was a senior
and we were sophomores.

'Here, Tommy, write him a quick note. He'll be glad to hear
from you,' Mom said.

Tommy seemed flustered by the pen and sticky note, but he
squeezed himself into a kitchen chair and did as she told him. I

grabbed a few sodas for us out of the fridge before we went up-stairs, and as I passed the table I saw he wrote (all in uppercase): HI GREG. YOU KILLED OSAMA YET? GO SPARTANS! TOMMY

'So do you wanna go for a drive?' Tommy asked when we got to my room. He looked like a monster on my little twin bed and I couldn't help remembering what Portia had said. It was the kind of thought that just creeped in all by itself and started whispering, *rapist, rapist.* I wondered what Tommy was really capable of with his strong hands and soft brain. There was that whole Lennie Small angle to consider. Even though the gearshift stayed between us every time we made out in his pickup, he still tried to move his hand down my shirt to my jeans. And every time I pulled away and said, 'No, Tommy.' Like a dog, like how you would train an over-eager Labrador. Then he would apologize without meaning it and eventually take me home. There was no gearshift between us in my room, though. The bed was here. The door was mostly closed and Mom was all the way downstairs, humming along with the radio.

'Maybe later.' I reached into my backpack for my script. 'I have to memorize the rest of my lines first, remember? Will you help me?'

'Seriously?'

I nodded and he groaned. 'Come on, Hattie. I can't read that stuff.'

'It's good for you.' I smiled, a flirty little smile, and sat down on the bed next to him, opening the book. 'See, you just have to read whatever comes right before Lady Macbeth's lines and then make sure I'm saying them right.'

I pointed out the highlighted text, but Tommy was concentrating on other things. He pulled me against him and landed a sloppy kiss behind my ear.

'Not now.'

When I tried to pull away he tightened his grip, keeping me close.

'Just a little,' he mumbled and moved to my mouth.

Somehow his other hand found the back of my head and held me still as he kissed me. I felt like I was suffocating and couldn't even picture Peter the way I usually did.

'Tommy,' I managed when he came up for air.

'What?' His hand squeezed my breast. How did he grow so many hands?

'Not now,' I repeated and managed to squirm away.

He grunted and lounged back against the wall, not even bothering to hide the bulge in his jeans. 'It's not ever with you.'

'My mom's here. And I really do have to learn this.'

'I don't understand why you're doing this play.'

'I don't understand why you play football.' I mimicked him in the same stupid tone as I cued the video camera on top of the dresser.

'Okay, okay.' He sighed and picked up the script, then squinted at it like it was in Chinese. 'This part?'

'You're a sweetheart.' I gave him a peck on the cheek and backed into the center of the room. While he worked up the nerve to say Shakespeare out loud, I let myself become Lady Macbeth. I looked at Tommy until the horny teenager faded away and he became my instrument. I looked at his fingers and saw a hand that was mine to wield, that I could drive to murder the king himself. I looked at his confused expression and saw the madness that we would soon share. I became cold, too cold to feel. By the time he cleared his throat to say his first line, I could taste my own death.

Somehow on the Friday of spring break we got a perfect day, the kind of nauseating perfection you only see in commercials. The sky was cloudless and the sun warmed you in your bones as it devoured the snowbanks. Dad immediately disappeared into the barn, getting his equipment ready for planting, while Mom paged through seed catalogs for her garden and hung sheets out on the line to dry. I was giddy because during my shift on Wednesday Peter had dropped off a flash drive with a single picture on it. It was a photograph of the barn.

'Enjoying your spring break?' he asked nonchalantly when he came back for the picture.

'It's nothing special.'

'Maybe it'll pick up by Friday morning.'

'Mmm, I hope so.' I tried to sound bored as I rang him up and contained the excitement that rocketed around inside me.

I left the house as if I was going to work and called in sick. Peter was waiting for me when I got to the barn. His wife and mother-in-law had gone to the hospital for a bunch of tests all day, so we hiked into the middle of their property, away from any roads or houses or outbuildings, where a giant oak tree marked the intersection of four fields. We'd both come prepared this time. I brought a quilt and the book he'd given me for Christmas and he brought a picnic basket and a bottle of wine. He flipped through the book and read some lines aloud while we picked at the cheese and crackers and sipped pinot noir from Dixie cups. I'd never had wine outside of church before and even though it tasted dry and coppery, I didn't mind. I'd rather drink wine with Peter than all the beer in the world with Tommy.

After a while I laid my head in his lap while he leaned against the tree trunk, read, and stroked my hair. I listened more to the tone of his voice than the actual words. I started to feel like a cat, like I wanted to rub my head against his thigh and stretch and roll in the warmth of the sun. Maybe the wine was getting to me.

'So he spends his entire worthless life searching for V.' Peter flipped the book shut and set it aside.

Usually I loved listening to him talk about books, to hear that crisp analytical tone in his voice as he lectured the class, but the more he'd read of this one, the more depressed he sounded, especially about that weird stalker character. I asked him who V was, to change his focus, and he perked up a little.

'That's the unsolvable mystery, the unknowable question. Pynchon would never be so prosaic as to attempt to answer it.'

I rubbed my cheek against his pant leg. 'Well, I didn't ask Pynchon. I asked you.'

He was quiet for a minute while his fingers continued to sift through my hair, starting at my scalp and smoothing the strands over his thigh and down to the ground. It was hypnotic, addictive. I wanted to lie in the sun and feel him stroking my hair forever. My eyes drifted closed.

'I should say that I'm not that prosaic either, but it's irresistible. She haunts you as you read, like a ghost drawing you through each page.' He paused again, hesitating. 'When I gave it to you I thought V was you, in about fifty years.'

I laughed. 'And you're the man searching for me?'

'I don't know. Probably. It doesn't matter who I am. It's about you, who you are. I still don't even know what to call you. All your names. All your identities.'

'It's just acting, Peter.'

'No, it's not. A person's actions dictate who they are. You can't be a Democrat if you vote Republican. You can't call yourself a vegetarian if you eat steak. And your actions, they don't add up to one single person. I watch you, Hattie. You gossip with Portia before class, egging on all her ridiculous ideas, feeding her one bullshit line after another. You let Tommy paw you in the middle of the cafeteria while you blush and giggle. You play teacher's pet with every single staff member I've talked with and they all think you're going to major in their field. And I can't find one hint that any of it bothers

221

you. You say you're just acting, but you're fracturing yourself into a thousand pieces, and every time I see another piece, you're gone again. You turn into someone else, a crowd of someone elses, and it makes me wonder if there's any such thing as Hattie Hoffman. I could have hallucinated this whole affair.'

He laughed bitterly. With my eyes still closed, I reached a hand up and drew my finger along the inseam of his pants until I reached the center.

'Do you think you're hallucinating right now?' I brushed my fingers back and forth until I felt his body respond.

'Hattie . . .' His voice sounded strangled.

'Would you like to hallucinate some more?' I reached for his pants buttons, and he grabbed my hand.

'Stop it.'

I sat up, annoyed. If I had done that to Tommy, he would have forgotten his own name, let alone any question he might have had about mine.

'What's your problem, Peter? Why did you even want to see me today?' I demanded.

'You like it, don't you? You like manipulating people. Does it make you happy to have Tommy panting after you? To have Portia mimicking you like some brainless clone?'

'No. That's not how it is.'

'The first time I met you, you told me you drop an alias whenever it stops being fun. Do you have fun knowing what you've turned me into? I loathe myself every time I think about us.'

'I don't want you to feel that way.'

'Said the actress.'

'I don't like it, okay?' I shouted, then dropped my head and breathed for a second. 'I used to. I used to love it, but now I just feel trapped. There's no person, no character I can put on that takes away this empty feeling in my gut when I'm not with you. I hate it. I hate that I can't escape it, I can't act it away. And I go through every day miserable because all I really want is . . .'

I faltered. It wasn't time to tell him yet.

'What? What do you want?'

'Nothing.'

'Stop lying to me.'

'God, you're such a teacher.' I turned away from him, unbelievably frustrated. Today wasn't going at all how I imagined. We should have been wrapped up in this quilt together, laughing, kissing, enjoying every stolen moment. Psychoanalysis should have been the last thing on his mind.

'You want to name everything, to analyze it and shove it into a little box in your head next to a million other boxes just like it. Labels and dates and a neat little synopsis for each one. Fine. I've got a synopsis for you. You want to know who I am? You want me to tell you something else that's true?'

My heart was racing all of a sudden. This wasn't the plan, but I could feel the words bubbling up in my throat. I couldn't hide it anymore. I spun back around and gripped his hand, clinging to it, hoping and dreading what was going to happen next.

'I'm Hattie Hoffman, actress, CVS clerk, and Pine Valley high school senior. I'm in love with Peter Lund and I want him to move to New York with me.'

His face froze. He stared at me for what felt like forever and I didn't know if he was going to hug me or yell at me. We'd never talked about the future. My future, yes, but not his. Not ours. This relationship existed outside of our lives; it had no sense of time or progress.

Suddenly Peter yanked his hand away, stood up, and walked to the edge of the branches hanging over us. I followed him.

'Peter? Say something.'

'What do you want me to say?'

'Say yes.'

He laughed again, but it was a hard sound now. It made my stomach clench.

'Oh, okay. I'll just go to New York with you. That sounds simple.'

'It is. It can be.'

'Where will we live?'

'We can sublet a room somewhere. There's a million listings on Pulse.'

'And how will we pay for that room?'

'I have over two thousand in savings. And I'll transfer to one of the pharmacies there.' I rattled off a few of the CVS locations I'd memorized from their website, touching his shoulder, but he pulled away.

'And you can teach,' I added.

'Do you even know what the licensing requirements are in New York?'

'Licensing?'

He laughed that awful laugh again. The conversation was turning on me. This wasn't supposed to happen. If I had taken more time and researched things, I could have answered him. I could have shot down his every objection. But no – he demanded I be honest and like an idiot I was. Now he wouldn't even look at me. I felt the desperation in my throat, closing it off like stage fright, and it made me bounce on my toes, quick bounces to try to shake it off.

'We'll figure everything out. We've got the whole summer to figure it out.'

'The whole summer?' He stretched out the word *whole,* using that sarcastic voice he got when he wanted me to feel like I was four years old.

'How long do you need? People move to New York all the time.'

'Our situation is a little more complicated than most people's.'

'Don't you want to go with me?'

He didn't say anything and I almost started crying right then. Then he put a hand over his face. 'I do.'

The hope and love surged through me so fast and fierce I almost couldn't breathe.

'Then come with me.'

'It's not that simple.' Finally he turned around. His eyes were full of despair.

'Actually it is.'

'I'm married, Hattie.'

'So get unmarried.'

'It's not that easy.'

'It really is, Peter. You say *I don't want to be married to you anymore. Here are the divorce papers. Goodbye.*'

'Her mother is dying.'

'Her mother was dying two months ago when you ran off to Minneapolis to sleep with me. She was dying an hour ago when you were kissing me under this tree.'

'Mary can't know about this. The last thing she needs right now is—'

'I don't care what the last thing Mary needs is. I'll tell her myself. She comes in to the pharmacy every week for her mom's prescriptions.'

'You wouldn't dare.' His voice went low and scared. He grabbed my arm.

I leaned in close, close enough to feel the heat of his breath, to see his pupils dilate and the blood beat against his throat.

'You have no idea what I would or wouldn't do, Peter. Remember? All my names, all my identities that make you so crazy?' I gave him a tight, angry smile, even as my heart was breaking. 'Who knows which one your wife might meet the next time she stops in for her meds?'

I wrenched my arm out of his hand, hard enough that it hurt, and marched down the hill and back toward the barn. I wanted to look back, to see if he was following me to apologize, but I didn't. I wanted to run, too, faster than anyone had ever run before, but I didn't do that either. I walked in the dried mud tracks of a combine that had plowed through these fields last fall, letting the tears come, feeling the ache in my arm where he'd grabbed me. By the time I got back to the pickup, I was sniffling and trying not to lose it completely. I drove home and walked in the front door to see Mom sitting at the kitchen table with my computer open in front of her. She looked from the screen to my face with heavy, disappointed eyes.

'We need to talk.'

DEL / *Wednesday, April 16, 2008*

I GOT back to the station that afternoon after talking to Fran, half hoping the DNA results would be sitting on my desk. Instead, Mona was waiting in my office, her hands quietly folded and eyes down as she sat in the visitor's chair. Winifred Erickson was with her. I thought about my phone call with Bud this morning, how he'd hung up on me, while I stood on the other side of the glass looking at them.

Jake came over with some warrants: two for outstanding tickets and one failure to appear. County business still had to go on.

'How long have they been here?' I asked as I signed the warrants.

'Twenty minutes maybe.' He kept his voice down. 'I tried to get them to wait in the conference room, but they just walked in there and sat down. Didn't say a word to anyone.'

I nodded. 'What else do you have?'

'The rest of Hattie's computer was pretty clean. A lot of temporary internet files and cookies for New York websites. It looked like she was browsing for places to live, even made a few inquiries by email. No confirmations, though. I didn't get the feeling she was ready to hightail it, just getting the lay of the land.'

Jake glanced around to make sure no one was nearby before continuing. 'No other communication with LitGeek, as far as I can see.'

'And her phone records?'

'Nothing. Tons of texts, all to friends, and a few every week with Tommy.'

'Anything off about the ones with Tommy?'

'Not much to 'em. Just stuff like "See you at 7:00" and "Running late." They mostly sent funny pictures. LOLCat and things like that.'

Jake caught my look and tried to clarify. 'Uh, internet pictures. With cats. That want cheeseburgers.'

'Uh-huh.' I finished signing the warrants and handed them back. 'I need you to send the entire case file, pictures included, to the FBI.'

'What?' Jake couldn't keep the volume down on his surprise. 'Are we turning it over?'

'No, we're getting some help.'

I gave him the information for Fran's contact, a forensic psychologist who evaluated crime scenes. Normally I wouldn't have much use for a psychological anything, but Fran said he was 'peerless' in the state, and I wasn't going to turn my nose up at anyone who might be able to point his peerless finger at our killer.

'I want a call with him today, tomorrow at the latest. And tomorrow we're bringing both suspects in again – right after Hattie's funeral – to go over their Friday nights in detail. Let's see if any stories start changing after they've spent all day with her casket.'

Jake got to work and I left the business and noise of the station behind and opened the door to my office. Winifred turned as I came in, but Mona didn't even lift her head. She looked like she was made of stone, with her feet together and hands folded over the big, faded purse in her lap. Her eyes saw nothing; everything about her was turned inward, locked inside.

I'd known Mona nearly as long as Bud, saw her pregnant with both Greg and Hattie. Other than the size of her belly, you'd never have thought she was expecting. Whenever the baby gave her a good kick from the inside, she'd said, *You just come out here and try that,* and rubbed the spot before carrying on with whatever she was doing. Now she worked part-time for the only lawyer in town, doing his typing and filing, while still helping Bud in the fields, taking care of the house, and putting food on the table to boot. She made a mean potpie, with whole mushrooms and big hunks of chicken in a white wine sauce and always served it sizzling right out of the oven. If you complimented her on it, she'd just shrug and say it was nothing fancy.

To tell the truth, Mona and I were probably more alike than me and Bud. Neither of us had much time for small talk. So I knew she was here today for a reason.

'Mona.'

I sat down on the other side of the desk. Winifred stood behind her with her hand on Mona's shoulder, giving the kind of silent comfort a friend should, but me, I had to put that desk between us. I had to look at her as next of kin, not as a woman I'd known for almost half her life.

'It never crossed my mind.'

She didn't seem to be speaking to either of us. Winifred and I glanced at each other and waited for her to continue.

'In all the months since Greg's been gone, I never once thought I could lose Hattie. It's been Greg, Greg, Greg. Greg stepping on a land mine in my head in the middle of the night. Greg's unit getting attacked. Greg's face still and pale in a coffin. Greg's been my nightmare and I thought I could trade them off. Greg's tour is up in July, and Hattie had it in her head she was going to New York. I'd get one back and start worrying about the other. That seemed . . . fair.'

Her gaze finally focused and she looked at me now, all the anguish in the world swimming in her eyes.

'I never thought I could lose her when she was so close to me. Not here at home, in Pine Valley.' Winifred held tight to Mona's shoulder with her bony fingers like she was keeping Mona upright, and shot me a look like women do when they want you to do something or they think you're making a mess of it.

'Mona, what are you doing here? This is the last place you need to be right now.'

'There's something you need to know. About Hattie.'

She reached up and patted Winifred's hand. 'Wait for me in the lobby, will you?'

'You sure, honey?'

'I'll be along in a minute.'

Winifred gave her a pat and me a warning look before she left and shut the door behind her. Mona paused again. She seemed to be collecting her energy.

'All these people keep asking about me. Doing things for me. I can't stand it. It's not about me, Del. I would feel this way for the rest of my life if she could just be alive. It wouldn't matter if I never saw her again, never hugged her. I would cut off my hands and feet just to know her heart was beating. That she was breathing and smiling and living somewhere. How can I live knowing she's not? I can't bear it, Del. I can't bear it.'

She pressed her lips together, fighting for control.

'You have to take it one day at a time, Mona. Just focus on what's next.'

She nodded. 'Winifred says you learn how to live with it, that the grief becomes your new child.'

'She lost two; she would know.'

Mona nodded and took a deep breath, changing the topic. 'Bud says you don't know about the DNA yet.'

'No, not yet. And I know Bud's upset.'

'We're all upset, Del.'

'No, I didn't mean about – I meant –' Christ, I didn't know how to handle women. Maybe if I'd been married for more than two seconds, I'd be better at this sort of thing. Mona saw my floundering and, despite what had just been robbed from her, still had the good grace to step in.

'Bud told me about your call this morning. He was angry. He expected more from you.'

'Mona–'

'I know, Del. You have to do your job. I know about disclosure and what you can and can't say. I used to read detective novels.' Her gaze dropped. 'For fun.'

'I'm not trying to keep Bud in the dark about anything.' I didn't even realize it was a lie until the words were already out. I kept talking, just like the lying criminals did, trying to justify it, to make it better. 'Once we get the DNA back, the whole game's gonna change. Hattie's killer's not going to be able to hide for long. Believe me.'

She looked up again and I saw she trusted me. She trusted her friend of twenty-five years to find her daughter's killer, and even though I knew I was doing the right thing keeping this Lund thing quiet, it still tore at me. It turned my stomach.

'Bud will understand later. He'll calm down.'

I knew he might understand if he ever had to find out the whole truth, but I didn't know if he'd forgive me for keeping it from him. I shook my head, needing to move on.

'What did you want to tell me about Hattie?'

'I've been thinking.' She took a deep breath. 'I didn't remember it when you came to the house. There was too much . . .'

She shook her head, looking like she was willing the tears back so she could get out what she needed to say.

'It was three weeks ago, during Hattie's spring break. She was supposed to be working on Friday, but when I stopped up at the pharmacy for my pills, she wasn't there. She'd left in the morning wearing her smock and her name tag. The girl who checked me out said she hoped Hattie was feeling better. I didn't say anything. I just nodded.

'When I went home, Hattie was still gone and she didn't answer her phone. She wasn't at Tommy's or Portia's. After another hour went by, I went into her room. I usually don't. Teenagers like to be left to themselves, you know, and Hattie never did anything that made me worry, so I gave her space. But when I still hadn't heard from her I went in and started looking around.'

She took a deep breath. 'It was in her computer.'

'What was?' I asked, wondering if I already knew the answer, but I didn't.

She pulled some papers out of her purse and pushed them across the desk.

'I printed it before she got home. I'm not exactly sure why. I knew I wasn't going to show Bud. Hattie was his little girl, his angel. He's loved that child stupid since the day we brought her home from the hospital.'

The paper was a chart of some kind. On the left side there was a column that said *Character* and then a bunch of names. I skimmed down until I saw *Tommy*. Next to the character column were other headings. Under *Through line*, she'd written *Sex and acceptance;* under *Needs* she'd written *To be told what to do, to fit in, to slobber all over me*; and under the last column, *Stage Direction*, was *Tell him he's just like Derek. Keep him in social scenes. No more private parties.*

'What is this, Mona?'

I looked at a few more. Bud's *Through* line was *Farm and fam-*

ily. The stage direction for Portia was *Talk about Portia as much as humanly possible without puking.* Hard not to smile at that one. I'd done a fair amount of talking to Portia lately, myself.

'That's what I asked her when she came home. She looked sad and a little windblown, red nose and eyes. She'd been outside somewhere. I demanded to know where she'd been and why she lied to her boss. She said it wasn't any of my business, that she was eighteen and an adult and could do whatever she wanted.'

'Typical teenager.'

'Typical teenager – not typical Hattie. I'd always gotten the feeling that Hattie told people what they wanted to hear. I couldn't ever prove it before, but a mother knows when her child is putting on a show. I can see their hearts, Greg and Hattie, whether they want me to or not. Hattie was a people pleaser, although I could never quite figure out if she did it because she didn't want to disappoint anyone or if she just didn't know what she wanted for herself.

'Anyway, she yanked the computer out of my hands and said it was her property; she'd paid for it fair and square and I didn't have any right to touch it. Then she stormed off to her room and slammed the door. I followed her in there and told her it was my door, that her father and I had paid for it fair and square, and she didn't have any right to shut it in my face. Then I asked her about that spreadsheet. I said, what are you trying to do with that? People aren't characters in one of your plays. She claimed it was just an exercise. Something to help her be a better actress like her camcorder was.'

Mona shook her head, remembering. 'I said something like, who do you think you're fooling? And then she started crying. I went over to the bed and held her for a while, stroking her hair just like when she was little.'

Mona teared up and wiped her eyes with a tissue. 'It'd been a long time since she'd let me that close. She was her daddy's girl. Always kept me at a distance. I never knew why . . . why she did that.

'But that day she needed me. She let me in a little. She cried and I held her and she said that the only person she'd been fooling was herself. I told her to stop thinking about what she could be for everyone else, stop putting on shows and people would respect her for it in the long run.

'She said it was hard to think about the long run, so I told her just what you said to me right now. Take it one day at a time. She had to figure out what she wanted and concentrate on that. I kept talking for a while, just rocking her back and forth and trying to get through to her. It felt like I had my baby girl back for a moment.

'She never told me where she'd been that day and I didn't push her on it. I didn't want to break that fragile bond, to have her shut me out again. Now, though . . . now I wonder if she was mixed up in something that got her killed. If I had just made her tell me, or grounded her . . .'

She broke off again and wiped her eyes with the tissue.

'You can't think like that, Mona. You can't blame yourself.'

'I don't blame myself. I blame the murdering bastard who did it. But maybe I could've prevented it. Maybe if I'd been more strict with her–'

'She'd have run just as hard in the opposite direction,' I interrupted. 'That's what kids do. It's how they're wired at that age.'

She wiped her eyes some more, nodding. 'I know that, Del. It's just these thoughts. These thoughts keep finding me. They won't let me go.'

'And we don't know she was mixed up in anything yet. Kids go out to that lake and have sex all the time.'

'But there was the envelope.'

'What envelope?' I sat up straighter.

'It came that night – a white envelope in the mailbox. No stamp, no return address, just Hattie's name on it. She took it from Bud and disappeared up to her room.'

'Did you find out what was in it?'

'No.'

'Have you seen it since then?' I wouldn't have noticed something that mundane when I'd searched her room.

'No.'

'And the next day she disappeared again.' I pieced the timing of it together.

Mona looked surprised. 'How did you know that?'

'Portia.'

She nodded. 'Portia dropped her off because her truck had broken down off the highway north of Rochester.'

'What was she doing up there?'

'She said she went shopping.'

'Shopping for what?'

'I don't know, but again – I didn't push her on it because she seemed happier. I figured she'd sorted out whatever it was that needed sorting. When Bud grumbled about the truck breaking down over supper that night, she cracked jokes and teased him. Told him it was a sign that Bud should buy her a new car, a convertible so she could drive with the top down all the way to New York. Then he told her that her allowance was now a nickel a week and she could save up for it herself. They went back and forth all the time like that, ribbing each other. She seemed fine, happy, like I said, not like she'd been crying on my shoulder the day before. Maybe it was just teenage mood swings. One day they're on the top of the world, the next day their life is over.'

I heard it in her voice, how she caught herself, how the sarcasm came back and punched her right at the end of the word and suddenly she doubled over. Silent sobs shook her shoulders, too deep for noise. Too raw.

Winifred, who'd been standing guard out by the file cabinets, hurried back into the office and held Mona by the shoulders. I grabbed some takeout napkins from a drawer and shoved them across the desk, but Winifred rolled her eyes and produced a handkerchief from her purse. Mona wiped her face, pulling herself together, while I felt about as useless as thumbs on a snake.

'Mona, I need you to do something for me.'

She managed to calm down and sat up straighter. The grief hadn't made her weak. A woman like Mona Hoffman – a true farm woman who faced every season and every storm with an equanimity that would make God jealous – thrived on action, on measuring out the task and getting it done. Even here, in the darkest days of her life, I knew she would do whatever I asked of her.

'I want you to look through Hattie's room again, and her truck, anywhere she might have left that envelope.'

'Okay, Del.'

'There's a few other things we need to know the whereabouts of, too,' I added on an impulse. 'Her suitcase and her video camera.'

'What?' Surprise broke through the other emotions.

I described them both briefly and said, 'We think they're missing.'

'The suitcase was her Christmas present from us. Bud bought it at Brookstone. She loved it.'

She said she would look for Hattie's things after they picked out the casket flowers for the funeral.

'We're having the wake tonight at the house. Just family.' Mona glanced away as she got up to leave.

I walked them out, but stood back while the old woman helped the younger one into the sedan. A news van hovered on the other side of the street, waiting for a break in the story. They'd be swarming around the funeral tomorrow, trying to interview anyone they could about the 'curse killing.' At least I could take care of that nuisance for Bud and Mona. I didn't feel capable of much else as I watched Mona's car pull away.

It was a long while before I went back inside.

PETER / *Friday, March 21, 2008*

COULD A body tear in half? I stood under the tree, one of Mary's sprawling oaks that had shown her what she wanted to do with her life, and watched Hattie walk away from me. Her ultimatum hung in the air. *Come to New York with me or I'll tell Mary about us.* She hadn't said those exact words – had she? – but the threat was there, glittering in her fearless eyes.

I watched her shrink across the field, her steps eating up the ground with a callous teenage confidence that would have told the sun itself to fuck off. My desperation grew proportionally with the distance between us. Everything in me burned to run after her, to haul her back here, tie her to this tree, and put her mouth to use until it couldn't speak a word of truth or lies. Give her exactly what she wanted and then find a car and drive. Show her everything. Make us both forget this town and ourselves and every terrible decision that had brought us to this place and time.

But New York? What did she expect me to say? Yes, I'll move

to New York with you? I'll throw away any chance of getting my life in Minneapolis back and go live on the streets of New York City with you? That's where we would be – on the street. Even if I could miraculously line up a teaching job for the fall, I wouldn't get a paycheck until October. I had a thousand dollars left in my savings account, which was nothing, yet Hattie thought her two grand would somehow support both of us in the most expensive city in the country?

She had no idea what she was facing. She had no friends there, no contacts, no plan. She needed me. God, she needed me almost as much as I craved her, and the temptation to give in to her insane demand practically overwhelmed me.

Except I couldn't forget Mary.

Mary kept me rooted to the spot, watching Hattie until she disappeared into the woods. I didn't give a shit about the rest of it – my job, my reputation – nothing in this Pine Valley life mattered anymore except Mary. She'd told me her plans to stay on the farm over a month ago and we'd been living in a stalemate ever since. I hadn't given her an answer as to whether I would stay and she hadn't brought it up again. We existed in parallel, passing perfunctory remarks like well-mannered yet distant neighbors. I knew she was waiting for me to make a decision, but I honestly couldn't tell whether she cared about what that decision would be.

Was it any wonder I'd set up this rendezvous with Hattie? Hattie, who'd curled up in my lap like *I* was *her* haven from the world, who'd pleaded with me and threatened to break me, like I was someone worth breaking.

I drank the rest of the wine and tossed the leftover food to a circling crow, then lay down and stared at the sky through the bared branches.

Would she really do it? Would Hattie talk to Mary the next time she came into the pharmacy? She'd told me over and over that she would do anything for me, that she was the right woman for me, but which version of her? Even if she wasn't a born actress, she was still eighteen, for fuck's sake. What wouldn't a scorned eighteen-year-old do?

When I couldn't stand thinking about it anymore, I gathered everything up and walked back to the barn. Hattie was already gone when I got there. Maybe she was home already, planning the best way to ruin me. It wouldn't take much. A quick phone call to Mary or a confession to her parents, and my life would be over.

I hurled the empty wine bottle against the barn wall, but it didn't even crack, so I kicked it into the pond that was forming on the far side of the building. It was tempting to toss her picnic blanket in after it. Instead, I left it in a dry corner wrapped around the book.

When I arrived back at the house, Mary's truck was parked in the driveway. She'd said they were going shopping in Rochester after the doctors' appointments, but it wasn't even noon. They were home early.

I tossed the picnic basket in the backseat of my car and then opened the front door quietly. If I had any ideas of sneaking upstairs, they immediately died when I saw Mary sitting on the couch in the living room, staring at me like she'd been counting the minutes until I got home. The TV was off. Elsa was nowhere to be seen. The overwhelming assault of guilt compounded as the seconds ticked by and Mary remained motionless. She'd hardly paused in the last year. Could there be any doubt about the reason for her still life now?

On a completely different level from the nausea and slamming of my heart, I wondered how she'd found out. I started scanning the pages of my life, looking for the subtext that must have spilled over and given me away. Or maybe I hadn't done anything. Maybe Hattie had already made good on her threat.

'Where were you?' Mary finally broke the silence.

'Out. Walking.' I didn't admit anything yet.

'Walking where?'

'In the fields. Back there.' I swung an arm in no particular direction. 'I wanted some fresh air and didn't feel like a run.'

Mary laughed without any humor. 'You live on a farm and you had to go walking to get some fresh air. That's it, isn't it? That's it right there.'

'What's "it"? What are you talking about?'

'Nothing.'

'Where's Elsa? I thought you were going shopping.'

'She didn't want me pushing her wheelchair around. I dropped her off at Winifred's for a visit.'

'Okay.' I waited for the accusation, the tears and the rage, but nothing came. She kept sitting there with that unreadable expression.

'Is there something else?' I took a step toward the stairs, instinctually retreating.

'Sit down, Peter.'

My ass hit the chair immediately. Part of me even welcomed what was coming next. It was the end of my marriage – new paperwork to file in front of the old – but the end of the deceptions, too, the end of pretending I was anything good.

'What's going on?' I asked. 'You're acting strangely.'

She took a deep breath and looked at her hands.

'I fainted at the doctor's office.'

'What?' Surprise rushed through my veins like some delicious drug. 'What happened?'

'It was silly. We just had to stay in the waiting room longer than I thought and we were sitting for so long and it was hot in there. When the doctor called our name, I stood up too fast and blacked out. I came around on the floor with a nurse and the receptionist standing over me. They helped me up and made me drink some water.'

'Did you even eat any breakfast this morning? You're taking care of everything around here except yourself. That's why you fainted.'

'I know. That will have to change.'

'Do you still feel dizzy?'

'A little.' She nodded. 'The doctor asked me some questions and then gave me a test.'

The thought of Mary being sick seemed impossible. She'd become Elsa's guardian and champion; she'd singlehandedly re-invented the farm; she paid the bills, cooked the meals, and cleaned the house, all with that Reever stoicism. She was the fucking bionic woman.

'What test?'

'It was positive.' Her voice was small. Suddenly I wanted her to look at me; I needed to see her eyes.

'What test, Mary?' I got up and crossed the room, dropping in front of her to make her look at me. When she did, I saw con-fusion and hesitation. I could tell she was working up the nerve to tell me. Whatever it was – and it was something clearly unrelated to the fact that she had a cheating, lying husband – was tearing her up inside.

'I'm pregnant.'

'What?' I shot up and stumbled back. 'What?'

My brain stopped working. The room went black at the edges, like I'd read in scenes with certain heroines and always dismissed as sentimental, hyperbolic writing. How could she be pregnant? Was it even mine? Mary wasn't the cheating kind, but we hadn't had sex in months, we hadn't . . .

Then the living room came back into focus.

'The day the window guy was here?'

'It must have been. They asked about my last period, said I was six weeks along. The dates match up.' Her fingers laced over her stomach, holding tight.

I ran my hands through my hair, wiped my mouth, trying to come to terms with what was happening.

'What are you going to do?'

'Start eating breakfast, I guess.' She released a quick, nervous laugh. When I didn't say anything, she continued.

'I picked up some prenatal vitamins and some saltines. Mom said I needed saltines.'

I still couldn't speak.

'I know we haven't been in the best of places lately.' My bark of laughter only gave her pause for a second; she was picking up steam. 'But this is what we wanted.'

'You're going to keep the baby.'

'Don't you dare suggest what I think you're going to suggest.' Her voice, still low, was like steel now.

'What am I going to suggest? How do you know what I think, when I don't even know what I think?'

'I know you, and I know we haven't been happy, but this is my baby.' Her hands broke apart, spread over the small, flat plane of her abdomen. 'This is our baby, our family.'

'You're raising it here.' All I could do was state the obvious, mumble each bald fact as it punched me in the gut.

'We've already talked about that. I'll need some help with the chickens. I can't lift all the feed bags on my own anymore. The wheelbarrow should still be fine. I'm not sure about the ammonia in the excrement, but at the most it would be an hour of your day. I made an appointment with an OB-GYN.'

She sat there on the faded couch with her gaze falling somewhere between us, outlining details I could barely comprehend. It all felt horribly wrong: Mary's tightly controlled pragmatism, my monumental panic. We were a parody of what this moment should have been, what it would have been if it had happened a year ago. Instead of a celebration she was giving me an ultimatum, the second I'd been handed in as many hours.

'You don't seem overjoyed by the news,' I managed.

'I was surprised.'

I made a half-strangled noise that suggested agreement.

'It's been better lately, though, hasn't it?' she appealed. 'You've been spending time with Mom. The principal says you're doing a great job with the play, that you're working with some talented students.'

'Jesus.' I couldn't take any more of this, not when Hattie's presence hovered at the edge of the conversation, threatening to spill into this nightmare. 'I have to think.'

'Peter–'

'I just need some time to think.' I grabbed my keys and left the house, gunning the car out of the driveway and flying over the gravel road. I hit sixty, then seventy, and the rocks that pummeled the underside of the car sounded like a stampede, a hundred desperate, hoofed creatures running for their lives.

Thirty minutes ago I'd been fantasizing about – why whitewash it? – the sexual torture and abduction of Hattie, and the abandonment of Mary in the process. Why hadn't I gone? Why hadn't I scooped Hattie up the minute she'd uttered the words and forced her in a car before she could change her mind? We'd be in Wisconsin by now. I could've sent Mary an email from Madison, blissfully unaware of this child. I could've escaped.

Now there was no escape. Was there? Jesus, could I leave Mary, pregnant and alone, branded forever as the woman whose husband left her for Hattie Hoffman, that girl who was in the plays and not even out of high school? He was her teacher, you know. I could hear their whispers, picture their sympathetic looks.

I sped toward Rochester. The melting fields blurred into rolls of

white and brown, and then subdivisions gave way to the car dealer-
ships and big-box stores that lined the freeways on the outskirts of
the city. I turned toward Mayo Clinic and downtown, slowing the
car as people spilled into the sidewalks for lunch hour, their faces
lifted, basking in the unseasonable warmth of the day.

It was warm the day I'd proposed to Mary, too. God, it seemed
like a lifetime ago now, but it was less than six years since that day
after graduation.

I zigzagged up and down the streets of the business district and
finally parked next to a café and started walking, thinking about
the girl I'd proposed to, everything I prized about her. I loved her
sweet, dependable personality. I loved how loyal she was to the
American classics, to Steinbeck and Cather and Thoreau. I loved
how she'd shop the thrift stores twice a year, always on the Daylight
Saving Time days so she never forgot, and she'd take back grocery
bags of her old clothes and sell them for half the money of her new
finds. She was so responsible with her money, not like me. I could
get by on ramen and tofu for a week, but then I'd go to the bar on
Saturday and blow two hundred dollars on drinks and cabs. I knew
I needed a wife like Mary. It made sense on so many levels that I
never wondered – like a lot of my friends did about their own girlfriends – if I could find someone better. To think that one day I'd
long to leave her for a deceptive, brilliant actress would have been
laughable.

I planned to propose at Solera, the same tapas restaurant that I'd
taken Hattie to in Minneapolis, but when I told Mary about the
reservation, she balked.

'It's too expensive,' she said. 'Thirty dollars for a bottle of wine?
That's ridiculous.'

She suggested a picnic instead, so on the Saturday after graduation we took the bus to the Stone Arch Bridge and walked to
the park on the north side of the river. Mary had prepared a cold

feast – a fruit-and-cheese plate, crunchy baguette, and wine poured into grape juice bottles so the park police wouldn't bother us. We lay out in the sun and watched the bikers and rollerbladers zoom over the bridge from our vantage point up on the bluff, eating and throwing our crumbs to ducks that became progressively bolder as the afternoon passed. As settings for marriage proposals went, it was absolutely ideal.

Dessert was my cue. I'd brought Mary's favorite chocolate cake from the bakery, but when I brought it out – while the jeweler's box bulged conspicuously in my pocket – I couldn't do it. I couldn't make myself say the words. Mary noticed my sweaty anxiety after a few bites and asked whether I was feeling okay. I lied and said I'd probably had too much sun. We packed up the picnic while I kicked myself, trying to figure out a way to propose now that I'd missed my moment. It wasn't until we were walking back over the bridge that Mary unknowingly handed me a second chance. She stopped, leaned against the railing, and smiled at the small rapids rushing in front of Nicollet Island.

'Isn't that just perfect?' she asked, and even though the question was obviously rhetorical, I seized upon it.

'Not quite.' I dropped the picnic basket, pulled out the ring, and bent to one knee. 'You can make it perfect, though.'

'Oh, my.' She breathed it, I remembered. Her hands came up over her mouth just the way I'd imagined. A few rollerbladers cheered and whistled as they shot past us.

She blushed, dropping her hands, but then abruptly sobered and looked intently into my eyes.

'Are you asking me something?'

'Yes,' I stammered, finally spitting it out. 'Mary Beth Reever, will you marry me?'

'That depends.'

Her answer caught me so off guard, I actually swayed. I remember the ground rising toward me for a second, then my standing awkwardly again, still holding the ring between us.

'Depends on what?'

Every nuance of her answer was still etched in my mind: her solemn tone, the careful set of her features eclipsed by the painfully perfect blue of the sky, the dignity of downtown and the spires of the Hennepin Avenue Bridge on the horizon. Every part of the cityscape seemed to sanctify what came between us right then, more so than even the minister did later at the wedding. He gave us someone else's words to say to each other; these were the vows we found for ourselves.

She asked me, 'Do you want to have children? I can't marry a man who doesn't want to start a family.'

'Yes, I do,' I answered instantly. I did want a family with Mary. She would be an exceptional mother.

A smile broke over her face and tears glistened on her smooth, apple cheeks. 'Yes. Yes, Peter Martin Lund, I'll marry you.'

Six years later she was pregnant. This Mary, who harbored little more than an echo of that glowing girl I'd twirled around on the Stone Arch Bridge, had managed to conceive her child.

I felt sick. The wine I'd drunk with Hattie turned into a pounding headache as I kept walking through downtown Rochester. The sidewalk crowds died down when lunch hour ended, exposing me as an aimless wanderer. I had no destination and was incapable of forcing pretend smiles when strangers extended their Minnesotan niceties at stoplights. After a while, my pace slowed. Then it seemed pointless to continue. I stopped in the middle of a sidewalk, staring at the dirt-smeared puddles eating at the concrete.

I didn't have any choice in the matter, did I? There was no escaping the responsibility of what I had promised.

At the same time I came to that sinking realization – knowing I was stuck in Pine Valley for the rest of my life – a woman talking on her phone walked out of a store, bumped into me, and apologized. I glanced up at the clothes in the store's window display and stopped breathing. The ache in my head swelled to beat the very air around my body. Without the capacity to think beyond it, I went inside and bought the outfit in the window.

I drove to the bank, withdrew the last thousand dollars from my savings account, and took it straight to the Hoffman farm, a place I'd only seen on Google maps before today. The house was sheltered by spruce trees and surrounded by wind turbines dotting the horizon. I couldn't see any of the home's windows and hoped no one was watching me as I placed a plain white envelope addressed to Hattie in the mailbox. Inside, I'd wrapped ten hundred-dollar bills in a note that read: 'Mary's pregnant. Go to New York. Know that I loved you.'

Then I went home to Mary with the outfit from the store – a tiny shirt and pants covered in fuzzy farm animals – lying on the seat next to me.

DEL / *Thursday, April 17, 2008*

TWO HOURS before Hattie's funeral, I walked along the perimeter of the high school checking security at the entrances in my best Sunday suit and a mud-splattered pair of galoshes.

The high school'd canceled classes today, which they probably would have done anyway, but since the Methodist church couldn't fit more than three hundred people, the funeral was set for 11:00 a.m. in the school gymnasium. We were counting on most of the kids, parents, and teachers showing up, the whole church congregation, not to mention Hattie's theater friends from Rochester, both of Mona's and Bud's extended families, and the rest of the town, too. All told, at least a thousand people.

A thick roll of clouds cast the town into a restless gray, but the forecast said no rain, so we likely wouldn't have to deal with road conditions. The boys were well into their assignments. Shel had taken up station at the parking lot entrance to direct traffic and keep things orderly. Jake was on media duty and reported there were already two news vans sniffing up and down Main Street. The rest of the crew was checking out the other locations and keeping an eye on the closed businesses. After the service was over, we had to lead the procession to the cemetery and block off the cross-traffic, escort the family cars back to the fire station hall, where the church ladies would serve lunch, and then direct traffic and keep an eye on things there for the rest of the afternoon. If either of my suspects didn't show up, I'd have to send a man out to locate them. I wasn't letting anybody drop off the radar today. I just hoped to God there wouldn't be any accidents on the highway, because there was no one to spare. Nancy would have to call in the state troopers.

I'd been up since four and spent a good long while deciding whether to wear the uniform or civilian clothes, while the Nguyens' cat looked bored in the living room doorway. I went with the suit and wore my gun and badge underneath the jacket. Jake had enough respect not to say anything about it when we made the call this morning to Dr. Terrance B. Standler, the forensic psychologist Fran had recommended. He answered right away and seemed polite enough, but tried to worm his way out of being helpful.

'Dr. Okada said you have an excellent DNA sample for the perpetrator and two strong candidates.'

'Yeah?'

'I usually reserve my time for cases that are more challenging for local law enforcement.'

Jake had given me a look and mimed a gun at the speaker phone.

'Did you look at the case file or not?' I asked.

'Yes, I have it in front of me.'

'Okay, then tell me if you have any useful information and save the snarky comments for later.'

He sighed.

'As you know, anger and power are the two primary drivers in most run-of-the-mill homicides, and there is evidence of both here. The abrasions of the sexual encounter are certainly power-based, but this is clearly not a case of erotophonophilia.'

'Come again?'

'Lust murder, homicides in which the killing itself is a sexual act. Here we have two separate acts. The sexual encounter, while aggressive, was clearly mutual although somewhat complicated by the presence of the condom. If it was used in this particular sexual encounter, the condom could be either a mark of respect toward the victim or an attempt by the male to keep his DNA off the victim. In any case, after the sex act, the victim got dressed again. There was a clear interlude.'

'Intermission.' Jake muttered.

'Excuse me?' Standler asked.

'Nothing.' I shot Jake a warning look and decided he could use a few extra shifts babysitting the DWI drunks after this case was closed. 'So it's likely they had an argument between the sex and the murder?'

'Yes, there was a decided turning point. The attack itself has a lot of hallmarks of a first-time killer, and first homicides are less likely to be planned. Statistically, we see a significantly greater amount of escalated arguments. Now, the wounds. The initial, fatal stab to the heart indicates strong momentum and precision. Although the attack was probably not premeditated, there is a clear presence of will. The postmortem cuts to the face can be indicative of one or two things. First, there is the spite motive.'

'Spite?' Jake interrupted. 'He'd already killed her. What more could he do to spite her?'

'Facial mutilation is often employed to take a victim's identity away, which – to some killers – is more important than the victim's life. It's an act to demonstrate the killer's power over the victim, that they have obliterated any threat that person posed to them.

Last year I reviewed a case where a beauty queen killed a rival and poured acid on her face. The victim's main source of power over the killer, her flawless face, was taken from her. Spite is a strong motivator, but the second possibility is even more so: fear.'

'Fear of what? Getting caught?'

'Not at this stage. You see the fear of getting caught later, when the killer took the victim's purse and threw it in the lake. No, this is a primal fear, often documented as an immediate first emotion following a murder. It can take the form of facial cuts, covering, or even disposal of the entire body. The killer tries to erase the victim's identity in order to erase the crime itself. It's essentially a remorse action.'

'He killed her and then felt bad about it?'

'I believe so. The sex and stabbing are both indicators of strong swings in emotion. It's possible that the killer's emotions swung back to regret and fear just as quickly. You're looking for a younger, excitable man, someone who may have difficulty fitting in or has a history of volatile relationships, either with the victim or otherwise.'

Jake and I looked at each other, and he tapped his finger on a name on the murder file. I nodded.

Whether or not Standler told us anything new, he'd sound mighty good up on a witness stand. I thanked him and made sure he'd be available to testify when the time came, then Jake and I headed over to the school for funeral duty.

The school maintenance guys and the funeral home staff had already set the place up last night, but the flower deliveries poured in all morning. After I finished the outside security checks, I escorted a couple florists inside the gym and took stock of the place.

The stage from last weekend was gone, broken down and stored away, and they'd pulled out the bleachers like a school assembly and filled most of the floor with chairs. All the floor seats faced a pulpit, mountains of flowers, and dozens of pictures and yearbooks set up at the front of the gym. I walked along the back wall, where students had stretched a paper banner and covered it with memories of Hattie.

She was always smiling.

She helped me with my English paper. A bunch of times.

We got the last season of Sex and the City from my sister. Hattie slept over and we watched it all night and rated the dresses. She thought they were way cuter than I did.

Sharing banana splits at DQ. NO STRAWBERRY SAUCE, PLEASE! Lol

She was such a good listener. (I saw that one over and over again.) *She listened to all my problems and tried to help.*

Hattie really listened to you.

There was a city skyline along the bottom of the paper with a girl stick figure waving from one of the windows.

I didn't notice until I got to the end that someone had hung up Hattie's dress from the play, Lady Macbeth's dress washed clean of the blood bath, white and pristine. It hovered against the wall like a ghost. She'd been wearing it less than a week ago in this same room. I'd been working that night, catching up on the paperwork that never ended when budget cuts knocked you back to just a skeleton crew, but I should've let it wait. I should've come to see her.

The hearse arrived and with it, Bud, Mona, and Greg. They followed the casket into a room off the gym where the family would stay until the service. Greg nodded at me as they passed, looking jet-lagged and rough around the edges. Neither Bud nor Mona glanced up.

Then they came, the whole town in twos and threes, no one walking alone. Winifred Erickson patted my arm as she shuffled in. The Nguyens openly cried and held on to each other. Hushed, angry voices filled the halls and the gym. Brian Haeffner came up, dressed in the string tie and mother-of-pearl clasp that he wore everywhere during election season.

'Del, what's happening? Your press releases don't say shit.'

'It's an ongoing investigation.'

'People are hurting here. They need to know what happened to Hattie.'

I could feel ears perking up all around us, red-rimmed eyes measuring our faces, waiting.

'We don't need anyone to get spooked right now.' I kept my voice down.

His voiced dropped too as he glanced around us. 'Del, this is the kind of case you got to wrap up quick or people will remember at the polls. It was already a slim margin last time on account of your age.'

'I haven't keeled over yet.'

'You might as well if this thing drags out too long.' He caught my look and jumped to defend himself. 'I'm telling you that as a friend. This is a career breaker.'

The last thing I wanted to talk about right now was my career. I gave a curt nod and walked away from my friend, the suit cuffs chafing every time I moved my arms.

I hadn't worn this suit since I bought it for my mom's funeral a few years ago. She'd been active in the church her whole life and everyone showed up to send her off to the pearly gates – including Bud and Mona, standing right by my side. The mood had been solemn, yet satisfied, too, like people knew she'd lived the best life any of us had a right to expect. We told funny stories about her and all sat down to eat and watch my sister's grandkids play tag around the flowers. Then that was that. Death was the end of a cycle that farm folks saw every day. They joked and ribbed each other about most everything else, but when it came to hardship or loss, they endured, without making a big fuss about it. I'd been to more funerals than I cared to count, and eaten so many ham and butter sandwiches I could practically taste the flour-dusted bun when a hearse drove down Main Street, but Hattie's funeral was something else entirely.

Grief and rage rolled off this crowd so strong I could almost smell it. I walked up and down the aisles as people took their seats, feeling eyes on me from all sides. The suit didn't fool anybody. They knew what was on my mind as much as I knew what was on theirs – murder.

I worked my way to the far side of the gym, scanning the crowd for my suspects. Gerald Jones from Rochester caught my eye and nodded. Although the volume in the room was building, I could still hear the two mothers who walked in front of me.

'Took him out of school and brought him down to the station.'

'I heard he was directing the school play that Hattie was in.'

'He was. I was here on Friday night, saw Hattie just a few hours before it happened. I got chills, watching her. And now the papers are talking about a curse.'

'Have you heard what happened at the rehearsal?'

'No, what–?'

The women spotted me and they both hushed and found some seats.

Farther into the room I located Tommy. He sat in the middle of the first row of bleachers that groaned under the weight of the football team. None of them were saying much; they stared at the front of the gym, their unused muscles just waiting to tense. Tommy wore a suit that was too small for him and looked like he wouldn't have heard the halftime horn if you blew it in his ear. His folks sat directly behind him, both of them watching me. I kept walking.

I found Peter Lund high in the farthest section of bleachers. A lot of teachers and school staff sat in the same area, but they'd left a space between him and the rest of them. The closest person to Lund was Carl Jacobs, although the two didn't act like great buddies. Carl folded and unfolded his program while Lund stared into the center of the crowd and seemed oblivious to that deliberate distance between him and the others. He wore a suit, too, and maybe his was snazzier than Tommy's, but he looked just as out of place in it, with bloodshot eyes and at least a day's worth of beard. I didn't see Mary Beth anywhere.

Fear, Standler had said. Fear and remorse drew that blade down Hattie's face, leaving her nothing left to show the world. Which one of them had the rage to kill her and then the gall to feel bad about it in the next breath?

I made my way back out of the gym and alerted the crew, letting them know I'd located both suspects. Then, taking a deep breath and smoothing a hand down my stiff suit, I slipped into the nearby classroom next to the gym, where Hattie lay among her family.

Her casket filled the front of the classroom, with lilies covering its closed lid and masking the horror inside. The preacher stood in front of it with his hands on Bud's and Mona's shoulders. Eyes closed and face up, he prayed.

'Heavenly Father, we know this was not your plan for Hattie. Our sorrow and anger are overwhelming. They choke us. We need your strength, Lord. We need you to help us understand how this could happen. Even though we know she is with You, we cannot contain our bewilderment, our need for justice. Help us get through this day, Lord. Help us put Hattie to rest, even as the sin of retribution burns inside of us.'

He kept on like that as another noise rose in the room – a soft sobbing from all corners. The men tried to hold it in, but the women broke down one by one, their faces in Kleenex, mascara dripping down their cheeks. The only one without his head down was Greg. He wasn't crying like the rest. He stared directly at me and I recognized a soldier poised for battle. He was his father's son, ready to take revenge on his sister's killer, like the preacher's prayer made flesh.

After the Amens I nodded to the funeral director to let him know it was time. I held the door while the pallbearers, Greg at the front, took their stations and carried Hattie out. Bud and Mona were the first to follow, and this time Bud saw me and stopped, holding up the whole procession.

'Del?' he asked, and I knew what he was asking. His face was wet. Mona tightened her grip on his hand.

'I'm so sorry, Bud.'

I put a hand on his shoulder, but he didn't acknowledge it. He breathed out slow, like he was fighting to control something in him that wanted loose and then kept walking, letting my hand fall into the air.

As the rest of the family exited, Jake appeared. He waited until the last of them were well into the gym before giving his report.

'News vans are in a holding pattern. They tried asking me a few questions, all general sniffing around, nothing about either of our boys. Shel's keeping an eye on them while they film their updates for the evening news.'

Piano music drifted down the hallway, followed by a thousand voices echoing off the rafters. I glanced at my program: 'Hymn of Promise.'

'Good.' I cleared my throat. 'Everybody knows their jobs

after the service. I'm going to go inside and keep to the back.
I'll–'

My phone buzzed. I pulled it out and saw a Twin Cities area
code. Jake and I both tensed before I punched the button.

'Goodman.'

'Sheriff Goodman, this is Amanda at the Minneapolis crime
lab. I have the results of your DNA tests for case number 094627.'

Like I had a hundred case numbers pending DNA results. My
pulse leapt as I waited.

'The specimen was an exact match to the second DNA sample,
donor name Peter Lund. I'm emailing the full report to you right
now.'

Son of a bitch. The married teacher.

'Appreciate it.' I hung up before she said anything else and
turned to Jake. 'It's Lund.'

His eyes steeled over and a muscle jumped in his cheek. 'We
don't take him now, do we?'

'And risk a damn lynch mob? Not in front of this crowd or
those news trucks camped outside.' I checked my gun in the shoulder holster. 'I'll show you where he is. After the service you shadow
him. Follow him to his car and then take him in. I'll be along after
I lead the procession back from the cemetery. Too noticeable if I try
to leave before then.'

I gave him Lund's position as we entered the gym, sidling up to
the end of the bleachers. Tommy was still in the front row, but with
everyone standing for the hymn, I couldn't see to the far side of the
room. Even though Jake was taller than me, I could tell he wasn't
having any luck either. The singing seemed to take an age, in verse
after verse they delivered Hattie up to the Lord, their voices a sharp,
grieving thunder that paralyzed us. Finally the song ended and the
crowd sat down. I craned my neck and located Carl Jacobs, sitting
alone in a sea of people.

Lund was gone.

Adrenaline shot through me, feeding my old bones with that familiar surge. The tension rolling off Jake told me he was in the same place. Everything became silent, deliberate. The preacher's voice fell away.

'Make sure,' I muttered and we checked and rechecked the crowd, but there was no trace of him. We left the service and I sent a text to the crew.

> Lund MIA. Exits and perimeter. ID and report only. Do not detain in public area.

Shel replied.

> No one out the front door in the last ten minutes. I've got front and east exits in visual.

We swept the front hallway, restrooms, and staff offices, and then moved toward the classrooms. I motioned Jake to take the upstairs and I stayed on the main level, looking in every room. Lund's classroom, where the principal had escorted me two days ago, was the last door on the right. As I got closer I could hear something – a loud, ragged breath. I unholstered my gun and crept along the wall, then ducked inside the room to see Lund standing at the window with his back to me. I couldn't see his hands.

'Stay right where you are.'

The only sign he heard me was a tremor that ran through his whole body. Chicken shit.

'Peter Lund, you're under arrest for obstruction of justice in the case of the murder of Henrietta Sue Hoffman.' I stepped cautiously forward, keeping the gun trained on his back. 'Hands where I can see them.'

Slowly he raised his arms and turned around. His skin was sallow and sick. He looked like he hadn't slept since Friday night.

'She wouldn't let me end it. She kept pushing and pushing.' The next words were hardly more than a mumble, but they tore into the room like a gunshot.

'She'd still be alive if she would've just let me go.'

PETER / *Thursday, April 17, 2008*

THE SHERIFF wouldn't stop pointing the gun at me. He ordered me to face the wall and put my hands behind my back, just as the younger officer came in and put me in handcuffs. I'd never been in handcuffs before. They were cold.

'Aren't you supposed to read me my rights?'

'I'm figuring the best way to get you back to the station without getting your head blown off by any of those fine folks out there.'

I hadn't thought of that. For two days I'd imagined all the possible scenarios after the DNA test came back. They could have come for me at school or at home. I knew they wouldn't let me drive in on my own, despite the obvious fact that I hadn't skipped town or disappeared from my life. I went to school yesterday, went through the motions of teaching as the entire staff and half the students watched me like I was the worst kind of predator. I sat across from Mary at the dinner table last night while Elsa, oblivious, rambled on about family names and all the possible horrors we might inflict upon our unborn child. Marcy. Etheline. Albus. I stared at the plate and listened for gravel crunching in the driveway, waiting for the swing of headlights through the living room windows. I could even see Sheriff Goodman pulling me aside after the funeral and shoving me in the back of his squad car while news cameras ate up the moment in greedy clicks, but it hadn't occurred to me that I might be shot by one of Hattie's mourners. I don't know why not. It made perfect sense. Winifred Erickson had killed her husband after she got tired of him and never served a day in prison. Of course they'd shoot me.

They decided to take me out the exit behind the cafeteria next to the dumpsters. A high fence gated off the area, trapping the stench of sour milk and mold. The deputy left to pull his cruiser around, leaving me alone with the sheriff. Even with the handcuffs, the smells, and the fury leaking out of the old man's eyes, it was still better than sitting in that gymnasium staring at the box that held Hattie's dead body. The details had spread like wildfire through the school on Monday morning: the stab through her heart, the slashes destroying her face, her body half-submerged in the lake. It was impossible to sit quietly in that room with her body, imagining her terror and her pain. I'd stumbled out of the gym before I broke down completely.

'I didn't kill her.' As the words came out, I wondered why I hadn't said them before.

He looked at me like I was the thing rotting in the dumpster. Then he read me my rights.

The deputy pulled up and they put me in the back of the squad car.

'Book him and let him sweat.' The sheriff slammed the door. 'I'll be along as soon as we get the procession back from the cemetery.'

The deputy nodded and pulled out of the alley slowly, like he'd been checking security around the building. Three media vans were parked on the street with cameramen and reporters milling in front of them.

As we pulled out of the parking lot, the reporters spotted me and suddenly cameras flashed and bodies swarmed closer to the car. I sat woodenly, indifferent to what any of this would mean for my life.

'Hmm, I guess the secret's out. Smile pretty.' He eased out into the street.

'I didn't kill Hattie.'

'Good one. Next you're going to tell me you don't fuck your underage students, either.'

She wasn't underage – I bit back the impulse before I could say it. He laughed low and mean at my silence as we cruised the few blocks down Main Street.

'Not going to bother denying that one, are you? Now shut up and don't give me any excuses.'

At the station he hauled me through fingerprinting and photos and shoved me in the first of three empty cells in the back room. Then everything was quiet.

There were actually bars on the cells. It seemed so clichéd. I paced and, without even trying, the list of names started forming – William Sydney Porter, Ken Kesey, Paul Verlaine, every Russian writer ever – and the discussion questions rose to frame them. How did time spent in prison inform their work? Compare and contrast the societal pressures against Oscar Wilde versus Solzhenitsyn. I could even see the handout I would type up and distribute to the students along the front row, igniting that flush of anticipation in Hattie's complexion. She would read every excerpt by the next class and then she'd insist–

Hysterical laughter dropped me to the cot and turned into a half-bellow. I covered my face and strangled the sound so the deputy wouldn't come back and threaten to beat the shit out of me for something I hadn't done.

I did not kill Hattie Hoffman.

She had killed me, in so many ways, over months of guilt and obsession and need. She had taken everything I thought I was and destroyed it with a coy wink in the middle of a chaotic classroom. When I'd met Hattie in the barn on Friday night, I let her demolish me. I gave in to screaming temptation and lost myself in her, rejected every responsibility, corrupted every decency for the chance to fly away with her, to attach myself like a barnacle to her shooting star. I made love to her. I kissed her goodbye and went home. I did not kill her.

But who had?

For the last five days it had consumed me, imagining her ending, her brazen heart breaking open and spilling on to those coarse, cold planks. Tommy. Tommy, was all I could think. That hulking arm always wrapped over her shoulders like she was some prized football trophy. The baby fat that still clung to his giant frame, his sudden shouts in the lunchroom, the fanaticism on his face during pep rallies. I'd watched him closer than he could've ever imagined, the secret lover stalking the public one. She'd wanted to torment me with him, and God, she had. He must have followed her there. It had to be Tommy.

That's why I kept going to school – to watch him, to see if his guilt would manifest in some physical way – but he hadn't been in class all week and I hadn't been able to confront him today in the overwhelming crowd. I needed to see his eyes when he looked at me. If he'd seen us together, if he'd killed her for it, I knew he couldn't hide it from me in those big, dumb eyes.

I paced the cell, a ten-foot length that made my legs stiff with the need to stretch, to run, and waited for the sheriff to finish burying Hattie.

At least two hours passed before the deputy came back. He brought me to the same conference room from two days ago, although this time I noticed recording equipment had been brought in.

'I want my phone call.'

He ignored me, so I repeated myself.

'You'll get it,' the sheriff answered as he strolled in. The suit from the funeral was gone, replaced by his uniform.

'Mary Beth already phoned here, if that's who you were going to call. Everybody else on the planet is calling, too. Some of those news vans are sitting right out there.' He pointed at the door.

'I didn't murder Hattie.'

'That's not what we're here to talk about.' He sat down across the table and fixed a piercing stare on me.

'Yes, okay, obviously I was having an affair with her. It was stupid and wrong. Believe me, I know how wrong it was, but I genuinely loved her. I could never have hurt her, much less stab her to death in cold blood.'

'We'll get there, lover boy.' The sheriff leaned back and crossed his arms. 'When did it start?'

I told him everything; how Hattie kept pursuing me after I'd found out who she was, how she started dating Tommy as a cover, the notes on her assignments, the trip to Minneapolis and every meeting after that. It was a relief to admit it, finally to be free of this secret that had hung over my life for the last half year. I told him how I found out Mary was pregnant from our only sex in months, how I'd ended the affair and withdrawn the last of my savings, hoping Hattie would use the money to go to New York.

'I wanted her to leave. I couldn't bear seeing her and didn't want her to have to see Mary pregnant.'

'Wouldn't want her to talk to Mary, you mean.' He hadn't said much throughout the entire story up to this point.

'No. I mean, yes, but I was thinking mostly of Hattie. I didn't want to cause her more pain.' I dropped my head. 'I took her innocence. I know I did. I thought the least I could do was help her realize her dream. I knew she'd find someone in New York who would make her happy and she'd forget about me.'

'That's a nice little story you've got there. I'm sure your lawyer will love it.' He checked a piece of paper in one of his files. 'Now, I've got one last pesky question for you. That envelope showed up on March twenty-first, three weeks before she died, when you wished her well and sent her on her way, so how is it that we've got your semen inside of her on the night of her death?'

'Friday . . .' I began, and took a deep breath. The sheriff leaned in.

'After the play, what happened?'

'I did go to Carl's, like I told you. We had a drink, but afterwards I went to meet Hattie at the Erickson barn.'

'Thought you said you ended the relationship.'

'I did. I mean, I tried—'

'You lie to me one more time and I will have your balls. Do you understand me?'

A muscle twitched in his jaw and his voice was like shards of gravel. I nodded.

'Good. What time did you get to the barn?'

'After ten. I dropped my car off at the farm and walked over. Maybe closer to ten thirty.'

'And then?'

I laid my hands deliberately on the table and tried to gather my thoughts. 'She wanted to give me my money back, she said. When I got there, though, I found out she'd already spent it. I didn't know that until after . . .'

'After you had sex with her?'

I had a sudden moment of clarity, a premonition of how this interview was going to proceed, and saw exactly how guilty it would make me look. Hattie had told me about the money. She told me and then she threatened me.

'I want a lawyer.'

———◆———

The sheriff didn't seem surprised by my request to invoke my Miranda rights. He'd switched off the recording equipment and tossed me in the cell with hardly a word. While I waited for the county defender to show up, the deputy led Mary back into the holding area.

'You've got ten minutes. Don't touch the bars. Don't try to hand him anything. I'll be watching.' The deputy nodded to the security camera and set a chair down for her before leaving again. Mary rested a hand lightly on her stomach. She must have played the pregnancy card.

She sat down and glanced around the room, her eyes flitting everywhere except to me. Eventually they settled on the security camera and she stared intently at its red blinking eye.

'I told Mom I was going to the grocery store,' she said to the camera.

'Mary.'

'She asked for peaches. She's been wanting peaches all week and they're eight months out of season. It doesn't matter, though.' Her head dropped. 'She won't remember that she asked for them by the time I get home.'

I swallowed. The weight of Mary's life smothered the already oppressive room. 'Aren't you going to ask me why I'm in here?'

'They told me.' She said it to her lap, while her hand made small, deliberate circles on her abdomen. 'They said you were here for lying. It's nice to know that lying is a crime, at least sometimes.'

'They think I killed her.' I tried to talk low, casting a glance toward the door and then the camera. They were probably listening to every word.

'Because you were sleeping with her.'

Shock jolted through me. There was no change in her tone or expression, no indication that she had any feelings one way or the other about the matter, except for the fact that she finally lifted her head and pinned me with her clear, passive gaze.

'They must know that by now,' she added, waiting for my reply.

I had no idea how to respond. *I'm sorry* came to mind, but it was ludicrous, unimaginable. Apologies were for spilled drinks and bumps in the hallway; they were the courtesies of people whose lives progressed along predictable, uncomplicated arcs. *I'm sorry* had no place between us anymore.

'How did you find out?' I asked.

She didn't answer right away. Instead, she got up and went to the door, peeking through its lead-glass window. After a moment, she came back to the bars and stood opposite me.

'I never imagined I'd raise the child of a murderer.'

'I'm not a murderer. I didn't kill Hattie. Christ, I couldn't even kill a chicken.'

She ignored me and spoke again in that eerie, passive voice.

'I don't know why I brought the knife.'

The words were so soft I almost didn't hear them. Then I was sure I heard wrong. The blood in my head started pounding and I lurched forward. She automatically stepped back, turning away.

'What did you say? Mary, look at me.'

She wouldn't. Her profile was stark, emotionless except for her concentration on the memory.

'I heard you drive up on Friday. I was in the barn, cleaning the knives. Always maintain your tools, Dad used to say. Clean them and put them away. I looked out and saw you walking away

270

from the house. I followed you. I didn't realize I was still holding the knife I'd been sharpening until we were crossing the Erickson woods. By then I'd figured out where you were going. And when I got there, I saw why.'

A dread too awful to name filled my chest. It was worse than when I'd first heard a body was discovered in the barn, worse than when Hattie hadn't shown up to Saturday's performance and I was seized with the knowledge of her death, worse even than when I thought Tommy had murdered her. Good God, it was Mary? The horror curdled in my stomach and broke over my skin in a clammy sweat.

'Mary . . .' I choked on her name. 'What did you do?'

She looked back at me and there were angry tears in her eyes now, but not a drop fell.

'I saw you with her, Peter. I saw how she looked at you like you were hers.' The anger flashed and smoldered. Her hand pressed tight on her stomach. 'How could you do it? After I'd worked so hard to build something here. Did you think you could hide it? That I wouldn't find out in my own hometown?'

I stared at the bloodless fingers of her hand, like she was shielding her long-awaited baby from this conversation and all of its consequences for our lives to come. What would she do to keep it safe? To protect her family? I'd seen that hand do things I'd never imagined possible; I'd watched it slice through the throats of chickens and calmly hang their bodies upside down to drain their blood. She was pregnant, more emotional than I'd imagined possible. The rage seemed to burn right out of her. Oh, God.

'Mary, what did you do? Answer me.' I gripped the bars, desperate

'You know exactly what I did. How can you ask me that?' The tears finally spilled over, glittering dangerously on her cheeks. 'And I'm telling the sheriff everything.'

'Everything?'

'I'm going to walk out of this room and tell him I saw you together that night. That I dropped the knife outside the barn, ran
home in shock, and haven't seen that knife since.'

'What?' I didn't understand. She was going to lie?

The deputy hovered at the doorway, talking over his shoulder
to someone. He was coming in any second. This could be my only
chance to find out the truth, but Mary didn't even seem to hear me.
She was seething now, months of silent rage finally overflowing and
finding purchase inside these concrete and steel walls.

'No matter what happens, no matter what you do or don't say
in here, I'm keeping the baby. And you will never, ever see it. I won't
even put your name on the birth certificate.'

'Jesus Christ, how are you going to raise a child in prison?'

'Me?' She spit it out just as the deputy opened the door and
walked in between us.

'Time's up.'

Neither of us moved for a second, our eyes locked on each other
for what might have been the last time.

'Ma'am?' The deputy put a hand out.

'No matter what happens,' she said again, just as the deputy
pulled her away and shut the door, leaving me alone and shaking
against the bars.

It felt like a long time before the sheriff came and got me, time
enough for one life to end and something else, something much
less lifelike, to begin. I sat on the cot with my head buried in my
hands, unable to erase the image of Mary's hate-riddled face, her
revelation, and her vow. She was telling the sheriff she dropped
the knife and left – an obvious lie from someone who had motive,
opportunity, a murder weapon, no alibi – and she was admitting
all this for what?

To put the knife in my hand.

It was the only possible explanation and I couldn't even work up any anger about it. Maybe part of her even believed it, that I was the one truly responsible for this nightmare.

I imagined our baby in foster care while I tried to prove paternity to the courts and the shitty father I would undoubtedly be if I managed to get custody. I cried. I cried for the unwanted child of a lost marriage, for the life I had thrown away like garbage and the one I almost tasted before it was ripped away, even for the world Mary had fought to create, her savage phoenix struggling to rise out of the fields of the dead. And I cried for Hattie, knowing now, absolutely, that I had caused her death. Because of me, because I had been too weak to resist, she would never become any of the thousand people that had been quickening inside her.

Eventually the tears ended and a numbing calm seeped in. There was, at last, lucidity as a final choice unfolded before me. I had all the details I needed to know, thanks to Pine Valley: the crime scene had been recounted all over the school; the purse, Winifred told Elsa, had been pulled from the lake; and if none of that convinced them, I still had a final piece of evidence they didn't even know existed, the coup de grâce.

After months of indecency, shame, and guilt, I felt an almost strangled joy when I realized I had this last chance to do something good. The child would be fine. This town would embrace it and Mary and take them for their own. My name would never be spoken to them. Walking slowly around the cell, I took deep breaths, filling my lungs to the bottom and feeling their elasticity, their wondrous capacity. This could easily have been Sydney Carton's state of mind as the wagon carried him to his fate.

Later, when the sheriff opened the door, I stood calmly in the middle of the cell, hands at my sides, waiting. A stranger hovered just behind, a fat, hesitant young man that Hattie could've wrapped around her finger with a wink and a glance.

The sheriff nodded. 'Your lawyer.'

'Good.' I looked straight at the sheriff. 'I need to make a confession.'

HATTIE / *Saturday, March 22, 2008*

PORTIA WAS royally pissed off by the time she dropped me at home. I didn't care. After the last day and a half, I had zero ability to listen to every stupid detail of her choir trip. I had threatened Peter, cried on my mom's shoulder, gotten Peter's hush money and breakup bombshell, run away to Minneapolis, almost gotten arrested by Homeland Security, had my truck die, and puked in a field. Her *unbelievable* chicken Caesar salad by the Country Music Hall of Fame? Sorry, Porsche. Not in my top ten right now.

She did take me into Rochester, though, and waited at the mall while I bought what I needed and stowed my new suitcase. I used one of Peter's hundred-dollar bills to buy her a thank-you shirt and I also found a dress, the perfect dress, a dress that made me want to twirl and dance and start my new life. I was done wearing costumes.

When Portia pulled into my driveway, I was surprised to see Tommy parked next to the house. He had his hands shoved in his pockets and was leaning on the hood of his pickup while talking to Dad. They both looked over when I jumped out of the car.

'Thanks, Porsche!'

'Whatever.' She rolled her eyes and started backing her car up before I'd even slammed the door. It was strange, knowing she was angry and not trying to deflect or spin it the way I usually did, but the real Hattie Hoffman had just stood up, in a big way, and I wasn't about to sit back down anymore.

I took a deep breath and walked over to Tommy and Dad.

'Where's your truck?' was Dad's first question.

'Broken,' I replied, grinning. I told them what happened and maybe I snuck in a few innocent lies about the specific chain of events, but that part wasn't important. They both grilled me on the exact noises and symptoms of the truck and decided the alternator might be the problem.

'I just replaced mine, same time I changed out the rims.' Tommy kicked his tire affectionately. 'I could help you tow it back and take a look at it.'

'Sounds good,' Dad started to say until I cut him off.

'No, don't worry about it, Tommy. I'm sure you've got plans.'

He looked at me like I was mental. 'I thought we were going to watch the UFC fight at Derek's house. Everyone's going, remember?'

'Right.' I'd completely forgotten. We'd talked about it on Tuesday, which seemed like a lifetime ago. 'I don't think I can go. I'm still not ready for the play and I'm kind of freaking out about it. After Dad and I bring the truck back, I'm going to run lines.'

Tommy started to look like he was going to argue, so I gave him an awkward hug. 'You should totally go. Tell Derek I'm sorry to miss it.'

After Tommy stuttered around a little, he eventually climbed into his truck and gunned it out of the driveway. Dad just kind of looked at me and I shrugged and said, 'UFC sucks,' which wasn't a lie at all.

He laughed, one of those big belly laughs that I've always loved, and we went to pick up my dead truck.

'Haven't seen you much lately, kid,' Dad said as we pulled on to the highway.

'There's been way too much going on.' Again, not lying.

'Tommy bugging you?'

I shrugged. 'He's a high school boy. I don't think he can help it.'

He laughed again and we fought over the radio station for a while, a loud, bickering tradition we both loved. I told him where the truck was and when we got there we worked together to hook it up. If I'd been born in the city like Peter, I probably wouldn't know how to connect a tow rope, or put boards down to haul a tractor out of the mud, or anything like that. They weren't things I could brag about when I got to New York, but it made me happy right now, knowing I could do my share, that Dad didn't need Greg or Tommy to help him. I'd made this mess and I was helping clean it up.

When we got back home I stayed out in the garage with Dad, handing him tools and pointing the light. I loved my father. I loved how he said everything with a joke lurking right behind the words, how he liked to be argued with, how he seemed so solid and good. He would stick out like a sore thumb in New York City, but maybe I could bring a piece of him with me. Maybe I would be half him after all.

As March turned into April, school became harder. That conquer-the-world feeling wore off after a few days and I had to work not to slip into old habits. Portia gradually started talking to me again, although she still acted put out every time I didn't instantly agree with her about something. I admitted to my teachers when I hadn't done the assigned readings and even got a detention when I freely confessed to skipping class because I thought math was not worth my time.

When I got pulled into the guidance counselor's office, her desperate last attempt to get me to consider college, I told her I had no idea what I wanted to do with my life, that I was almost as scared as I was excited to move to New York, and that I was going to give myself a year to figure it out or start thinking about East Coast schools. She looked at me, sighed, and said, 'That's the most sensible thing you've ever said.'

At night I recorded everything on Gerald's camcorder. I told it the story of my life, pathetic as it was, every stupid, crazy, awful thing I had done and it felt good – being honest at last – even if it was only with myself.

But the worst part of my new life was forcing myself to sit in Peter's class every day, trying not to cry every time he glanced in my direction. I couldn't help noticing, though, that he looked terrible. His color was pale. His usually clean-shaven jaw carried a shadow of beard most days, and then razor marks where he'd been careless when he did shave. His clothes looked wrinkled and his lectures were fumbling and depressed.

Portia noticed my bleak stare and mistook it for boredom.

'He's really off his game,' she commented as we left class on the day of the dress rehearsal. 'It's the curse. It's catching up with him.'

I glanced back to see Peter staring sadly out the window. 'You know what, Porsche? You're probably right.'

We sat together in physics, neither of us bothering to take notes. Portia doodled a series of drunk cows on her notebook – her witty nod to her parents' customers at the liquor store. I looked at my own blank notebook page for half an hour, wondering stupid things like why they punched three holes in it and not four, what Peter's kid would be like, and if they'd still use notebooks by the time he or she went to school.

Every time Peter looked at this kid, he was going to see a prison, the thing that had made him give up any chance of happiness with me. God, was this how people were made? Was the whole planet full of cheaters and assholes running around making new cheaters and assholes? I had been one of them, too, the worst one of all. Mom warned me that I had a lot to learn about the world. I wished she would've mentioned how much the learning was going to hurt.

'I hope you're going to have some respect for the curse tonight,' Portia said as we walked into the cafeteria for lunch. 'This is our last run before opening night. We can't have any slip-ups.'

'Whatever.' I headed for the football players' table, not even bothering to get food. Some of the guys on the far end were telling a story that involved milk cartons for props, but Tommy let his attention lapse long enough to pat me on the leg and smile when I sat down next to him. I'd stopped seeing him outside of school, trying to gradually distance myself until it would feel natural to break up. I didn't want to hurt him more than I had to.

I watched Portia get her lunch and pause at a table to talk to one of the guys from the lighting crew. For the last few weeks Peter had been completely phoning it in at rehearsals. He didn't act openly miserable, but the depression was just under the surface and everyone noticed it. Portia started taking over for him on stuff like costumes and the set construction. She'd become the unofficial director at this point and we all knew it, even Peter, because he'd started asking her opinion on certain scenes in our last few rehearsals.

When she finally sat down at the table, she started right in on famous female directors – which ones she liked and how underrepresented women were in the profession.

'It's not like a complete boy's club,' she said between bites of bread stick. 'There're plenty of female role models. Penny Marshall is the box office queen, but I think Sofia Coppola really sets the style for the next generation of filmmakers.'

Even though I wanted to roll my eyes about her sudden career obsession, it was actually a good fit for her. Portia'd successfully directed the rumor mill for years. Maybe that's why we'd been such good friends: she'd been my director and I'd been her actor.

'You gonna make movies, Portia?' Tommy asked.

'Yeah. The U doesn't have a great film program, but it's not a bad place to start.' Portia talked to the table near Tommy's hands. She never looked directly at him.

'You should put Hattie in your movies. She can be your star.' He flung an arm around my waist and drew me closer on the bench.

Portia smirked at me. 'She's welcome to audition.'

'Hey, let's get together tonight, since you're going to be busy this weekend with the play.' Tommy's fingers clung to my ribs, like he was scared to lose his grip on me. He'd definitely noticed my avoidance of him outside school and was in denial.

'I'm busy tonight with the play, too.'

'It's the dress rehearsal,' Portia added.

'That's not going to take all night, is it? I'll pick you up after-wards. Some of the guys are getting together at Derek's. We're going to figure out plans for the cabin this summer.'

He'd been bringing this up a lot lately – some annual trip to a cabin up north where kegs, bonfires, drunken streaking, and loose girlfriends were the norm.

'I told you I don't know if I can get off work for that.'

I tried to put some space between us, automatically glancing toward the corner table where Peter sat with Mr. Jacobs. He had a book open where his lunch should have been and his head in his hand, but he wasn't reading the book. He was staring at me. As soon as our eyes met, he dropped his gaze and turned a page.

Oh, God, I still loved him. Despite everything, despite his preg-nant wife, despite the fact that in a few weeks I might leave and never see him again, I still loved him with everything I was. Even the pain was all mixed up with love inside me.

For the first time, I didn't want to use Tommy to make Peter jealous. And I didn't think I could use Tommy to make me feel better, either, even though he had grown on me over the last months. He was sweet and simple, trying to plan these high school trips for us, always talking about going to the U and how much I would like it there. In his eyes, the future was all mapped out. I always knew what he was thinking and what he would say next, and he loved everything about me. He reminded me of a dog again, one that kept following me around and wagging its tail no matter what I did. But you can't have a relationship with a dog.

'Well, you're not working after the rehearsal tonight, right?' Tommy asked, still hopeful. 'Come to Derek's and you'll see how awesome the cabin is going to be.'

'I don't know how late it's going to go.'

He looked so disappointed that I couldn't help adding, 'You can come see me tomorrow on opening night.'

He groaned. 'Boring.'

'You'll love it. There's witches and sword fights and severed heads. Blood everywhere.' I was being totally honest. Tommy seriously loved horror movies.

'Are you the innocent, screaming girl?' He laughed, completely forgetting he'd run lines with me only a few weeks ago.

'No.' I patted his hand and moved it off my waist. 'I make the blood run.'

After school I put on my costume, which was just a simple white sheath. I thought it looked too Greek, but Christy Sorenson was in charge of costumes and she didn't want to hear it. They'd made them in Family and Consumer Science and had to sew four sets each, one for each performance and an extra for the dress rehearsal, because we were basically going to ruin them each night. After Macbeth murdered the king, he and I put our crowns on, but then before every scene we had to drizzle more and more red corn syrup on our shoulders, like the witches were making the crowns bleed. That was Peter's idea. He told us, back when we were deciding set design and interpretation, that you had to make Shakespeare visual. Most people couldn't follow iambic pentameter very well, but everyone knew what a knife meant when you pulled it out. So the whole play was heavy on stage direction and gestures. There was a lot of sword waving, which the guys loved. Obviously.

Portia gathered everyone together in front of the stage after we dressed and then physically hauled Peter over by the elbow. She shoved him next to me, completely exasperated.

'Um, okay everyone.' He looked around at all our faces except mine. I hoped I wasn't as flushed as I felt with him standing so close.

'Hold hands, everybody,' Portia directed from Peter's other side, grabbing her neighbors' hands. 'We have to form the power circle.'

Everyone thinned out into a big circle and connected up, until Peter and I were the last ones apart. He slipped my hand into his before it became awkward and held it gingerly.

'You've all worked so hard,' he began slowly, clearing his throat. 'Look at this set,' he said. Everyone turned and admired it.

'It's on par with anything I've seen at the smaller professional theaters in the cities. Great construction, guys. And the costumes. Christy, they're exactly how I imagined them. Clean lines, timeless. Beautiful job. The lights and sound are all a go, mainly because Portia's been riding the crew like Peter Jackson. Thanks, Porsche.'

I started. I couldn't help it, hearing him use my name for Portia like that. It rolled so easily off his tongue as he warmed up to the speech, and I remembered the times I'd rambled on about my best friend to him, all the things he knew about her that he had no right to know. How she craved drama. How she hid shirtless pictures of Ryan Gosling in her nightstand. How she hated that her parents made her speak Hmong during Sunday dinners. How she wanted so badly to fit in and stand out at the same time.

No one else seemed to notice his slip. Everyone laughed and grinned at Portia, who beamed.

Peter continued, using his full-on teacher voice now. 'This isn't a happy play, but it's an important one. Here we see Shakespeare looking deep into one man's soul after he murders his king. He's not an evil man. Evil is simple. It's a child's explanation for why people do bad things. The truth is always more complicated and worth pursuing. Shakespeare pursued the truth in this play. Of course, he threw in the witches and the bloodbaths to boost ratings' – everyone laughed except me – 'but at its heart, this is a psychological study. Why would a man commit a terrible crime, something he knew was wrong even before he did it?'

My palm started to sweat. Gradually, so slowly that I didn't even notice it at first, his hold on my hand grew tighter.

'Ambition,' Portia answered.

'The witches told him he'd be king,' added Emily, who played the Second Witch.

'His wife made him do it,' said Adam, who played Macbeth. I stuck out my tongue at him, and he winked back.

'You're all correct,' Peter answered, 'but the underlying theme is desire. What happens to him – what could happen to any of us? – if we pursue our darkest desires? What do we lose of ourselves when we cross that line? What does it cost those around us?'

His fingers squeezed mine.

'Macb – MacBee,' Peter amended, drawing a gleeful smile

from Portia, 'crossed that line anyway. He took what he wanted, regardless of the consequences, regardless of society's conventions, of the mental anguish, or even of his own life. That's what makes this play so timeless. He's just an ordinary man who understands, I believe, at least in part, what his temptation will cost him, and he succumbs anyway.

'This is what you'll show our audience this weekend: the consequences of a man's ugliest and most powerful desires. After all the work everyone has put in, I know you're going to crush it. You'll have no mercy on this poor bastard's soul.'

Everyone broke apart and clapped and cheered. I didn't move. I didn't know what to do. I just stood there, not looking at Peter, while the rest of the cast and crew yelled. He gave my hand one last lingering squeeze and then walked away. I turned and slipped backstage, waiting numbly for Act 1, scene 5, when I would make my entrance.

Even though it didn't go perfectly, the dress rehearsal was pretty good. One of the thugs dropped his sword at one point, right when he was supposed to be killing Banquo. Banquo laughed, but then the thug pretended to snap his neck and Banquo obediently fell over dead.

Adam had his lines down and worked up some pretty good emotion during the monologues. Some of the cast hadn't liked that he looked so babyish, but I did, because it helped me appear like I was manipulating him to commit the murder in the first place. I was almost a foot taller than him in my heels and I really laid on the power in our first scene where we plan the murder. Harsh, high tones. Severe expressions.

My best performance, though, was the sleepwalker scene, my last scene. The crown slipped sideways in my hair and my dress was almost completely red down the front. I looked more like the murder victim than the murderer now, which was the whole point.

Our treachery was killing us. I paced upstage in agony, holding my hands in front of me like I couldn't figure out how they were connected to the rest of my body. I stared blindly into the gymnasium walls and over the space where the heads of the audience would be, where Peter sat by himself in the dark. I didn't even realize I was crying until the room blurred. I poured my heartache into the scene. In rehearsals I had played this act just as strong as the waking scenes, shouting sleeping instructions to myself to shake off the murder.

'Wash your hands, put on your nightgown, look not so pale!'

But now my lines hinted at desperation, like I knew I was heading over the abyss into madness and could not understand the fall. My voice trembled, threatened to break.

'I tell you yet again, Banquo's buried. He cannot come out on's grave.'

If Lady Macbeth had been frightening in her cold, murderous calculations, now her unconscious confession was shocking. From the very first read, I'd seen her as a strong villain, a Cruella de Vil with no heart or conscience. The sleepwalking scene was just a hiccup, I thought. Now, though, I saw how it revealed everything. She was as tormented as Macbeth: her desire was her undoing. After my final exit, I went directly to the greenroom and sat in a daze for the rest of the play.

I had to keep Peter in my life. I had to. New life or old life, it wouldn't matter without him. My desire was my undoing – I knew it and I still couldn't turn away. We wanted each other beyond all reason or caution, regardless of the consequences, just like he'd said in the power circle speech. I had to find a way to talk to him.

After the last scene, I heard everyone applauding and walked back out to the gym, my mind racing.

'Where did you go? I've been looking everywhere for you,' Portia said, running up to me.

I looked at her and suddenly smiled from ear to ear.

'Macbeth!'

I yelled it again and again, laughing at Portia's horrified glare, at everyone who ran desperately to the doors. They all left the gymnasium and I could hear the trample of the crowd as they made the long circle around the halls outside. A single, abandoned spotlight lit the stage and Peter stood on the opposite side of it from me. Our eyes struggled through the light and we stepped forward to the edges of the shadows.

'I still have your money.' I said the first thing that came to mind, even though it was a lie.

'Hattie, please,' he whispered.

'I want to give it back to you.'

'I don't want it.'

The thunder of feet got louder. They were past the halfway point.

'Tomorrow night. After the play. Meet me at the barn.'

I could hardly see his face through the spotlight. He moved forward slightly, revealing only the curve of his head, the rising of his chest and the uncertainty of his stance. Mirroring him, I took a step closer, feeling the kiss of the light touch my lips. It connected us, heated us.

'I can't,' he said.

'You have to. You have to say goodbye.'

'It's impossible. Don't ask me to.'

The feet stopped outside the double doors and there was a muffled chant, a sonnet they'd all memorized to banish the evil I'd invoked.

'I'll wait all night, Peter. All night for you.' I couldn't hide the longing in my voice. 'Come get your money and say goodbye.'

The doors burst open just as Peter turned away and the noise of everyone drowned out anything he might have said in reply.

DEL / *Thursday, April 17, 2008*

I CHARGED Peter Lund with the murder of Henrietta Sue Hoffman at 3:02 p.m. on the day of her funeral.

It didn't sit right with me, him confessing right after Mary Beth came to visit. She went in to see her husband, then calmly gave us a sworn deposition that she'd followed Peter to the rendezvous, seen Peter and Hattie together, dropped the knife, and left. She described the dimensions of the murder weapon perfectly.

'Why did you keep this to yourself for six days?' I pressed. 'Why didn't you say anything when I was over at the farm?'

Mary Beth smoothed one hand over her stomach. 'I had a lot to come to terms with, Sheriff. I'd just found out my husband was cheating on me and our unborn child. I hadn't thought him capable of that, let alone murder.'

'You were talking murder with Winifred Erickson that day. Don't tell me it was about chickens.'

She nodded, dropping her head. 'You're right. I'm sorry I lied to you about that. We were talking about abortion.'

'Why did you lie?'

'I was ashamed, I guess. I didn't know if I should have this baby, considering.'

Jake and I exchanged a glance and I leaned in, waiting for Mary Beth to raise her head and meet my eyes. When she did, I took off the gloves.

'Maybe you did some considering on Friday night when you saw the two of them together. Maybe you took some revenge on your cheating husband.'

'I didn't.' She hardly seemed bothered by the accusation, let alone surprised. 'If I was going to kill anyone that night, it would have been him, not her.'

Jake's eyes widened a bit.

'So what you're saying is you've been thinking about killing your husband and your baby in the last week, but you didn't have anything to do with Hattie's death.'

'That's right.'

I stared at her and she stared right back. Eventually she nodded her head a little, like she'd just told herself something important, and said, 'If you'd had the week I've had, you would've thought the same things.'

'What did you do after you dropped the knife?'

'I ran home. I remember it was cold, but that's about all. When I got back, I turned the lights off in the barn and went into the house. I thought about sitting up and confronting Peter when he got home, but in the end I didn't even want to look at him. I slept on the cot in Mom's room instead.'

'You went home and immediately fell asleep? After seeing what you saw?'

'Not right away. I cried for a while, soft, so Mom wouldn't

hear. I figured I'd be up all night, but the next thing I knew it was dawn. I guess the baby made me tired – I've even been napping in the afternoons lately. On Saturday I was trying to figure out how to confront him, whether I was going to kick him out right away or what, when Winifred came over to tell us about the body.'

'What was Peter's reaction to the news?'

She shrugged. 'He was already up at school for the Saturday performance.'

I went through the whole night with her again and her story didn't waver. She was somber, dry-eyed, and pale, answering questions directly without fuss or too much explanation. Jake and I stepped out after another half hour.

'I don't know, Del.' He wiped a hand over his mouth, avoiding the eyes of everyone else who'd come back to the station after the funeral. The phones were still ringing off the hooks.

I sighed. 'We've got nothing to hold her with at the moment. Right now all we can prove is she supplied the murder weapon that we don't have. We'll have to wait until Lund's DA shows up to get his story and go from there.'

I walked Mary Beth out myself to make sure the reporters kept their distance. Cameras flashed from the other side of the parking lot, but no one came up to harass her. They probably didn't know she was our suspect's wife.

'What'd you decide about the baby?' I asked as she opened her truck door.

She seemed distracted by the reporters, then shook herself and climbed up into the dusty cab. 'Women use sperm donors all the time.'

'You know, Mary Beth, when your parents had you, it was like they'd gotten a second life.'

Her face seemed frozen, waiting.

I glanced at her stomach. 'Maybe it'll be the same for you.'

For the first time since she walked into the conference room she looked like she might cry. She closed her eyes and nodded and said she hoped so, before closing the door and driving away.

The DA, such as he was, arrived over an hour later. Jake had gone out to get Dairy Queen for everyone, but I couldn't eat. I drank a quart of coffee and did some paperwork, warning Nancy not to disturb me until the lawyer showed up. When he did, looking about twelve years old and nervous as hell, Jake and I took him back to introduce him to his client. Then Lund cold-cocked us all with his announcement that he wanted to confess to murder.

Jake was excited, I could tell, but I couldn't quite latch on to the feeling. Lund had gone from swearing up and down he hadn't killed Hattie when we arrested him to coolly confessing that he had, less than two hours later. I pulled him and his lawyer into the conference room and grilled him on the details.

'How did you get the knife?'

'It was lying right outside the door.' He spoke quietly to the table, not looking at a single person.

'I was trying to leave after we had sex. I thought it was just one last time and that she would give me my money back like she promised, but she said she'd already spent it. Then she threatened me. She said she was going to tell the guidance counselor at school about us if I didn't agree to go away with her. I saw the knife and picked it up.'

'And then what?'

He closed his eyes. Everyone inside the room was absolutely silent, even the lawyer.

'I was just going to scare her with it. I didn't plan to hurt her, but she kept insisting that I leave Mary and go with her to New

York. I just wanted her to go away. I wanted my life back, before any of this had happened. Before her. Before I moved to this god-forsaken town. I backed her into the corner and pointed the knife at her, told her to leave me and my family alone. She . . . she started laughing and I just snapped. I stabbed her.'

'Where?'

It took him another minute to answer, but when he did his voice was the same. Soft. Emotionless.

'In the chest. She fell over.'

'And then what did you do?'

'I slashed her face. I didn't want to see her dead face looking at me. I wanted to make it go away.'

That fit with the remorse bit the profiler talked about and was consistent with the wounds.

'What did you do with the knife?'

'I threw it in the lake along with her purse. Then I went home and burned my clothes and took a shower.'

'Where did you burn your clothes?'

'In the fire pit behind the garage. I used lighter fluid and made sure all the ashes had scattered.'

'Did your wife or your mother-in-law see you come home?'

'No.' He paused and swallowed. 'I didn't see anyone. I went straight to my room – the office, I mean – and stayed there for the rest of the night. I couldn't sleep. I was thinking about . . . the future.'

I rubbed my chin and leaned back in the chair. Lund's head hung from his body like some useless, dead weight and he sat abso-lutely still; I could barely tell he was breathing.

'Why her purse?'

He glanced up at that, for the first time in the interview, but his eyes skittered immediately away.

'Why'd you take her purse, Peter?' I asked again.

'I needed to get the key.'

Jake's eyes flashed and I leaned back in.

'What key?'

'She had a key to a locker at the Rochester bus station. She'd said everything we needed to leave town was in there. She had a suitcase ready to go and two one-way tickets, in both of our names, to New York City.

'She held it up when I asked about the money and explained what it was. Then she put it back in her purse and started threatening me. Later – afterwards – I realized I needed to take the key; otherwise the whole affair would be discovered. I didn't know then about the condom, that my DNA would be identified. So I took her purse and took the key out of it, then threw it in the lake, too.'

'Where's the key now?'

He lined up his knuckles on the edge of the table and took his time before replying in a low, offhand tone. 'In my desk at work.'

'You didn't go to the locker?'

'No. I was going to wait until the case was closed and then destroy the . . . evidence.'

I stared at him: his bent head, his carefully placed hands, the sag of his shoulders under the fancy suit. It fit. It all fit, and everything I knew about being a lawman told me I was sitting across from Hattie's killer, but something still nagged at me.

'You went to a lot of trouble, didn't you, Lund? Thought this all through.'

He shrugged. 'I thought I did.'

'So tell me this: How'd you go from swearing up and down that you had nothing to do with Hattie's death not three hours ago to signing your life away now?'

'Mary.' He answered immediately.

'Protecting Mary?'

'That's what I was trying to do – protect my family. I didn't know until Mary came today that she'd seen me and Hattie together. She . . . said she'd testify against me, about what she saw. At that point I knew there wasn't any hope in lying further. I wasn't going to get away with it.'

Lund looked up again and met my stare. 'To be honest, I'm kind of relieved. I'd just like to get all this over with and start serving my time. Can I do that?'

He glanced at the lawyer, who seemed to remember he was there as more than just a rapt audience member, and the two of them asked to have a minute alone to discuss sentencing options.

We tossed him back in the cell with his lawyer for company and drove to the school, found the key, and took it to the Greyhound station in Rochester. Inside the locker we found Hattie's missing suitcase, still gleaming and smelling like new, and an envelope holding three hundred-dollar bills, a note from Lund breaking off the affair, and two one-way tickets to New York, exactly as he'd described.

After we photographed and bagged everything, I turned to Jake and nodded.

'Book him. Murder two.'

———

I left the terminal and drove straight to Bud and Mona's. It was heading toward evening, and even though the burial and lunch were long over, it looked like half the funeral procession had followed them home. Over a dozen vehicles were parked in the driveway, on the lawn, and along the road.

One of Mona's sisters let me in and showed me to the living room. Photo albums were scattered everywhere and tagboard posters with pictures of Hattie were propped up against the walls. People crowded on chairs and the floor, surrounding Mona and Bud on the couch. Some were laughing and looking at pictures, some were crying, some were doing a bit of both, but they all stopped and fell silent when I walked into the room.

When Bud saw me in uniform, he took Mona by the hand and they stood up together.

'Let's get some air,' he said.

We walked out toward the silo with Bear the retriever shadowing our steps. The sky roiled with fat spring clouds that kept the sun at bay, making our path muddy and precarious.

Once we got out of view of the house, Bud and Mona turned toward me. I didn't beat around the bush.

'The DNA came back.'

Although neither said anything, a fire lit in both their eyes, a terrible anticipation.

'It was Peter Lund, Hattie's English teacher.'

'What?' Mona staggered backward.

It took Bud a moment to find his voice, but when he did it was at a full bellow. 'Her goddamn teacher? He forced himself on her?'

'No.' I looked him square in the eye. They deserved better than the truth, but the truth was all I had to give them. 'They'd been having an affair since January.'

I registered the fist coming at my face and let it happen. Mona's scream followed me to the ground, drifting in and out of my ears as the blow rang through my head and Bear barked and jumped around everyone. Bud stood over me, fists up, ignoring Mona's attempts to haul him back.

'That's a filthy lie, Del. A filthy lie! Don't tell me Hattie was bedding some sick, pervert teacher. She wouldn't do that.'

I rubbed my jaw and spoke to Mona, filling in the details, from the emails last fall all the way to the meeting on Friday night.

Mona was crying hard by the time I finished, still holding on to Bud's arm. Bear had quieted down and was standing guard by his master. Bud stared through me, past arguing but no less wrathful.

'I'll kill him.'

I stood up cautiously. 'You're not going to kill anybody, Bud.'

'Where is he now?' Mona managed to ask and Bud echoed her, but in a different voice, a planning voice.

'Yeah, where is he?'

'He's in custody. Locked up. It's done.'

Bud's expression didn't change, so I tried again.

'He gave a full confession this afternoon and he's not going to see light from the free side of a cell anytime soon.'

Mona leaned against the wall of the silo and covered her face while Bud's hands were still fisted at his sides and veins popped in his forehead. A crow cawed from some hidden place nearby. I didn't know what else I could say. There was no peace here, no sense of justice. I'd done what I'd said I would, sitting on their couch not five days ago; I'd handed them a murderer, but stole the last bits of their daughter in the process.

Greg appeared around the barn, walking toward us, looking as grim and hell-bent as his father. I touched Mona's shoulder and made my way back to the cruiser, leaving them to their despair.

◆

We never found the knife. I had a dive crew search the bottom of Lake Crosby for three straight days and all they came up with was a few rusted boat motors. I wanted that knife. I dreamed about it every night between Lund's confession and the arraignment. Sometimes Hattie was in the dreams, watching me search the barn, the fields, the lake. I couldn't find the damn thing even in my own head.

Fortunately, you didn't need a weapon to prove murder two in Minnesota, not when you had a spot-on confession, a body, and a mountain of other evidence.

Peter Lund's arraignment was broadcast on every television from here to Florida. My sister called afterwards to tell me she'd watched it on two channels in Tallahassee. The news crews mostly hung around the courthouse, but some still came out to film their bits on Main Street or in front of the school.

I stood at the back of the courtroom near one of the bailiffs. Bud and Mona and Greg sat in the front row on the prosecutor's side and friends and family crowded in behind them. No one was talking. I didn't see Mary Beth Lund anywhere, but Winifred Erickson stalked in just before the judge entered and sat matter-of-factly down in the same row as Carl Jacobs, behind the county defender.

When the judge called for the defendant, every pair of eyes in the room watched as Lund appeared. He walked quietly, looking at the floor, and sat down as meek as a kitten. I could only see the back of his head from then on, and he didn't so much as move a muscle until the judge asked him how he pled.

'Guilty, Your Honor.' His head tipped up when he said it, straight at the judge, and not a lick of emotion or insanity colored his voice. He might have been ordering office supplies.

There was a trickle of reaction from the seats. The judge ignored it, set the sentencing hearing for three weeks out, and that was that.

On her way out of the courtroom, Winifred stopped to chat.

'I'm blowing that barn up. Next week.'

'You need a permit for that.'

'It's on your desk. Can't look at the thing anymore. Makes me sick.'

She nodded behind her, where the Hoffmans were huddled in with the prosecutor, probably getting told that it was going to be a twenty- to thirty-year sentence.

'I've already told Bud and Mona. Whether you sign the damn permit or not, I'm blowing the thing to kingdom come.'

HATTIE / *Friday, April 11, 2008*

THE BARN rose up out of the lake like a water monster, all dark and gloomy on the horizon, like a horror movie set warning people away, but I was excited to see it. Tommy pulled into the parking lot by the beach and let the car idle.

My body still hummed from the play, the adrenaline of being onstage in the lights and sensing that hushed fascination from the audience. Everything had gone perfectly. No scenery falling over, no injuries, no fainting. Everyone remembered their lines and Adam and I totally knocked it out of the park. So take that, Portia. I knew after the dress rehearsal she was secretly hoping I'd fall over and break my arm, so she could play Lady Macbeth and act all smug and knowing about the curse. Maybe something would happen tomorrow. The whole gym could fall down tomorrow, for all I cared. Nothing mattered to me except tonight.

I waited around for a long time, after most everyone else had left, trying to catch a glimpse of Peter. I hoped he'd give me some sort of sign that he was coming tonight, so I took my time getting changed. I threw the bloody costume on to a chair, hung up my crown, and changed into my new sundress with the delicate straps and soft yellow folds of skirt. There was still no sign of Peter when I came out, but Tommy was there. His eyes lit up when he saw my dress and I knew what I had to do. He was even happier when I told him to drive us out to Lake Crosby. Bad as it felt, I just gave him a small smile and stayed quiet during the ride.

Now that we were here, he cracked open the paneling on the driver's-side door and pulled a flask out of his secret compartment. He took a long pull and gave it to me.

'What is it?' I sniffed and made a gross face.

'My dad's Jim Beam. Try it.'

I didn't get more than my lips wet before gagging on the stuff. Tommy laughed.

'That's even worse than beer.'

'Won't drink. Won't have sex. You're just Daddy's little angel, aren't you?' He was smiling as he said it, though, scooting over to my side of the seat. He tried to wedge an arm behind me, but I pushed myself back into the corner.

'Tommy, we have to talk.'

'About what?'

'I can't go out with you anymore.'

'What?'

I repeated it without looking at him, feeling the hot confusion of his stare. It was so tempting to fall back into the part just to avoid hurting him. Focusing on the barn, I took a deep breath and reminded myself what I'd just told Portia less than an hour ago – I was done acting.

'What are you talking about? Did your shift get changed or something?'

'No.' I kept my voice steady. 'I want to break up.'

I could feel him pulling back, retreating to his side of the cab. It was a minute before he asked why.

'Because we're going different places. It's not going to work out.'

'It's because of the sex stuff, isn't it? Look, I'm sorry. I won't do it anymore. I promise.'

If he wanted to play it that way, fine. It wouldn't be a lie. 'You know how I feel about it. You were just starting to make me really uncomfortable all the time. On the defensive, you know?'

'Okay, all right? I won't bring it up again, not even at prom.'

'Prom?' The word totally threw me, like it wasn't even in English. I'd been so consumed with the play and Peter, I hadn't given prom a single thought.

Glittery dresses, slow dances, standing in front of the house while Mom and Dad took pictures. It seemed so . . . high school.

'We'll go with the whole gang. The guys are talking about renting a limo and everything.'

'I'm not going to prom.'

'Everyone's going.' He said it like that was the only argument he needed to make. If only he knew how I felt about everyone.

'Not me.' I couldn't even imagine how awful it would be. Dancing in the gym with Tommy, trying to keep his hands from drifting, while Peter stood in the corner with the chaperones, miserable. I'd spend the whole night trying to think of ways to talk to him and he'd hate it, afraid one of us would say too much, look too long.

I hung my head in my hands. 'Some girls aren't meant to go to prom, Tommy.'

The seat dipped as he slid my way again. As soon as I felt his thick fingers rubbing into my back, I sat up quickly. His face was a shadow full of hesitation and hurt.

'Get back, Tommy.'

'What did I do, Hattie? What did I do that was so wrong?'

His voice broke and I could see his Adam's apple bobbing in the glow from the parking lot light. I couldn't stand it anymore, couldn't sit here listening to him cry for a girl who didn't even exist.

I yanked open the door, grabbed my purse, and jumped out.

'Where are you going?'

'Anywhere I want.'

His expression turned bitter. 'Everybody told me not to go out with you, that you were just a freak who wouldn't give it up. I guess they were right.'

'Then go find someone else to take to prom, Tommy. I'm sure there's some little junior out there who'll be happy to let you fuck her.'

I slammed the door and headed to the dark edge of the parking lot, where the trees were waiting to swallow me from sight. I heard a window open behind me.

'Where the hell are you going?'

'New York,' I yelled, without turning around. 'Get lost, Tommy.'

I ran into the weeds and found the trail, then waited until the truck's engine fired up and spun out of the parking lot, gravel flying from the tires. My stomach was rolling from yelling at him and being so mean, but it was better this way. He wouldn't try to make up with me on Monday now. He would tell Derek and all the other football guys what a bitch I was and they'd trash me and feed Tommy some beers and that would be that.

As the roar of the truck faded, I started noticing other noises. The first of the spring frogs sang in the lake. Last year's dead weeds rustled in the breeze and somewhere not far off an owl was hooting. It might have been coming from the barn. As the night settled in around me, the bad feelings all disappeared and I realized I was free, finally done with that awful role I'd created for myself.

I floated down the trail as the moonlight bounced off the water, guiding my way. The stars were out and there wasn't a cloud in the sky. I'd miss this. You probably couldn't see the stars in New York City, not even from Central Park, but here – where the only interference was the tiny glow from the parking lot behind me – I felt like I was standing on the edge of the solar system. There were thousands of lights, winking and shining, pulsing in the night. I could see satellites and planets and the only thing breaking the horizon was the barn in front of me. It was spectacular, a feast of light, the whole universe laid open, and I felt the way I'd always felt looking up at it, like I was huge and tiny at the same time. Yes, I would miss the stars.

Inside the barn I lit the lantern I'd left in the corner and checked the time.

10:17. Still early. Peter could be just locking up the school now.

I didn't mind waiting: it gave me the chance to rehearse what I was going to say. I wasn't playing a part anymore – I was all done with that – but it didn't hurt to be prepared, to know that the words coming out of my mouth were exactly the ones I wanted to say. The last time I'd tried being open and honest with Peter, everything had come out wrong and I wasn't going to make the same mistake twice. Not when this was our last chance.

After I finished rehearsing, I started dancing around the floor, partly to stay warm, because I hadn't brought a sweater to put on over my sundress, and partly because Tommy had put that prom idea in my head. What would it be like to go to a formal dance – not the Pine Valley High School prom in the gymnasium – but a real one in a ballroom, with a beautiful dress to wear, escorted by a man in a tuxedo? I started waltzing, holding my arms out around an invisible partner, one-two-three, one-two-three, just like Dad taught me in the living room after we saw *The Nutcracker* when I was ten years old.

I got so caught up in the thought, watching my shadow twirl and shift along the walls, that I almost screamed when I turned toward the broken window and saw the outline of a person.

My heart raced and I dropped my arms, tripping over a loose floorboard. After a pause, the figure drew forward, and I saw it was Peter. He stared at me with the strangest expression. I would have thought he'd laugh to see me acting so silly and young, but his face was transfixed. He walked out of sight and came around to the door, stepping just inside. Our eyes locked and held.

I didn't say anything, didn't want to break the spell. I walked over to him and reached out, drawing one of his hands to my waist and lifting the other in the air beside us. I circled my free hand over his shoulder, leaving a proper distance of space between our bodies. We almost matched up, practically eye to eye. I could see his objection coming, could feel the magic leaving him, so I pulled him gently toward me, starting the steps. One-two-three. One-two-three. And, like a miracle, he began waltzing.

Our pace was slower than mine had been. He moved me deliberately around the room, skirting the edge of the lake, never looking away from me. Neither of us smiled. I could feel my blood pumping warmer and faster, creating that reaction in the pit of my stomach that always happened whenever Peter touched me. I could tell he felt it, too.

After circling the dry half of the barn for what felt like an eternity, we moved to the middle and broke out of the waltz. Peter let go of my waist and spun me, slowly, one, two, three times from the length of his arm and stepped back, until only his fingertips brushed the edges of mine and then were gone. He let his arm fall to his side and we stood apart, breathing heavily.

'I don't know what I'm doing here.'

'You're dancing with me.' I tried to keep it simple, even though Peter never let anything be simple. He sighed and I knew complications were coming; they were climbing up his throat right now. I stepped forward and held my hand up. 'Just wait. Wait.' I took a deep breath, remembering what I wanted to say.

'You're going to be a shitty father.'

Peter opened his mouth. Closed it. Then said, 'Thanks.'

'I've thought this all through. I know you, Peter. I know you think you have to do what's right for the baby and stay with Mary, but she's never going to leave Pine Valley. So you're either going to be trapped here forever, hating every minute of it, or you're going to eventually get divorced anyway and drag the kid through some awful custody battle, making him believe it's his fault Mommy and Daddy hate each other, and leave him – or her – psychologically scarred for life.

'Then what? You'll move back to Minneapolis to try to start over, alone, never seeing your kid anyway because you're too far away for the every-other-weekend deal that most dads get. And by then I'll be in my twenties or thirties, probably married to some Wall Street guy that I only liked in the first place because he kind of looked like you, hating him because he doesn't understand me at all, and having his children, which I'm pretty sure I don't want.'

Peter was trying not to smile. 'What's his name?'

'Barry.' I shook my head like I'd said it a million times, and it was stuck to me like chewing gum on my shoe. 'His name is Barry. Can you believe it?'

'Yes, I can. Don't forget that Barry has a good job. You probably have a time share in the Hamptons. Barry can give you the kind of life that you deserve.'

'Barry is an asshole.'

Peter burst out laughing and I plowed ahead, acting like the put-out wife.

'He never helps with the kids and stays out at happy hours

with his friends all the time. When do you think was the last time he even took me to see a play, much less let me audition for one?'

Peter's laugh trailed off and he shook his head at me, smiling. 'God, I don't think there's a Barry in the world who can stop you.'

I walked over to my purse and pulled out a small, black-handled locker key, then came back and put it in his hand.

'Here's your money. Kind of.'

As he stared at it, his forehead crinkled up the way I loved. 'What's this?'

'Our future.'

'*We*' – he emphasized the word as all the amusement drained from his expression – 'don't have a future, so what the hell is this?'

'Greyhound station, locker number twenty-four. Our tickets are inside.'

He made a strangled noise and spun away from me, balling the key into his fist. The barn floor shrieked as he paced too close to the water. I kept talking, careful to keep my voice neutral.

'We leave the week after graduation and I've reserved space in a hostel for a few weeks until we find a room to rent. With the rest of your money and my savings, we've got enough for a down payment and two months' rent. I can transfer to three different CVS locations that have openings while you figure out your New York teaching license, but I think in the meantime you should work at one of the publishing houses.'

He swung back around, as angry as I'd ever seen him. 'You're delusional.'

'I prefer the term go-getter.'

'You lied to me. You said you wanted to return the money and say goodbye.'

'I do.' I stepped forward. 'I want us to say goodbye together, to this barn, to this town, to this crappy situation. It doesn't have to end this way, with both of us miserable and apart. We can escape. We can start our life together.'

'You want to start a life with a man who would abandon his wife and unborn child?'

'I want you, Peter. Just you. Not the labels you keep trying to put on us. I haven't thought about anything except us in weeks. Here's what I know.' I put my hand on his arm and, even though his muscles were tensed and rigid, he didn't pull away.

'I know that when I met you I was untouchable. No one affected me. No one made me want to laugh or cry. I felt like I was above it all, but beneath it, too. Does that make sense? I was like a shell of a person. And you were this light that gave me the courage to see inside myself for the first time. But I didn't know that you were broken, too. You made all the wrong choices, all the choices I might have made if I hadn't ever found myself. You needed someone to save you just as much as I did. And now that we have, now that we've found each other, we can't turn away from it. I can't live the rest of my life knowing I had you and gave you up.'

I felt the tears running down my face and saw them in Peter's eyes, too. He had trouble speaking, and swallowed.

'But Mary. How can I leave her like this?'

'How can you stay with her when you're in love with me?'

'I'll hate myself if I leave.' When he tried to pull his arm away, I grabbed his shirt with both hands.

'You'll hate yourself more if you stay.' I backed him into a dry corner of the barn; our shadows got smaller and smaller. 'And she'll hate you, too, because she'll know. Girls always know. She'll know you see someone else every time you make love to her.'

'Hattie '

'And your kid will hate you for making his mother unhappy.' I pushed him until his back hit the wall and he grabbed my wrists to try and force me off. But I just got louder and stronger.

'And the school will hate you because you don't fit in there. Because you're better and smarter than them and you know it. And this town will hate you because you'll never be one of them. You'll shrivel away into nothing here. You'll be an old, bitter, useless–'

He lunged at me, stopping my mouth with his own, kissing me brutally, boxing my head in his hands. I gasped at the force and he spun me around and slammed me into the wall. I cried out, but he didn't stop. Thank you, God.

'Peter.' I chanted his name as he wound my hair in his hands, wedged his knee between mine, and drove me up.

'Is this what you want?'

'Yes.' I found his belt and unfastened the buckle. 'Yes, always.'

He moaned my name, like it was being ripped out of him, and then there was no more talking. We fell onto the floor, not even bothering to undress, desperate for each other. It was hard and fast and rough and when it was over he collapsed and pulled me to his side, holding me tight.

We lay quietly for a while, letting our breathing return to normal. Then I pushed myself up to an elbow and smiled at him.

'I should have insulted you a long time ago.'

'I'm amazed you ever found anything positive to say to me.'

'I'm very creative.'

He smiled, but it was like a shadow passing over his face. I laid my palm along his jaw, so gently, and stared down at him.

'Come to New York with me.'

He mirrored my move, reaching up and stroking my face. 'I don't think I can.'

Then he closed his eyes and dropped his hand to cover them. 'But, God, I don't think . . .' – my heart dropped – 'I can leave you.'

'Wh-what?'

He sat up suddenly, pulling me with him as everything was confusion, then he took me by both arms and gazed at me, swallowing.

'I love you, Hattie Hoffman.'

'I love you, too.' My chest was pounding now, harder than it had all night. All my cards were on the table. There was nothing left to say, nothing left I could do. It was his decision.

'I don't have much money,' he said.

'Neither do I.'

'I'll have even less after paying for child support.'

'That's fine.'

'I don't know what I can do for work before I get my New York license.'

'You'll work in publishing, LitGeek.'

'We'd have to tell your parents before we go.'

That stopped me.

'I'm serious, Hattie. I can't live a half-life anymore. We do it all the way, or we don't do it at all.'

It was my turn to swallow. 'My father will kill you.'

'Then I'll die with a clear conscience.'

I took a deep breath. 'Okay. We'll tell them together. After I lock the gun cabinet.'

'I'll tell Mary by myself. When school is over.'

We stared at each other, smiles slowly lighting up our faces. My breath came fast and shallow, the excitement bubbling up.

'You're coming to New York with me?'

He looked jubilant, and all of a sudden I saw how he must have been as a kid. His face open and hopeful, not weathered by unhappiness.

'I'm coming to New York with you.'

I screamed and launched myself at him, grabbing him close and laughing as we tumbled over each other on the floor. I planted kisses all over his head until he found my wandering mouth and kissed me long and deep. I don't think anyone had ever been as happy as I was at that moment. It felt like I couldn't even contain it, it wouldn't all fit inside of me, it was spilling out my fingers and eyes and chest, pouring light into the darkest corners of this wretched barn.

'I love you, I love you,' I kept saying, until a noise outside made us break apart and turn toward the window, but there wasn't anything there except the wind, which made me shiver. Peter rubbed a hand over my goose bumps and sighed.

'It's getting late.'

'No, it's early.' I smiled, loving that I would get to contradict him for the rest of our lives.

'And you're cold.' He rubbed his way up to my shoulders. 'Why don't you have a coat?'

'Farm girls are tough.'

'They'd better be, because the hard part is next. Telling everyone. Breaking ties.'

I looped my arms around his neck. 'Then I'd better have some more of the kissing part, to get ready.'

After a few more minutes, he broke away again. 'We really should go. Are you going to be okay getting back to your car?'

I almost forgot I didn't have a car here, but I didn't mention it. I wasn't going to start our new life by becoming helpless. I'd just call Portia and have her pick me up at the parking lot. She was probably still at Dairy Queen with the rest of the cast and crew.

'You go on. I need to do something first.' I grabbed my purse.

'What about this?' He picked up the locker key that must have fallen on the floor at some point.

'Keep it. I told you I was giving you your money back tonight.'

'And you're just a model of truth and honesty.' He walked over to me and wrapped his arms around my waist, grinning.

'Just like you. We make a great couple.'

He gave me one last kiss to tide us both over until we could meet again and then he left. I started to reach for my phone, but became overwhelmed by euphoria. Everything flashed through my head, each moment and decision over the past year that had led me to this point in my life. I spun around a few more times, hugging myself, and then dug the camcorder out of my purse, eager to recount every last second of the miracle that just happened.

DEL / *Saturday, May 10, 2008*

WINIFRED BLEW up the barn on the morning of the fishing opener. Usually Bud and I spent this day motoring the patrol boat around Lake Crosby, catching a mess of crappies too little to do anything with besides throw back. We went to Lake Michigan later in July, between planting and harvest, when Bud could afford a week away and after I'd dried out the Fourth of July idiots. That was our serious fishing trip. The opener was just so we could feel the line casting out over the water.

The boys pulled practically all the lake patrol during the season. They confiscated alcohol and handed out tickets for not wearing life vests, but mostly worked on their tans. Everyone loved the lake shifts and I let the crew have them, except for the opener. That day had always been mine and Bud's.

We hadn't talked since I'd arrested Lund and Bud knocked me down. I wanted to call but didn't know what to say, and the days kept filling up with county business. Tommy'd become erratic and was pulled over for drunk driving. His parents talked the judge into giving him leniency on account of his loss. The station had a tractor turn over on the highway, a complaint of livestock theft, and a ninety-year-old who knocked over a light pole because his car was in the wrong gear. I filled out the paperwork and set up the detours, feeling all the while like I should apologize to Bud and not knowing what for. I passed him in town once or twice and we both lifted a hand from our steering wheels and kept driving in different directions. Finally, after the arraignment, I signed Winifred's permit and called him. I told him I'd be on the lake during the blast for security.

'I'm going with you,' Bud said, and hung up.

On the morning of the blast, we dropped the boat in and parked the cruiser in front of the entrance to the lot at 5:00 a.m., well before dawn. I posted the *Lake Closed* sign next to the newspaper notice on the gate.

'Warm already,' I commented as we pulled away from the dock.

Bud sat in the passenger seat, looking ahead at the black water. His face was unreadable as he nodded. 'It's gonna be a scorcher this year.'

Neither one of us spoke after that. The demo wasn't scheduled for another hour, so I killed the motor and drifted into one of the better inlets, handing the bait to Bud. We cast out the lines in silence and waited. Every once in a while I turned to check the crew's progress. They milled around the barn, a bunch of dark figures against the faint orange lightening up the horizon. A few days ago they'd strung up a net to catch the bits that were going to blast into the water, making it look like the barn was caught on a giant flyswatter.

Bud didn't turn around. When he got a bite, he didn't even pull the fish out. *Pull it up,* I wanted to say, but the words wouldn't come. We both watched the line tug this way and that until the fish thrashed free of the hook and swam away.

After a while the sun showed its face, throwing the cattails and weeds into that hollow first morning light. I reeled in my line.

'It's time.'

Bud followed suit and set his pole aside without comment.

'Better do one last sweep of the perimeter and then we can set up in the middle of the water. We'll be well clear of the blast radius.'

He nodded.

I slowed down when we got to the launch, making sure nobody was trying to slip by the cruiser and set in anyway. There were plenty of cars lined up on the road, but folks were lounging on their hoods with binoculars – they'd come for the show. There'd been a lot of grumbling on the timing of the thing, and now no serious fishermen were bothering with the lake at all today.

I motored over toward the east side by the barn, giving the demo crew a quick nod to let them know we were clear.

'Fifteen minutes,' the foreman shouted from the bank. I waved and headed back to the middle of the lake.

Bud's stare seemed to harden when we pulled up near the barn, but he still didn't have a word to say. Even though we'd shared plenty of quiet moments over the years, most of that had come from my side. Bud had always been the one who reached out, ready with a joke or a story about the kids. I'd lived with my silence until it was like a wife to me and I didn't think twice about it. Bud's silence was unnatural. I didn't know how to break through it. There was a barrier between us now, a hard place that used to be easy.

I positioned the boat and killed the motor. There wasn't any breeze today, which was good. As the seconds ticked by, I couldn't help tensing up, feeling that old nausea.

'Damned if I'll ever get used to explosions again,' I said, just to say something.

We watched as the last of the men cleared out of the barn and drove their 4x4s in the direction of Winifred's house, where they'd set up the controls. It was soon now.

I wiped a rag over my forehead, which felt sweaty and cold. Bud let out a long, loud breath.

'Don't suppose you've got any of that confiscated booze around here.'

I was surprised – Bud didn't drink. 'I don't. No one's been on the water yet this year. And usually the boys'll split whatever we do take. It doesn't last long.'

'Probably best anyway. It's just . . . I can't . . .'

'I know.'

'You don't know.' He shook his head and his eyes seared into the barn. He wouldn't look away from it.

'You don't know the first thing about having your daughter's life ripped away from you, making you feel about as powerless as a gnat. And then to find out she was sleeping with her teacher – her married teacher. It was like I didn't know her at all. I didn't know my own flesh and blood.'

'Hogwash. Course you knew her. She was a teenager, Bud. They think they're in love and do stupid things. They all snap out of it eventually. Hattie would have, too.'

'And him.' His rage took over again.

'I sat across from him at Hattie's conferences not two months ago and listened to him tell us what a bright, talented girl she was. And all the while he had his dirty hands under her skirt. God, he should rot in prison his whole life just for that. But then to take her life . . . to stab her in her heart . . .'

Bud's entire body was shaking now, the anger was pure and boiling in him and it had nowhere to go.

'It's not enough, Del. Prison's not enough. I need to do something to him. I want to throw him in that barn right now. I want that son of a bitch blown into fish bait for what he did.'

'Bud–' I didn't know what I was going to say. I didn't know if there was anything to say to something like that, but it didn't matter because the blast tore open the morning sky.

The barn exploded in a series of flashes and flying wood, then the smoke billowed out, hiding everything. Without thinking, I had snapped my hand to my holster and crouched behind the windshield of the boat. Bud didn't seem to notice. As the smoke drifted away and the smell of dynamite singed the air, I eased up a little and took us closer to the shore. These demolition guys knew what they were doing. The barn was now a scrap heap of wood and rubble, half on land and half caught in their giant net.

After a few minutes, the 4x4s returned and waved toward the boat to let us know we were all clear.

'Well, that's that.' I started to turn the boat around when Bud leaned over the side.

'Wait.'

He pointed at the water. Two sunnies had bubbled up to the surface, dead as doornails. As we stood there, another popped up. Then another.

'There. Over there.'

'Look at that one. He must be a three-pounder, at least.'

All around us, fish floated on their sides, their silver bellies shining like a hundred streaks of light in the morning sun. We couldn't count them all. They were everywhere.

'Must have been the shock wave.' I'd felt it go through me, but assumed it was as much in my head as anyplace else. Seeing all these dead fish, though, well, it took the thing out of me. The tremors were already gone.

We stood side by side, staring at the water.

'Let's go grab a drink, all right?'

'Mmm.'

I turned us away from the floating fish bodies and the demo

crew swarming around the rubble, pointing the boat back to the launch. Just as we docked, dispatch came over the radio.

'We've got a ten-fifty-two involving two vehicles out on highway twelve, right along the stretch by the lake. Del, are you still in the water?'

'Just getting out, Nance. I'll be there directly.' I was already halfway to the cruiser. 'Sorry, Bud. You'll have to come along and sit tight, unless you want to stay here. I'm sure Mona'd come by to pick you up.'

But he was already in the passenger seat, buckling up. I hit the lights and gunned past the line of cars. A few of the watchers swung their binoculars on us.

'What's a ten-fifty-two?'

'A crash with injuries.'

It didn't take long to find the accident. A semi was halfway to jackknifed on the shoulder and the driver stood nearby, frantically waving us down. As we pulled up, the pickup underneath the semi became visible, or what was left of it anyway. It was one of those monster-truck types by the look of it – a modified F150.

I parked the cruiser in the middle of the lane to keep traffic to the left.

'He ran right into me.' The driver started in as soon as I opened the door. 'There was this huge freaking boom and then this truck came at me. I couldn't get out of the way.'

'What are you hauling back here?' I checked his fuel line to make sure it was intact.

'Produce. Strawberries from California.' He stopped outside the wreckage, leaving me to work my way under the belly of the semi.

'Hello there! Sheriff Goodman here. Can you hear me?'

There was no answer.

I saw a pair of boots walking around the far side of the truck.

'Del!' It was Bud.

I ducked through by the wheels and met him on the other side.

'It's Tommy's truck,' Bud said. 'Tommy Kinakis.'

'Help me get the driver's side door open.'

We yanked it until there was a few feet of space to crawl through and I poked my head inside.

Tommy looked like he'd been swallowed by the steering column of his truck. The whole dashboard was crushed against the seats, with Tommy slumped in between. Blood dripped off the wheel and over the shredded fabric, where some empty liquor bottles were lying. I reached to take a pulse without any hope. The boy's eyes were open and blank.

I backed out of the wreck and shook my head at Bud, then called dispatch for an ambulance on a DOA.

'Jesus, he's dead?' The truck driver held his head like it was going to fall off and paced in the ditch next to his cab. I left Bud to go talk to him.

'Tell me again what happened. Slow it down this time.'

'I was supposed to drop half the load in Rochester and half in Red Wing. I just left Rochester and was thinking I should have gassed up, and then this huge boom came out of nowhere.'

'Demo crew blew a barn up right over that hill. Less than a mile away.'

'Oh. Oh, okay.' He took to wiping his forehead.

'So after the blast . . .'

'It was then, right at the boom, that this truck ran into me. He was coming from the opposite direction and it looked like he just spun out, going at least seventy. His back end kind of swerved and I hit the brakes and tried to move to the shoulder. He was under me before I knew it. I heard the crunch and the whole rig jolted to a stop. I jumped out to see if he was hurt, and all I could make out was his head, but he didn't move and he didn't answer me when I yelled, so I ran back and called it in.'

'No other cars coming at the same time? Anyone else see it?'

'No, none. It's pretty backwater out here. Maybe there was some afterwards, I don't remember.'

'Del!' Bud shouted and I looked to see him half inside Tommy's truck.

'Watch for that ambulance,' I told the driver, and jogged back. Could Tommy actually be alive? I hadn't felt any heartbeat.

'What is it?'

Bud withdrew, staring inside the truck like someone had just poleaxed him in the back of the head. He held up a finger and pointed.

I checked inside, but nothing had changed. Tommy was still dead. I didn't smell any fuel.

'The door,' Bud spat, and then I saw it.

The inside panel of the driver's-side door was cracked open, and there, stained dark with dried and crusted blood, was Mary Beth Lund's chicken-butchering knife. The knife I'd dreamed about, the knife we couldn't pull out of that lake. I leaned in farther and saw a rectangular box with buttons underneath the knife. I'd bet a thousand dollars it was Hattie's missing camcorder.

'Son of a bitch,' I whispered.

Bud stepped up next to me and we stood there, staring at Tommy's mutilated body, watching his blood congeal.

'Lund,' Bud said, quiet and low, and I knew he was thinking the same thing I was thinking. Peter Lund had confessed to a crime he didn't commit. Maybe he thought he was protecting someone else or maybe he wanted to pay for his other sins, but in all likelihood he was going to rot in prison for the next twenty to thirty years, and the only thing in the world that would prevent that was right in front of us.

I glanced at Bud. In the distance came the wail of the ambulance and another police siren. There was no time to think it through.

No time to wonder about the morality of a man's actions, whether he owed more to a friend or to the law and the country that depended on that law, no time to sift through the dozens of questions that would haunt me in the middle of the night for years to come, sitting up in a pitch-black living room staring at the neighbors' cat and feeling like I had no right to wear a badge, that I had failed the institution I'd given my life to and not even knowing what that meant. The sirens came closer and closer and I turned to Bud, my oldest, broken friend, and I gave him back a crumb of what he'd lost of himself.

'It's your call.'

Tears coursed down his unshaved cheeks. 'I don't know, Del.'

'Decide for Hattie, then. Choose for her.'

I watched as Bud's hand slowly reached out, to either pry open that hidden compartment or to seal it from the world's eyes forever. To reveal who had murdered his daughter or to sentence her lover to a lifetime of penance.

His hand shook while he decided.

DEL / *Sunday, May 11, 2008*

JAKE AND I watched the tape from the beginning. Hattie's image filled the interrogation room, bright and bubbling one minute, big-eyed and somber the next, telling us everything she had done in the last year of her short life. This was the diary I'd expected to find when I'd searched her room all those weeks ago.

When the scene switched from her bedroom to the dark, splintered boards of the barn, we both sat up straighter. Everything in me tensed and went cold. Hattie was oblivious to any danger, bursting with details about her rendezvous with Lund and their plans to run away together. She was glowing, pulsing with life and hope. Then a squeaking noise pulled her gaze away from the camera and her face brightened.

'Did you forget '

Her smile died. She tripped backward, away from the camera and from the person who'd just walked into the barn.

'Tommy.'

'You lying whore.'

Hattie backed up until only her top half was visible. 'What are you doing here?'

'I was looking for you.' Tommy stepped into the frame, holding Mary Beth's knife in one hand. 'I went home and then came back. I drove along the back roads looking for you, to give you a ride because I felt bad about what I said.'

'That's sweet.' Her voice shook as she said it.

'Then I checked the barn.'

He kept walking forward, slowly, until he was in the far corner of the frame with Hattie, facing away from the camera.

'And I see you sitting in Mr. Lund's lap, making out with him like he just fucked you four ways from Sunday.'

'Tommy, I can explain.'

'I don't need any explanation, Hattie! I got the picture! You won't have sex with me, but you're giving it away to one of our teachers. Does he give you good grades? Do you give him a blow job for every A?'

'I'm in love with him, Tommy.' Hattie's eyes kept bouncing to the knife.

'So you're cheating on me with a teacher. Letting him do all the things you tell me you won't do. Were you laughing at me behind my back? Laughing at me while screwing him?'

'No. No, I never laughed at you. I never . . . thought about you.' She took another step back and the floorboards creaked. She had to be close to the water's edge now. 'You were a really good boyfriend, Tommy. Really. I'm so sorry. I didn't mean to hurt you. I didn't think.'

Suddenly she pointed to the blade in Tommy's fist. 'What are you doing with that?'

'I'm going to get some answers out of you. I watched him leave and waited for you to come out. Then I found this.' He lifted it for the first time, pointing it at Hattie's chest.

'Can't you just put it down? We'll go somewhere, anywhere you want, and we'll talk. I'll tell you anything you want to know, the whole truth. I promise.'

'Did you fuck him here?' he demanded, his voice rising.

She hesitated before answering. 'Yes.'

'Then I want to talk right here.'

They were only a few feet apart now.

'How long have you been screwing our English teacher?'

'Since January.'

He stumbled back at that, opening up a little space between them. Hattie's eyes flickered toward that gap and then back to his face. There was a tightly controlled panic in her features but a concentration, too, like she was working something out in her head.

'January? You've been sleeping with him almost since we started dating?'

'Tommy, I started dating you so I could sleep with him.' That backed him up another step and her voice picked up volume and confidence. 'He didn't want anyone to find out about us, so I got a boyfriend. An all-American, football-hero boyfriend. It was the perfect cover.'

'Oh my God. Oh my God.' Tommy's hands went to his head and he started rocking back and forth.

'I wasn't trying to hurt you, but I wasn't trying not to, either. I really didn't give a shit about you, Tommy. It was never about you.'

Next to me, Jake shifted in his chair and whispered, 'What is she doing?'

Understanding came swiftly. 'She's trying to back him up. Every time she says something terrible, he retreats. See?'

I gestured to the space between them on the screen, the escape route she was clawing at the only way she knew how.

'You.' Tommy had gotten a hold of himself and pointed the knife at her again. 'I thought you were good, that you liked me. I spent so many nights thinking that I was the bad one, because I wanted . . . but you're just like tonight. Aren't you? You're just like onstage.'

'What?' All concentration fell off Hattie's face, replaced by shock. Her eyes were white circles on the screen.

'You're that queen. That evil bitch who makes men do terrible things. It's you, isn't it? You . . . manipulate people.' He fumbled for the word, but then spat it out like bile. 'You use them to get what you want.'

Out of the corner of my eye I saw Jake's hand go to his face, and then everything happened quick.

Tommy took a step forward and Hattie tried to run past him in the space she'd been working to open. As she disappeared from view, Tommy lunged after her and his arm swung around in a vicious side hook. It was a crushing, instantaneous blow. A flash of movement, a yell, a cry, and it was all over. Hattie fell backward, and for the briefest second she was visible again, mouth open, eyes wide, before hitting the floor with a muted thud.

Tommy looked paralyzed for a moment, still half crouched, and then he dropped out of view.

'Hattie? Hattie? Hattie!' He pleaded and then stood again, rocking violently.

'No, no, no, no, no, no.' The rocking got bigger and bigger. His head started shaking in time to the words. 'Not Hattie. It's not Hattie.'

He chanted the same refrain for an age, swaying in that childish, dazed way and covering his face. Then he knelt on the floor, still denying what had just happened in a voice that became strangled and oddly punctuated.

He was making her face disappear.

When he appeared again, he had her purse and the knife was gone.

'Prom. The cabin. She wants to go. Everyone's going,' he said as he passed the camera. His face was flushed, eyes glazed and seeing nothing. A full minute went by before he came back, muttering and crying, his words unintelligible now.

Leaning down, he grabbed the knife and backed into the center of the frame. He stood still for a moment, sobbing openly by this point, then spun around as if to flee. That's when he spotted the camera.

His crying stopped and he stared into the screen like he could see us sitting here watching him, the living transfixed by the dead. He looked down at the knife in his hand and then walked forward with a sudden purpose. The view and noises turned to a jumbled mess before everything went black.

It was a long while before either of us moved. The room blurred out of focus and I didn't stop it, letting the grief I'd held down for the last month finally rise up and grip me. When Jake eventually got up to turn off the TV, he was good enough to look the other way.

PETER / *Monday, June 9, 2008*

THE SHERIFF'S cruiser idled in front of the prison's front gate, waiting for me. No one told me he'd be here, just like no one mentioned they were going to release me in the middle of the night, waking me from a sound sleep as my cellmate blinked dumbly into the guard's flashlight.

Somehow I wasn't surprised. After the DA had called with the news, I doubted anything could surprise me again.

They'd found a tape, a video recording of the murder from Hattie herself. Tommy Kinakis had killed her. And Tommy was dead, too. After a few weeks of paperwork, my conviction had been overturned.

I walked under the security lights of the entrance and passed the window at the gate, where an armed guard's stare contemptuously summed me up. The suit I'd worn from the courthouse to the prison hung limply on my frame. Other than the wallet in my back pocket, I had nothing.

Quietly, I got into the back of the cruiser. The sheriff didn't turn around or give any sign that acknowledged my presence other than to put the car in gear and pull out of the parking lot. The surrounding hills were black and only a few other headlights lit the freeway as we headed south toward Minneapolis. The time on the dash read 1:07 a.m.

'Where are we going?' I asked after ten miles or so.

It felt like he took another ten before replying.

'You'll see.'

He was probably dropping me off on some shitty street corner on the north side, maybe in gang territory. It didn't matter.

I had no idea what I was going to do now. For the last few weeks, the question had buzzed around my head like some inconsequential fly. I ignored it and ate my plastic-smelling lunch, or ran around the track, or fell asleep to the sounds of metal crashes and laughter echoing down the block. It was easier to exist that way, in the future of oblivion I'd planned for myself. But suddenly another future was here, an alternate reality for which I was completely unprepared.

I didn't have a profession anymore. My teaching license had been revoked while I was still at the Pine Valley jail and even if it hadn't been, I couldn't pass a background check at any school in the country.

I didn't have a wife anymore either. The divorce papers were my first piece of mail after I was transferred up to St. Cloud. I added my signature next to Mary's, sent the forms back in the pre-stamped envelope, and assumed that was the last contact we'd ever have. Then I got the call from the DA, changing everything, and Mary showed up out of the blue during the next Sunday's visiting hours.

She looked good – fuller in the cheeks again and a little more color in her lips. She wore a dress I didn't recognize. It billowed softly in a pattern of delicate green leaves as she walked into the visiting room, not exactly a maternity dress but nothing like the tight-waisted vintage pieces she used to wear. The fabric settled on a slightly more rounded stomach when she sat down. I didn't let my gaze linger.

Neither of us wanted to speak first. We stared at the empty table between our hands and it was a full minute before Mary broke the silence.

'You've heard?'

'Yes.'

Another lull, and then she cut to the heart of the matter.

'I thought it was you. I thought you were going to lie about it like you'd lied about everything else. That's why I went to see you at the jail – to make sure you were going to confess.'

She spoke to her clasped hands and I noticed her wedding ring was already gone. There was no tan line on her finger.

'But you thought it was me, didn't you?' she continued. 'After we heard about Tommy, I went over our conversation again and realized how I must have sounded. You confessed because you thought it was me.'

'Yes. I'm sorry.'

She nodded and breathed deeply, as if letting go of something she'd been holding too tightly. I changed the topic, asking about Elsa and the farm, and we exchanged some stilted small talk before she stood up to leave.

'When will you be out?' Her glance flickered up and then around the room.

'I don't know. Soon, I guess.'

'What are you going to do?'

The million-dollar question. I stared at the cracked and pot-holed pavement racing through the headlights of the sheriff's car and remembered the curve of Mary's jaw as she refused to look at me. She'd smelled like wind and sun.

I'd told her I'd figure out a way to pay child support.

She'd looked embarrassed, nodded, and walked away.

I still had a few friends in the city who might let me stay with them while I found a job. As I started thinking about places to work, we drove through the suburbs and into downtown. The skyline, with its golden glow punctuated by Foshay Tower's delicate spire, was an old friend after a long absence, familiar and yet awkward in its familiarity. The streetlights made my eyes water after so much darkness. It wasn't until we crossed the Mississippi into St. Paul that I realized most of the bad neighborhoods were behind us and he still hadn't kicked me to the curb. A few miles farther, when the cruiser turned south on a freeway that led all the way down to Rochester, another possible future presented itself.

Maybe he was taking me back to Pine Valley. In the middle of the night. With no witnesses.

My pulse leapt, creeping up the back of my throat as the situation became obvious. The sheriff was friends with the Hoffman family. Good friends.

'Can you please tell me where we're going?' I asked again, leaning forward toward the partition this time.

The sheriff laughed, but it was a humorless sound.

'Seem a little nervous back there. Worried about your homecoming?'

'Mary and I aren't married anymore. She doesn't want me there.' I tried to keep my voice calm.

'Imagine that.'

His glance flickered toward me in the rearview mirror, then back to the road. The cities disappeared behind us like a mirage in the night. Was he taunting me with them? It struck me that this man had learned the most intimate details of my life and I didn't know a single thing about him. He could be married, gay, Jewish, atheist, or all of the above, but none of that really mattered. It didn't tell me what kind of person he was.

He wasn't wearing his hat and I noticed his age for the first time. His gray hair was meticulously trimmed above his collar where sunburnt lines creased his neck. Even though his hands held the wheel in the proper ten-two position and he sat straight in his seat, there was no undue formality in him. He looked like someone set on a course of action, with decades of right on his side.

'Would it make any difference if I told you how sorry I was?'

The reflection of his eyes in the mirror turned dark. 'I don't see how.'

I shook my head, unable to disagree. Regret didn't change a thing.

With every passing mile my resignation increased. It didn't replace the panic and I couldn't help that. My body didn't want to die. My heart thudded painfully and it was hard to get enough air in, but I made myself lean back and pressed my palms steadily into the seat on either side of me. If this was my last car ride, I wasn't going to spend it wallowing in fear. We climbed another hill, passed through a dark thicket of trees, and descended into a valley of fields where crops reflected pale lines of moonlight, zigzagging their way back to the sky. Even in the darkness I could identify the soybeans from the corn, and a little ways farther a field was dotted with what I recognized as dairy cattle. Strange, how the knowledge was there, unattached to any memory of receiving it. Then something occurred to me.

'Was Hattie scared?'

The sheriff must have seen the tape. He had witnessed Hattie's last moments, which I had imagined a thousand times, my horror uncontainable for not knowing the extent of hers.

He sighed, and the heavy sound of it made my muscles tense, waiting for the blow. I held my breath.

'She was,' he finally said.

'What happened?' I managed to get out.

An eternity passed before he answered and suddenly I wanted to lunge through the partition and wring the information out of him. My hands had turned to fists. I was shaking.

'Please,' I added, squeezing my eyes shut. 'Please tell me.'

When he spoke, his voice was quiet.

'He surprised her with the knife. Cornered her. She was scared, but she told him everything he asked. She told him the truth. Then she tried to run and was dead before she hit the floor.'

He sighed and I didn't trust myself to speak. I leaned into the window, out of his view, and wiped my eyes as the murder scene unfolded in my head. I watched Hattie fall. She fell over and over, never reaching the ground, caught in that last moment for infinity. My mind couldn't make her live and wouldn't let her die.

'It didn't sit right.' The sheriff spoke after a few more miles, breaking the silence so abruptly I almost missed it. 'Most of the pieces were there. DNA. Confession. Everything in that locker.'

His tone had changed. It didn't sound like he was talking to me anymore, but I answered anyway.

'I thought I was doing the right thing. For once.'

He nodded slowly, eyes never leaving the road. 'I suppose you did. Damn near cost us the truth.'

'So it's my fault Tommy killed her?'

'Tommy Kinakis was no murderer. The two of you tore that boy apart. Point two-five alcohol in his blood when he hit that semi. Now his folks put their home on the market and won't even show their faces in town. And I think . . .'

The pitch of his voice rose suddenly before cutting off. Though I could only see fractions of his face, he seemed to be reining in a flare of emotion, and when he spoke again his voice was strangled.

'. . . I think Hattie's to blame.'

He breathed deeply, steadying himself.

'I loved that girl – I loved every cheeky, smart-ass hair on her head – but the truth is she killed him as much as he killed her. And neither of them meant to. Just stupid kids.'

A flash of oncoming headlights eclipsed his profile as he shook his head. 'Stupid kids who'll never grow up and figure out they're better than that. Never go see the world and realize what it means to come home. That their life's only worth the friends they find in it.'

Long miles passed with only the sound of the rhythm of the wheels over the asphalt. There was nothing to look at except the dark, burgeoning fields, no distraction from the choices Hattie, Mary, Tommy, and I all made that had brought us to this place and time. I'd confessed to something I didn't do, thinking I could trade it off for the wrongs I had committed. Now there was no avoiding the past. I rode toward it, heart thumping in sick anticipation of the reckoning I knew I deserved.

It was after three in the morning when the lights of Rochester began glowing on the horizon. The roads remained empty as we came into the commercial district.

When we passed the turnoff to Pine Valley without exiting, I sat up straight. Confused, I swiveled around to make sure I hadn't misread the sign and then looked back at the sheriff, who was still calmly driving the speed limit. It wasn't until the Mayo Clinic became visible on the horizon that he exited, working his way through the residential streets, and pulled into a nondescript gas station. He parked away from the pumps, letting the engine idle.

I waited and after a minute he slid open the partition between the seats.

'Don't suppose you remember what day it is.'

I didn't. I hadn't thought days would mean much anymore.

He reached into his glove box and pulled out some pieces of paper, pushing them through the window. I unfolded them toward the gas station lights, reading, and my mouth fell open.

They were the bus tickets Hattie bought for us. A one-way trip to New York, leaving at 3:38 a.m. on June 9, 2008. I hadn't thought about these tickets since I'd confessed to murder. The brief stolen giddiness Hattie and I had shared in that barn seemed like a dream now, a hallucination that couldn't have been real. Yet here were the tickets in my hand, the paper creased and crisp, with both our names typed in neat black letters. Before I could even process what was happening he passed an envelope back, too. It had Hattie's name on the outside, in my handwriting, and held a note and three hundred dollars.

'That's not evidence anymore,' he said, facing away from me.

'I don't understand. I thought . . .' As I stumbled over what I had thought, a Greyhound bus lumbered into the gas station lot and parked with a grumbling whoosh of its engine. A few blinking, rumpled people climbed out and wandered into the building.

'Better get going.'

I looked at the tickets and money again and then the back of the sheriff's head.

'Why are you doing this?'

He sighed and I didn't think he was going to answer. Then he shut the glove box and cleared his throat.

'Bud Hoffman's been my friend almost as long as you've been alive. I'm not going to let him do anything he might regret later. Better that you get gone.'

He turned around then and looked at me for the first time that night, not like a police officer looking at a criminal or a righteous man looking at a sinner, but with a strange kinship born of loss, like two men passing in a graveyard. There was something quiet and consuming about the sheriff's look and several moments elapsed before I swallowed and nodded, folding the tickets in my palm.

As I climbed out of the car, I realized I'd just learned everything I needed to know about the sheriff of Wabash County.

Crossing the parking lot, I breathed deep, tasting the Minnesota air for the last time. I handed my ticket to the driver and boarded, then stared at the car across the lot until the bus revved into gear. Without any visible emotion, the sheriff picked up his hat and put it on, straightened the brim over his brow, and eased his cruiser out on to the road. As he passed my window, his fingers lifted an inch off the steering wheel. By the time I raised my hand in return, he was already gone.

The bus rumbled out of the city. The musty upholstery and hint of sweat from sleeping travelers confirmed that I was actually here – this was really happening. I leaned into the cool pane of the window and stared at the country. Hours passed and the sky lightened. The hills rose and fell like a silent soundtrack and it was only now that I'd been exiled from them that I fully appreciated their beauty. An ocean of plants flourished here, roots secure and leaves bathing in the dawn of a new day. I saw Mary in this land and Hattie, too, despite everything she had claimed; I saw her spirit and determination.

As the sun broke over the horizon in fiery oranges and reds, I opened the envelope the sheriff had given me and pulled out the note.

Go to New York . . .

Although it was my handwriting, the words were hers, whispered in the air all around me, breathing in the land rushing past, and they filled my chest with a buoyant kind of pain, a lover's keepsake that I would carry for the rest of my life, guiding me toward an impossible atonement.

. . . Know that I loved you.

ACKNOWLEDGMENTS

First and foremost, I must thank Emily Bestler for not only her fabulous editorial eye but also her dedication and enthusiasm throughout the publication process. It's an honor to be an Emily Bestler Books author. Many thanks to Claire Miller for being my first reader when the book was just a rough sketch of images, and to Brandon Holscher for providing me a theater primer. Thank you to Investigator Renee Brandt and Officer Brandon Howard for giving me a glimpse into their law enforcement worlds and correcting many of my erroneous assumptions. (Up to a year for DNA!) My thanks to Sharon Amundson for her expert mystery reader's feedback. I am indebted to Josh Wodarz for all his advice and support, and most of all for his ability to see the book as it could be and not as it was. Thank you to Ellen Goodson for finding that quiet Friday afternoon and mug of hot coffee. Gratitude is a poor word when I think about what Stephanie Cabot has done to turn this manuscript into an international release. Superagents of the world, you have nothing on this woman. (Her husband even comes up with brilliant titles.) My thanks always to Tom and Linda Montgomery, for never telling me I couldn't fit six quarts into a five-quart jug. And, of course, thank you to Sean Montgomery for keeping me focused on what's really important – his RV.